LEAH & JAKE

ruin their

FRIENDSHIP

AMANDA BRAUN-BOE

To those who have serious opinions about homemade desserts, including, but not limited to, cinnamon rolls, pies, and donuts, and would argue about whether éclairs and Long Johns are the same thing, like Jake, Dennis, and Craig, this one is for you!

Welcome to the Alexandria Lakes Area! Thanks for choosing my book. A quick note before you begin: even though this is a rom-com with a lot of banter and baked goods, it also contains elements that may not be suitable for all readers. These elements include cheating, divorce, parental death, an uninvolved parent, strong language, and explicit sexual content.

Once again, thank you so much for deciding to spend time with Leah and Jake. None of this would be possible without you!

Amanda

I'm a-wondering if she remembers me at all
Many times I've often prayed
In the darkness of my night
In the brightness of my day.

— "Girl from the North Country" by Bob Dylan

1

A FEW MOONS—*COUGH*—MANY MOONS AGO...

Iwas six and on the hunt for a new best friend after Chrissy Hanson and I had a falling out over *My Little Pony*. We always played a game called Pony Royalty, but my ponies were never allowed to be kings and queens because they were thrift store finds, splattered with mud from trotting through puddles in our backyard. Chrissy's were new, with perfect pink manes and ice cream-stamped butts. This all came to a head when I threw her ponies out of her second-story bedroom window into the cold Minnesota winter. In kid language, she told me where to stick it.

For a few months, I only had my brother Steven to play with, but he was three and more interested in throwing Cheerios at the wall. This all changed one day in March, when my parents announced we were having the new family from down the road over for supper. My mom prepared tater tot hotdish, which, even as a child, I thought was a good way to scare them back to wherever they came from.

"Their last name is Bradley." Mom shoved the casserole into the oven. "They're from Ireland. And they have a little boy you can play with."

"Just don't wreck this one's toys," said Dad.

Apparently, the mom, Bonnie Bradley, had some office job and an opportunity came up where she could transfer to the States. They must have thought coming here would be an adventure or something. And they had family nearby, so the place wasn't totally new to them.

When they showed up, I hid around the corner to scope the new boy out. My parents and the Bradleys were already talking about dips and wine and other boring stuff.

But where was their son?

I came out from my hiding spot and huffed. That's when I looked out the sliding deck doors, and there he was. He sat on the white porch swing that hung from the maple tree in the backyard, and he was playing Game Boy.

Whoa.

"I thought our kids could play," Mom said to Bonnie. "How old is Jake?"

Bonnie bravely plunged a cracker into my dad's creamy corn dip. "He's ten."

"You don't have to worry about his size or him being rough and tumble," said Bonnie's husband, Craig. "All he wants to do is build things with Legos and play Game Boy."

Now this was something I could get behind. I ran to my room, grabbed *my* Game Boy, opened the sliding deck door, and charged into the backyard. Spring in Minnesota meant melting snow, plenty of mud, and winter temperatures that refused to let go.

I stood in front of Jake Bradley, my Game Boy in hand. It took him a moment to realize I was there. He was a beanpole, with brown hair and blue eyes. He looked at me like he wasn't sure how to start a conversation. So, I did it for him.

"I'm Leah Roth."

His eyes were huge. "Jake Bradley. We just moved here."

I'd never heard an Irish accent before, but I didn't say anything about it because I didn't want to look stupid in front of a potential friend. And I was lonely since Chrissy decided to be a prissy brat.

"I have a Game Boy, too." I held mine up.

Jake smiled a little. A lonely smile. "What do you play?"

Castlevania.

"Holy shit," he said, impressed. "I mean, I'm sorry. Don't tell my parents I said that."

I giggled. "What do you play?"

"*Teenage Mutant Ninja Turtles*." He looked relieved that I wasn't going to rat him out.

I sat next to him on the swing and looked at his screen. He went back to playing while I watched.

"You like your new house?" I asked.

He shrugged. "It's all right. All the snow's kinda cool. Nice Christmas, maybe. My cousins, Felicity and Kenneth, live in Mankato. But Kenneth's a bit of an eejit."

I nodded, not sure what else to say. There weren't too many boys in the neighborhood, and the ones I knew zipped by on skateboards. I was more of a rollerblading kind of kid.

Finally, a thought occurred to me. "My dad says the maple tree is haunted."

I pointed to the tree, whose large, low branch held up the swing.

Jake inspected the tree like he was waiting for something in the empty branches to spring out. "Sounds a bit silly." His eyes shot to mine. "The ghost of who?"

"I don't know. Want to climb it?"

"Sure!" said Jake.

In a minute, our small hands guided us up the cold, naked tree. Jake gently pulled me to a higher branch. About all you could make out from up here were trees in every direction. They lined our property outside of Alexandria and obscured all the lakes in the distance, but through a few trees, I could just make out Jake's new house down the road.

"Cool." Jake scanned the area. "I like it, even if it's not haunted."

"My mom made tater tot hotdish for supper."

A line formed between his eyes. "What's that?"

"Not good," I said. He looked like a deer in the headlights, and I dissolved into giggles. "Don't worry. I hid some cookies."

After a moment, his shoulders lowered and his face smoothed out. He joined me in laughing about supper. "I have a regular Nintendo, too." He traced the bark with his dry finger. "We just got *Bubble Bobble*. We can play it tomorrow, if you'd like."

"Sure," I said, excited.

Looking back on it, it was strange that when the Bradleys came over, Jake went right out to the porch swing that would become *our* spot. It was like the swing was waiting for him. It was like *he* was waiting for *me*. Like *I* was waiting for *him*. I never could have known when I charged out to him through the snowy mud that he would become my best friend in the world. The boy I tried to force to sing along to the Spice Girls. The teen I embarrassed on the way home from school. The man who held my hand in the delivery room when I had my son. And I never could have realized how close our families would become.

Until he started working at the restaurant after high school, Jake spent the better part of every summer back home in Ireland, rooming with his grandma and hanging out with his cousins. The first summer he went back for a visit, Jake and I had already become best friends. Playing countless hours of *Contra* solidified that.

We stood in his driveway, hugging for a long time before he got into the car. We both cried, not caring who saw.

"We'll talk on the phone all the time," he said, squeezing me. "I'll bring you back some Taytos. We'll have a sandwich."

Jake said he was going to a town I'd never heard of called Westport, in a place I'd never heard of called County Mayo. My six-year-old mind spun. All I knew for sure was that Ireland felt very far away, and my friend was going there. And apparently, we had to work out when to call each other because the time wasn't the same.

On the day he left, I made my parents buy me a map of Ireland. They helped me follow the black lines and dots all over the sheet until we found his town, right there on the West Coast. After that, I made Mom and Dad bring me to the library so I could check out books on Ireland and see what the place was all about. Being only six, I had a hard enough time reading and writing my name, but they figured they could read the books about Ireland to me like a bedtime story. One faded page told us that Westport was a town designed in the Georgian architectural style. When Mom got to that, I asked her what the heck it meant. My parents exchanged a glance and grabbed a dictionary.

There were several odd things about Jake's trips to Ireland. One was that neither my parents nor his ever chewed us out for spending so much time on those long-distance calls to each other. The other weird thing was that when he came back, things were never awkward. We never worried that the other had made cooler friends or that we'd outgrown each other. Instead, Jake always returned with an armful of candy and silly stories. Then we'd hug, and I'd tell him about the gossip from around town. We'd play Nintendo, go to the mall, and do one of my favorite things: hang out in the kitchen while Jake made something—

pancakes, cookies, or muffins. I'd never met a kid who liked to cook before, and I definitely didn't mind being a taste tester.

Our childhood was measured that way, and in all the other important things: in haircuts given to plastic ponies, in bets on who could keep sour Warheads in their mouth the longest, in laps around the block on Jake's bike while songs from R.E.M. and The Cranberries drifted from radios in open garages, in the fingers we'd cross as we slid a movie into the VCR, hoping the worn machine wouldn't eat the tape, and in double helpings of worms and dirt that we'd steal from the fridge when no one was looking.

It was like that until I was ten.

I sat on my bed reading *The Boxcar Children* while Steven sat cross-legged on the floor, sticking bulbs into his Lite-Brite. I didn't pay much attention to the phone ringing downstairs until I heard the upset, muffled talking that followed. I slid off the bed and walked down the hallway, Steven too focused on his picture to notice. As I tiptoed down the stairs, the sounds got louder. It was crying.

My parents never cried.

My feet were ice on the linoleum kitchen floor as I peered into the living room. My parents stood by the end table. Mom had the corded phone in her hand but held it away from her like it burned. I couldn't see her face, but her head was bowed. Dad's eyes were red. He rested a hand on her back.

My mom choked the words out. "He says it's Bonnie."

I didn't know what that meant, but it made my stomach hurt. I darted back up the stairs before they could see me, but I stood by the top to listen in. I only caught fragments of what they said.

Bonnie was in Rochester for work.

Wet roads.

Fog.

No one else was hurt.

I held my breath as I scurried back to my room. Steven sat

on my bed, looking at my book and accidentally breaking the spine. I didn't get mad. I didn't care.

I locked my bedroom door and threw my stuffed animals in front of it, like I thought I could keep everything bad out. Like as long as we stayed in my room, whatever scary thing that had happened wouldn't come true.

For a long time after Bonnie's death, I closed my eyes and saw those terrible moments at the funeral home: Craig's hand glued to Jake as he held his son close, Jake's face puffy from the tears he had already cried and the tears he was *about* to cry, burnt coffee, congealed funeral potatoes, and little Steven tugging my shirt, confused.

After the funeral, Jake and I sat on our swing. As I sat next to my friend, watching his red-rimmed eyes stare out into nothing, I realized for the first time that your life is made up of two different parts—the part when your parents were with you and afterward, when they were gone. My stomach turned as I realized Jake was going to spend so much time in the second part. There was going to be so much that Bonnie wouldn't be there for. So many memories without her in them. And there was nothing anyone could do about it.

Life's not fair. And like a kid, I thought I was the first person to realize this.

I didn't know what to say to Jake. I didn't know what to do. The only thing I could think of was to hold his hand. I clamped down on his clammy fingers. They were cold, even though it was a hot summer day. I worried that Jake didn't want to hold hands, but after a moment, his raw eyes met mine, and he gave me a faint smile. Then he squeezed my fingers.

For a little while after Bonnie's death, I worried that Jake and Craig would move, but my fears quickly evaporated. After only four years, it was clear that our families would be intertwined forever. Our parents owned a restaurant together, plus we had dinners together, celebrated holidays together, went on trips together—even one to Ireland once—and we bonded by rolling our eyes at Steven's progressively stranger hobbies and collections. The Bradleys were always there for us, and we tried our best to be there for them.

It didn't take too long for me to realize that my friendship with Jake was something I'd never want to ruin.

2

EARLY SPRING, AGE 38

I scurried around a small church in Alexandria, Minnesota, a town of just under 15,000 people that I'd lived in or around my whole life. Alex was a town of lakes—Lake Le Homme Dieu, Lake Agnes, Lake Ida, Lake Carlos, and those were only a few. They ran through town and surrounded it. The streets curved and angled around the gentle lap of waves, the pavement broken up by water, trees, and the hum of boats.

The rest of the bridesmaids and I put on the finishing touches to our hair and makeup. My friend, Monica, curled my long brown hair while I slapped on dark lipstick and a kitten eye at warp speed.

I adjusted my blue velvet dress as Jake walked up, grinning. He looked at ease in his dark suit, sliding next to me. He was a lanky six-three, and I was barely five-five, so I had to look up to tease him. His hair was chestnut brown, and, as always, he had a little stubble on his face. Relaxed, self-deprecating humor was the name of his game. His bright blue eyes sparkled when he joked around or playfully gave someone the finger. He was great if you needed to get through an awkward silence, but the right thing could wind him up. The 2010 milk shipment debacle at B&R Café was a big one. He walked around in frantic circles for a day with the expression of someone on a skateboard about to faceplant into a railing.

I knew there were days when his marriage made him anxious too, but he mostly kept that to himself.

"How are things?" I asked.

He chuckled. "Since I talked to you yesterday? Grand." He gave me a casual glance. "Your dress is pretty. Is that velvet? It's all coming back."

I swooshed around. "Yeah, I think I wore a velvet dress for Christmas when I was seven."

"I think I have photographic evidence of that. Next will be stirrup pants."

The wedding planner scurried over. His face was stamped with a large frown. "You two." He pointed at us. "For the love of God, don't you dare trip when you walk down the aisle like you did at the rehearsal."

Jake's eyes twinkled. "I don't think we tripped, really." Jake nodded toward Monica. "Pretty sure Monica kicked us when we went through the doors."

"Don't you throw me under the bus," said Monica, with her hand on her hip. "You two are as uncoordinated as Electric Slide night down at our bar."

"I've never witnessed Electric Slide night, but somehow I believe you."

Jake's cousin, Felicity, was the no-fuss, sporty bride. She was tall like Jake, with a head of curly black hair that she usually had up in a ponytail. Her wedding dress was a simple, off-white, strapless gown with a longer train.

As Felicity and her fiancé, Mark, said their vows, my eyes drifted through the church and finally settled on Jake with the groomsmen. We made eye contact, and he smiled, his eyes bright. But I'd been his friend since I was six, and I detected sadness there. Was he thinking about *his* vows?

My eyes unconsciously drifted out to the pews, where Jake's wife of nearly ten years sat in the second row with the rest of our family. Ashley was pretty, with reddish hair, brown eyes, and understated yet fashionable clothing. But it was kind of hard to look past her bored, impatient expression. I always thought Ash acted like life had been dumped on her, and now she was stuck with it. She seemed like she was just passing time with Jake, and as his best friend, that didn't sit well with me.

Ashley wasn't paying attention to the service. Instead, her eyes wandered across the church to Kenneth, Felicity's brother, and Jake's other cousin. Ashley raised an eyebrow at Kenneth, who stared down at his lap. She probably wondered what Kenneth was doing there. *Everyone* wondered what Kenneth was doing there. He'd recently been in and out of jail for breaking and entering and theft. Nothing big-time, like a jewelry store heist, but enough to get him branded a loser. It wasn't a secret that Felicity drove to his house and gave him a verbal thrashing.

My gaze shifted back to the bridal party. Jake's eyes met mine again, and I looked at the back of Felicity's dress to make sure everything was in place. At least that was what I told myself. Most of the time, Jake and I laughed over bad movies and took our kids bowling. But then sometimes, something would flash inside me, and I couldn't look into Jake's eyes for too long. Certain things seemed to bubble up—things that were better left where they were. Because he was my *friend*, damn it. And he was just being kind. Just being funny.

And you both have kids, for God's sake, I thought, bitching myself out. *And he's married.*

Our kids sat in the pews, wedged between Ashley and Steven. Daisy, Jake and Ashley's nine-year-old daughter, and Henry, my eleven-year-old son, played the old Game Boy I recently found in the attic. Played it on mute, of course.

"Is this some kind of joke?" Henry asked when I first offered them the Game Boy. Henry was lanky with messy brown hair. "This is even older than a DS."

"I think it'll be cool to see how old people had fun," said Daisy, grabbing it. Daisy was a short little thing with light brown hair, a face full of dimples, and an affinity for tie-dye.

I stared at them. "I'm not old." They stared right back. "Do you even *know* how old I am?"

"Twenty-five is old," said Henry.

I sighed. "Stabbed through the heart by my own son."

The reception was in an events room attached to B&R Café, a restaurant my dad co-owned with Jake and his dad. Our families had been in business together since Jake and I were kids, and somehow, we were all still friends. Although there had been a blueberry shipment incident a few years back…

The place was decked out with crisp tablecloths and white, glittery tulle cascading from the ceiling. A million tiny, sparkling lights were everywhere. With all those candles, it looked like a place where you could conduct a séance.

"This room is blinding," said Henry. He sat next to me at our table, blinking rapidly.

"It's supposed to be romantic…duh," said Daisy.

"Then romance hurts," said Henry.

I cracked a smile. "Truer words were never spoken."

My parents sat down at our table and sighed. My mom, Gail, had shoulder-length light hair and loved silky button-up blouses. She seemed to have a firmer grasp on reality than the rest of my family. In 1997, during the debacle over Steven's mysteriously acquired traffic cone collection, Dad spiraled into anxiety, worried that we'd all wind up in the pokey. Meanwhile, Mom sat back, cool and calm, doing a crossword puzzle.

My dad, Dennis, was stocky with salt-and-pepper hair and a deep love for clothes that made him look like he belonged to a bowling league. He was terrible at bowling.

"I don't know what this punch is, but it tastes like Fruity Pebbles," said Dad, sipping it.

"It'll pair well with the dry chicken," said Mom. "Weddings always have dry chicken."

"Mom!" I said, scolding her as I kicked her foot.

"Say what you will about the food," said Craig, sitting next to my dad. Then, under his breath, he added in Irish, "Bheadh ár mbia níos fearr. We didn't make it. Just let them use the room. It was catered by some coffee shop in Saint Cloud."

Craig was a tall, lanky guy like his son. He reminded me of a teddy bear, always ready to give you a hug or a firm pat on the back. His philosophy was to go with the flow. Because you never know what might happen. He had experienced that firsthand.

"If a coffee shop did this, there better be scones," I said.

My brother, Steven, slid down into a chair across from me, looking sullen. Steven was big on collections and hobbies that made him look weird. He decided at the age of five that he was an artist, but the art he planned to make wasn't going to be a statue or a painting. The art was *him*. He was a lot of yarn, fabric, stickers, and paint smashed onto a canvas. He had pointy cheekbones and a thin nose. His dark, curly hair stuck up like a cross between a mad scientist and Wolverine. He only ever wore sports coats with a T-shirt underneath.

"Well, shit," he said, slouching in his chair. "Here we all are at a table together, talking and eating like we do every Sunday. We could have skipped the wedding and eaten Shake 'n Bake somewhere more comfortable."

I eyed him. "Where's your date?"

He shrugged. "She decided to go to the extreme ironing competition instead."

My dad uttered some kind of inaudible, annoyed noise.

"It's a legitimate sport," said Steven. "People do EI all over the world. She could take first place in paddleboard ironing this weekend, and I'm stuck at this stupid thing."

"Weddings aren't stupid," said Mom. "They're a declaration of love. It's a very beautiful thing…with dry chicken."

Steven usually had nothing against weddings. The way he belted out Celine Dion and sometimes played the guitar at them was proof of that. And most of the time, he was the king of laid-back and casual. But as he sat across from me, his nervous eyes kept scanning the room. I knew why. One of Felicity's close friends was Margot Crowley, Steven's ex-girlfriend. They broke up five years ago, but Steven still felt the sting and rarely talked about her. I didn't know if he wanted Margot to be there or not.

Everyone at the table exchanged glances as Steven stared down at his punch. Our eyes said it all. Nobody had seen Margot. Maybe she wasn't there, or maybe she was hidden in a dark corner. Avoiding Steven was Margot's second job.

Steven pulled the plastic cup away from his mouth and smelled his drink like it was battery acid. "Aren't weddings supposed to be places where single people find love? How is anyone supposed to love anyone else while drinking Fruity Pebble punch?"

I laughed down at the table.

"Where's *your* date?" Steven asked.

"Shut up, Steven." I stuck my tongue out at him. Our running gag since he was six was to constantly pretend we were annoyed with each other.

"Mom doesn't have a date," said Henry. "So embarrassing. You should have let me set up that Tinder account."

"You could've asked Lance," said Steven.

I felt like making a gagging noise. Lance was Henry's father, and therefore, the last guy on the planet I would ask to be my wedding date. He was probably busy anyway, doing push-ups while a thin woman in a crop top sat on his back for added resistance.

Jake and Ashley strolled up. Ashley looked like she had gotten a head start on drinking. My whole family gaped at the wide smile that took up her whole face and the way she had her arm wrapped around Jake. She *never* had her arm wrapped around Jake. Daisy stared at her parents like they were grossing her out.

"Hello again!" said Ash, smiling at us.

Jake looked surprised by her attitude, too, especially when she reached up and kissed his cheek.

"I'm going to get a drink," she said to Jake. "Then will you dance with me?"

"Of course, Ash," said Jake. He almost blushed at the thought.

"Get me one of whatever you've been drinking, kid," said Craig.

"Sure thing," said Ashley, patting her father-in-law on the shoulder as she walked away.

I pulled out a chair for Jake, and he sat next to me.

"Thanks for looking after my wayward daughter," said Jake as he eyed Daisy.

Daisy shrugged. "Henry and I were hanging out."

Jake nudged Henry, making him look up from his Game Boy.

The smile on Jake's face was like a kid up to no good. "I got it."

Henry's eyes lit up. "Really?"

Jake reached into the inner pocket of his suit and pulled something out. It was a small bag of chips. He laughed and tossed it to my son. "They might be a little crunched from the mail and then from keeping them in my jacket. I had to hide them for the dramatic reveal."

Henry studied the chips. Jake and I exchanged a smile.

"What are they?" I squinted through the darkness, trying to make out the words on the bag.

"They're All Dressed potato chips," said Henry. "Jake and I were talking about them the other day. They're super popular in Canada."

"We thought we better give it a lash. Find out if they're delicious or disgusting. It's going to be very scientific."

Daisy scooted closer. "They're gonna be gross, Dad. I can smell them from here."

Jake laughed. "He hasn't even opened the package yet."

Henry ripped open the bag and offered us each a chip. Henry and Jake ate theirs right away. Daisy and I gave each other nervous glances, daring each other to go first.

"They *do* smell strong." I inspected my chip. Daisy and I laughed when we finally bit the bullet.

"A taste explosion," said Henry.

"Ten out of ten." Jake ate another one, studying them. "I have no idea what the flavor is. But it grows on you."

"Tastes like mold," said Daisy, scrunching her nose.

We all laughed.

"I'm not sure about these," I said. "I think the ketchup ones were better."

Henry and Jake kept eating the chips.

"What should we try next?" asked Jake.

"Poutine!" said Henry, excited.

"What's that?" asked Daisy.

"Isn't it fries?" I asked.

Jake nodded. "With gravy and cheese curds."

Daisy and I looked at each other and shook our heads again, giggling. *No, thanks.*

"We'll show them, Henry," said Jake. "We'll get them hooked."

Henry had known Jake his whole life, so they were close. If the kids had a movie night, Jake would make snacks he knew Henry liked. Sometimes Henry had slumber parties with Daisy over at Jake and Ashley's house. Then Jake made homemade pizza, followed by root beer floats. After that, the kids usually raced around on a sugar high. It filled my heart when I saw them together. Jake loved Henry. If I were honest with myself, Jake was the closest thing to a father figure Henry had ever known. Way more of a father to him than his biological one. It was a bittersweet feeling. I was glad Henry had Jake, but everyone who knew Jake was lucky.

When we got up for snacks, I pulled Jake aside. "What's with Ash? Was she replaced by a pod person?"

"No idea," said Jake, glancing around the room. "She's been grumpy about the wedding all week. But this morning, when we got up, she was excited about it. She and Daisy laughed while they got ready. It was nice."

"It sounds nice," I said, trying to be supportive.

Jake looked at everything except me. I could see the tension in him. His jaw shifted.

"It's going to be alright," I said, over the music, squeezing his arm to reassure him.

He finally made eye contact. "I know. Ups and downs. That's the way marriage is."

When the DJ put on *Macarena*, Jake reached out his hand and asked me to dance. We laughed as we went through the moves.

"This is what my brain thought was important." I put my hands on my hips. "I could have geometry stored in my brain. Or piano lessons. But nope, I chose to remember 1990s dance moves."

"Look at you," said Jake, watching me to keep up. "I don't know what I'm doing."

"Sure you do. We used to dance to this all the time."

Jake laughed. "I don't think so. That was all you. You loved this song."

I shook my head. "No, you can't pin that on me."

"Pretty sure you did."

"I loved the Spice Girls," I said.

Jake winked. "I liked them too, but for a different reason."

Just when Jake was getting the hang of it, the music changed to a much slower song.

"This is better," said Jake, gesturing for me to come closer. "We can have a good cry to Ed Sheeran."

I put a hand on his shoulder, and he placed one tenderly around my velvet waist. And there it was, that little sizzle when his fingers touched my dress. Like he was on bare skin.

Damn it, Leah. Don't think about it.

This was one of those times, just like in the church. A time where all the joking fell away, and everything suddenly seemed serious and immediate. I couldn't ignore how good Jake smelled. Caramel and musk. My chest felt like it was filled to the brim with something winged, trying to crash out. I couldn't deny that I wanted to dance with Jake, *really* wanted to, but it would have been safer to hang out by the food, laughing and hunting for another slice of chocolate cake. And my stupid body was betraying me. Heat pooled in my stomach. My hands turned embarrassingly sweaty. I hoped he didn't notice.

Leah, you're a jackass. If you were going to say something, you should've done it years ago, before his wedding. You're out of luck, idiot.

I should've said something lighthearted, but instead, I swayed with him to the music, stuck in the king of awkward situations. God, he had nice arms. Who was I kidding? All of him was great. Long, lean muscles. Over the years, I'd seen him many times without a shirt when we went swimming at one of the lakes. The man was *fine*.

Did I blush? I felt his eyes on me, but I gazed around the room.

"Hey." His voice was quiet. I had no choice but to look at him. For a minute, I thought he'd say something I was afraid he'd say. And if he ever said anything like *that*, our friendship would be ruined, and our families would explode. Plus, I was *not* a woman who did *things* with a married man, even if we'd known each other forever. Just because I saw him first didn't mean I had dibs. He wasn't a slice of pizza, for God's sake. "Did you see what Felicity and Mark are giving as wedding favors?"

I let out a little relieved laugh.

He doesn't think that way about you. You're his best friend. That's good. That's what you want.

"Twin Bings." I smiled. "Are they saving you a whole case?"

Jake grimaced. "Of all the candies in the world… They could've at least picked Salted Nut Rolls."

Now that we had eased into a conversation, the awkwardness fell away. Of course, it had probably only been awkward for me.

"Can you believe Kenneth is here?"

"He didn't have much of a choice," said Jake. "He's Felicity's brother. I guess Joe and Tina have had a lot of sleepless nights because of him. I always knew he was a tool. When we were little, he wiped his runny nose on his shirt and then traipsed around like that, snot everywhere. That was the first sign."

I giggled and scanned the room. "I don't see him."

"He's probably in the bathroom sticking decorations down his pants," said Jake.

"Monica's in charge of the gift table. She's been watching it like a knight who's sworn an oath."

A smile crept over Jake's face. He tried to be Fred Astaire by twirling me around. We both cringed, thinking I'd trip in my heels, but I let out a laugh when I spun back into his arms intact. He grabbed my waist again, his smile growing.

"Have you danced with Ashley yet?"

"She's MIA." His eyes flickered. "She owes me one when I find her."

3

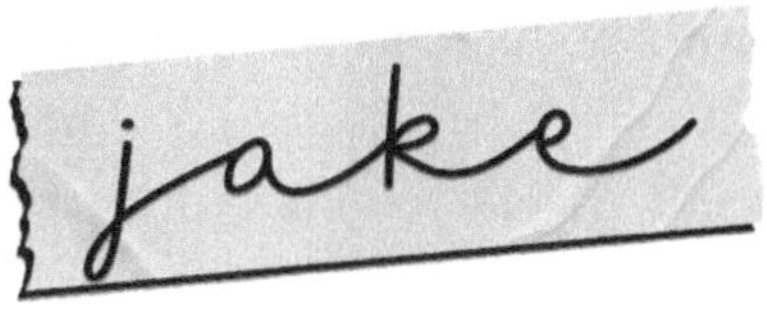

"Have you seen your mom, Dais?" I asked.

"Nope," said Daisy. She and Henry were making origami animals out of expensive wedding napkins.

I gave her a pat on the shoulder and nodded to Dennis and Gail. They nodded back, understanding. We always watched each other's kids. Daisy was in good hands with the Roths.

Nothing like a wedding to remind a man that his life was imploding. All the glitter, candles, and booze made everyone else smile, but they weren't doing much for my mood. I seemed to be nursing a hatred for "Come and Get Your Love" that I never knew I had until hearing it twice in under thirty minutes.

When had love stopped feeling like sweet songs and shared smiles and turned into a puzzle I couldn't solve, into long silences I couldn't stretch across? At the beginning, everything you did seemed to make them laugh and smile. So many inside jokes and stolen kisses. And then suddenly, it was like a light switch going off, and everything they liked about you before made them slide further away from you on the sofa.

I walked around the ballroom, congratulating Felicity and

Mark, drinking some punch that tasted faintly of cereal, and making a stupid joke with some guy I barely knew. I was good at jokes. Jokes were easy. They were a nice blanket to cover things I didn't want to talk about.

I had been making jokes since my mother died.

Out of the darkness and twinkling lights, Ashley bumped into me out of nowhere, like she had rematerialized back into the world.

"There you are," I said, smiling a little. "You still owe me that dance."

Ash rested her hands on my chest. "You remembered? That's my baby."

She gave me a naughty smile, like she had plans for me. I liked that idea but would've liked it more if she wasn't banjaxed. She wrapped her arms around me and rested her head on my chest.

Ash had never called me *baby* in her life. There had been a *honey* or two in the first couple of years, but then that all fell away. I put a tentative hand on her back, and we swayed to the music. She didn't say anything, but that was okay. Couples were like that sometimes. Comfortable silences.

My eyes drifted around the room to a small group of people talking and laughing. Leah and her brother Steven were there. She saw me and instantly smiled.

Leah knew my marriage was imploding. I could tell when she squeezed my arm. I just hoped Daisy didn't know.

Hell of a night, I thought, dancing with Ashley.

Something was wrong. More wrong than usual. Ashley had been running hotter and colder than ever. And she'd tossed her normal routine out the window. We never knew where she was, and it made me nervous. Now, if someone wanted to go out and do something in the evening, that was wonderful. That was great. But when you started having a secret schedule, and then got angry at your family for asking about it, it didn't inspire a hell of a lot of confidence.

My eyes drifted to Leah, who stood chatting in her usual animated fashion, nothing but bright eyes, moving hands, tousled hair, and freckles. She scrunched her face and stuck her tongue out at me when I glanced over. Somehow that made me feel a bit better, despite everything.

There was something about Leah. I wondered if she knew there was a spark about her, an energy that drew people in and made them feel safe. I'd sensed it the moment we'd met as kids. She wasn't afraid to speak her mind and was a fierce protector of the ones she loved. When you were with her, you were home.

There *had* once been a time when I'd thought...when I'd *hoped* that we could be more. There were nights when I stayed awake, staring at the ceiling, wondering if I had a chance in hell. But there were a lot of romance movies where the goofy best friend didn't fare well. And I was pretty sure that would be my fate as well, given the marathon-running, muscled guys that Leah usually went for.

But despite that, there had been a moment on the porch swing in her parents' maple tree when I wanted to take that chance. I even planned what I was going to say, but I fucked it up royally. Our families were having a Halloween party. Despite the cold weather, the swing was still up. It was always up for us. We wiped the frost off the wood and sat down, even though Leah wore tights and a short skirt under her green wool coat. She nestled next to me with those perfect curves. Leah's ass was, well, fuck me. I flexed my jaw, willing my body not to react to our proximity.

We stared up at the stars, and she leaned her head on my shoulder. I was going to do it then—I *should* have done it then— but she was my best friend, and I was terrified of ruining our good thing. If she didn't feel the same way, what would have happened to our friendship? What would have happened to our families?

I didn't kiss her. I didn't say a damn thing. And after a long while, her dad slid open the deck door and told us that dinner was ready.

But for years after, I replayed that moment in my mind. And each time, I did it right. I took her hand and told her we had always made a pretty good pair, and I wanted to be a pair with her for the rest of my life.

I snapped out of my reverie as Ash repositioned herself in my arms, giggling. We smiled faintly at each other. She put her head back down on my chest and we kept dancing.

I didn't like to think of that memory anymore, or how I could've met Leah under that tree to fix it. To do it right. She probably never felt the same as I did, and I would've just made a fool of myself. Two weeks after we sat there on Halloween, Leah met Lance. Mr. Fecking Personality. Four weeks later, she was pregnant. And not long after that, I went out on my first date with Ashley.

I'd buried all those foolish feelings for Leah long ago. We were just friends.

"What happened to your hair?" I asked Ash.

She nervously touched her frazzled locks. "What?"

"It's all messed up in the back."

She ran her hand through her hair but didn't answer me.

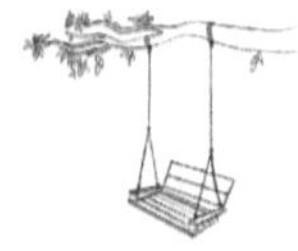

That night in bed, Ash slipped in, pulled the covers up, and turned away from me. I stared at the ceiling for a moment, then I scooted closer to her and put a hand on her side.

"What are you doing?" she asked, almost asleep.

I felt like an instant idiot. "I thought we could cuddle."

Ashley craned her neck to look at me. "We haven't cuddled in years."

My eyebrows lifted. "That's what I mean."

She turned back to the wall. "Not in the mood."

I rested my head in my hand. "You used to enjoy cuddling with me. You used to enjoy having sex with me too. Now I could mark the times on the wall like a person marking days trapped on a desert island."

She looked at me again. "We're not newlyweds."

I tried to keep my voice at a whisper level. Still, I couldn't hide the exasperation in my tone. "Yes, that's a true statement. I thought we had a good night—"

"Parts of it were good," said Ashley.

"Well, then…" I said, trailing off. I had no idea what I was trying to convince her of. "Is there a problem, Ash? Is there something you need? Because I want to give you what you need. I want to make you happy."

I thought that was a nice thing to say and something I'd like to hear myself, but all it elicited from Ashley was a long, fed-up sigh, like this was the breaking point, and I was nothing but the world's most annoying dick.

"Ash?"

Finally, she flipped onto her back and stared at me. "I don't want to cuddle with you because you're too needy."

Um... "What is that supposed to mean?"

"You're too nice."

Fecking hell. "Well, I've known my fair share of assholes, if there's one you'd like me to mimic."

"You have too many needs. I wish you were feral. I wish you'd just take me. A man's man. I don't want you to ask about my feelings. I don't want to ask about yours. I want you to be something tough and wild."

My mouth hung open. The song "Troglodyte (Cave Man)"

ran through my head. My wife had described a man who was the exact opposite of me. Great.

"I thought women liked being asked about their wants and needs," I said, still gaping.

"Not me." She sighed. "Why can't you be like...Rip from *Yellowstone*?"

I didn't think my eyes could go wider. "Are you fecking crazy? That's a character from a television show. The man's not even real."

Ashley shrugged.

"Doesn't he smash people's faces in?" I asked. "Doesn't he goddamn kill people to keep secrets?"

I stared at Ash. She stared back.

"Is there a second option for a man you'd prefer I be?"

Ashley didn't respond.

"Son of a bitch," I whispered. The feeling drained from my face. "So...I make you incredibly unhappy."

"No." Ashley scooted closer. This was the closest we'd been together in bed for a long time. "I'm still drunk. And I'm half asleep. You know that I get grumpy at night. I don't mean any of this. Go to bed. We'll have sex tomorrow."

She was like a mother offering ice cream as an apology. I still didn't know what to say, but Ashley was already back on her side of the bed, curled up, and pointed away from me again.

I crossed my arms and gazed up at the dark light fixture. "I love you, Ashley."

But she was already asleep.

4

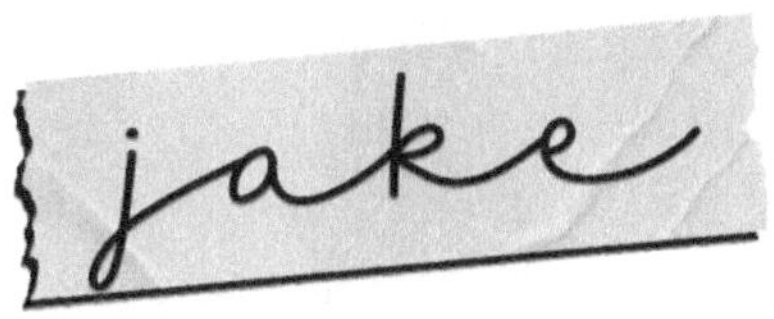

I woke up to an empty bed and light streaming in through the windows. I sighed and got up. I felt like shit, and I wasn't even hungover. I couldn't even recall if I had a drink at the wedding.

"If I did, it was weak," I said, pulling on my pants.

I walked down the stairs to find Daisy sitting at the kitchen island, dressed in a tie-dye shirt with her hair up in a ponytail. She poured cereal into a bowl and smiled. "Morning, Dad."

"Morning, sweetie," I said. "Time got away from me. Do you want waffles instead?"

Daisy shook her head and poured milk into her bowl. "This stuff is good."

"And it meets all possible sugar requirements you might have for the day," I said, kissing her head. "I'll have some too."

"It tastes like that punch at the wedding." Daisy laughed as she took a bite.

Her grin cracked me up. "That's true. Not sure what was going on there."

I poured the last of the cereal into the bowl. "Ash," I called out to wherever she was in the house. "We have to get cereal next time we're at the store."

"Mommy's not here," said Daisy.

"What was that?"

"She left a long time ago."

I poured milk. "Went for a run."

Daisy shook her head. "I heard her car, and I looked out the window. I couldn't fall back asleep."

I abandoned my cereal and walked across the kitchen like I was seasick. I opened the door to the garage, and the gaping space where her Buick had been didn't lie.

"It's on Blink," said Daisy.

I walked back into the kitchen, trying to sound light. I didn't want Daisy to be worried that Ash had left. "You've been watching too many detective movies with Steven."

Daisy rolled her eyes. "My bedroom window is right by the driveway. Duh."

What could I say to that?

I sat back down but pushed my cereal aside. I grabbed my phone and went to the app. One of the cameras pointed at the driveway. We had gotten it so we'd know when packages were delivered. My hands were sweaty as I scrolled through videos.

"Four-thirty in the morning!" I said, forgetting to put on an air of nonchalance. "What the actual fuck?"

Daisy dissolved into giggles.

"I mean…shit. I mean, I'm so sorry, sweetie. I shouldn't have sworn. That was very bad."

"Grandpa Craig swears worse than that."

I raised an eyebrow. "That's very true."

I called Ashley as discreetly as possible, but Daisy seemed content as she wove a bracelet out of plastic threads. There was no answer. I called again fifteen minutes later. Still no answer. I texted her. Nothing. It was Sunday morning, and it felt like my wife had fallen off the face of the planet.

"Is everything okay?" asked Daisy.

"Of course."

Leah showed up five minutes after I called her. "Hey, people!" Her face was relaxed. For Daisy's benefit, I guessed. "How are you liking that big box of crayons, kid?"

"It's awesome!" said Daisy. "There are eight different greens."

Leah nodded. "That's because I only had a ten-pack when I was a kid. And they were RoseArt. I know what it means to be deprived."

Steven moseyed in behind Leah and pushed his way into the kitchen.

"You brought your brother," I said, but Leah looked as confused as me.

"Nope," said Steven. "Just out for a walk and saw Leah's car." Steven surveyed the kitchen. "You have any food? Pastrami, maybe?" His eyes settled on my forgotten cereal. "Is that Fruity Pebbles? I love when it's mushy."

"Don't you have food at your fancy new townhouse?" I asked.

Steven sat next to Daisy, frowning. "Me and the new place are experiencing a lovers' spat. Pretty sure I'll get kicked out within a year. Not sure I can swing the rent."

"Didn't you think about that before taking the place?" I asked.

"Wasn't your girlfriend moving in?" asked Leah.

Steven mowed through the cereal. "She texted me this morning. We are finito. Alone again, naturally. She met some new fella at that EI competition. You know what he specializes in?" Steven sighed. "EI rock climbing."

Leah and I exchanged a glance. Daisy eyed Steven like he was something from a different planet.

"Does that mean he irons while climbing up the side of a cliff?" I asked. "How does that work exactly?"

Steven slouched. "I don't know. And I don't want to. I need a new hobby." He nudged Daisy. "How do you feel about collecting all the elements on the periodic table with me? It might get dicey when we get to the radioactive ones."

Leah pulled me aside, whispering, "So, Ash left super early? She didn't say anything?"

"Nope." I crossed my arms. My stomach was nonstop crashing waves.

"Did you argue?"

How to answer that? "I don't know what the hell it was. But I...don't think she's happy with me." I lowered my voice even more as my palms got sweaty. "She hasn't been happy with me for a long time."

Leah waved away that comment, like she couldn't imagine someone being unhappy with me. There was that banging heart again, the dumb fuck.

Steven didn't always have the firmest grasp on reality, but he must have sensed we were having a conversation I didn't want young ears anywhere near. He asked Daisy about her recent drawings, and she pulled him to her room to show them off. From down the hall, I heard him complimenting the shading she'd done on a bird. Daisy loved drawing animals.

Thanks, Steven, I thought, trying to relax.

"I'm sure everything's fine," Leah said. "Ash likes to exercise. She could be at that fitness place. Monica says it's loud there, so maybe she didn't hear her phone. I don't go to gyms since Lance owns one. I see a deadlift machine and walk the other way."

I tried to push down the worry. "Maybe you're right."

"Has she done anything else weird lately?"

I shrugged. "She goes out some nights, but that's because she's taking a pottery class at the community center."

Leah nodded, thinking.

Steven wandered back out into the kitchen. "Daisy's drawing me a tiger." He looked me up and down. "Pottery class, eh?" He suppressed a laugh. "Were you born yesterday?"

I flipped him off.

Steven jammed more cereal into his mouth, talking around it. "Sweet, naïve lamb."

"There's nothing wrong with Ashley doing that, you jackass. That's a good thing. We should all expand our horizons. Try something new."

That was funny, coming from me. Mr. Peanut Butter and Jelly Sandwich for lunch for the last fifteen years.

Steven smirked.

"What?" I asked.

"I know there's nothing wrong with hobbies. I have a hundred." He shifted. "But you think that class exists?"

My face turned hot. Steven's smile was positively evil. He grabbed his iPhone and proceeded to do something that was probably unwise. It dawned on me that quite a few people were now privy to my imploding marriage. The tile floor seemed like a good place to pass out.

"What are you doing?" asked Leah.

"The community center has a list of courses online," said Steven. "That's how I found out they were doing that class on whittling soup ladles."

"That ladle hardly held any soup," said Leah. "And it was terrible soup."

Steven scanned the website. "The ladle was bad, but the soup was alright. Who doesn't love Lima beans?"

I shook my head. "I don't think this is a good idea. Everyone is entitled to their privacy."

But they were entranced by Steven's phone. Finally, he raised his hand in victory. "Hot damn!"

I was officially nervous. "What?"

"Right now, the community center is offering Introduction to Watercolors, Intermediate Basket Weaving, and something called The Simplistic Beauty of the Haiku. I should take that sometime." He dramatically raised an eyebrow. "No pottery classes."

We stared at each other, understanding what this implied but saying nothing.

"I'm sure she's at the gym." Leah put on her best reassuring voice. She was trying to be supportive, but I felt like I might puke up my small intestine.

Steven balked. "She's not at the gym. She's four blocks away."

"What the hell, Steven?" Was my whole body clammy? Was that normal? "Why didn't you say that right away?"

He shrugged. "I wanted to see how this played out." His voice was calm. "Isn't the human condition fascinating?"

Leah mumbled and rubbed her temple. "Tell us what you know."

"I was out for my morning constitutional—"

"It's a walk, Steven," said Leah. "You walk on Sunday mornings. You're not an 1800s gentleman with a top hat and tails."

"Not with that attitude," said Steven.

I didn't think I could take much more of this. It was supposed to be a nice morning. Eating cereal and playing a card game with Daisy.

"I go out early," said Steven. "That way I can get all around town. People watch. You see some funny things." He eyed me. "This morning, I saw Ashley's car. It's on Kingston Road."

"Kingston Road?" I asked, confused.

Leah's eyes widened, realizing what this meant before me. "Oh my God."

"She's at Kenneth's," said Steven.

Steven agreed to watch Daisy while we went to Kenneth's.

"I'll drive," Leah said, as we got into her car. "You're too wound up."

There was no arguing that. I felt like I had lockjaw; my face was so tight. My mind swirled with a million terrible possibilities. Kenneth? Surely not. "Why would she be there?"

Leah didn't respond, but her hands tightened on the wheel.

"Kenneth steals DVDs," I said. "Who the fuck wants DVDs anymore? He breaks into elderly people's houses and takes whatever cash they have sitting around, for God's sake."

We stopped at a light. Leah tried to flash me an optimistic smile, but it didn't work. "This is one of those times when things seem dire. But I'm sure there's a perfectly logical explanation. We'll laugh about it tomorrow."

That was probably true, but instead, I looked at her and said, "If my wife is screwing my deadbeat cousin, you're going to have to peel me up off the floor."

There it was—Kenneth's house—and Ashley's car was in the driveway. It was like a weight pressing into my chest. I stared at it and had a bout of raspy breathing. I fumbled with the door handle and stumbled into the driveway.

Leah zipped out of the vehicle and walked with me to the door. "Remain calm." She touched my arm. "Do you want me to stay in the car or go in with you?"

"*I* don't even want to go in there." But I didn't want to face this alone, no matter how embarrassing. "You might as well come. It's a good day for emotional carnage."

I reached a sweaty hand to the doorknob.

"Maybe it's locked," said Leah.

But I twisted that bastard right open, quick and quiet, before hesitating.

Leah stared at me. "This is crazy. It can't be what we think it is."

The door didn't make a sound when we entered. I'd been at Kenneth's house a few times before his downward slide into assholery. He had odds and ends, vaguely reminiscent of the 1980s. We peeked into the kitchen, living room, and laundry room. Nothing. The place was silent. Oppressively silent.

"Where are the bedrooms?" asked Leah in a whisper. The thought made my face hot.

But then there was a sound above us that answered that question. Leah's eyes widened. My stomach dropped.

My ears rang as we tried to ascend the stairs without making them squeak. The noise became easier to distinguish with each step. It felt like something was draining from my face, through my body, and right out to the floor. Leah gave my arm a reassuring squeeze as we rounded the corner to the bedrooms.

My whole body was cold. I pushed the bedroom door open and stepped in. It felt like I had tunnel vision when I saw the bed. There was rhythmic movement under the puffy white comforter. Leah stood next to me, her mouth wide.

I didn't know who made a sound first, but finally, Kenneth's blond head came up for air. When he saw my face, he looked like a man afraid he was about to be beheaded. He nervously nudged Ashley, who stuck her head out, grumbling, her hair a tangled mess.

Ash and I stared at each other for a second. Her mouth was a little "*o*."

My nostrils flared. "Aren't weddings fecking romantic?" I was like an overtightened stringed instrument. "I guess this settles the question about whether you're leaving me."

"Shit, shit, shit," said Kenneth, grabbing for his pants.

"Give me my clothes!" Ashley yelled. Leah and I turned and left the room. "Jake, wait!"

We were almost down the stairs when I heard a commotion coming after us. Ash zoomed into the living room, trying to stop me. Her shirt and leggings looked as though they had been thrown on in a tornado.

"I cannot believe this," I said, eyes on fire. I couldn't feel my feet moving. I couldn't feel anything. "What am I going to tell Daisy, for Christ's sake? She's waiting for us to come home and play UNO."

Ashley stood between us and the front door. "I need to talk to you."

Leah's face was plastered with shock. She also looked like she wanted to jump out the window to escape this awkward situation.

"I think the picture you gave us up there is worth a thousand words, Ash." I stared into her eyes. Did she feel like crying, too? "And I'm sure as fuck not talking about it here, in Kenneth's house."

"We can't talk about it outside!" said Ashley. "The whole neighborhood will hear us."

"Too late," said Leah.

Ashley stared her down. Leah took a deep breath. I could tell she was trying not to say what she *really* wanted to, but her face softened. "You can talk in my car."

Leah strolled down the street like Steven on his constitutional. There was worry on her face. She glanced back at me every once in a while, probably wondering if I'd had my heart attack yet.

I was in the driver's seat, and Ash was next to me, staring at the glove box. I didn't know where the hell to start. When did she stop loving me?

"That's yer man, then?" I asked, finally. "Rip from *Yellowstone*? The guy you want me to be like? He breaks into people's houses! He stole an old lady's TV. He stole a beef brisket from Hy-Vee. What the hell, Ash?"

"He doesn't do that anymore." She crossed her arms. "He made a mistake. A lot of people do things they wish they could take back."

I rubbed my hands up and down the steering wheel to keep some grip on reality. It probably wasn't a good sign for our marriage that she started by defending her boyfriend. "Okay, we'll put that little nugget aside for now and focus on all the other horrors." I swallowed my emotions. "You're going to have to draw me a map, Ash, so I can understand how the fuck we got here."

Ash bit her nails. Ashley's nails were always immaculate. "A few months ago, Kenneth pulled into the bank while I was working the drive-through. We talked. And laughed. Then he kept coming back."

"Is he your two-times-a-week pottery class?"

Leah made another round back up the sidewalk toward us, but she never got too close to the car.

Ash nodded.

I grabbed the steering wheel harder. It was the only thing

keeping me conscious. "And…I really hate to ask this… Do you sleep together every time you see him?"

Ashley's face sank. "Yes. But the wedding was supposed to be the last time."

"The wedding!" I felt an adrenaline surge. Then the truth smacked me in the face. She was excited to go to the wedding because she found out Kenneth would be there. She was flirty and happy at the reception because she was eager to meet up with him. And then, in bed later, she was angry because it was me she was next to, and not him. "That's why your hair was all crazy. You…What…Met up in the bathroom?"

Ash bit her lip. She didn't answer straight away. "I'm sorry."

I tried to inject humor into the situation just as I always did during times of stress. "Totally fine. No worries."

We sat in silence for a moment. Ashley's eyes were fixed on me. But I stared straight out the window. Finally, I made eye contact. "We've been married ten years." My heart felt like it was in bits. "I'd kind of like to know… How much of that time did you actually love me?"

Ashley's stare was full of sadness. Stupid question. I regretted it immediately.

She put a hand on my shoulder, like when we first dated, but this didn't feel like then. "I'm sorry, Jake." She paused. "I don't think I've ever loved you. I like you. I *want* to love you. But I don't."

My ears were ringing again. She never loved me. *Huh.* This didn't feel like life, but an amazing simulation. "Then why did you keep dating me? Why did you *marry* me?"

"Because I couldn't trust Kenneth," she said quietly.

My eyes widened. "You're going to need to say that again."

"I knew him." She cleared her throat. "Years ago, before you and me got together."

Somewhere soon, I'd need a toilet to throw up in. "So…I'm

the other man?" It was getting hard to breathe. "It doesn't even feel remotely sexy."

"We went out for a while. Kept it quiet. But I couldn't depend on him. He never felt stable. You were stable. And attentive. And I liked that at first. But…I was going to come back later and pack a suitcase and tell Daisy. I don't want to hurt Daisy."

We were quiet for a long time, watching people walk by. Nobody seemed to notice us. That was the way insane days were. Days when your wife left you. Days when your mother died. The sun kept coming up, and people kept walking by like nothing was amiss.

"Don't you ever wake up and wonder where the hell the time went?" asked Ashley. "Or wonder what you've been doing with your life? It seems like I was just sixteen, and now, boom, look at us. It goes by too fast not to do something about it. Not to make things happen for yourself."

I couldn't hide that I was offended. "This was making things happen?"

"Yes!" I was surprised by her sudden defensiveness. "Not like you. Not like *her*."

Ashley pointed to Leah down the street, who was talking to an older woman.

"What's Leah got to do with it?" I asked, getting defensive right back.

"She has *everything* to do with it."

Holy shit.

"I've never given her so much as a peck on the cheek."

"That's the whole damn problem, Jake."

I had lost the thread of something somewhere, but I was wound up. "What?"

"Some women might be intimidated that your best friend is a woman. Not me. Know why? You're the same. You let life happen to you. You take the easy road. You don't grab the things you want. I've seen the way Leah looks at you. And you let the moment fizzle away."

What the hell was happening? "You're mad at me because I *haven't* cheated on you?"

"I'm mad because this whole thing is stupid. Your life had this big, built-in romance, and instead of seizing it, you pissed it down your leg. Her son's first name is your middle name, for God's sake."

I tapped my finger on the wheel and avoided looking out at Leah.

"You don't take risks. You've eaten a peanut butter and jelly sandwich every day for lunch for the last fifteen years. You work at the restaurant your dad and Leah's dad started—"

"I didn't fall into that job," I said, cutting in. "I've been cooking and baking since I was eight flipping years old. I'd have that kind of job even if they hadn't opened the restaurant."

Ash ignored me. "And Leah works at the furniture store her great-grandpa started. Your jobs would be fine if you stepped out of your element and fought for one tiny thing you wanted…"

My chest was tight. "I thought I was fighting for *you*. Isn't that what marriage is?"

"I don't want you to fight for me. Why don't you take a second to realize I'm leaving you, and it's not the end of the world? Because you have feelings for that woman wandering down the sidewalk like a weirdo, worried about you. You have a thing for her. Deep down you know it. I might be an asshole. But I'm not the only one."

I felt like I was standing in a storm, pelted with hail and debris. I'd had feelings for Leah years ago, but that was in the past. She was my friend.

Just my friend.

And Ash thought…

My mouth was suddenly dry. The car hadn't seemed hot at first, but now it was unbearable. All the strands of my life were unraveling, and I couldn't pull them back together.

"Maybe you can't admit it now," said Ash. "Maybe you've pushed it back for so long that you don't even see it anymore, but it's there. You two vibrate on the same wavelength." I marveled at how she kept her voice so calm. "I don't know what you're going to do with the rest of your life, Jake. But you should think about taking a chance. You should think about living."

I swallowed hard.

Ashley put her feet up on the seat, holding her knees to her abdomen for comfort. "We have to figure out custody with Daisy."

Whose life was this? I felt shell-shocked. My eyes drifted up and down her. She tucked her light auburn hair behind her ear, like she had so many times before. It made me think of our first date, our wedding day, and the day we found out she was pregnant. Did she really think I didn't care?

Ashley must have read my mind because her face softened. "I know, Jake. I know you love me. But I also know that deep down, your heart belongs to Leah, the same way my heart belongs to Kenneth."

It felt like there was something raw and naked sitting in the car with us. I couldn't stand the heavy, hanging silence. "I'll always care about you. I hope you know that."

Ash took a deep breath. She always did that when trying to stop herself from crying. "And I didn't mean that. About you being an asshole. You're not. You're a nice guy. But I guess I don't like nice guys."

I nodded slightly. "And don't you use that word to describe yourself, either." She smiled faintly. "Sometimes people just aren't a good fit. And apparently, those people are us."

Ashley let out a whisper of a laugh. "There's one positive thing about all this."

My burning eyes said otherwise. "I'm curious to know what that is."

"You never have to make small talk with my dad again."

5

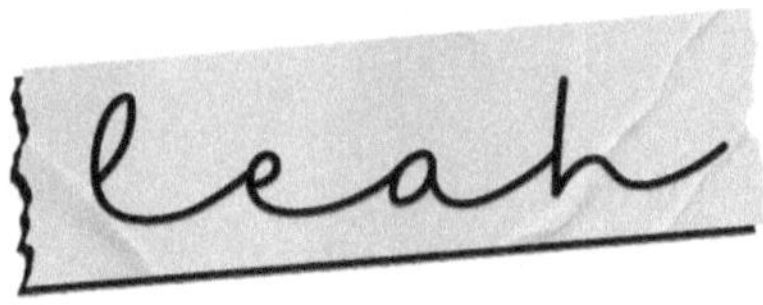

Sunday nights were family dinner nights at my parents'
house. It was something the Roths and Bradleys had
done since that first tater tot hotdish. There were only a
handful of times when Craig or Jake didn't make it. I thought
marital strife was a good reason to take a week off, but Jake was
insistent that he and Daisy would be there. Ash never usually
came with them, so her absence wouldn't be a red flag. But I
figured it was probably better if I showed up early to break the
news to my parents so they didn't slip up and say something
super awkward, which was pretty much our family custom.

I pulled into my parents' driveway, but we didn't get out.
Henry had a large container of Oreo fluff on his lap.

"You made way more fluff than usual. Is it for drowning
sorrows?"

"I don't know where you learned to talk like that," I said,
leaning back in my seat.

"It's DNA." He looked at me. "Aren't we going in?"

"We have to go over a few things first. Daisy might be pretty
sad. This is going to be a hard time for her, so you need to be an

extra caring friend, okay? Think about things before you say them."

Henry nodded. "Okay. But I think you're being kind of weird about it. In my class, there are only like two kids whose parents aren't divorced."

"That doesn't mean it's not sad." I thought about the math. "And it can't be that many."

Henry gave me his patented look of pure sass.

"I think you should dig around in your pockets and try to find a better attitude, mister. I don't know where all this sass is coming from."

"DNA," said Henry, unbuckling his seatbelt. "Like I said. Grandma says you were the same way."

"Then maybe I should do to you what your grandma did to me when I was sassy."

"Take away your phone? Oh, wait. You were a kid before phones existed."

I wasn't going to dignify that with a response. "No, I'm going to make sure there are treats in the house, but only ones you hate. So watch it, or you'll be snacking on nothing but Circus Peanuts, Bit-O-Honey, and Necco Wafers."

There was horror in Henry's eyes. "I'll be good."

We got out of the car and headed to the front door.

"Let me tell my parents about the divorce," I said. "I want to slip it into the conversation so nobody accidentally puts their foot in their mouth when Jake, Daisy, and Craig get here."

"Uncle Steven will probably do that anyway."

Probably.

Jake gave me the SparkNotes version of his talk with Ash but was pretty quiet on the drive back to his house. Who could blame him? He rested his head against the passenger-side window, staring out at the sunny spring day. It should have been cloudy. It should have been raining. The day didn't fit the mood.

I was all smiles as I nearly threw the container of Oreo fluff at my mom. Henry sighed, like he thought I was drinking too much coffee again. I was, but that was what I did when I was nervous, even though coffee always made me *more* nervous.

I was on edge about Jake and Daisy showing up. It reminded me of how I felt when Bonnie passed away. What could you do when someone you cared about was grieving? I mean, *really* do? You could listen; you could say supportive garbage. But garbage was all it was because you couldn't take their pain away, even though you wished you could.

"Everything alright, Hun?" Mom asked. Dad and Steven sauntered into the entryway, eyeing me.

Henry looked at me, then looked at Steven. Steven picked up on my son's energy. He stared holes in me, hungry for information he hadn't received when we relieved him of babysitting duty earlier.

"Great." But the words caught in my throat. "Need any help with the lasagna, Mom?"

We all walked toward the kitchen. My parents' house was an open-concept log cabin with rough, exposed beams and river rock. With the crackling fireplace, it should have felt cozy. So why did it feel like pure ice?

"You can start the garlic bread if you want," said Mom.

"Not so much garlic this time, though," said Dad.

"Sure thing." I searched through the cupboards. "Is Craig here yet?"

"Nope." Steven leaned against the wall. Knowing. Stupid Steven.

"I'll put some cheese on the garlic bread too." I opened the fridge and stuck my face in the cheese drawer. "Oh…Jake and Ash are getting a divorce. Hey, where's the garlic salt?"

My family stood still for a beat. Then another. Then another. Then all hell broke loose.

"What?" Dad asked, mouth gaping. He dropped his bag of Old Dutch chips.

"Ha!" Steven pointed at me. "I knew it. Where's my twenty? Someone owes me money."

"Did you just say what I thought you said?" asked Mom.

"Yep." Henry jumped onto the nearby sofa and grabbed his Game Boy and a bag of gummy bears hidden in the cushions. "It's a whole thing."

"How did this happen?" asked Mom.

"Ash cheated on him with Kenneth," said Steven. "Didn't she?"

I nodded.

Steven smiled. "Damn, that's salty." A look of pride swept over him. "I was instrumental in finding the evidence. I should have been Sam Spade."

"Kenneth!" said Dad. Actually, he screamed it. He needed to sit down. "Dirty bastard. I never trusted that guy. When he was a kid, he took Leah's Lincoln Logs right off the deck. I know it was him. He was the only one out there. That's when it started. His life of crime."

Mom was usually unflappable, but if she fiddled with the pendant on her necklace much more, she was going to rip it off. "Jake can't be coming for supper tonight."

"He says he is." I needed something to do. "Anyone want coffee? We should have coffee."

Henry ate a gummy bear. "I can't have energy drinks, but you've had fifteen cups of coffee since noon."

"I can't help it." I poured the grounds into the filter. "I'm nervous."

"What are you nervous about?" asked Dad. "You're not the

one who has to face everyone after having your heart shredded back and forth over a cheese grater."

Mom cringed. "Good grief, Dennis."

There was a weird smile on Steven's face. He picked up his guitar from the recliner and started strumming as he stared at me. "Nothing like a little heartbreak music."

I shook my head. His smile widened, still playing. "I know what she's nervous about. Jake's broken-hearted now. But eventually, he won't be. Eventually, he'll be back on the market."

I wanted to flip him off like Jake. "Shut up, Steven. His wife left him nine hours ago. Stop being crude."

Steven stopped playing and chuckled.

"Hell no," Dad said, stomping toward me. "At no time in the future will you date Jake Bradley."

I cut a baguette in half for the garlic bread, irked. "I never said I was."

"Because we all know your track record for relationships," said Dad, ignoring me. "We own B&R together. If you two start dating and things go to hell, your friendship will be ruined forever. And then *our* friendship will be ruined with Jake and Craig forever. I can't stand next to Jake making chicken salad after you break his heart." He put his face in his hands. "How can you do this?"

Steven chuckled. "It's starting already." He slid down next to Henry.

Mom patted Dad's shoulder. "You'll give yourself heartburn with hypotheticals again, honey." She nodded to me. "I think we need that coffee now."

I spread butter over the bread, then added garlic and Italian herbs. My hands shook the whole time. "My track record with men is not terrible."

"There was Brian," said Dad. "Didn't he date two other girls at the same time?"

"There was the guy who wanted his pet snake to sleep on a pillow next to you guys," said Henry, giggling.

"Sometimes I wonder if Mr. Slither has killed his owner yet," I mused.

"Vincent was alright," said Mom. "Why did you break up? He smelled so good."

I threw the garlic bread in the oven and wiped my hands. "He moved to Fargo. I wasn't going to drag Henry up there. We weren't that serious."

"And there was Lance," said Steven, laughing. "No offense, Henry."

"None taken," said Henry, staring at his game.

"Okay, fine, I tend to date guys that look like they're auditioning for Steven's band…"

"The Big Damn Deal will take off someday," said Steven. "Give it time."

"Either they're weirdos or you end it before things get serious," said Dad.

I pressed my lips together. I felt like going full Miss Piggy on these people. "What's this got to do with Jake?"

"You've got a big-time crush on him, hun," said Mom, matter-of-factly. She took a sip of coffee while everyone else nodded.

I made noncommittal noises and waved my hand as if they were all nuts. "I do *not*…have a crush on… He's my best friend. My *buddy*. My *pal*."

Steven leaned his head back. "I seem to remember several times when you had a little too much hard lemonade and said—"

"My c*hum*!" I cut in. "My *cohort*."

My family stared at me, totally unconvinced. I stared back at them, totally awkward.

Supper with the Roths and Bradleys was usually a loud, rowdy gathering with plenty of laughter and teasing, but now it was painful and slow, like surprise dental work. Jake stared at his plate, making a few light jokes. Everyone knew that everyone else knew, but we didn't say anything. Instead, we sat in near silence. Was the clock always that loud? Daisy and Henry were the lucky ones. They disappeared early to play games in my old room.

After about fifteen minutes of poking at our food, I couldn't stand it any longer. "Steven."

He looked up, startled. "Yeah. What? Sure."

"Have you…uh…" *Any conversation, Leah. Come on.* "Do you think you'll be able to find a roommate?"

Jake gave me a small smile, like he appreciated me breaking the silence.

Steven stabbed his lasagna. "I figure if it doesn't pan out, I can always move in with you."

Everyone at the table was suddenly horrified.

"That's a terrible idea!" *Hell no.* "I have a smaller house than you, and I have a kid. Where would we put all your collections?"

Steven was placid as usual. "The rock collection is down to a hundred and fifty now. And most are smaller than bowling balls. And I could store some of my geodes here again."

"Nope," said Dad.

I glared. "You should think about selling more chairs."

"Not everyone likes to push recliners on the masses like you. When I pinched my finger putting that one in the moving truck, I swore an oath." He sighed. "But I could push coffee tables."

Jake and I sat on our swing in my parents' backyard. He leaned forward, elbows on his knees, staring at the ground. I sat back, not knowing what to say.

"Thanks for giving everyone a heads-up," said Jake. "I was afraid I'd have to talk about it all night."

I wanted to comfort him. What was I supposed to do? I rested my hand gently on his back, and he gave me a sad smile.

"If there's anything else I can do, let me know," I said. "I can get food for you guys or set up some playdates with Henry and Daisy. And if you want to start a collection like Steven, I could buy you fifteen can openers."

Jake brightened at that. "That might be nice, actually. I can never find one when I need it." He tried to smile. "Sorry that I ruined dinner."

I gave him a lighthearted nudge. "Knock that off. You didn't ruin anything."

"Say that to my wife." Jake leaned back in the swing. "Say that to Daisy."

I couldn't hide my surprise. "Stop that right now. You haven't ruined Daisy."

"Haven't I? When she looks back on her childhood, there will be the time before we split up, and then the time after we split up… Ash had a long talk with her before we came over— told her what was happening. She listened to Ash and nodded. She cried, but her face was like stone." Jake's eyes turned glossy. "Now…who does that remind you of?"

"She'll see Ashley all the time. You were resilient. So is she. Give yourself a little credit."

Jake scoffed. "I wasn't resilient. I was a mess, and you know it. The last thing I said to Mom was, 'Don't forget we're going swimming this weekend.' How stupid. I could have told her I loved her. I could have said a lot of things." He rubbed his palms together. "But you never think this is the last chance to say the things that matter."

We looked at each other until I couldn't look anymore. "I wish there was something I could say to make you feel better. Or something I could do. I'm so sorry."

He chuckled softly. "Don't be sorry. You're great. Sitting here with you like this makes me feel better. You made me feel better back then, too." He glanced at me. "When you wore that weird Halloween costume. That was the first time I laughed in months."

"I was one of the little girls from *The Shining*. It was so easy to tell."

Jake smirked. "I thought you were Judy Garland from *The Wizard of Oz*."

"I was proud of that costume." I laughed. "It didn't make sense because Monica chickened out and wouldn't dress up like the other girl. It wasn't my fault that it was out of context. I was adorable."

Jake opened his mouth to say something but stopped as he shifted his focus to the house. "I can't believe I was married for ten years to a woman who never loved me for any of it." He let out a defeated sigh. "Classic me, isn't it? That's like spending ten years with the person who annoys you in line at the DMV."

I gave him another nudge. "You're still not as bad at relationships as me. Remember what we used to say when I got back from the bar after a date?"

Jake smiled, remembering. "I would ask you how your night went." A crinkle formed between his eyes. I liked that.

"And I always said that nobody had to worry. I was still going to die alone."

We both let out quiet laughs.

"They weren't all bad," said Jake. "Vincent was okay."

"How about Lance?"

Jake shifted in the swing. He always hated Lance. "Nope. You know someone's a miserable little fuck when they sneak around while someone wonderful is at home, feeding their baby."

I wasn't going to blush. "He thought he was hot with all the chicks."

"The dick pics he sent to women behind your back…"

"He even had that catchphrase. Who has a catchphrase?"

Jake rolled his eyes. "All the ladies go into a trance for Lance."

We made eye contact. Now our laughter was real. Honest.

"Yep." I sighed. "That's Henry's father."

Jake grinned for a moment longer, but then it dissolved. There was too much other crap to think about.

"Alright," I said. "You know I'm not big on hugging. But come on. You look like you need one."

Jake was surprised. But he only hesitated for a moment. He leaned in and wrapped his arms around me. He smelled like caramel and coffee. And home.

We stayed like that for a long time, drifting slowly back and forth in weather too cold to swing in.

"Thanks, Leah," he whispered in my ear.

"What are friends for?"

6

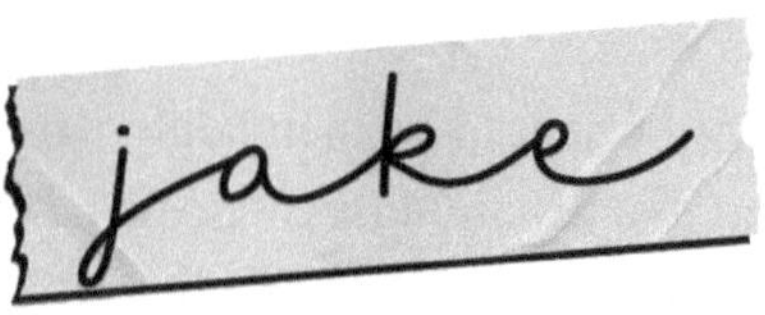

When you'd been married for almost ten years, it became hard to distinguish *your stuff* from *my stuff*. It was just *our* stuff. But somehow Ash was able to pick through it and get what she wanted. I didn't care what she took. None of it mattered anymore. She could've ripped the toilet out of the bathroom, and I wouldn't have batted an eye.

TV and movies taught me that divorce meant people sorting out who was going to get the house, but Ash had no interest in it. Maybe that was another thing she never really liked. Shows also led me to believe that a long custody battle might be about to ensue, a fear that initially caused stabbing pains in my stomach. But that didn't happen either. We were going to split Daisy's time between us as equally as possible. Ash was renting a house in Ottertail, where her parents lived, and was excited about setting up Daisy's room.

A nice divorce—that's what our family and friends called it. Friendly. Civil.

I didn't know where my life was going, and I always felt like I was about to throw up.

"As soon as I get everything put away, you can spend the night." Ashley kneeled on the driveway and kissed Daisy on the forehead. "Does that sound alright?"

Daisy gave Ash a slight smile. "Can I bring my lava lamp?"

Ashley laughed. "You can bring whatever you want. Just ask your dad first."

Daisy brightened more after that.

"I'll see you tomorrow, baby," said Ash. She pulled Daisy close and hugged her. Ash tried not to cry. That about did me in. We made that child together. When I looked at Daisy, I saw Ashley's eyes. Ashley's ears. And now Ash was getting in her car and leaving.

People got divorced all the time. But the sensation was new to me; that was for damn sure. The whole thing felt too strange. Someone who'd been a huge part of my life was going to step out of it like she'd never been there in the first place.

I patted Daisy's shoulder as she walked by me back into the house. When Daisy was gone, Ash and I strolled up to each other. She had her hands in her pockets. Her car was absolutely filled, ready for the journey.

"I know you hate Kenneth," she said. "I don't want you to worry that I'm going to have Daisy over there when I'm hanging out with him. Their paths won't cross. I swear."

I tried to smile, but I could only nod.

She gave me a small frown. "Thanks for being so nice about everything."

I didn't know what to do with my hands. "It's fine. No worries."

Ash opened her mouth, hesitating. "I'm sorry, Jake. I know I hurt you. And I didn't want you to find out like that. You were always so great to me."

What should I say? I looked at my feet, then at her. My eyes felt hot. "I thought you were pretty great yourself, Ash. Don't worry. It's going to be okay."

She stepped closer to me and whispered, "I should have been better to you." Tears were about to pour out of her dark eyes. "And I'm very sorry. I hope someday you can forgive me."

I reached out my arms and wrapped them around her. We both had tears sliding down our faces. I'd hugged her so many times. Her perfume always smelled expensive. Something floral. I never found out what it was.

"I forgive you, Ashley," I whispered. "Don't cry. We can't cry out in the driveway like this. It'll give people the wrong impression. They'll think you're leaving me."

Ash rested her head on my chest and laughed through her tears. She glanced up at my wet face and wiped my tears away. "I'll always be grateful for you."

"And I'll always be grateful for *you*." We were quiet for a moment, staring at each other. "And I'm really grateful that you did the laundry and I did the cooking because you were fecking terrible at it."

Ash laughed again. She leaned forward and kissed my cheek.

I waved as she got into her car, and in a moment, she was gone.

I stood in the driveway for a long time, watching the darkening sky, thinking about endings and beginnings. A more optimistic person would have considered this an opportunity to change their life. But staring at the sky, all I could think about were my failures, and all I could see was gray.

7

It had been over a month since Ash moved out, and I was fairly certain we were still the main source of gossip in town. Down at the restaurant, the waitstaff tiptoed around me like I was the temperamental boss of a slick, New York City restaurant, instead of the owner of a homey diner with great coffee. Our pies were also quite good.

I walked out of the kitchen with a coffee cup in hand. It was a rainy Wednesday, and less busy than usual. Dennis and my dad sat at a table arguing over changes to the menu again.

"No one likes the cranberry muffins, Craig," said Leah's dad as I walked up. "Jake, do you like the cranberry muffins?"

"Sure," I said, sitting.

"That's my boy," Dad said. "I don't think we should do anything to the muffins. Take away that awful sour cream and raisin pie."

"That's Leah's favorite," said Dennis.

"Her favorite pie is cherry," I said. They both looked at me. I cleared my throat. "I think we could take an ax to the poppy seed muffins. I don't understand them. They've been on the menu forever, and hardly anyone buys them. Who wants a muffin that tastes like a seed?"

"And they mess with drug tests," said Dennis.

"There you go," I said. "Two reasons."

"What are you still doing here, anyway?" Dad glared at me. "Faigh Saol. Don't you ever punch out?"

I shrugged and took another sip of coffee. "Where the feck am I supposed to go? Everyone looks at me and whispers."

"I heard that Martin Reed was caught pissing in his front yard," said Dennis. "Someone got a picture of it and everything. In a week, nobody will be talking about you anymore."

"That's good," I said. "Well, probably not for Martin Reed and his little penis…"

"You could go home sometime," said Dad.

"What's the point when Daisy's at Ashley's? There's nobody home except me and our cat, Purrito. And Purrito looks at me like I'm nuts when I talk to her."

"How did you ever name your cat Purrito?" asked Dennis.

"Daisy picked it. She was four."

"That's as weird as the name Leah and Henry gave their cat," said Dennis. "It's…uh…"

"Karma," I said. They both looked at me again.

I took a last sip of coffee and glanced at the clock. "But I guess since it's my lunch break, I'll head down to the furniture store."

"Greet the rest of my family," said Dennis.

I made three lattes and headed for the door. "I won't greet Steven. He's on my list."

When I got to A-to-Z Furniture, a few customers were looking at the mattress selection while Leah helped them. Steven sat in a massage chair, his eyes closed.

"How can you sell that chair as new when you've used it every day for the last three weeks?"

"Because it's a crooked world, and I'm a crooked man."

When the customers were gone, I gave Leah and Steven their lattes. We sat behind the service counter.

"You're early today," said Leah.

"Yes, well, our fathers thought I should go. Something about me working for the last three hundred and thirty-six hours."

"I can't believe you brought me a latte," said Steven.

"I made sure it was a flavor you don't like—hazelnut."

Steven took a sip and frowned. "Damn."

Leah sneered at her brother. "Serves you right."

Leah and Steven always wore burgundy clothing for work, with name tags pinned to their chests. Leah had on a sweater-style dress that ended right above her knees. She also wore dark tights and high heels. For some reason, I found I needed to look at the floor.

"He didn't want that Tinder account, jerk."

Steven drank the coffee he hated. "I was trying to help. You need to get out there."

"Ash and I have been split up for a whopping month and a half," I said.

"I got my heart broken by a woman who sells grandfather clocks," said Steven. "Four days later, I met someone new."

"You were with that woman for a week," I said. "I was with Ash for ten years."

"More like nine years, six months, and twenty-one days," said Steven.

Leah rolled her eyes. "You're an idiot."

I fiddled with my drink. What Ash said about Leah had been running through my head lately. Perhaps that was why I couldn't look at Leah. And damn, those fecking heels. "I don't think I could do online dating. Meeting women in bars is depressing enough."

"Especially the bars around here," said Leah.

Very true.

"Go out. Have sex. You'll feel better," said Steven.

Leah drank her latte. "You're so romantic."

I felt so hyper-aware next to Leah. I shifted my jaw. "I don't think I could meet a woman and have sex with her two hours later. I don't even become charming until about hour five."

Steven put down his cup, pointed at Leah, and began cackling. Leah's face went pink.

Fuck me! I didn't mean that. I'm such a prick.

"Shut up, Steven!" Leah scowled. She kicked her brother as he got up. "I don't have sex with all of them. And even if I did, what's it to anybody? So I like sex. Big whoopity doo!"

My heart thumped in my head. Leah talking about sex wasn't helping that hyper-aware feeling. Steven's laughter echoed as he walked into the break room.

"I hate that guy," said Leah, then she called out to Steven again, "Hey, asshole, get me my sandwich when you're in the fridge."

"I'm sorry." My face was never going to cool down. "I didn't mean that. There's nothing wrong with meeting someone and having sex on the first date."

"Don't worry about it." Leah's look to me was calm and relaxed. If she felt as awkward as I did, she didn't show it. "I hardly have sex with any of them…unfortunately. I *would* if I could find someone normal." I didn't say anything to that but planned to mull her comment over at length sometime later. "You know how many guys you have to go on a date with to find one that's slightly normal? I'm assuming the women on there are just as weird. Well, I *know* they are. Because I'm on there."

My heart slowed down to a normal pace. We looked at each other and laughed. Leah's eyes went squinty. That sometimes happened when she was happy. It always knocked me out.

One day, when A-to-Z Furniture was swamped, I offered to pick Henry up from school when I got Daisy. The kids slid into the backseat, looking annoyed.

"How was school?" I knew how this conversation was going to play out. It was always the same.

"Boring," said Daisy.

I hid a smile. "What did you do?"

"Nothing," they said in unison.

"That's funny." I took a right turn. "I used to say the same thing to my parents when I was your age."

"You can remember that far back?" asked Henry. Daisy giggled. "I found a recipe for a sweet potato milkshake during recess. We could make it sometime."

"That sounds great. We haven't whipped up something weird in a while."

Daisy rolled her eyes. We were a mystery to her. "Why is it always weird? Why can't we make sugar cookies?"

Henry pulled a pair of sunglasses out of his backpack. He put them on and tried to act very serious. "We do it for the kicks."

I chuckled. Sometimes Henry reminded me of a tiny Steven. What a frightening thought.

Daisy wasn't impressed. "You're just as weird as those boys at school."

"No," said Henry. "I'm weird. They're *jerks*."

My ears perked up. "Why are they jerks?"

"They said my shirt was stupid."

He was sporting a T-shirt with characters from *Princess Mononoke*. "Isn't anime in anymore?"

"If anime is out, I don't want to be in," said Henry.

"They didn't cross a line, did they?" I asked. "Do you want me to say something?"

"Dad!" Daisy put her hand in front of her face, like the very idea embarrassed her.

"I don't care what they say," said Henry as he leaned back, relaxed. "Hayao Miyazaki isn't stupid. *They're* stupid."

I stopped at a light. We were almost at the furniture store. "Kids used to be jerks like that to me sometimes when I was at school with your mom."

"How come?" asked Henry.

I did an over-the-top shrug. "Well…my voice sounds a little different than most people around here, don't you think?" Henry and Daisy pretended to be oblivious. I got a kick out of that. "When I was a kid, it was even more pronounced. Plus, I was used to saying things the way we did back home."

Henry lowered his sunglasses. "You still say things differently sometimes."

I glanced at him in the mirror. "You think so?"

Henry's eyes widened like I was oblivious. "Especially when you get back from visiting home. Then you're all like…*what's the craic*?"

I hid a smile. "I can't help it. We have the best slang."

Daisy nudged Henry. "You should hear all the words my great-grandma says when she gets mad about something."

"Moving here was an adjustment until I made friends with your mom and everyone," I said. "The first couple of days, I made the mistake of saying *sham* to people. And there may have been a *feck* or two. Kids teased me for that. And they nagged me for the way I pronounced some of my t's."

"I bet Mom didn't tease you," said Henry.

The memory warmed me. "Nope. She thought the way I talked was cool. Classy, even…or whatever a six-year-old's version of classy is."

I pulled up in front of the furniture store. "After a while, everything settled down. And I got used to the phrases people say around here. Although I still don't think there's a better insult than calling someone a gobshite."

"What's a gobshite?" asked Henry.

I smiled. "Those kids who made fun of your shirt."

Daisy gave me a knowing glance. "And what about what you and great grandma and everyone say when we're at her house?"

I grinned as we piled out of the car. I walked between the kids, giving them each a heckling tug on the shoulder. "How could I forget? When we get to her house, suddenly everything's *arseways*."

That weekend, Leah and I took the kids to the bowling alley. It was something we did all the time. In the past, Ash would sometimes come along, and sometimes not.

The place was busy with the sound of falling pins, laughter, and kids running around to the arcade in the back.

Leah held up her arms in fake exasperation. "What's going on?" It was her second gutter ball in a row. She walked back to Henry, pointing at him and pretending to be annoyed. "You jinxed us. You said we were having a great game."

Henry laughed, shrugging. "If we suck, we suck, Mom."

"I hope you're still laughing when Jake and Daisy do their victory dance."

The great thing about the bowling alley was that it had food, and it wasn't even terrible. Actually, the pizza was nice.

Leah decided the problem must be her bowling ball. She went in search of her lucky one while I watched the kids. I breathed out built-up tension as she walked away. What the fuck was wrong with me? This all started the day I noticed Leah in those tights and high heels. Now I couldn't keep my fecking eyes off her.

When we first got to the bowling alley, Henry and Daisy were more interested in playing in the attached arcade. So it was just Leah and me bowling. Every time she bent over to throw her ball, I had to glance at the ceiling to stop my dick from getting hard. Then she did a silly dance. That smile. The way she moved. *Jesus.* It was a blessing when the kids came over and decided they wanted to play after all.

It wasn't like I'd never spent time with Leah. And she was always sexy. So what was the deal?

You're single. She's single. And the torch you carry is looking more like a bonfire.

I told my mind to shut the hell up.

After my turn, I walked back to our table just as a waiter wandered over. I didn't recognize him. "Here are your wife's fries."

His words were like one of the bowling balls smashing my fingers. I quickly recovered and was able to manage a normal, human smile.

What the fuck is going on?

First, Ash told me to make something happen with Leah. Then my mind and body turned into a teenager. And now this.

The kids were right behind me, taking their turns. Either they hadn't heard the waiter's comment, or they pretended not to, but they gave each other a strange glance.

A few minutes later, Leah returned, all smiles. She held a bright purple ball in her hands. She did a little shuffle with it and put on a sing-song voice. "You know what this is?"

I smiled. A goofy, awkward smile. My body liked the way

she held that ball. Liked the way her narrowed eyes stared into mine.

You goddamn idiot.

Leah winked. "Oh, yeah, it's Tiffany." I tried to push down the weird stuff that was happening inside me. "And I always win with Tiffany. What do you think about that?"

I took a deep breath and laughed. I told her we were going to put her team out of its misery.

But later, I thought about that waiter's comment. We were two kids and two adults. It wasn't surprising that he thought we were a family. The idea was like an electric shock in my body. The good kind.

I wondered what Leah would have said if I told her what I really thought when she did her silly dances. If I told her what I thought when she and Steven dissolved into one of their fake fights. I wondered what she'd say if I told her what I really thought of *her*.

Somewhere in the mix of Ashley leaving, Steven insisting that I go on a date, and my body being stupid, that old familiar thought began poking my mind like a kid tapping you again and again to tell you something. I was keenly aware that there was now nothing stopping Leah and me from going out on a date, and yet I did nothing.

Just like Ash said. You don't make things happen.

I told myself it was stupid to think about things like that. Ashley and I just split up. It was too soon. It wasn't too soon for Ash, of course, because that was the whole reason we weren't together. Just the week before, I'd been forced to duck into the pharmacy when I saw Ashley and Kenneth walking down Broadway toward me, hand in hand. They strolled into Margot's Bookshop Café.

I hope her espresso machine is glued down, I thought.

People moved on at different speeds. Some people who had

split up probably didn't go on a date for two years. Maybe some didn't for ten. And some probably died alone.

And some were too afraid to admit their feelings to the woman they'd known since childhood.

That night, I couldn't sleep, so I started snooping through my bedroom closet. I grabbed a small photo album and sat on the bed. It was filled with childhood photographs of the two of us. I flipped through the pictures, smiling: Leah and I playing Game Boy, Leah and I walking in the park, and Leah and I on her birthday.

I flipped the page. Leah and I on Halloween. The one right after my mom died. We sat on our swing, holding hands. There she was, dressed up like one of the girls from *The Shining*. Leah stared straight at the camera, not smiling to keep in character. I didn't wear a costume. Said I was too old, even though it was for a party, but the truth was, I didn't see the point. The sadness about Mom left me drenched, and I didn't know how to dry myself out.

But there I was in that picture, holding Leah's hand, a tentative smile on my face. Photographic proof of how her friendship had helped me during that horrible time.

It was a bad idea to date Leah. We were friends. If we got together, it would be good until the world fucked it up, or *I* fucked it up. Something would fuck it up somehow, and then what would happen?

You wouldn't have a friend; that's what would happen.

I put the album on the bed. I wasn't scared. It was just a bad idea.

But then I looked at the open photo album, and our two hands joined together. For a second, my fingers tingled, and I let myself imagine what it would be like to have Leah next to me in bed.

Fecking amazing.

I swallowed, then I thought about what it would be like to trace one of my fingers up Leah's thigh.

My body was on board with that thought. My dick hardened almost immediately. I sat there, thinking about her perfect hourglass figure, thinking about how it would be to have her bent over with me behind her. Or how it would be to have her naked breasts pressed against my chest. We'd spend all night exploring each other's bodies. I'd trace my tongue across her, stick my tongue inside her. I wouldn't want her to come fast. I'd want to taste her longer than that. I had a sneaking suspicion that Leah was a fecking dream when she moaned.

My cock was rock hard. I sighed. I knew what I was going to do now, at one in the morning, unable to sleep. I was going to take a shower and jerk off, thinking about Leah and her curves, and I was going to love every goddamn second of it. I hadn't done that since before dating Ash.

A better man would think of something unsexy, like spoiled eggs, and call it a night, but I didn't feel like being a good man tonight.

I grabbed a pair of sweatpants and wandered into the bathroom. I stayed hard just *thinking* about thinking about her.

I turned on the shower, sighed, and stepped in.

8

"Mom, what are you doing?"

I stood in my bedroom closet, staring at potential outfits. My parents were having a get-together to celebrate their forty-fifth wedding anniversary.

Henry charged into my room and took a photograph. I bought him a Polaroid camera that shot the pictures out right away, just like my parents always had on family trips.

"That'll be a good photo." My hands were full of clothes. "I'll look like I'm crawling out of a cave."

Henry shook the photo while it developed. "You're not ready yet?"

"I don't know what to wear. Do you think this is a dress thing or a jeans thing? These jeans with the frayed ends are kind of stylish when I try."

Henry rolled his eyes. "Who cares? Wear pajamas. It's what most people do."

"I don't want to look like I'm going to Walmart. I want to look cute."

"Gross." Henry strolled toward the hall. "We're supposed to be there at six."

"What a responsible, punctual child I raised." I kept talking as he walked away. "Just like me when I was a kid. I remember this one time at school when... And he's gone. I'm talking to no one."

I picked a shirt off my bed, considered it, then set it back down. Nope.

I pulled out a summery white dress with yellow flowers, but it was still cool out.

I wandered back to my closet and rummaged around. I pulled a black jumpsuit with off-the-shoulder straps out of the back. I held it up and smiled.

I hummed as I stepped into the cool fabric. After a moment, I realized that I was humming the old song "I Could Write a Book." We always used to sing it in choir back at school, and it reminded me of Jake when I had a big crush on him.

Where did that come from?

That was a stupid question. My head had been full of stupid thoughts lately, all about Jake. I'd always had a thing for him, but now that he was single again... Yikes, I was acting like a teenager. Maybe because I hadn't had sex in a while. The last couple of guys I was with were nice enough, and the sex was... *fine*. But for some reason, it seemed like whenever I told a guy to keep doing what he was doing, he'd immediately switch the tempo, and my orgasm would evaporate.

I was having a better time with my vibrator than anything else lately, but that wasn't a good thing. One night, I was about to come when Jake's name was suddenly on my lips. And that didn't stop my orgasm. Nope. That sent me right over the edge.

Yep. I was in trouble.

A few minutes later, I put on the jumpsuit and stood in front of my full-length mirror. I nodded. It *was* cute. It had a cinched waist and wider ankles, which created a pleasant swooshing sound when I walked. I liked the way my shoulders were naked, and my curly hair hung down on them.

I shook my head at my reflection. "What the hell are you doing? Four days ago, you spent thirty seconds planning what you'd wear today—jeans and a shirt with a Peter Pan collar. So what's this, Leah?"

"And why are you talking to yourself?" asked Henry, leaning against my doorframe. He took another picture and bolted away.

I called after him. "Bring that cake and punch out to the car, would you?"

I pointed at my reflection. "You're tempting fate. You're trying to sabotage your life. And your friendship." I put on an annoying, high-pitched voice. "I want to look cute for Jake. I want Jake to notice me. Aren't I special?" I cleared my throat. "Idiot."

I gazed at the clothes on my bed and shrugged. "But I might as well wear the jumpsuit since I already have it on."

Jake had been acting weird lately. He always seemed to be staring at me like I had something on my face. And living with a son had taught me that there was a good possibility I always had something on my face. Henry's pudding phase when he was seven was a good example. So every time I was with Jake, I checked myself in reflective surfaces.

When we got to the party, I took the two sheet cakes into the kitchen and placed them on the counter.

Mom and Dad walked up, all smiles.

"Have you tried the dip?" asked Dad. "It might be my best one yet."

"I don't think a dip that includes sauerkraut can be worth consuming," said Mom.

Dad examined me. "It's good that you're dressed up."

"Dennis…" Mom said it slowly, like a warning.

"I can't help it," said Dad. "I'm excited." He nudged me. "The Piersons…You remember the Piersons? They brought their son along. His name is Tim. About your age. Just got divorced. Isn't that great?"

I stared at Dad. "Probably not for Tim. Depending on the circumstances."

Mom pressed on. "We know you don't like getting set up, Hun. But he seemed like a nice guy. Kind of stocky. Like a boxer. Must work out, but not in the dedicated Lance kind of way."

Mom pointed over to the living room, where Tim stood with his parents, nodding and saying a few brief words. He *was* stocky. Clean-shaven. My height. Sandy-brown hair. Attractive, but…

"I don't think he's my type," I whispered.

Mom arched an eyebrow. "What *is* your type?"

Interesting question. I'd dated all sorts, including an amateur magician who tried to see how big he could grow a handlebar mustache. Don't get me wrong, I was a big fan of a nice, slutty mustache, but talking about mustache wax for the better part of our dates was too much.

My parents stared at me, and my heart did a two-step. The truth was that life had taught me that my type was Irish guys who moved down the road from you, had brown hair, a little bit of stubble, liked to bond over Nintendo, enjoyed laughing at terrible movies, and always stared at you like you had something on your face.

"I don't know what my type is."

"He's an accountant," said Dad. "And you're terrible at math. It's a perfect match!"

"I'm not terrible at math," I said.

"What's seventy-five times two hundred and ten?" asked Dad.

I stared again. "You tell me."

Dad looked around. "Let me get a calculator."

I was halfway through stirring the punch when Daisy and Henry ran up.

"Hey guys," I said. "How was that science test, Daisy?"

"I got an A," said Daisy, all smiles. I gave her a high-five. She flashed Henry a knowing glare. "How many A's do *you* get on science tests, Henry?"

Henry shrugged. "I guess my mom likes you more. She tutors you better."

I blinked. "Uh-huh. That's definitely what the issue is." That's when I noticed the weird bundle in his arms. "What's that?"

Henry placed it on the ground. It was a long, rubber snake that was just realistic enough to be disturbing. He grabbed the controller from his pocket and pushed some buttons, making the snake spin across the floor.

"That's fairly terrifying," I said.

"I think it's kinda dumb," said Daisy.

Henry had a wicked grin. "Steven gave it to me to scare people."

"Sounds about right," I said. "But don't use it at the party, huh? You'll give someone a heart attack."

I liked to stick near the kitchen at parties. Being near the food gave me something to do with my hands when I felt awkward making small talk. I chatted with people as I leaned against the island. I had a view of almost the whole house. I felt like a cowboy in a corner, ready for a showdown.

I watched my parents talk to Tim, my parents talk to Jake, Jake talk to Craig, and Craig talk to my parents. Daisy and Henry sat in the living room, watching me and whispering. What was that about?

Jake stood near the hallway, talking to Steven. He wore a dark blue Henley shirt that rested snugly on his toned arms and chest. The man looked fine. Damn. And the way his body moved when he walked, his tall frame making cool, easy steps. His 6'3" physique towered over many in the room, but his relaxed humor made him approachable. He was the kind of funny guy who had no idea he was sexy.

I wiped the sweat off my hands.

Jake hadn't talked to me yet. That was weird. But each time I started a conversation with someone, I felt his eyes on me. I reached up to see if something was on my nose.

Maybe he's staring because he has the hots for you. He's been acting weird since he split up with Ash.

I wasn't going to entertain stupid ideas like that. Jake saw me as a friend. That's the way it had always been. That's the way it would always be.

I was thankful when Monica wandered over.

"What's up with you, sweet friend?"

She smiled through a long sigh. "Remember how I said me and Tony were taking the kids to his parents' house in South Carolina?"

I nodded.

"What a nightmare," she said. "Their basement flooded. We spent two weeks cleaning."

"Oh, no, that's terrible. You didn't get to hang out at the beach at all?"

"Not much," said Monica. "Plus, it rained a lot." She paused. "What's going on with you? Why have you been in the kitchen all night?"

I gestured to the living room. "My parents are trying to set me up with that accountant."

"The guy in the red?"

"Yep."

Monica examined him. "He's cute. What's the problem?"

What is *the problem?*

I shrugged. "I don't know. Not my type."

From the way she looked, Monica didn't buy that. "And you figured this out from zero seconds of conversation?"

I took a sip of punch. "Sure did."

Monica hid a laugh. "I know what's going on." She nudged me. "Why don't you ask him out?"

"The accountant?" I asked, confused.

Monica rolled her eyes. *"No.* You know who I'm talking about. Now that he's not with Ash, what's the problem?"

I sputtered, trying to deny it. "No. That's so…not even what I was thinking."

Monica watched me, knowing. "Look at you. You can't even say it with a straight face. You can't lie to me. I remember listening to Bon Iver in our early twenties. And I remember what you said when you had a little hard lemonade in you."

My body tensed. "That was a long time ago. And my hard lemonade days are over."

Monica's gaze shifted to Jake in the living room. "Deny it all you want, but you have the hots for him. Big time."

You're so obvious. "I do not. I've decided to die alone, actually."

"He's been staring at you all night," Monica whispered. "It's incredibly obvious. Like you're in middle school."

"That's because I probably have something on my face."

My parents stood in front of everyone and gave a little speech about how long they'd been together.

"What can I say?" Dad asked. "The woman has good taste."

They told a little story about how they'd met. I'd heard it so many times. My dad spotted my mom at a restaurant during some brunch buffet. She was there with her cousin. When she got up to get a pop, Dad walked over and started talking. *Coke or Pepsi? Why not risk it all and mix all the sodas together?* And that was it. He asked her to go to a movie that Friday. After that, they were inseparable.

I didn't mind being alone. After all, I had Henry, and my family was close by. But I always thought I would've found someone by my mid-twenties. Was that stupid to think? It felt stupid now. I didn't think life would still have this wandering chord. This aimlessness.

But you did find someone, I thought. *And he's walking right up to you.*

I tried to smile as Jake made a beeline toward me. Steven trailed slowly behind. As Jake approached, beer in hand, I had to admit I wasn't hiding in the kitchen to avoid Tim. It was because I was nervous to talk to Jake.

I was *never* nervous to talk to Jake.

So stupid. What the hell did you wear this jumpsuit for?

"Having fun holding down the kitchen?" asked Jake.

I flashed a smile that was way too toothy. "Sure am."

There was that stare again. His jaw flexed. "You look great."

"Do I have something on my face?" I touched my cheek.

An awkward smile played on his lips. "Not at all." He took a sip of beer.

"You look great too," I said, trying to recover.

And the way he smelled—caramel and musk. I had to get over it.

Jake cleared his throat but didn't say anything.

"I look nice too," said Steven, walking up. "And I smell great. It's Giorgio Armani. At least, I think that's what the magazine insert said."

"You better not be thinking of bringing that remote-controlled snake to work," I said. "You'll terrify the customers."

"That's the whole point," said Steven.

"Why are you wandering the kitchen?" Jake asked me.

Steven grinned.

I eyed Steven. "Do you know?" He nodded.

"What am I missing?" asked Jake, confused.

"My parents are trying to set me up with Tim the accountant."

Jake shifted. Why did he look uncomfortable all of a sudden? "Ah. Which one is he?"

I sighed. "The one in the red shirt, sitting by the fireplace, poking at his food and staring off into space because he doesn't know anyone."

"Your parents must have pointed you out." Jake looked Tim up and down. "Why doesn't he talk to you?"

"For the same reason I don't go over to him," I said. "Not interested."

Steven leaned against the cupboards. "Maybe he thinks you're homely."

I narrowed my eyes. "Thanks."

"Poor bastard." Jake stared over at Tim. "I hate when I'm at a party and I don't know a soul. It's painful. And the time drags on."

"We should go talk to him," I said. "Make him feel less awkward."

We all nodded. That was a great idea.

None of us budged.

"Of course, I hate when strangers try to make small talk," I said.

"Because they always ask the same questions," said Jake. "*What do you do?*"

"Yep," said Steven.

"*Crazy weather, eh?*" asked Jake.

"Yep," said Steven.

"*Where do you live?*" asked Jake.

"Nobody asks interesting questions." I smiled at the possibilities. "We should ask him what children's movie emotionally crushed him when he was seven. That's what I wish someone would ask me. A question where you really get to know someone."

Jake chuckled. "We could ask him what song he likes to have a good cry to at three in the morning."

"I know mine," I said.

"'A Case of You' by Joni Mitchell," said Jake.

Steven and I stared at him.

"It is," I said, surprised. Bizarre sensations fluttered around my body. I pushed them away and tried to be funny. "And yours is 'Eternal Flame' by the Bangles."

Jake got a kick out of that. "How did you know?"

"Mine's 'Wake Me Up Before You Go-Go,'" said Steven.

When it was time to serve dessert, Jake helped me take one of the big sheet cakes out of its box. It had bright blue frosting with flowers all over it and *'45th Anniversary'* piped in white icing.

Jake took the cover off the second cake while I moved the first over to the kitchen island, where we had forks and plates set up. Steven moseyed over to help, but he shouldn't have, because, unbeknownst to him, Henry and Daisy got bored with the remote-control snake and left it abandoned in the middle of the floor. Steven didn't see it until it was too late. He stepped right on it, ankle rolling. He thought he was falling, so he reached his hands out to brace himself, but *I* stood right in front of him with the cake in my arms. He plowed into me like a linebacker, squishing the cake between us. In a second, there was white cake and blue frosting all over my boobs and stomach.

Jake stared at us, shocked. Scratch that. *Everyone* stared.

There was cake all over Steven, too, but he didn't mind. He scooped a large smear of it off his brown sports coat and took a bite. "It's all good. There's another cake, right?"

The blue dye sank into my black jumpsuit. This was the first time I'd worn it, too.

"Yes, Steven." I was monotone. Chunks of cake and butter-cream slowly fell off me, plopping to the floor. "There's another cake."

Jake and I stood in my parents' guest bathroom. We laughed as I scraped the cake off myself and into a garbage can.

"Serves me right for trying to look cute," I said. "If I wore sweatpants, this wouldn't have happened."

"You still look cute," said Jake. "Now you've got an abstract art thing going on."

I ignored his use of the word '*cute*' and frowned at my outfit. "Do you think it will stain?"

"Considering that everyone who's eaten a slice of the other cake has a blue tongue, I figure there's probably more dye in there than a person's supposed to eat in fifty years."

"That's great. Is this one of those things you're supposed to use club soda on?"

"You'd probably need twenty gallons of it."

Jake smiled. There was that look again. My stomach fluttered as his eyes rested on me.

I was about to say something when Jake beat me to it. "Wait one second." He leaned in, scraped a dollop of cake and frosting off my stomach, and dotted it on my cheek. "You have something on your face."

I stared at him, wide-eyed and mouth open. I couldn't contain my laughter. "I cannot believe you did that! You never do things like that!"

"I've had two beers and three coffees." Jake's eyes sparkled. "Anything's possible."

Then something weird happened. I must have had an out-of-body experience. I suddenly had the urge to flirt. Okay, we were *already* flirting, but I wanted to make it obvious.

I scooped frosting off the chest of my jumpsuit, leaned in, and spread it over his lips.

I blinked. "Ha!"

Why did I do that? What was I thinking?

It was Jake's turn to stare at me, stunned. The side of his neck twitched as he licked the frosting off his lips. That was so sexy, considering where it had just been. He nodded. "It *is* good cake."

I decided to push it more. "Of course, it tastes good." I held his gaze. "It was on me, and I'm one hot mama. Don't you think?"

Jake was speechless, and there was something about his

expression. If I didn't know better, I would have thought I made him weak in the knees. My breath caught in my chest. That wasn't possible. I had a crush on him, but he didn't have one on *me*.

We stood in silence, watching each other. Jake opened his mouth to say something when a camera flash nearly blinded us.

Henry and Daisy stood in the doorway. Henry smiled as he pulled the picture out of the camera.

I pointed at my son, feigning annoyance. "I forgot that I'm mad at you."

"It's like you always say, Mom. That's one for the Christmas card."

I gave him a warning with my eyes, but the kids laughed— an evil laugh, too. They disappeared down the hallway.

Jake and I cracked a smile, our weird moment gone.

"I don't think they respect our authority," said Jake.

"My little Steven wannabe is not keeping that picture."

Jake laughed. "Then let's get them."

9

SUMMER

I wasn't sure what was going on with me and Leah. I'd been in my share of relationships. I'd flirted, thanks, but I was no encyclopedia on it. So…were Leah and I flirting now? Yes? No? It seemed like it, especially in the bathroom at her parents' party. When Leah smeared that frosting across my lips, I almost said something.

Of course, I started it by wiping that cake on her cheek. There was something about her in that off-the-shoulder outfit. Leah was always beautiful, but for some reason, it took me all night to get up the nerve to talk to her. I was afraid I'd get tongue-tied and look like a dick.

The next time I saw her, I thought things would be weird, but we laughed, joked, and heckled Steven like nothing had happened.

I wasn't sure if that was good or bad.

The restaurant was busy during the breakfast and lunch rush, and cranky customers complained that we didn't give them enough ranch dressing.

I took a break in the midafternoon when the place quieted down.

My dad wiped down some tables and sauntered over to me. "What's the deal with ranch dressing?"

"I don't know, and I don't want to know."

My dad plopped down in the seat across from me and sipped my tea.

"Hey!"

"Relax," said Dad. "You came from me, you know."

I tried to block that image. "Nice."

I was in the middle of eating a PB&J, but it was obvious that Dad wanted to have a chat.

He twiddled his fingers on the table. "That's a peanut butter and jelly sandwich."

I stiffened. I knew what was coming.

"Your mother always used to make you those. We never ate peanut butter before we moved here. You two thought it was so weird and funny. Gloppy and thick. Cuimhní maithe."

I was quickly losing my appetite. Good memories? Sure. But hard memories, too. Maybe the pain was proof of the good times. "I know."

My dad smiled. "You make omelets, burgers, and grill a mean steak for everyone else, but come lunchtime, you always have that."

I put the sandwich down. "Is that bad?"

His smile turned wistful. "No. It's kind. You're remembering." He paused. The silence prickled. "You know…I meant to say something at the Roths' anniversary party, and then afterward…but I kind of lost my nerve."

I sipped my tea. "I can't imagine that."

"I wish me and your mom could have had forty-five years."

I didn't want to have this conversation. Of course, I *never* did. "Me too."

His voice was quiet. "You know, you're older now than she ever was. That's strange to think about."

My eyes felt hot. "I was older than she ever was when I was thirty-five."

He thought for a moment. "That's true. We started a family when we were young. That's the way it was back then, I guess. Now people take longer to figure things out, which is grand… but."

I pushed my plate away. This conversation wasn't going where I thought it would. "But what?"

"It's been a while now since Ash moved out." Dad gave an encouraging nod. "She's moved on… You know, you deserve to be happy. You know that, right?"

I raised an eyebrow. "What exactly are you trying to say?"

"I know I've given you crap about going out with Leah. Saying it would ruin the friendship."

I leaned back in my chair with a sarcastic grin. "Yes, I seem to recall the years of you and everyone else telling me that…"

Dad stood up. "But she makes you happy, doesn't she, Jake? She makes you *very* happy. I can see it. Everyone can." His breath caught. "So perhaps you should tell her how you feel."

I stared. This was not the advice I expected.

He gave me a firm pat on the back. "Perhaps you should tell us all to go get fucked."

The kids hadn't been on summer break long, but they were already bored. On my weekends with Daisy, sometimes we'd walk with Leah and Henry at the park. Then, afterward, we'd get ice cream.

We all grabbed our Blizzards from Dairy Queen and wandered down the street to eat them at our picnic table next to the quiet swimming beach.

"I can't believe you like M&M Blizzards," said Leah as we sat next to each other. The more she teased me, the bigger the bites I took. "So tame."

"Look at yours," I said. "Peanut butter cup. Too rich."

"You eat a peanut butter and jelly sandwich every day!" She gestured to Daisy. "Tell him, Daisy. Tell your dad he's crazy."

"You're both wrong," said Daisy. "It's cotton candy or nothing."

"I think they'd be better loaded with gummy bears," said Henry.

"You don't want that," I said. "They get too hard. You'd break a tooth off."

Henry shrugged. "That's okay. A few of mine are still baby teeth."

Leah spotted Monica and Tony walking through the park with their kids, so we waved.

Something flashed across Leah's face. She got up. "I'll be right back. I have to ask Monica when her sister's baby is due. I need to get a gift."

Leah ran across the park, Blizzard in hand.

When I looked back at the kids, they weren't eating. Instead, they stared at me. It felt like a high-stakes meeting.

"Something up?"

Daisy somehow sounded forty. "We have to talk."

Henry put his elbows on the picnic table, all business. "Listen, it's pretty clear that you think my mom is a fox."

I nearly choked on my ice cream. "Excuse me? Did you just say a *fox*? Have you been watching films from the 1960s?"

What the hell has been going on lately?

Neither of them responded; they just kept staring.

"And I…don't think that," I said. *Lies.*

"*Dad.*" Daisy knew. How did she know? "Come on."

Leah was still nearly half a block away, chatting with Monica. I turned back to the kids. "Have you been talking to Grandpa Craig?"

They shrugged. Just what I thought.

"Listen, Daisy, I realize that things are a little weird right now, but we can't force something to happen." I pushed the words out. "Leah and I are just friends."

They didn't buy it.

"What if I told you that my mom is madly in love with you?" asked Henry.

The ice cream turned into a cold rock in my throat, and various parts of my body seemed to be going numb. "I'd probably go over to that trash bin and throw up."

Daisy gave me a quizzical look. "Because you don't like her?"

"No, Dais, as you get older, you'll realize there are multiple reasons why you might want to throw up in a park trash bin."

This couldn't be true. I had feelings for Leah. Leah did *not* have feelings for me. Leah probably wasn't even flirting with me at her parents' party. She probably spent too long in the kitchen, exposed to fumes from Dennis's bizarre dip.

Could she have feelings for me? *No way.*

But I couldn't stop hope from burrowing into my heart.

"I know you might want us to get together, but…"

Henry leaned closer. "Whenever the four of us aren't hanging out, I spend all my time with my mom, grandparents, and Uncle Steven. I *know* stuff. I can tell you stuff. She was just talking to Steven about you last week."

I thought I might lose consciousness.

What was Leah saying to Steven about me?

I pushed the thought aside. It wasn't possible.

"Leah's coming back," whispered Daisy. She had a trouble-maker's smile.

I cranked my head. Leah strolled through the green grass back toward us. I turned to the kids. "Don't say a word about this when Leah gets here."

Henry's eyes narrowed. "But my mom says it's important to talk things out."

I tried my best to keep my composure. Were Leah and I like this when we were kids? No, we never would have blackmailed our parents… Maybe.

"I'm so serious right now, kids! I've never been more serious about anything."

"What's it worth to you?" asked Henry, dead serious.

Leah would be back in a minute.

"We'll come back tomorrow for ice cream," I said, "and sometime next week."

Daisy and Henry exchanged a smile.

"I think we can make that work," said Henry.

That night in bed, I stared at the ceiling. Was it possible that Leah had feelings for me? I scanned my memory, trying to pinpoint moments when she might have given me a look. But as soon as my mind went there, I shook my head.

No. Kids had imaginations. When I was seven, I spent half the time trying to convince people that I was a T-Rex.

You don't make things happen.

Ashley's words stabbed me. What if Leah *did* have feelings

for me, and I never said anything? That would be pretty fecking stupid.

But what if I told her, and she didn't feel the same way? Or what if I told her, and she felt the same way, and it all went to hell? Then what?

The thoughts and opinions of everyone I knew swirled around in my head, but it didn't matter what they said. It didn't matter what they thought. It was up to me and Leah. What did she want to do? What did I want to do?

I sat up in bed, wide-eyed. "Holy shit." I stared into the darkness. "I'm going to tell her."

I slowly slid back down to my pillow, opened my mouth, and whispered to the darkness, "Please God…or any other momentarily available higher power. Please don't let this get fucked up."

10

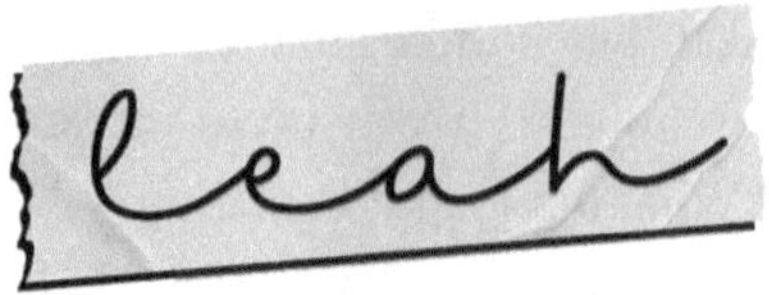

It was a hot summer day. Steven told Henry and Daisy to meet him at my parents' house. They were going to scour the attic for our old Super Soakers, then spend the afternoon chasing each other through the backyard.

"It'll be ice-cold water," I told them. "Steven's evil like that. Just warning you."

Originally, I was all for joining them. I hadn't given my brother a water balloon to the face since I was fifteen. Meanwhile, Steven was the master of hiding by my front door and spraying me with the hose on my way to work. But then Jake and I started talking about bad movies. We hadn't watched one in a while. What was the deal?

You're nervous to sit next to Jake in a dark room.

My mind was a jackass.

There was no reason to be nervous or have weird stomach pains. And there was no reason to dress up, damn it. What was I trying to do? The bathroom incident was a step too far. I almost said something and ruined everything.

I grabbed a pair of jeans and a shirt out of my closet, hardly even looking at them.

You don't need to be cute. You need to be normal, for the love of God.

I opened the door and tried to act calm.

Jake looked perfect in a brown T-shirt that showed off his strong, lean arms.

Shit.

He had a weird smile on his face, like he was nervous, but that was probably just me.

I tried to ignore everything as we stood in the kitchen, making popcorn. We made pointless small talk. We never did that. Why did Jake look like he was sick? Was there something on my face?

But below those thoughts were other thoughts. Thoughts that I had when we danced at Felicity's wedding. Thoughts that had bubbled up a million times before.

I wanted to be alone there with Jake. I wanted him to be next to me.

And I wanted to sit close to him in a dark living room.

This is bad news.

"You look nice," said Jake.

I snapped out of my crazy thought tornado. I was like a cyborg, answering questions while hardly paying attention, but his comment got me thinking. That was another thing about Jake. He always complimented me, and it was probably usually a lie. He'd seen me in the morning, half drooling, with hair plastered to my face.

"Thanks," I said. "You look pretty nifty yourself."

You're an idiot.

But Jake chuckled. Jake always chuckled when I said something weird.

I *always* said something weird.

We sat next to each other on the sofa, sinking in. I put the popcorn bowl between us, not knowing why.

We watched a lot of bad movies on that sofa. And if I was

honest, there had always been feelings for Jake swimming around in me. But I was never nervous about spending time together alone. So why was I now?

Because now he isn't with Ash.

I told my mind to shut up.

An hour into the movie, my nervousness was gone. We had our feet up on the coffee table, laughing at the terrible movie.

"This is almost unbearable," said Jake. "I never thought anything would be worse than *Deathbed: The Bed that Eats.*"

I leaned my head against the cushion and laughed. I laughed so much that Jake grinned and a crease formed between his eyes.

"I'm serious." He chuckled. "What the hell is this again?"

"*Manos: The Hands of Fate.*"

"Jesus Christ. How did you discover this?"

"They did it on *Mystery Science Theater 3000*," I said.

"I don't know what that is."

"Yes, you do." I threw a piece of popcorn at him. "Me and Steven used to watch it all the time when we were kids."

Jake shrugged, oblivious.

"Come on. It started in Minnesota!"

Jake grinned. "I'm not originally from here, remember? That's why I still have this cadence to my voice that other people don't."

"Is that what that is?"

Jake kept his gaze on me. "Yes. I don't sound like this because I'm from southern Iowa." Something shifted in his eyes. "It makes me sexy and mysterious."

My neck felt hot. "Does it?"

Oh, no. We were flirting again.

"I think so. Don't you?"

Instead of answering, I took another piece of popcorn and chucked it at his head. He chuckled quietly.

"I can't believe you've never heard of *MST3K*," I said, looking down.

His voice sounded off. "I really haven't."

"But you're a nerd. Wait…how about this…" I did a weird sing-song thing to my voice. "'He tried to kill me with a fork-lift!' Do you know that?"

Jake could hardly keep it together. "What the *hell* did you just say?"

My face was hot from embarrassment. "You have to know that. That was one of the little songs they did."

Jake tried to catch his breath. That crinkle between his eyes was killing me. "I have no idea what you're talking about… Wait…say it again."

He leaned forward like he was trying to catch every word. He was so close…

I hardly got the line out because I was half-laughing. "'He tried to kill me with a forklift!'"

Jake's whole face was bright. It made me shy to look at him. "I guarantee that I have no idea what you're talking about."

I dismissed his nonsense with a wave. Why the hell was I using so many hand gestures? "Oh well. I guess that'll have to be next movie night, huh?"

But Jake didn't answer. He kept staring at me. Time felt like it stopped, and there we were, with that stupid popcorn bowl between us. For some reason, my hands got sweaty. I didn't know what to say.

I tried to laugh it off. "You're looking at me like I'm a weirdo."

Jake still watched me, but his expression changed. His jaw shifted, and his eyes were… Had he ever gazed at me like that?

You're nuts, that's all.

But it made my shoulders weak. What was happening?

I don't know, but holy crap, his eyes are amazing.

His voice was rough. Quiet. "That's not how I'm looking at you."

God. The words sent a chill through me. I didn't know what to say. I didn't know what was happening. Was he being funny? Was I reading this wrong? Was it possible that I passed out from too much caffeine and was now unconscious on the floor…and this was a dream I was having? The possibilities were endless, and I felt nervous. I felt like I was sitting there, anticipating something…but what? This was Jake, my friend. I had feelings for *him*. He didn't have feelings for *me*. I knew I should brush his comment off, but…

"Then how are you looking at me?" I asked quietly.

He sat up straighter, grabbed the popcorn bowl, and set it on the end table. I felt naked with nothing between us.

His whisper was sweet and jagged. "I have something to tell you."

Now *I* sat straighter. Adrenaline rushed to my face. "Is something wrong?"

Jake's smile was nervous. He took a deep breath, his eyes focusing on me again. "No, it's nothing like that. It's just… I don't know what you're going to think."

That didn't stop my weird adrenaline face thing. "Now you're scaring me."

He scooted toward me half an inch, and my skin tingled. "You've always been there for me. First with my mom. Then with Daisy. You're my best friend in the world." He didn't speak for a second. It was the longest second of my life. Was I supposed to say something? Why was I so nervous? "But for me, there has been something under that for a long time."

Was this an out-of-body experience? He was like Charlie Brown's teacher, telling me things my mind couldn't make sense of.

"But I didn't say anything because of our kids and my marriage," he continued. "And life, I guess. And because I was afraid. And because, apparently, I let life happen instead of making it happen." He breathed again. "But I want to make something happen."

I stared, wide-eyed.

No. Way. Is there a camera on me?

"I don't know if you've ever guessed this." The words came out in a slow trickle that heated me from head to toe. "But I have feelings for you. I've had feelings for you for a long time." Heat traveled up my body. I didn't breathe. Jake's eyes stayed on me. "There's nothing I'd change about you, Leah. I'm mad about you."

His words hung in the air. His nervous eyes could hardly look at me. I couldn't believe what he was saying. A warm tingle spread across my chest and through my arms. I was pretty sure that if I stood up, I'd fall face-first onto the floor.

Jake felt the same way. He had felt it for years. Holy shit.

Your body requires oxygen, Leah…like, soon!

"You have feelings for me?" I finally asked. It didn't even feel like me talking.

His jaw twitched. "Yes."

I felt tears behind my eyes.

I guess I'll look nuts now.

I wiped a tear away. Jake scooted closer to me. He grabbed my hand. The last time we held hands was when I had Henry. And wow, did his fingers feel good. Warm, safe. But there was a worried expression on his face. I was giving him the wrong impression.

"I'm sorry, Leah," he said. He had never sat so close to me. I felt his warm breath on my face. "I'm an idiot. Ignore me. Just ignore everything."

My body felt like it was going Mach 4. I shook my head. "I

don't want to ignore everything. I thought it was all my imagination."

"It wasn't your imagination." Oh crap, did his face sink a little? He didn't think I felt the same way. "I adore you."

My heart pounded harder.

Dang. Put on your seatbelt because you are terrible at relationships, and this one actually matters.

The room felt so still. I took a choppy breath. "I never thought you'd feel the same way." That did it. Suddenly, everything was fast and slow at the same time. Jake froze. His gaze whipped from our interlocked hands to my eyes. Surprise was slapped across his face. He couldn't do anything but stare. "I never thought I'd get that lucky."

Everything turned soft around the edges, like my vision was lined with glitter. Suddenly, there was no space between me and Jake. His hand was resting on the back of my neck, and his lips brushed up against my ear.

"Come here to me, mo fhíorghrá," he whispered.

They were the most beautiful words I'd ever heard.

I'd be lying if I said I never wondered what kissing Jake Bradley would be like. I thought about it *a lot*. And it was just the way I imagined it would be. A lot of the guys I'd been with kissed like it was the first level of a video game, and they were hurrying through it on their way to bigger and better things. Shoes kicked off and pants unbuttoned. Kissing was only step one. But Jake kissed me like he was clearing his schedule. Like he could do this all afternoon, all night, and into tomorrow. His kisses were tender and deep, like he was exploring something he planned to remember forever. He kissed me like it meant something. Like *we* meant something.

When I thought he might stop, I pulled him closer, and his breath caught. His touch became more frenzied. Our kisses became needier.

He grabbed my waist. "Leah."

I tugged him toward me. I couldn't get him close enough. Each brush of his hand sent warmth careening through me.

His words were raw. "Kissing you is fecking amazing."

Now that I had a little, I wanted a hell of a lot more.

I nibbled his lower lip, and he groaned against my mouth.

"You like that?" I whispered.

I felt his hard dick through his pants as I leaned against him. His hands slid down my back and cupped my ass. I moaned and pushed against his cock. Jake held me there. His groan was hoarse.

His lips brushed against mine. "Fuck yes."

I could have had sex with him right there, but I wanted to take my time. I didn't want Jake for fifteen minutes. I wanted him all night.

Reluctantly, we pulled away from each other, our chests heaving. Jake's smile was hazy as he cupped my cheek. He looked at me like I was someone he cherished. Men had looked at me in a lot of different ways after a first kiss, and I liked a lot of those looks. But nobody had ever looked at me like that. I couldn't explain how it made me feel.

That wasn't true. It felt like home.

Wonderful. Terrifying.

The movie still played, but I didn't know what was going on.

I sat in front of him, leaning back against him. I tried to stop my body from shaking. He wrapped an arm around me. It was warm and soothing. I grabbed his hand and played with his fingers.

He leaned forward, his whisper tingling my neck. "That was one hell of a first kiss."

I turned my head, kissing him deeply, sliding my tongue against his. He brushed my collarbone. I felt it down to my toes.

I held his arms against my stomach. "Are we doing this?"

"We're doing this," he said. "If that's what you want."

"Only since I was twenty," I said.

He had that surprised look again that quickly turned into a wide grin. "Jesus. Really?"

I nodded.

He couldn't hide the happiness on his face. He rubbed my fingers. "Should we go out on a date?"

Yes, please.

"That sounds great."

I tried to play it cool.

I was *not* cool.

"What should we do?" I said.

"I have a few ideas."

There's a problem with this plan, Leah. I mean, besides you.

I sat up straighter. "Oh, crap."

"What?"

"What will our families think?"

Jake lifted a shoulder like he wasn't worried. How was Jake *not* worried? "I don't think they'll make a big fuss about it."

The next night, we were gathered at my parents' house for the Roth/Bradley dinner. Dad slammed the casserole dish onto the table. Jake and I jumped.

"I think this is a bad idea," said Dad.

I raised an eyebrow. "The casserole?"

"Not the casserole. You and Jake's relationship."

Jake and I exchanged wide-eyed looks of horror.

Steven pointed at us and elicited a whooping laugh.

"Careful with that casserole dish, Dennis," said Mom. "My grandma gave me that. I didn't care for her, but it's a nice dish."

Steven wiped away tears. "I give it four weeks. Maybe five."

"Shut up, Steven," I said.

Jake flipped off Steven with a grin. "No one's breaking up with anyone."

His words made my chest ache in a good way.

"They already have little inside looks," said Mom. "That's cute."

Steven laughed harder.

What the hell? "How does everyone know about this already?"

Nervousness washed across Jake's face. "The other day, the kids suggested I should ask you out." He scratched his neck. "They thought you wouldn't be averse to the idea."

I cocked my head at Henry and Daisy, pretending to be annoyed. "You don't say?"

"Don't look at us," said Henry.

"Grandpa Craig gave us each twenty bucks to say something to Dad," said Daisy.

Jake swallowed hard. "Excuse me?" He looked back and forth between Daisy and Craig.

"How could you do that, Craig?" asked Dad. "What if they break up, and it ruins the friendship?"

Craig let out a long sigh. "They've been mad about each other for years. It was starting to annoy the piss out of me."

Jake leaned toward me, his whisper tickling my cheek. "I want to go on record and say that I care about you very much, and I wanted to ask you out anyway. Please don't let insane people give you second thoughts."

I rubbed my thumb across his hand. "Don't worry." Then I pressed a light kiss to his lips.

There was an uproar at the table. Dad made anxious noises, Mom *awwed*, the kids were grossed out, Craig cheered, and Steven did a hyena impression.

"I don't know how you were all so sure that I'd asked Leah out," said Jake.

"Easy," said Steven. "Me, Daisy, and Henry were down the street, waiting and spying. We saw you two give each other a goodbye kiss when you parted ways."

I pursed my lips. "I thought you were having a water fight."

Steven shrugged. "We ran out of balloons."

11

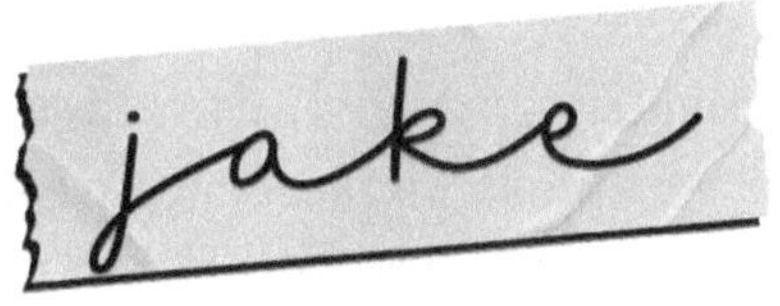

Steven sold some of his collections to make extra cash for the townhouse he couldn't afford. I was floored that he had so many takers with that Number 2 pencil collection, but I guess it takes all kinds. The guy he wanted to sell his rock collection to didn't have much in the way of cash. But he did have a movie projection system that piqued Steven's interest, so they made a trade.

I wasn't sure who was more excited about the projector, Daisy or Henry. Steven was becoming everybody's favorite uncle, which was a terrifying notion. The kids wanted to have a sleepover at his place, watching movies all night and eating fake whipped cream straight from the spray can. I was a little hesitant at first.

"Light-hearted movies," I said.

Daisy sounded like a teenager already. "Dad!"

Steven tried to give me an oblivious look, but I wasn't buying it.

"I'm serious. Nothing nightmare-inducing, alright? No screenings of *The Exorcist* at midnight."

"Of course not," said Steven. That devil-may-care smile of his didn't inspire optimism.

With the kids occupied, Leah and I decided it would be a good Saturday night for our date. My knee did a weird nervous shake the whole drive over to her house.

"Stop being thick," I whispered. "Nobody wants to have sex with a goblin."

My breath caught thinking about holding her on that sofa. Or the way she had been pressed against my cock. But I wasn't going to rush things. I wasn't going to push. It was only our first date, after all.

But our relationship had been a long time coming.

"Stop psyching yourself out, you fecker!"

Leah answered the door, all smiles. She wore a summery white dress with blue flowers all over it. It had tiny straps and a plunging neckline that made me readjust my stance. The way it rested against her perfect curves accentuated her ass in a way that made my chest tighten.

It took a lot of effort not to stammer like a fool. "You look beautiful."

Understatement of the year.

"You look great, too," she said. "I've always wanted to tell you that you look sexy in blue."

My face felt warm. "Really?" Did I look as nervous as I felt?

"Yep. It's your color." She winked. "You look sexy in brown, too."

Dear God.

When we got into the car, she turned to me. "So…what are we doing?"

I swallowed my nerves and flashed her a sly smile. "Returning to the scene of the crime."

Leah was all laughs as we got out of the car. She blinked at the mini-golf course. "You can't let it go, huh?"

"Old grudges die hard." I wrapped my arm around her waist like it was the most natural thing in the world. Because it was. And God, it felt good to be that close to her skin. She kissed my cheek. "We're going to relive the Great Crime of 2010, when my golf ball mysteriously rolled by itself into the waterfall when I wasn't looking, and both you and Steven somehow got your balls through the castle in one shot, even though it's the hardest obstacle on the course."

Leah couldn't stop laughing. "We did!"

I narrowed my eyes, my face close to hers. Damn, I could do this all night. "Still lying, after all this time. I know for a fact that you two had extra balls hidden somewhere."

She gave me a playful swat. "That would be crazy. Why would we go through that much work to win at mini golf?"

I widened my eyes, pretending to be exasperated. "I have no idea. I still wonder about that all the time. I lie awake at night, baffled. That's why I didn't tell you we were coming here. So you couldn't shove golf balls in your purse."

That made Leah laugh even harder. Yep. That's what I suspected. I kissed her.

"Damn it," she said, smiling.

"Stop making me laugh," said Leah. "I can't hit straight. That's cheating."

"And you'd know all about that, wouldn't you?"

Leah broke down again. She could barely hold her golf club. She ran a hand through her long, curly hair and tried to regain her composure. "Okay, come on. Get in the game."

"Will she get her ball across the bridge, or will it fall into the water?" I asked.

She eyed me. "Will *yours*, after my turn is done?"

"What are you going to do, knock my ball off course again?"

She hit her ball. It went coasting through the bridge without incident. The breeze picked up, playing with Leah's dress. Between that and her spicy perfume, I was having a hard time paying attention to the game.

"Maybe I'll throw you off your game by telling you that I like to talk dirty during sex."

Yep. That would do it. I tried to ignore how one sentence made me suddenly hard.

She looked me up and down. "I bet you like to talk dirty too. Don't you, Jake?"

I didn't say anything. I stood there like an idiot, grinning.

She grinned back. "That's what I figured."

Leah feigned annoyance. "If you get through this pirate ship, I'll be so mad."

I winked. "I can't do worse than you."

"It only took me three tries."

The hell? "Four! The cheating begins again!"

Leah giggled, grabbing my arm. "Your stance is off. Let me show you how to do it." She stood in front of me with her club, practicing a hitting stance. But when she bent over, her ass brushed against my dick.

I scanned the area to make sure we were alone, then I bent forward toward her, brushing against her ass again. "I'm not sure the manager appreciates you making me hard on hole four."

She shuddered, grinning. "I could flick it to make the erection go away."

My lips brushed against her ear. "I guarantee that you flicking my cock won't make my erection go away."

Her laugh was silent as she peeled herself away from me and readjusted her dress.

"Now I definitely won't make it through," I said.

I positioned my club and tried to concentrate.

Leah's eyes drifted to the pirate ship. "I love the ocean. Do you?"

"I suppose. I never thought about it."

Her voice felt far away. "I'd love to see it again."

I looked up from my club. The only time Leah had ever seen the ocean was when we all went to Westport together. "You would?"

"Yeah. I want to sit on a dock with my legs stretched out and my toes in the ocean."

My heart beat faster. "We could go sometime."

Her eyes twinkled. "Really?"

I paused as I scanned her. "Yes."

"I'd like that."

"Good," I said, hitting my ball. "Because we're doing it."

My ball sailed through the pirate ship with no problem.

Leah gave me a look. "I guess I'm not good at distracting you."

I slid my arm around her waist again, my hand tingling against the fabric. "That's not an accurate statement."

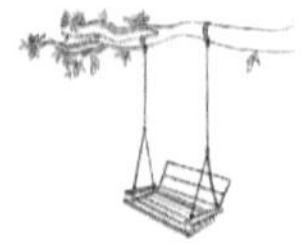

We walked down the sidewalk hand-in-hand. The sun was setting, and the sky was bright with pink and purple clouds. The lakes spread out around us, shimmering.

"You should have worn your winner's ribbon," said Leah.

"That wouldn't make me look crazy."

"When Steven and I tied, we wore our ribbons for three days."

I gave her a comical glance. "Yes, I seem to remember that."

"Where are we going now?" she asked, nudging me.

"We better eat before the growling in my stomach attracts predators."

We meandered around Lake Carlos. "Way out here?"

"I stumbled on a cool place a couple of weeks ago," I said. "I think you'll like it."

We rounded the corner. I pointed at a red food truck parked at the end of the street. There were little tables set up and a long line of people waiting.

Her face lit up. "I love food trucks."

"It's a food truck that's nothing but macaroni and cheese."

She turned to me, her mouth wide. "It's like a dream come true!"

I rubbed her hand with my thumb. "Let's fill ourselves with carbs."

We sat on a bench by the lake, eating macaroni and cheese out of cardboard-like bowls.

"This is great. This is more bacon than macaroni and cheese. How's yours?"

Leah was in the zone. "I didn't think you could get this much cheese in macaroni and cheese. We should bring the kids here."

Her comment made a warm sensation spread across my chest. My heart was being a bastard again. We took the kids out all the time. To the lakes. To the arcade. Out to eat. I thought back to that guy at the bowling alley who mistook Leah for my wife. If we all went out together now, it would be different.

Take your foot off the gas. Calm the fuck down.

I tried not to think about it, but it was a thought I liked.

"But *your* macaroni and cheese is better," said Leah.

I shook my head.

"Yes," she said. "All warm and gooey with the breadcrumbs on top. That's my favorite part of Thanksgiving."

I turned my head. "Really?"

"Yeah," she said, eyeing me. "Well…after seeing you."

Her comments were throwing me again. "You see me all the time."

She hummed. "I know. It's great."

I looked at my food, feeling nervous and lucky at the same time. "I hope that means you want to go out on another date."

Her shoulder brushed mine. "Definitely."

We were quiet for a moment. I placed a hand on her knee, but she didn't react. She kept looking forward. I made little circles on her kneecap with my finger. She smiled, scooting closer.

"I love *all* the food you make." She placed her hand on my leg. "You're so talented."

My chest tingled as she made idle, lazy strokes.

"What country's currency did you receive to say that?"

She squeezed my leg playfully. "Hush. You make the best bread. There's nothing like fresh bread. And the desserts—that chocolate pie? Please. And whenever I'm at the café, I get the pancakes. So nice and fluffy." Her hand slid higher on my leg, and a longing throb shot through me. "Remember when we were kids? You came over on Saturday mornings and made pancakes. I stood beside you cracking eggs, but I always got shells in the batter." I couldn't stop looking at her. "You were talented even back then."

I wrapped my left arm around her, resting my hand on her hip. "I used to make you pancakes for breakfast all the time."

God, it felt good to hold her.

She leaned in, her head against my shoulder. "I know. What happened?"

"Do you want me to?" My blood heated. I knew damn well what I was implying. "Sometime soon?"

She nuzzled into my shoulder. "That would be nice."

My heart beat so fast, I was afraid she'd hear it. "I remember you singing while you picked the eggshell out of the batter. You used to sing a lot."

She sat straighter. "Now I only sing when we act like idiots doing karaoke in the car. Or when I'm trying to embarrass Henry."

"You used to walk around the yard, playing and singing. You sang in high school, too."

"In choir. But not in college."

"You have a pretty voice. It's unique."

She shook her head. "My voice is… It's not like some people, who blow the roof off. It's just an average voice."

I leaned toward her ear. My whisper made her shiver. "There's nothing average about you."

By the time we got back to the car, it was pitch black. I wasn't sure what to say or do. The streetlight splashed across Leah, making her blue and white dress appear golden, but she was always golden.

My hands were sweaty and my body throbbed. I had to say something, so I cleared my throat. "It's getting pretty late." I hesitated. "Do you want me to drop you off at home?"

I was nervous about what we were doing, one way or another. I looked into her eyes. I couldn't decipher her expression.

Her voice was hushed as she shifted. "Do you…*want* to bring me home?"

That got the adrenaline pumping. I fiddled with random things in the car. The center counsel was suddenly fascinating. "Not particularly." My face felt hot. I held my breath, wondering what she'd say.

Her words were slow. "There's no pressure. If you don't want to do that tonight, we…" Leah stopped talking. She put her hands up to her face, like she didn't want me to see her. "Oh, God. I am *so* embarrassed."

I had no idea what was happening, but her embarrassment was the most adorable thing in the world. "What? Why do you have your hands over your eyes?"

"Because I'm mortified! I was going to say that we don't have to have sex tonight…but I don't even know if you *want* to have sex with me. I just assumed. How stupid. Forget I said anything. Don't look at me."

I chuckled and pried her hands from her eyes. "You're so cute when you're embarrassed." I took a deep breath. "Look how I was at the golf course when you brushed against me. I've had feelings for you for a long time, so it's a pretty good bet that I'm…interested in having sex with you."

That car was like the vacuum of space. Neither one of us made a sound or moved.

"You're looking at me like you think it's a bad idea for us to spend the night together," she said.

I didn't take my eyes off her. "That's not how I'm looking at you. I'm looking at you like I've never wanted to *not* go slow so bad in my life. But I don't want to pressure you."

Leah fiddled with the hem of her dress. "With some people, it might be fast. But it's you. With you, everything feels different. *You're* different."

The car was quiet again. She was different, too. Everything felt different with Leah. Comfortable. Safe. Loving. I looked at her, and she looked at me.

"What should we do? What do you want to do?"

Her eyes sparkled in the streetlight. "Let's go to your place."

It had never taken me so long to unlock my front door. Leah stood beside me, rubbing my back as I fiddled with the key. I felt every finger.

Leah threw her purse on the cupboard while I flipped the kitchen light on. We stared at each other, awkward and heated. The way her chest rose and fell with each breath was enough to drive me mad.

"Usually when you look at me like that, I get nervous." She

stepped closer. "I always wonder if it means you want to kiss me."

My breath was raspy. "It does." Internally, I was shaking. But when I took her in my arms, everything inside me went still. She was so soft. "You're sure you want to do this?"

She pressed a light kiss to my jaw. "I'm sure. Are you sure?"

My heart pounded. There was so much I wanted to say. I wanted to tell her I loved her, but I'd look like a fool if I said it so early on. And the words were all caught in my throat anyway. So I put my forehead against hers and willed my heart to calm down. "I've never been more sure of anything."

There was a sheen on her eyes as her lips met mine.

Leah. Every square inch of my soul was hers, and she didn't even know it.

I ran my fingers across her elbow.

She gave me a hazy smile. "That sends a shiver through my whole body."

"You like it?"

She nodded. "And your eyes—I've always loved your eyes. The way you're looking at me makes me feel half-drunk."

She was like pure energy, charging me all over. "Everything about you does something to me—your smell, your eyes, your laugh…"

She peppered kisses up my neck, then nibbled my ear. "But I'm too short."

God, her fecking mouth. "You're perfect. I could pick you up and carry you off."

She bit her lip. I could have made love to that look. "I bet you could haul me to the bedroom like I'm a feather."

I could hardly speak. "Do you want me to?" She nodded.

I slid my hands down her back and rested them on her ass. Dear God. It was perfect. I held my hands there and gazed into her eyes as she grinned. I squeezed her ass. God. How many times had I wanted to caress her ass? I got a little taste that day on the sofa. Now I didn't want to stop. I rubbed and cupped, driving myself crazy. Leah leaned into me and let out a small moan.

That set me off.

"Fuck, Leah." I pulled her tight against me, still touching her ass. I kissed her neck, intoxicated from feeling her.

"Pick me up," she whispered, her breath raspy.

I lifted her up to me. My heart pounded in my ears. She wrapped her legs around my waist. Fuck. She was pressed right against me.

I carried her to the bedroom and set her gently on the bed. She tugged me down with her. Her lips were too damn soft. I broke away and burrowed into her neck. "Do you know how long I've wanted you?"

I breathed in the perfume behind her ears. Her hair tickled my cheeks.

She slid a hand under my shirt, scraping her nails against my chest. I jolted against her touch, wanting more. Her fingers teased lower. My breath caught as she grabbed me through my jeans. "I'm so glad this is happening, Jake. I want you so much."

"Fuck," I whispered, pulling her mouth to mine.

"Do you like that?" She squeezed my dick. Jesus. I throbbed under her fingers. This was better than any dream I'd ever had. "You're so hard."

"I've been hard all night," I whispered back. "I want you so bad I can taste it."

Abruptly, she stood, gesturing for me to sit on the edge of the bed. My heart pounded as she slowly sat down on my lap, her legs wrapping around my waist.

"Is this okay?" she asked. Then she ground against me once, nearly making my eyes roll back in my head.

I held her tight to me, thrusting back against her. *Jesus.* "It's a lot better than okay."

"I want this to take a while," she whispered, and the hairs on my arms rose. "I want you to tease me so much that I'm begging you for it."

"Fecking hell, Leah." She stuck her tongue in my mouth, and I sucked it, bucking against her.

The pressure of her body against me was amazing and unbearable at the same time. She pulled my shirt off and ran her hands across me, still grinding. "You look so good, Jake. Your chest and arms. So sexy."

She ran her tongue across my left nipple, and I groaned. "Jesus, Leah. You feel so fecking amazing. Tell me what you want."

Her eyes narrowed, grinding forward again. "Have you ever thought about this? About us together like this?"

My breath turned raspy again as I cupped a breast through her dress. "Yes."

She smiled. "What did you think about?"

My hands ventured down to her ass again. I grabbed and squeezed. "I've thought about touching your breasts. I've thought about what it would feel like to press my hips down onto yours." I licked her neck. "I love your hips. Do you know how many times I've gotten hard watching you walk away? Do you know how many times I've dreamed of taking you from behind?"

Leah let out a small gasp. "I love how tall you are. I've thought about you holding me against a wall and fucking me. I've touched myself at night thinking about you riding me hard on a table or the floor."

I stilled, staring at her. "Are you serious?"

She grabbed my dick through my jeans again. "Yes."

I put my hand on hers to make her squeeze me harder. "Jesus. Fecking. Christ."

We pressed against each other, our kisses fevered. I couldn't get enough of her.

She leaned forward, her voice a whisper. "Unzip my dress."

My hand shook as I pulled the zipper down. She let the straps fall down her shoulders, the dress pooling at her hips. She wore a lacy purple strapless bra.

I ran my hand across the lace. "Christ, you're sexy."

Leah swore and held my hand to her. My blood boiled.

"I want you to touch me," she whispered. "Touch me all over."

"Fecking hell." I hardly got the words out. The bra was off in a second. Those perky breasts. I groaned as I became intimately acquainted with them. *Damn.* I couldn't stand it. She was so soft. Her breasts fit perfectly in my hands. I sucked on her pointed nipple, making her moan, and that made me suck even harder.

When she said my name, it was a sultry whisper. "Jake."

That word went straight to my dick. "I've dreamt about you moaning my name. I want my name on your lips when you come, Leah. I want you to yell it so loud that you fecking make me deaf."

Leah's smile was evil. "You know what I've always thought about?" I looked into her eyes, breathing hard. "I've thought about you reaching up my dress, pushing my panties away, and touching me."

My heart pounded wildly as I licked and thrust against her. "Is that what you want me to do, baby?"

"Yes."

"Thank Christ." My shaking hand went under her dress and slid up her leg. She shivered as my fingers got close to her pussy, her legs still seductively wrapped around me. Her thin, lacy panties were damp. *God.* I pushed the lace aside and touched her gently. That first touch. *Damn.* I circled my thumb against her clit. She moaned my name again. Fecking hell.

I kissed her as I teased her with my fingers. "Leah. Holy shit. You are so wet."

She pressed forward, taunting my finger. "I've been wet since this morning."

My heart skipped a beat as I slowly plunged a finger inside her. "Is that okay? Tell me if it hurts."

But her answer was a breathy intake. She pushed herself against my finger and moaned.

Goddamn.

"You don't know what you do to me, Leah." I'd never seen anything quite as perfect as her riding my hand. She didn't even have to touch me. I could have come just from that. I plunged in and out, groaning. I pulled my finger out and added another. She ground against me harder. I couldn't take my eyes off my hand. "Come for me, mo fhíorghrá. Just like this."

She leaned her head against my shoulder as I plunged into her again. She moaned and bucked against me. I didn't want this to end.

"No." She grabbed my shoulders. "I want you on top of me. I need you on top of me. Please."

"Jesus," I said. "You don't have to ask me twice."

She lay down as I discarded my pants and underwear. By the time I knew what the fuck was going on, she was naked before me, her dress thrown on the floor. Holy hell, she was perfect. Her round, delicious hips and her perky breasts. Her dark hair cascaded over her nipples. That set a fire in me all over again. Those curves. She was wonderful.

She stared down at my hard dick. Her gaze lazily drifted over my body, and I got harder just watching her watch me. Then her eyes drifted to mine. That smile killed me.

I crawled onto the bed, and she sat up, grabbing for my dick. "God, you're big."

My breath caught, but I playfully evaded her grasp. I knew if she got her hands on me, I'd come in a second, and I wanted to make this last for her. "I'm sure I'll be a perfect fit for your tight pussy."

I kissed her neck, gently guiding her to lay back down. Then I crawled down to her ankles and ran my tongue up her legs. I felt frantic to touch every part of her. "I love your freckles. I'm going to lick each one."

She shuddered. "God."

I hovered over her pussy, blowing a breath against it. She twisted beneath me. "Is that the kind of teasing you like?"

Before she had a chance to answer, I eased her legs apart and licked her inner thigh. I kissed the soft skin. I rested my fingers gently on her, opening her to me. She shook slightly as I ran my tongue up her. *Hell. Yes.* "Just what I thought. Fecking divine." Then I lazily plunged my tongue inside her.

Her breath caught, and she jerked. "Jake!"

The way she said my name made me crazy.

"You taste so good, Leah. I could eat you all day."

I rested my hands on her inner thighs to keep her open. She gasped as I stuck my tongue in her again. I licked her up and down as she grabbed at my head. I moved my hands under her ass, running my nails across her. She moaned, but her body remained still. I pulled away and looked at her. Her face was pink. Her lips were swollen. This was everything.

"Grind against me, Leah." I nipped at her. "Grind me while I fuck you with my tongue. I want you to come on my face."

"Jesus, Jake. I never knew my best friend was fucking naughty."

I chuckled.

She moaned as my tongue plunged into her again. She ground down against my face, and she wasn't subtle about it. Good. I didn't want her to be.

Hell. Yes.

She thrust harder as I lapped her up, squeezing that ass I loved so much. I nipped and licked. She tasted exactly the way I thought she would. Exactly the way I dreamed.

I lifted her butt and plunged my tongue in as far as it would go. She pressed against me in a tight spasm, her whole body shaking. I knew she was close. She grabbed my head as she moaned up to the ceiling.

"Jake! God!"

Her words made me shudder. Made my dick throb. I made her come with my tongue, and I couldn't wait to do it again. I lifted my eyes and licked my lips. She peered at me, her eyes hazy and content. She was a dream.

She grabbed my arm and pulled at me. "I can't stand it, Jake. I need you inside me right now."

Damn, I wanted her bad. I was about to explode.

I crawled on top of her, leaning down and brushing my lips against hers, her scent in my mouth. She pulled me close, and I put my weight down, my dick pressed between us. She wrapped her legs around me. Holy fuck, that felt good.

"I could get used to this," she said, looking up at me.

My mouth found her nipples again. "You're delicious."

She ran a hand through my hair. "I'm on birth control. And I don't have anything. You don't have to wear a condom…"

The words bounced around in my head. My eyes met hers. "I don't have anything either…but…are you sure?"

She nodded, grinning. "You're going to come inside me, Jake."

I shuddered. "Is that what you want?"

Her nails ran down my back to my ass. "Yes."

"Fuck yes."

I lifted myself slightly, freeing my dick from between our bodies. I positioned myself and gave her entrance a teasing flick. She closed her eyes and moaned, making my whole spine tingle.

I flicked her again, and she squirmed. "So fucking naughty, Jake."

I chuckled. "Do you like that?"

She tugged at me. "More."

I brushed up against her again. I think I was torturing myself more than her. She smiled and reached around. She cupped my balls. *God, yes.* I bucked against her.

"Get in my pussy right now."

She pulled me closer with her legs. I couldn't take it any longer. I plunged into her a little, careful not to hurt her. She let out a deep breath, eyes closed. I stayed there for a moment, then I pulled out. Her fingers dug into my back. Our breath was raspy as I plunged in again, a little further this time. I couldn't tell if the moans were coming from her or me. When I was all the way in, I waited for her to adjust. But she was ready, squeezing her inner muscles against me.

"Holy fecking shit."

She moaned and crashed into me like a wave, grinding in fluid, steady movements. I took her ass in my hands, pushing myself as deep into her as I could go. It was clear that neither of us was going to last long. Her groans were liable to set me off any second.

She lifted herself a little so I could plunge in further. Her mouth opened as she glanced between our bodies. "Look how deep you are."

I looked down at her hips meeting mine, at my dick going in and out of her. "Fuck me, Leah. You feel good. I love seeing my dick go in you."

She bit my nipple, sending shockwaves through me.

"I want to make you come so hard, Leah. I want our first time to be so good for you, mo ghrá."

She moaned, biting my neck. "Do I make you feel good? I want to make you scream."

"So good, baby. You feel fecking divine."

I felt the heat rising. I wouldn't last. And the way her hips met my thrusts—bloody hell.

Her moaning got louder, her movements jerky. I held her tight as she lifted her mouth to my ear. "It's our first time, and you're already so good at fucking me."

I burrowed my head into her neck and gave her a long, languid thrust. She arched her back and moaned, holding me tight. She looked so beautiful when she came, her eyes closed and her hair streaming down to the pillow.

The tension built in me like a wave. I wasn't going to be able to stand it. Holy shit, she felt good. I thrust against her, even though it felt like it would kill me.

I finally exploded, clutching her and shouting her name as I rode out the orgasm. I was in awe of her, in awe of us, and in awe that this was finally happening.

Our jerky thrusts softened out until both of us stilled. We stared at each other for a few moments, smiling and shaking. We gave each other long, lazy kisses, me still on top of her. She nuzzled her nose against mine.

"Leah," I whispered. "You were amazing."

She smiled. "I don't think I've ever felt this good."

We kissed, Leah biting my lower lip. It didn't take long for our kisses to turn feverish again. My body ached as I licked her all over in a frenzy, caressing and exploring all the places I never thought I'd be lucky enough to embrace. And when she shifted on top of me, I thought I'd lose my mind. Her hands were on me, finding, touching, and taking everything I'd always wanted her to have—my body, my heart, and my soul.

Something woke me in the middle of the night. The tap of light rain on the window. I was on my back, my blurry eyes trying to make sense of my surroundings. I glanced to my left. Leah slept on her side, pointing toward me. It hadn't been a dream. She was there, and we were together. Part of me still wondered how I had gotten so lucky, but I damn well wasn't going to question it.

What had I been afraid of for so long? Nothing was ruined. The Earth hadn't splintered. This was bliss. It felt like home. *She* was home. And the world wasn't going to fuck it up.

I wasn't going to fuck it up.

I placed my hand on Leah's side. Her eyes dreamily batted open. Without a word, she scooted over, wrapping her left arm around my chest. She reached up and kissed me before resting her head on my shoulder. A moment later, she was asleep again. I felt her chest rise and fall against me. I felt her heart beating. I wrapped my arms around her and kissed her head.

She was my home, and nothing was going to ruin that.

We held each other until the early morning rays streamed in through the curtains.

12

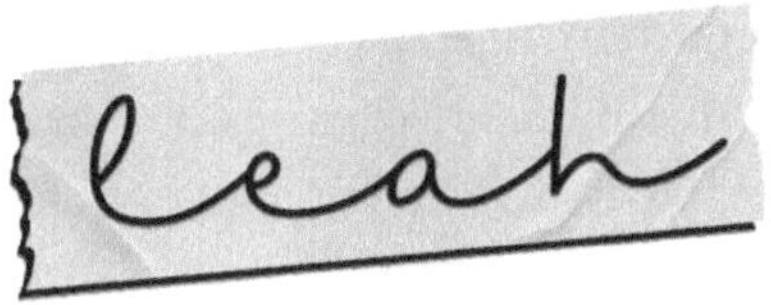

I opened my eyes and kissed Jake's chest.

He ran his fingers along my back. "Good morning."

My voice was tired but happy. "Good morning. What time is it?"

"It's early. You can sleep longer."

"I can't go back to bed. I'm with a sexy guy. It's pretty distracting."

Jake looked around. "Where?"

I gave him a playful nudge. "Oh, please."

He leaned in and kissed me. "How do you feel?"

I smiled. "Couldn't be better. How about you?"

"Fabulous. If I knew having sex with my best friend would feel this good, I would've done it a long time ago."

I let out a quiet laugh and kissed his chest again. "It's not like the movies, though. If this were a movie, I'd have a full face of makeup. We're talking concealer, thick eyeliner, mascara—everything. Sties be damned."

Jake ran a hand across my naked, freckled face. "If this were a movie, I'd be ten years younger, and I'd be played by an American with a terrible Irish accent." We leaned in toward each other and laughed. "Plus, I'd have pecs like I work out seventeen hours a day."

I grazed my fingers across his firm chest until he trembled. "Don't act like you're not sexy." I smiled. "I like you just like this."

He kept his eyes on my fingers. "Is that so?"

"Yes. You're just my type."

That made him curious. "What's your type?"

"Irish transplants who are terrible at mini golf."

He leaned back and laughed.

"Plus, that whole exercising seventeen hours a day thing wouldn't work," I said. "We wouldn't have time to plan a second date."

"No, we wouldn't," he said, playing with my hair.

"Then I'd feel pressured to work out. And with my history of gyms, we both know that's not happening."

We laughed quietly again until it turned into soft kissing. I messed up his hair and pulled him closer. "If this were a movie, we'd also have minty breath in the morning."

I stood by the stove as Jake flipped a pancake.

"They smell so good." I nudged him with my hip. "Is there a secret ingredient?"

Jake put a finger to his lips. "MSG." He winked. "Don't tell anyone."

I cracked a smile and blew on my mug of coffee. "I wonder what the kids are up to."

Jake glanced at the clock. "Steven's probably filling them with sugar. Most likely washing down a case of donuts with Coke."

"I don't know. Remember that time he fed them chili for breakfast?"

Jake tossed a pancake onto a plate. "There's an interesting wake-up call for the old digestive system."

We took our plates to the table and sat down. He had jam, fruit, maple syrup, and whipped cream for the pancakes. I grabbed the syrup, then put it down, pretending to search for something. I gave him a quizzical glance. "Where's the Log Cabin?"

Jake stared me down, pretending to be exasperated. "As you know, there is no pancake syrup in this house. If it passed through that front door, an alarm would go off."

I laughed in his face. I didn't even like pancake syrup, but it was funny to get him on a roll. Maybe next I'd bring up Spam.

"We have real maple syrup here," he insisted. "I know the guy who makes it. Pancake syrup is *not* real. It's corn syrup with food coloring."

I kept heckling him. "I don't know. Is it really an American breakfast without corn syrup?"

Jake pointed his fork at me. "You better watch out, or for your next birthday you'll get a big box filled with Hungry Jack and that weird apricot stuff from Perkins."

"Don't you dare." I poured maple syrup on my pancakes.

We sat there quietly. Jake glanced at me like he wanted to say something but didn't know where to start. "I…uh…I had a great time last night."

"Are you referring to the amazing sex?" My eyebrows lifted. "The best sex of my life?"

His eyes widened. "The best in your life? Truly?"

I sipped my coffee, staring him down. "Definitely. I've never been with a man who moves his hips like that. I mean, when you were thrusting." I smiled as I took another sip. "It was like you didn't have bones."

Jake's face reddened before he grinned. "You should've seen

me nail Dance Dance Revolution back in the day." He was quiet for a moment. "The feeling's mutual, by the way. Last night was the best of my life." His smile was nervous. "How could it not be, with you?" I blushed. "But not just the sex. Everything was wonderful." His eyes met mine. "Every moment was fantastic."

I suddenly felt like a teenager. It was crazy how he gave me butterflies, like I'd never gone on a date. "I thought it was pretty great, too."

His eyes stared into mine. "Yeah?"

I smiled right back at them. "Yeah."

We ate for a minute in silence. Somewhere in the distance, a wind chime jingled.

This was nice. With Jake, everything was different. I rarely spent the night at a guy's house. First of all, it was always awkward, and second, I had a son. I didn't want Henry to think I was prioritizing strange men over him, and I didn't want him to think that they were going to be permanent. Because they never were. To be honest, I usually knew that before I entered the restaurant to meet them.

With Jake, there was no awkward banter, no tissue-paper-thin reason to slip out the door. There had only been a little nervousness before sex—the anticipation of being with someone you care about. Someone you've wanted for so long. But now everything was relaxed. I didn't feel the urge to bolt. I didn't feel the urge to find some reason why this wasn't right.

What would I say when Henry asked about Jake? He and Daisy seemed eager for us to be together. I was surprised their attempt at matchmaking didn't make me feel pressured. As I ate pancakes with Jake, a realization hit me: I wanted all four of us to be together. I'd loved Daisy since the moment I leaned down and saw her bright little eyes staring up at me, her tiny hands reaching out and batting at my fingers. She and Henry were best friends. They were always listening to music, playing, and teasing each other, the way Steven and I did when we were kids.

The thought of us morphing into a family made my heart flip.

Jake watched me. "Everything alright?"

"I was thinking…" I said, trailing off.

"Oh no, you're leaving me for Lance."

I batted that comment away with my hand. "No. I was just thinking that I'm not…freaking out about this. *At all.*"

Jake's fork paused on the way to his mouth. The tips of his ears turned pink. "Oh."

I ran my finger around the edge of my plate. "I'm not trying to run out the door at warp speed. I'm not thinking about getting a friend to text me with a sudden emergency. I mean, that would be difficult since you're usually that friend."

Jake smiled down at his plate like he was shy to look at me.

"This is new for me," I said. "It's nice. It's never been this nice."

His gaze lifted to me again, and something about the early morning light made the sparkle in his eyes seem delicate. A tender pang spread through me as I realized I held his heart in my hands like it was a fragile plant. That scared me, but I told myself not to be scared. Because this was Jake. He knew me, and I knew him. And I wasn't going to mess this up.

He shifted his jaw. "It's never been this nice for me either. And we don't even have to worry if our kids will get along."

I leaned forward. "I *know*. That would be hell, right? We totally bypassed that one. We already do a bunch together." Why was I blushing? I felt like I was going to stumble on my words. "But we could do more. If you want… If you think it would be alright with Ash."

Jake reached out and took my hand, warming my fingers. "That sounds great. We could all play mini golf."

"Perfect. I can get them to cheat, too."

Jake pointed. "You finally admit it."

I dissolved into laughter. "I couldn't help it! It was too easy."

We sat there smiling like a couple of goofy twenty-year-olds.

I broke the silence. "So…nothing is standing in the way of us doing this?"

A grin stretched across his face. "I know. Let's mark this on the calendar. We have nothing to worry about."

I stood, leaned forward, and kissed him. "I think this day is definitely calendar-worthy."

13

One time, when I was twelve, I came down with a nasty case of the flu. I was nauseous and freezing. My parents made me stay in bed with blankets heaped on me. On the second night, my mom sat down on the edge of my bed with a bottle of liquid children's medicine.

"Maybe this will work better than the stuff you took yesterday," she said. She filled the little medicine cap and made sure I drank it. Then she put a hand on my forehead to check my temperature.

I rested my head on the pillow, expecting the next day to be filled with more soup, blankets, and long baths. But when I woke up in the morning, it seemed like every bird on the block was singing right outside my window. I listened for a full two minutes before I realized how much better I felt. It was as if something had been stripped from me in the night, a heaviness that had been tossed aside like all those blankets. I felt light. I felt new.

That's how I felt after Leah and I got together. Every morning was full of birds, and everything felt new.

To the untrained eye, our lives looked about the same. I still went to the café every morning. Leah still went to the furniture store. I still brought her and Steven coffee during our lunch breaks. But there was a slight shimmer to life that was missing before. Whenever we saw each other during the day, I'd give her a wink. I liked doing that. It always made her blush like she was twenty, and then she'd look me in the eyes and smile until it took up her whole face. Nothing but happiness and freckles. And that made *me* feel like I was twenty.

I looked like a fool, but I didn't care. The days were soft and breezy. And my heart didn't worry. That was a new sensation.

"Can I have pie for breakfast?" asked Henry. Leah and Henry started coming to the café for breakfast more regularly. Daisy was with them on days that she wasn't with Ash. Since it was summer, the kids bounced around between hanging out at the restaurant, the furniture store, Leah's parents' house, or one of our houses, depending on who was where.

"I don't know," said Leah, considering. "What do you think the chances are of grandma and grandpa feeding you fruits and vegetables later?"

Henry tried to formulate a lie, but Daisy couldn't help herself. "None! They let him eat whatever he wants."

"Hey!" said Henry, annoyed. But Daisy laughed in his face.

Henry had oatmeal with a side of fruit.

I was back in the kitchen, getting ready to make Scotcheroos. I liked to make pies and cakes for the dessert display, but people always bought out the Scotcheroos right away. I was grabbing for the peanut butter when I saw Henry wandering around up front.

I washed my hands and walked out to him. "What's up, Henry? Aren't you supposed to be at your grandparents' house?"

Henry shrugged. "Yeah. Grandpa's teaching Daisy to tie flies. But I don't know… That sounds lame. I told them I wanted to hang out here."

I smiled. We hadn't made anything for a while. "Are we baking something, then?"

Henry was all for that. "Can it be weird?"

"*I* think they are. We're making Scotcheroos."

Henry wasn't impressed. "That's not baking. That's stirring."

"You've got that right." I patted his shoulder. "But that means you get to eat one faster."

Henry stirred the sugar and corn syrup on the stove. "How long does this have to heat up?"

I poured cereal into a large bowl. "Until it boils. Be careful. Hot sugar and syrup are no joke. Your mom will kill me if you get burned."

Henry rolled his eyes. "I'm not seven. I make stuff all the time."

Funny. That's how I was as a kid.

"What have you been trying lately?"

Henry stirred the mixture. "Mom likes my quesadillas. I put lots of chilies in them."

I walked up beside him, surprised. "That sounds good."

"I can make you one sometime."

"Great." How many times had my dad and I talked like this when I was Henry's age? "What else?"

"Lots of stuff. I watched this guy make peppermint patties on YouTube. So Mom got me the stuff. They were good."

My mouth hung open. "Peppermint patties? Fair play, Henry! That's awesome."

I turned off the heat. I pointed at the peanut butter, and Henry plopped it into the boiled sugar mixture.

"It's fun." He stared at the pot, his voice lowering. "I do it because of you."

I stopped stirring. "Because of me?"

"It's awesome making stuff with you. And all the weird snacks we try." He took a breath. "And I like how you always bake me a cake for my birthday. Or pie."

I'd loved Henry since the first moment I saw him, pink and screaming bloody murder. I felt my heart go up into my throat. I patted his back.

Henry stirred the vanilla into the peanut butter mixture, and then I dumped the whole thing into the bowl with Rice Krispies.

"Isn't this supposed to be Special K cereal, not Rice Krispies?" asked Henry.

I lowered my eyes. "Don't tell anyone."

Henry smiled, stirring the mixture. "I bet you're pretty happy I got you and my mom together, huh?"

I let out a laugh. "Is that what you did?"

"Duh."

I poured the sugar and cereal mixture into a cake pan and flattened it out. Then I put chocolate chips, peanut butter, and butterscotch chips in another pot and placed it on the stove.

"I bet you wish you got together a long time ago," said Henry.

This kid was never afraid to say what was on his mind. I grinned. "I think it happened the way it was supposed to. After all, if it hadn't happened this way, I wouldn't have Daisy. And your mom wouldn't have you." I nudged him. "I don't think I'd like a Henry-less world very much."

Henry looked deep in thought. "Maybe I'd still be here, but just kinda different. I'd still be half the same because of my mom. It's just the dad half that would be different." He glanced at me. "I guess my dad half would be you."

Leave it to kids to knock you right on your ass.

I nearly dropped my wooden spoon. My mind flashed to the night Henry was born, when I stood in the delivery room with Leah. The nurse had given me a scratchy outfit to wear. My body didn't know whether it wanted to be nervous or excited, so it chose both. I could barely put the damn outfit on from the way my hands shook. But I calmed down when the nurse told Leah that everything was going great.

"You can hold your husband's hand if you want to, honey," the nurse said.

We never corrected her. Leah grabbed my hand, nodded, and started pushing.

I looked down at Henry. "Yeah, I guess I would be."

Henry stared at the chocolate. "Maybe I'd be me, but my nose would be different. Or I'd have some other talent. Instead of being good at English, I'd be good at science." Henry thought. "Is that how that works?"

I shifted. "No idea."

I poured the melted chocolate mixture over the cereal and spread it around. Now all we had to do was wait.

"I wish my dad was different." Henry sighed, staring at the counter. "He always has a new girlfriend. And the only thing he likes is working out. Some of his weights are super heavy."

It had been a while since I'd encountered Lance, but he was one ripped sucker. He was all protein powder and pecs.

I didn't know what to say to Henry about Lance. I didn't want to badmouth him in front of his son, even though the guy made me throw up in my mouth a little bit. "Sometimes people have different interests."

"He *did* take me to that monster truck thing in the Cities that time."

"Was it fun?"

Henry's eyes sparkled. "And loud. It was cool." He frowned at the dirty pans. "I like making stuff, but I hate cleaning."

I chuckled. "Tell me about it."

Henry was quiet. He looked at the counter instead of me. "I wish you were my dad."

It felt like a heavy weight smacked into my chest. The good kind.

I mussed up his shaggy, dark hair until he laughed and elbowed me.

"The feeling's mutual," I said, resting my hand on his back.

I cut us a couple of Scotcheroos before they were set up. We both took big bites, the chocolate smearing across our faces.

When I got to A-to-Z Furniture with our coffee, Steven was at the register ringing up someone. Although Steven was supposed to be paying attention to his customer, he stared at me during the entire transaction. When the customer left and I walked forward, Steven hummed "I Want You to Want Me."

"You're in a good mood today," I said.

He wiggled his eyebrows. "Why wouldn't I be? Love and its calamitous aftermath make for good music."

Leah walked out of the break room with three sandwiches. "Shut up, Steven." She smiled at me. "He's been heckling me all morning. People get into relationships all the time."

"They get out of them all the time, too," said Steven. "It

might not be funny *now*, but when you break up, the chuckles will commence.”

“Classy.” Leah was monotone. “We’re not breaking up.”

My heart beat faster. Leah and I exchanged a glance.

“Because your track records are so good,” said Steven. “They’re like mine, and that ain’t a ringing endorsement.”

“This is different,” I said. “We’ve had feelings for each other for a long time. It’s not like we met out of the blue.”

“Take it from me, that might be wiser,” said Steven, staring at the ground. “The crashing and burning wouldn’t have so much smoke.”

Gail walked up, her eyes on Steven. “Help me with these people. They want that big recliner loaded into their pickup.”

“But my pastrami.” Steven turned glum. “And my heckling.”

“The heckling will keep,” said Gail. She gave me a friendly wave as she pulled her son to the other end of the store.

Leah handed me a sandwich. “Are you hungry, or did you eat?”

I leaned forward and kissed her. “I had a PB&J at the café.”

“Really?” She pretended to frown. “And I made you one and everything.”

I took the sandwich. “You did?” Nobody had made me one since…

My dad never even made them, knowing what it meant. He always made grilled cheese.

We looked to see if there were customers around. There weren’t. I pulled her close and kissed her again.

My lips brushed her ear. “I’m still a little hungry.”

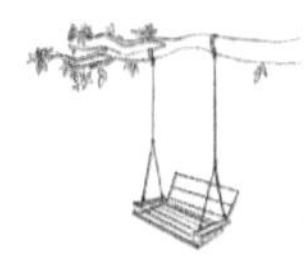

Steven was back in a flash. He sat next to us in the break room, bemoaning his sandwich. "Pastrami has lost its allure." We stared at him, drinking our coffee. "Mom didn't need my help. She wanted me out of the way so you could have alone time. Can you believe that?"

"Sure can't," said Leah, humorless.

"*And* she said she doesn't want me taking a lunch break with you anymore. What does she care? This is the dead time. Goddamn."

"Maybe she's doing it for your benefit," I said. "Leah and I could be talking about personal things back here."

Leah snagged this train of thought. "I could be asking Jake if he's seen my missing bra."

"And I could ask her which one she means because I've now seen several."

Leah narrowed her eyes. "You might start to feel like the third wheel."

Steven shrugged, unperturbed. "What the hell's new about that? From day one, you guys have had some kind of energy field between you. And I'm like the scientist studying your activity."

"That's a disturbing thought to fall asleep to," I said, eating my sandwich.

"And now that you two have admitted your feelings, I can finally say this: Leah, once, when you were twenty and still living at home, you and Monica went out pontooning on Lake Ida. Jake came over and saw you in your swimsuit. He checked you out bigger than shit."

Leah's eyes widened, turning to me like I'd been caught. "Did you?"

"I don't remember that, but I probably was. You went swimming all the time. And you always looked... Do *you* remember?"

"Hell no," said Leah.

"There are lots of other gems like that," said Steven. "It's hard keeping track… Oh, and Leah used to listen to sad indie and folk music when Monica and I came over. It didn't take too many Bon Iver songs and hard lemonade before she was talking about her feelings for you."

Leah kicked Steven in the ankle. "Fuck off, Steven! I was in my early twenties."

"Really?" I never would've imagined that while I was listening to sad songs and thinking of Leah, she was listening to sad songs, thinking of me. She said as much on our first date, but hearing it like this… I could've told her how I felt that cold Halloween. *Damn.* "What did you say about me?"

Leah was completely pink. It was adorable. She tried not to laugh as she looked at me. "I don't know. I guess I thought you were the cat's meow."

I wanted to pull her onto my lap and kiss her, but Steven still sat there, studying us like a mad scientist.

He cleared his throat loudly. "If anyone's wondering, my love life is going great, too. I think after all my years of heartache, I found a balm to my pain."

"Is that so?" I asked, incredulous. "This is quite a step in the other direction from you searching around Felicity's wedding for Margot."

Steven gave me a relaxed stare, refusing to be embarrassed. "What can I say? My philosophy on life is to live for the moment, enjoy music, and make sweet love while you can."

Leah tried to block that mental image with her hand. "Ick. Shut up."

"What's she like?" I asked.

Steven grinned. "She doesn't make butter sculptures like Dee, but she plays the banjo."

Leah and I exchanged a glance.

"She's a banjo-playing real estate agent." Steven stared off dreamily. "She wears three rings on each hand. There's nothing sexier than that. Plus, she has blonde hair that goes halfway down her back, and it's the straightest hair I've ever seen."

Leah put her sandwich down and crossed her arms. Steven was, by that point, completely lost in a trance.

"I'm very happy for you," she said.

After supper one night, we took the kids out for a walk. They ran around the park like they had each eaten a bag of candy, while we strolled behind, holding hands.

"Wait, I've got something for you!" Daisy raced back toward us. She opened her hand, showing Leah something. It was a green and blue bracelet made from woven plastic threads.

"You made this for me?" asked Leah. She smiled, but her eyes were glossy.

"Yep!" said Daisy. "I made one for Henry, too. But this one turned out better."

Leah gave Daisy a knowing glance, and they giggled. Daisy helped Leah tie the bracelet around her wrist.

Those two were so sweet together. They made tie-dye shirts, shared inside jokes, and teased Henry. And Leah and I dating only brought them closer. Sometimes Daisy pushed me out of the room so she could ask Leah a question. She always wanted to sit next to Leah on the couch, which was fine with Henry because he was way too cool for that. Sometimes I'd wander into the living room and catch Daisy dozing against Leah's shoulder. I wished I could capture every second. And I didn't let my mind tell me it was too good to be true.

Leah hugged Daisy. "I love it."

My chest felt tight and relaxed at the same time.

Henry wandered over, curious about what we were up to. He

pretended to be annoyed. "Hey, Mom's bracelet is nicer than mine."

Leah pulled them in, smiling. "Hey, you guys. I have an idea to run by you." She flashed me her shining eyes. "When your dad and I were younger, our parents always brought us to the drive-in movie."

The memory came back to me like the bright lights of a camera—sitting in lawn chairs next to the car, Leah and I sharing a hot fudge sundae, Steven stealing our Mike & Ike's, and Leah falling asleep before the movie was over, halfway slumped on me. Good memories. Before my mom died. Before I thought I was a cool teenager and Leah was a goofy kid. Before she was in college and I realized I had feelings for her.

"Don't those movies start late?" asked Daisy.

"When the sun goes down," said Leah.

Daisy and Henry gave each other a high five.

"Cool, we can stay up even later than we did at Steven's," said Henry.

"What?" Leah and I asked in unison.

"When can we go?" asked Daisy.

"We just have to run it by your mom," I said.

Daisy bubbled with excitement. "I'm getting nachos."

"And I'm getting one of those slushies that turn your tongue blue," said Henry.

They ran to the playground, laughing and talking a mile a minute.

I wrapped my arm around Leah, and she leaned into me. "Are you happy?"

"*Very.*" She rested her cheek against mine. My skin warmed from her touch. "How about you?"

It was hard to say all of what I felt. "This is what I was hoping for."

"Me too," she said, gazing at me. Her dark eyes were hypnotic.

"I'd like to do something else too," I said.

Leah hummed. "Like get scuba certified? Or learn to play the spoons?"

I ran a hand through her long hair. "Maybe. But I was thinking another date first."

"Ah. I see. I guess that sounds fun too. And maybe we can embarrass other diners by playing the spoons at the restaurant."

I couldn't help grinning as I kissed her soft lips. "Sounds like a plan."

14

When I was a kid, we dyed our hair with Kool-Aid before football games and other events. So I thought it would be cute and nostalgic to do it for the drive-in movie. We gathered in my tiny kitchen. Somehow, dyeing our hair turned into getting Kool-Aid and undissolved powder everywhere it wasn't supposed to be. It would probably stain the cupboards and counter, but the kitchen was old and cruddy anyway, and we couldn't stop laughing.

"You first, Mom," said Henry, wanting me to be the guinea pig.

"No way. We're in this together." I mixed grape Kool-Aid for me and Henry. I thought it would show up best in our dark hair. Then I mixed pink lemonade for Daisy. I added the hot water and squirted in some conditioner while Jake draped towels over the kids' shoulders.

I nudged Jake. "Are you sure you don't want your hair colored? This blue raspberry has your name on it."

He stared at the white sink, now stained purple. Then he gave me an amused glance that looked a lot like *no chance in hell.* We all laughed again.

"My hair appears to be slightly dyeing itself, thanks," said Jake.

I spread the mixture all over their heads and then mine. Then we waited.

"I didn't know you knew how to do this," said Jake.

"You should've come to more football games," I whispered. "I looked flashy and fantastic with this and my glitter cheeks."

He put his arm around me. I felt a pang of happiness rush to my heart. "I was thinking about wearing these, though."

He grabbed a pair of sunglasses out of his pocket and put them on. The frames had Mario, Luigi, question boxes, and Yoshi all over them.

I gave him an approving nod. "Very nice." Daisy and Henry came over to look. "Do we have eBay to thank again?"

The characters were so big on the frames that when Jake smiled, his cheeks brushed against them. "You're damn right. I figured if we're going to get nostalgic, we have to go all the way."

He whipped three more pairs of Mario glasses from his shorts pocket and handed them to us. We put them on like we were doing our best James Dean.

"This is gonna be sweet," said Henry.

I leaned in close to Jake. "Thanks." I pointed to the glasses. "And they're nice enough for every day."

The four of us broke out laughing again.

When it was all said and done, Henry and I had hair that bordered on red, while Daisy's was bright pink.

"There are some serious 1995 vibes going on," I said, inspecting us in the mirror. "And I'm loving every second of it."

"Now we just need some Blessid Union of Souls playing in the background," said Jake.

"Are we staying at Jake's house tonight?" asked Henry.

I shook my head at four pairs of dirty socks on his floor. This kid. "Yes…If that's okay with you."

Henry rolled his eyes. "Um, duh. Daisy has all the good Game Boy games over there."

I stifled a laugh, grabbed a spare backpack, and plopped it on his bed. "Pack a few essentials. Toothbrush, socks, phone charger." I eyed him. "Toothbrush, *hint hint*."

Henry stared at the backpack. "Am I keeping this over there? For, like, next time?"

We stared at each other. The words came out of me all jumbled up. "I guess you could."

Henry nodded. Was this one of those moments when he wanted me to leave the room because I cramped his style? Or was this a heart-to-heart thing? I chose the latter and sat on his bed.

"Are we all moving in together?"

My whole body went soft and mushy. I opened my mouth like an alligator. It took a long time to say anything. "I don't know, kid. We haven't been dating that long. But maybe…at some point." I finally breathed. "How do you feel about that?"

Henry was repelled. "How do I *feel*? Don't say that, Mom. You weirdo."

"I plan to embarrass you way more than that." I hugged him close. He rolled his eyes. "Come on, would that be okay or not?"

"Gee, I wonder. Because we're totally not always together anyway. And you've been in love for, like, *ever*."

"But it would be different," I said, jiggling him. "It would be all the time. Day and night."

"Sounds good to me. As long as Daisy shares those games."

I raised an eyebrow. "And *you* could share the PlayStation games."

Henry turned sullen. "Oh, that." I ruffled his shaggy hair. I was about to get up when he poked my arm. "So, is that what you want to do? Do you want us all to live together?"

I didn't have to think about it for a second. That wasn't like me.

"Yes."

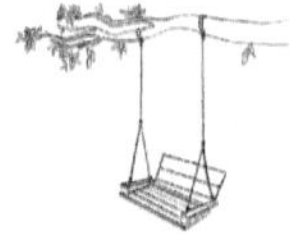

We sat at the drive-in, waiting for the sun to set. The sky to the west was pink and orange, reminding me of Daisy's hair. She and Henry sat on lawn chairs next to the car, sharing popcorn.

"So is this movie super old?" asked Henry.

"*The Goonies* came out around the time I was born," I said.

Henry's eyes widened. "Yep. Super old."

"My dad's older."

"You laugh now but wait." Jake's eyes narrowed, taunting them. "Someday you'll be friends with a coworker, getting along brilliantly, and then you find out they were born when you were sixteen. Then the slagging starts. Apparently, everything you like is hopelessly uncool."

I smirked. "Personal experience?"

Jake let out an over-the-top sigh. "That waiter, Sam, is brutal."

Jake slid onto the hood of the car and then held out a hand for me.

"Living on the edge." I took his hand and pulled myself next to him. "Didn't our parents gripe when we sat on the hood like this?"

Something about Jake's smile was illuminated by the setting

sun. He was so alive and free. I would've gone with him anywhere. "Somewhere, our parents sense what we're doing. No doubt they're screaming."

Jake wrapped a blanket around us, and I cuddled into him. It was chilly for a summer night, but the kids seemed oblivious. They watched the movie in their pajamas, laughing and teasing each other.

"I almost forgot." Jake grabbed the hot fudge sundae that sat next to him on the hood. "Here."

I leaned closer. "You remembered."

The sunset and shadows danced across Jake, making his eyes sparkle even more than usual. "It's hard to forget anything about you."

When we got back to Jake's house, it was late. The kids slept in the car the whole way back. I thought, as I glanced back at them and then over at Jake, that everything felt purple. A kind of hazy relaxation I never wanted to end. I could've spent my whole life like that, glancing at every person in that car in pure, concentrated happiness.

Jake carried Daisy to her room and tucked her in. I was guiding Henry into the spare room when Jake came over. "You need anything, Henry?"

Henry shook his head, half asleep. Then he reconsidered. "Can I have some water?"

Jake nodded, disappearing down the hallway. I told Henry goodnight and wandered to Jake's bedroom. I heard Jake bring Henry water and laugh about something.

Jake came into the room, still smiling. "He said the movie was good for being old as dirt."

I grumbled. "That kid sure knows how to wound me."

Jake went into the attached bathroom to change and brush his teeth. I put on my pajamas and thought about how natural this all felt.

When Jake came out, his eyes scanned me. "You're fecking adorable."

I stared at my outfit and tried not to laugh. "Pretty sexy, right? I think the combination of plaid pajamas and red Kool-Aid hair is real special." I posed. "What do you think?"

Jake took a step closer. "You want to know what I think?" He was dead serious. His voice lowered. Something about it made my heart beat faster. He reached out his hands and grabbed mine. I stepped up to him. "It's the same thing I've been thinking all night."

My heart was in my throat. I could barely breathe. "What?"

He pulled me close and rested his forehead against mine. He took a deep breath. "I love you, Leah."

His words were a whisper that sent shockwaves down my spine, but it wasn't fear. It was joy. I held my breath as I let go of his hands and rested them on his cheeks. "You do?"

Jake kissed my forehead. "Yes. I wanted to tell you that first day, but I was afraid it was too fast. I was afraid I'd scare you." He looked self-conscious. "But it's probably still too fast. You don't have to say anything back. I don't expect that. Honestly."

His rough whisper danced in my ears. I ran my hands down the back of his neck. I leaned in and kissed him deeply. When I pulled away, I hovered an inch from his lips. "Nothing about this scares me. I love you too. It's always been you. It's *only* been you."

Jake's hands settled on both sides of my face. We gazed into each other's eyes.

"Leah, I—"

But the words caught in his throat. A single tear ran down his cheek. I wiped it away as tears started sliding down my own face.

His face was raw with emotion as I kissed the place where his tear had been. "I love you so much." I slid my hands into his soft chestnut hair, teasing him as I whispered, "You're mine, you hear me?"

Jake's lips suddenly met mine, the kiss deep and sensuous. My body was instantly a hundred degrees. I moaned into his mouth.

When he pulled away, his eyes glistened. "You're damn right, I'm yours. Leah. I love you so goddamn much."

"I love you, too, Jake." I nestled into his neck, licking and nibbling. He slid his hands underneath my clothes, cupping my ass. I narrowed my eyes and pushed against the hard cock I could feel through his cotton shorts. He groaned into my neck. His hands were still on my ass as he pulled me against him. I needed him. I couldn't handle it. I pulled his shorts and under-wear down, exposing him. He breathed hard, watching me.

I pushed him backward and made him sit on the edge of the bed. His chest rose and fell as I shimmied off my pajama pants. He stared at my purple, lacy panties. His eyes met mine.

"Can I fuck you, Leah?" he whispered. His eyes were still raw from tears. "I want you so bad."

"God, yes."

My breath caught as he leaned forward and tugged my panties down.

"Jake!" I gasped.

He pulled me onto his lap, my legs wrapped around him. His shirt was off. I threw mine to the ground, but I didn't settle myself on his penis yet. Instead, I held him, swirling my thumb across his head until a drop of moisture came out.

"Atta girl. Tease my cock." He watched me touch him, his face red from pent-up emotion. He knew what I needed. My nipples were so hard, they hurt. He cupped my breasts, working the nipples between his fingers. I gasped into his ear.

"We have to stay quiet," he whispered, giving me an evil grin.

"I guess I can't scream your name."

He chuckled as he sucked on my nipple—those lips of his. *Holy shit.*

I lifted myself slightly and hovered over his cock. Jake stared down at his dick and the space between us, eyes on fire. "I need to fuck you so bad."

That did it. I lowered myself onto him, going slowly to torture us both. He groaned, his eyes watching as his dick went inside me.

"I'll never get tired of watching your tight pussy gobble me up," he whispered when he was all the way in.

I ground against him, and he lifted into me, the fluid motion of his hips lighting me up. He looked so sexy when he thrust like that. Like he was made of water. He rested his hands on my hips, steadying me and pushing me onto him.

I smiled at his focus. "You *do* like watching, don't you?"

Jake nodded, pulling me down onto him again. "It's hard not to. You're perfection."

Even sitting on him, I wasn't at the level of his head. I leaned against his chest, running my nails across it as I thrust into him.

He worked my nipples again. My whole body ached for him.

I gently bit at his chest, making his breath catch. "Are you all mine, Jake? All mine forever?"

"You better believe I am. Ride me like you own me. Make me beg for it."

I could only whimper as heat built inside me.

"Fuck yes." He was covered in sweat. We both were. I loved the slick, sloppy noise we made. I could tell Jake liked it too. He ran a finger across my wet breast. "Leah. God. Damn."

Before I knew what was happening, Jake grabbed me and stood up. My eyes met his. That evil grin was back. My legs still wrapped around him, he carried me to the adjoining master bathroom and shut the door behind us. He stepped right into the walk-in shower. I let out a breathy laugh as he put a hand on the knob.

"Should I?" he asked.

"Yes."

He turned the water on, and it plowed into us, drowning out the noise and splashing against Jake's back. He pressed me against the tile shower wall. The cold ceramic was a shock against my hot skin. I moaned as he thrust into me. The way the water looked as it slid down his tall, lean form made my heart beat faster.

Jake was hypnotized, watching droplets slide down my breasts and drip from my nipples. "Fuck. You're dripping wet. So sexy."

"God." I couldn't handle it. I felt the pressure building. "This is just how I wanted to get fucked by you."

"Hell yes," he said, holding me to the wall. "You know how many times I've jerked off in here pretending to hold you like this?"

Our pace picked up. "I'm yours, Jake."

He shuddered as his fingers dug into my ass. His breath was haggard as he ground against me. "I'm all yours, too." He groaned. "That's the way. Do you want to come?"

It was too much. He felt too good. "I want you to fuck me until your arms give out."

The pressure built on his face. His whisper tickled my ear. "That could be a long damn time."

Maybe it was the rough way he said it, but the orgasm came out of nowhere, pulsing through me. Jake must have known it was coming. He wrapped his hand around my mouth.

Jake's face twisted, and his movements became jerky. "Fuck. I'm coming so hard. Damn, Leah."

He burrowed his head into my neck as he came in a shaky, tight spasm. I held him tight against me as he groaned. His shudder rippled through me. I was seeing stars. From the way he shook, Jake was, too. We didn't take our eyes off each other. That had been… *Damn.*

We stayed slammed against the wall until our heartbeats finally slowed again.

I stared into his eyes. "I love you. Forever."

Water dripped down his face. "Forever. Only you. Forever."

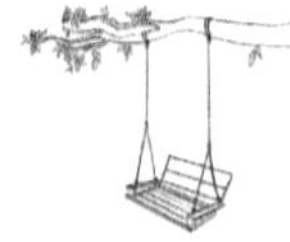

I glanced at the clock—3:00 a.m. And we weren't even close to being tired. We were in bed, wrapped in the blankets, talking quietly. "Look how late it is."

Jake placed delicate kisses on my stomach. "I never even stayed up this late when I was eighteen." He grinned. "But I'd go to bed this late all the time if nights were like this."

I let out a contented sigh and ran my hands through his hair. "You know what that time means?"

Jake slid up to my face. "What?"

I kissed his nose. "What song do you have a good cry to at three in the morning?"

Jake let out a quiet chuckle. "Seriously?"

"Steven and I told you ours."

Jake ran his finger across my lips. "'Girl from the North Country.' Whenever I listen to it, I think of you. It was written about you, you know."

I grinned. "Pretty sure Bob Dylan wrote that in the sixties."

"It's still about you. There are a lot of songs about you. I could give you a list."

I felt so relaxed. I didn't care if I ever fell asleep.

"What does Ashley think about all this?" I asked, finally.

Jake looked surprised by my question. "I don't know. She doesn't say much."

Now I was really awake. "What do you mean? Is she upset about it?"

His eyes were soft. "No. Not like that. I don't know what she thinks. We only talk about Daisy. I tell her what we're doing with Daisy, and she tells me what *she's* doing with Daisy. That's about it." He took a breath. "She's been quiet lately."

I nodded, thinking.

Jake nestled into my neck. "You don't have to worry."

"I don't want her to resent us." I held him close. "I don't want her to think I'm trying to steal Daisy."

Jake peppered kisses along my neck. "We both get equal time with her."

God, I loved him. "I guess. I just don't want anything to wreck this."

Jake looked into my eyes. "Nothing's going to wreck this."

And I believed him. I'd never been with someone like that. I'd never felt someone's love for me radiate through my body. It made me want to cry.

We breathed each other in until we both gently fell asleep.

15

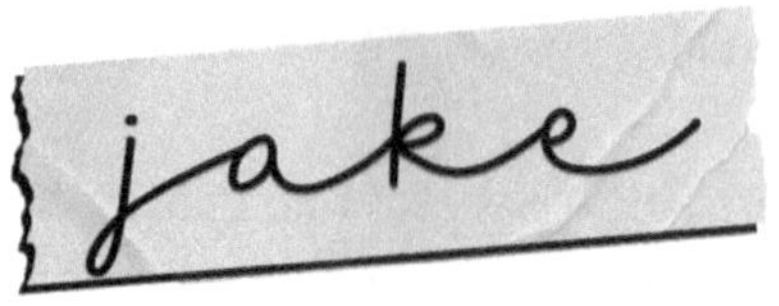

Leah and I had been going out for two months. It was bizarre to think about. It still felt like a dream, but, on the other hand, we slipped so comfortably into each other that it felt like we had been together forever.

So I tried to ignore the nagging thought circling my happiness like a lion circles a gazelle. Ash. Leah wanted to know what Ashley thought about everything. That was a very good question, one I'd been pondering myself. The past had taught me that I never knew exactly what was going on with Ash or what she was thinking. When she first moved out, she'd come over to get Daisy, and we'd stand on the driveway, talking. If I brought Daisy over to Ottertail, Ash was perfectly happy to sit on the steps and chat.

But as time went on, Ash turned quiet. Her answers were short and monotone. Sometimes she picked up Daisy and seemed reluctant to get out of the car.

Perhaps she *was* annoyed that Leah and I were doing so much family stuff with Daisy and Henry, but I decided not to jump to conclusions. *Me.* I was the one who used to pace up and down the kitchen, pondering hypotheticals to go crazy over, but this time I decided not to worry.

How unique of me.

When we got to Ashley's house, Daisy bounded out of the car. I followed behind.

"Have any fun plans with your mom this weekend?"

Daisy's ponytail bobbed with each step. "We're riding our bikes to the lake."

I rang the doorbell. "Sounds fun."

When Ash answered the door, she scooped Daisy up. Daisy's feet dangled an inch off the ground.

Daisy let out a muffled giggle. "Mom…"

"I missed you," said Ash, hugging her. I was glad that nothing was weird between Ashley and Daisy. But there was definitely something weird between *us*, because when Daisy waved goodbye and ran into the house, Ash looked like she wanted to close the door and pretend I wasn't there.

"Thanks for bringing her," said Ashley, quietly.

I tried to keep everything lighthearted. "No problem."

The desire to escape was stamped across her face.

Should I leave? Should I say something?

"Do you want to talk for a bit?"

That took Ash by surprise. She hesitated, then nodded and sat on the front steps. I slid down next to her.

Now that I had brilliantly suggested talking, I was desperate to figure out what the hell to have a conversation about. I had to ask if she was alright with the way we were doing things with Daisy, but I couldn't start there. Even used car salesmen asked about the weather first.

"Getting the house all squared away?"

Ash nodded. "I painted the living room yellow."

There was another question I knew I could ask, but did I really care how that dick was?

"How are things with Kenneth?"

Apparently, I did.

Ash was as surprised as me. "He's good." There was something weird about her voice. She didn't want to offer up anything other than the bare minimum, but then her posture softened. "We're going to the Florida Keys at the end of the summer…if that's all right with you. If you can watch Daisy."

"Of course," I said. "Florida sounds fun."

"Yeah." She stared at the sidewalk. "Should be."

She managed to make her fun trip sound like a medieval public execution.

There had been days in our marriage like this—quiet, non-expressive, lonely. Something was up.

"Listen, I was wondering if you're okay with the way we've been doing things? Leah and I have been bringing the kids out a lot. Is that alright?"

There was a strange flicker in Ashley's eye. "Of course. You two always brought the kids out bowling and stuff."

"I know, but you were there too, sometimes. I don't want to step on your toes."

Her smile was…downright weird. "Thanks. But it's fine." She kept her eyes on me. "You're always nice, you know that?"

I didn't know what to say. "I just want to keep Daisy happy."

Ash stared off into space. "I'm glad about you and Leah. That's great, Jake." She took a breath. "I've been meaning to say something."

It was a surreal experience sitting next to your ex-wife and discussing your new love.

"Thanks," I said. "It's been great."

"You're happy?"

I nodded. "I'm very happy."

We didn't say anything for a moment. I wondered if I should leave.

"Do you remember when we went to Westport?" she asked.

Talk about a question out of nowhere.

I spent a lot of time back home in the summer when I was a kid and a teenager. After graduating from high school, I made it my goal to keep going back once or twice a year to visit family and friends. Ashley went with me once, a couple of years after we were married. It had been a typical family trip. We spent part of the time laughing with my relatives and part of the time stressing out about stuff that didn't matter. We argued and then had to pretend we weren't arguing when relatives walked into the room.

But we danced, too. There had been good times with Ash. There had been times when we clicked.

"I remember," I said.

There had been other trips, too. When she was thirteen, Leah, Steven, and her parents went with my dad and me. I could still close my eyes and see Leah taking pictures at Westport House. She grumbled each time Steven photobombed a shot. The cool air was like a soft laugh as we wandered the gardens. Leah captured Steven in a headlock. Dad laughed as he snapped the picture. I could still see them running down the path, their chatter disappearing around the next bend.

Something struck me. Leah said she wanted to stick her toes in the ocean, but I couldn't remember her doing that on our trip to Westport. She'd never stuck her toes in the ocean, *period*. I wanted to change that. I wanted to bring her to the ocean. I wanted to bring her back home now that things were different.

"I should've been nicer on that trip," said Ash.

I snapped back to reality. "Nicer?" I brushed off the comment. "You're grand."

"We fought about stupid stuff. Blankets and toothbrushes, and how rude your grandma was."

I didn't try to fight the laugh that came out. "Everyone knows my gran is rude. Ask my dad."

Ash finally gave me a real smile. "I wish I could go back and do a lot of things differently. *I'd* be different."

I wasn't sure why, but suddenly I didn't want to be there. There was a twist in my stomach, a slight misgiving, but I didn't show it. I forced a pleasant smile, standing again.

I stared at the driveway so I didn't have to see if Ash noticed my discomfort. "Leave the past where it is. That's what Gran always says. Anything else is madness."

Ash nodded like she agreed, but her eyes were sad and tired.

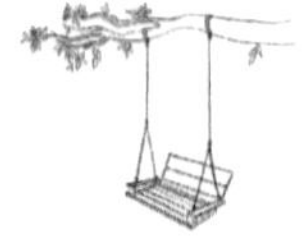

I was at the restaurant the next morning, making muffins when my phone rang. It was Leah. I was like a fecking teen when her name popped up. Except cell phones were bricks when I was a teen. "Hi, darling, what's going on?"

There was coughing on the other end. "Eh. I'm not coming for breakfast."

Her voice was rough.

"What's wrong?"

"I feel like crap." There was a muffled sound. "I have a temperature. Eh. Is this how getting kicked out of a car feels?"

"We'd have to ask some Hollywood stunt people."

Her coughing sounded far away. "Get them on the phone. I want to know."

I thought about her must-have whenever ill. "Does your electric blanket still work?"

"I have it set to lava."

"I'll come over at lunch."

More coughing. "You'll get sick."

I chuckled. "That's a risk I'm willing to take."

The conversation with Ash had left me unsettled. I knew I had to tell Leah, but what would I say? It's not like I knew anything definite. Maybe something was off with Kenneth, the shithead.

When I got to Leah's house, she was on the sofa, an electric blanket wrapped around her like a cocoon. The end table was a shrine to beverages—coffee mugs, tea mugs, and water.

Her face was puffy, and her nose was red. I ran a hand through her tangled hair. God, I loved her, even when she looked like she needed to throw up her small intestine. She pulled the blanket over her head and moaned.

"Conditions haven't improved since this morning?"

Her only answer was another moan. She lowered the blanket. "Henry's been spraying Lysol and telling me I'm toxic." She coughed. "I think he's right."

I rubbed her back. "What can I do?"

"Talk to me about something…*anything*. Sitting here makes me think about it, and then I feel sicker." Another cough. "I need a distraction."

There were a lot of things I could've talked about. I could've said there was drama at the restaurant involving our parents and a missing shipment of cranberries. I could've told her elderly Mrs. Mason had been trying to show me her new tattoo all morning. And I could've told her Steven had spent the previous evening telling me way too many personal details about him and the banjo-playing real estate agent.

But I also knew I could tell her about Ash.

"Something weird happened yesterday."

That perked her up. "I like weird."

My eyebrows rose. "This might be *too* weird. Remember how you asked about Ash?"

Leah nodded.

"When I brought Daisy over, I decided we should have a chat…but I don't think she wanted to talk to me."

Leah sat up. "What did she say?"

"I asked if she was okay with the way we've been spending time with Daisy and Henry. She said she was."

"Was she upset?"

"I don't know. She started talking about the trip we took to Ireland. Then she went on about wanting to be a different person."

Leah's eyes were like an owl's.

"What?" I asked.

"Maybe things aren't good with Kenneth."

I leaned back on the sofa. "Shocker."

She gave my arm a playful nudge. "She might want you back."

My eyes said it all. That would be the day. "I find that highly unlikely. When we were in your car that day, she made it *pretty* clear that she didn't want anything to do with me."

Leah stared at me for a long time. It made me nervous somehow. I couldn't read her. "Do I make you happy?" There wasn't any anger in her voice. Her tone was soft, like fingers through my hair. "Do you ever wish you were still with her?"

I was too stunned to speak. Then we made eye contact, and I chuckled. She smiled. I leaned in and kissed her, flu be damned.

"Are you crazy?" I grinned. "You know how long I've been

in love with you, Leah." I gave her a gentle tug. "You don't have to worry about that."

She stroked the back of my neck. Every small hair stood up. "I know. And I've loved you for a long time, too. But…I want to make sure you're happy." She breathed in. "Would you tell me if you weren't?"

Like that would ever happen.

"I'd tell you," I whispered. "But you're going to have a long wait. Because I've never been happier in my life."

She nestled into my shoulder, and I reached my arm around her.

"Have you eaten anything?" I asked.

"I haven't eaten since lunch yesterday. I started feeling like crap last night. I brought that garbage can out here in case I throw up."

I put my hand on her forehead. She had a temperature. I hated seeing her so miserable. "I brought you a little something in case you felt up to eating."

I pulled a bag off the end table and handed it to her. She peered inside and gave a hoarse laugh. "It's a peanut butter and jelly sandwich."

I nodded. "It'll cure what ails you."

"I'd kiss you again, but I'm told I'm toxic," she said.

"I think it's worth it."

Her lips were soft and warm.

"Don't you have to get back?" she asked.

I ran my hand through her hair again. "I have a while yet."

"No guy has ever taken care of me when I'm sick."

I held her a little tighter. "Better get used to it."

She pulled the sandwich out of the bag and fiddled with it. Finally, she took a bite. She chewed slowly, trying to decide whether it was a good idea or not. She swallowed and sat there, waiting.

"Nothing like wondering if you're going to puke, right?"

"No kidding," she said, taking another bite.

She stared at the sandwich. A line of concern formed between her eyes. "I've always wondered…what's the deal with peanut butter and jelly sandwiches?"

Oh, God.

My stomach sank. Fecking sandwiches. Why the hell did I always eat them and bring them up when I had no desire to talk about them? Bollox.

I tried to smile, but there wasn't much humor in it. Leah sensed my sadness. She rubbed my hand gently. "Is it because of your mom?"

Son of a bitch.

"I never ate peanut butter when I was little." I inhaled slowly. "Not until we came here. We bought it as a joke. And my dad always cooked…you know that…That's how they thought up the café. He taught me. Mom hated cooking and baking. It was a running joke how much she detested it." Leah's hand was firm over mine. "One time when I was sick, my mom wanted me to try to eat something. I didn't want soup or anything, so she made me a peanut butter and jelly sandwich. I don't know why, but it suddenly became our thing. An inside joke, I guess. If I needed to bring treats to school, she'd laugh and ask if she should whip up a bunch of peanut butter and jelly sandwiches. She always packed them in my lunches…"

Leah turned to face me, her head on my shoulder. I rested my left hand gently on her back. There was something so nice about the way she sat there, listening. Caring about what I said. And I had come here to take care of *her*.

"Keep going," whispered Leah.

I frowned. "You're sick. I'm supposed to be taking care of you."

"You are." She kissed my cheek. "You're distracting me, remember? But…I'm so stupid. If these are bad memories, you don't have—"

"It's okay," I said, looking into her eyes. I took another breath. "After she died, I couldn't eat them. I didn't want to. Then… You remember my graduation?" Leah nodded again. "I sat, listening to the commencement speaker, thinking I was supposed to be happy. But…I wasn't. Not at all. She'd been dead for four years, but that day, it felt fresh. I pretended to smile in the pictures, but…I was one miserable bastard."

Leah pulled the blanket around both of us.

I swallowed back a sick feeling in my gut. "I drove around that night, thinking about stuff. After a while, I got hungry. So, I stopped at the grocery store. I walked down the aisle, and there was the peanut butter." I let out an annoyed laugh. "Isn't that fecking stupid? Having a sentimental attachment to a sandwich, for Christ's sake."

Leah jiggled my arm. "It's not stupid. It's sweet. You're a great guy."

I shook my head. I wasn't sure about that. "I bought peanut butter, grape jelly, and a loaf of bread. I went back to my dad's place and made a sandwich. I ate it over the sink in the dark." I stared at my lap. "I wanted to feel like she was there somehow." I breathed in so my voice wouldn't quake. "She was supposed to be there. And that's the only way she could be."

Leah's eyes were glossy. She turned her face away to hide her tears.

"Somehow, that became my connection to her. I was only fourteen when she died, so what did I really know about her?" My voice finally wobbled. "I only knew the things a kid would know. I never got a chance to know what her hopes and dreams were." That notion did something to me. *Jesus.* "What were her hopes and dreams? Did she and my dad ever want more kids? I suppose I could ask him sometime. I could ask him that…and a bunch of other things. But whenever I want to broach the subject, I seize up."

Leah ran her hand across my face. I leaned over and kissed her. I *really* needed to kiss her.

"I've eaten them off and on ever since graduation. They make me feel better, I guess. Before she left, Ash told me I'd eaten one every day for lunch for the past fifteen years." I desperately wanted to lighten the mood. "If that's true, there's a chance I may be suffering from malnutrition."

Leah let out a laugh. She wiped a few tears from her eyes, and then she dabbed one away from mine. "I'm so sorry, Jake. She was great."

I needed to hold Leah tight. My voice was a whisper. "You know I care about the things that bother you, right? This isn't a one-way street. I feel like I've emoted all over you. And you're sick, for Christ's sake. You can tell me things, too. I want you to. You can tell me about the things that bother you."

I couldn't tell if her face looked that way from talking about my mom or from something else on her mind. The sadness. The hesitation.

"Tell me," I whispered.

She played with the blanket. Nervous. "It's stupid… I don't know where it comes from… Sometimes I get the strangest feeling."

I kissed the side of her head. "What feeling?"

She let out a slow sigh. "That I'm not someone made for long-term relationships." Her eyes met mine, like she was telling me not to worry, but my stomach still turned. "You know they never last. And a lot of that is my fault. When things get hard, I'm gone. Actually, I leave before they *get* hard." She rubbed my hand. "I'm not saying anything about us." She squeezed my fingers, and I squeezed back. "I'm just saying how it usually is. I always get out of relationships before my heart gets broken. Part of me thinks I don't deserve to be happy."

I pulled her close to me again, meeting her gaze. It was so strange to hear her say that, knowing my own fears. We were like two sides of the same coin. She was afraid she couldn't hack it in the long term, and I was afraid I'd fuck it up because it all seemed too good to be true.

It was nice to open your heart to someone and not worry about how they would react. It was nice not to feel judged. I wanted to spend the rest of my life telling Leah my secrets and keeping hers. Telling her my thoughts and listening to hers.

I whispered in her ear. "There aren't a lot of things I'm certain about, Leah. But if there's one person in this world who deserves to be happy, it's you."

She rested her forehead against mine. "Comments like that are why you're my best friend."

16

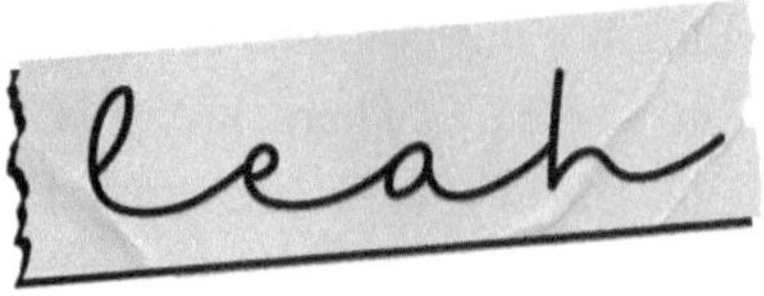

"It's just a few cranberries," said Mom. "You two need to get over it."

We were at my parents' house for dinner. Some cranberries had mysteriously disappeared from the café a few weeks earlier, and my dad and Craig still couldn't let it go. Jake and I exchanged amused looks with Daisy and Henry.

"It wasn't a few cranberries," said Dad, furrowing his brow. "It was a whole box of cranberries."

"Who steals a box of cranberries?" asked Craig, mystified.

"Maybe it was me," I said. "I could eat Thanksgiving dinner all year."

Jake made a face like he was begging me to egg them on.

"How many cranberries were in there?" asked Daisy.

"Must be a lot since they've been complaining about it forever," said Henry, sighing.

Craig and my dad argued about the calculations.

"Must have been about fifteen bags," said Craig.

"No…Twenty for sure," said Dad.

Steven was too quiet. He poked at his ham.

I pointed at him. "Sounds like something *you'd* do."

Steven's head bounced up, startled. "It does, doesn't it?" The whole table looked at him. He relaxed into his chair. "But it wasn't."

"Personally, I think it sounds like Kenneth," said Jake.

Craig nodded at his son. "That's what I said. Cad leathcheann."

"He *did* steal meat from Hy-Vee, didn't he?" asked Mom.

Jake leaned back, amused. "He stole a whole beef brisket."

"Imagine how that looked to people in the parking lot." I stifled a laugh. "A dude running through the rain with a brisket under his coat." I let out a quiet hum. "He *absconded* through the parking lot with a large quantity of meat."

Jake's eyes sparkled. "Yes, *absconded*. That's great. Nobody *absconds* anymore. Makes him seem like Al Capone." He leaned in toward me. "No one *runs afoul,* either. More people need to run afoul of things."

Under the table, my foot rubbed his. "After he ate all that brisket, he ran afoul of his digestive system."

Jake and I laughed, oblivious to everyone else. It took a few seconds for us to realize they were all staring.

Steven pushed his plate away. "They're doing that cutesy thing again. Where they enjoy each other's company." He sighed. "Damn it to hell."

I rolled my eyes. "Don't you and the banjo player share moments?"

Steven's smile grossed me out. "Ours are *actually* cute, though. I play the guitar, remember?" He lifted his eyebrows. "It's a musical, magical time."

My mom patted Steven on the shoulder. "I'm happy for you, sweetie. There's a lid for every pot. But that must be one hell of a lid."

Jake and I sat on the tree swing. Daisy and Henry were inside, fighting over turns on Steven's guitar.

"I'll be sad when this swing is finally shot." I ran my hand over the chipped white paint. "Look at this arm. It's warping again. Needs to be fixed."

Jake inspected it. "That's what happens when we keep it up all year round, I guess."

"But that's what I always liked best about it." I winked. "How else was I supposed to get my best friend alone so I could flirt with him?"

Jake danced his fingers slowly across my hand. "That's very true. I would've missed out on a lot of longing glances without this thing. Giving you a longing glance from the other side of your parents' kitchen island doesn't have the same panache."

I let out a quiet laugh. Jake watched me with those eyes of his. Even if he had a face mask on, you'd be able to tell he was smiling by the way they lit up. I loved how emotions played over his face.

I put my hand up to block his vision. "Don't look at me."

He grinned. "Why not?"

"It makes me shy."

He slid his arm around my back and whispered to me. It sent a shiver down my legs. "We've been going out for a while. I still make you shy like it's our first date?"

I tried to shrug it off but failed. "It's the way you look at me. I can't help it. It makes me happy." I poked his chest. "What about you? I don't give you butterflies anymore? Is the spark gone?"

He caressed my hand with his fingers. "The spark will never

be gone. The butterflies will never be gone." He kissed my fore-head. "I promise." He paused. "I was thinking about something."

"What?"

"I was thinking about how you wanted to dip your toes in the ocean. When we went to Ireland, you didn't get a chance, did you?"

I sat a little straighter. "Nope. Steven chased me off the beach. He had something slimy in his hands and kept threatening to throw it at me."

"We have to get you to the ocean," he whispered. I leaned into him. "Maybe…" He paused again. Was he nervous? I wasn't sure, but it was sexy as hell. "I…I want to bring you to Ireland again."

Excitement surged through me. "That sounds great!" I was talking a mile a minute. "I can meet your grandma again. Does she still swear all the time?"

I couldn't contain my enthusiasm, and Jake couldn't hide his relief. A laid-back smile tugged at his face. "That'll never change, I guarantee it. But we don't have to go there first. I want to bring you somewhere you *really* want to go." He was so cute. How could I *not* want to go to Ireland? "You've talked about going to Washington or Oregon. We can dip your toes there."

"I want to go to Ireland with you. I want to see your family." I gave him a light kiss. "I want to see your friends."

Jake's eyes were soft. "And I want them to see *you*."

"When should we do it?"

Jake didn't miss a beat. "How about this fall?"

"That soon?"

Jake shrugged, teasing. "Cooling on the idea?"

I was already mentally planning what to pack. "Absolutely not. But what about the kids?"

"We'll bring them with us," said Jake. "I'll get everything squared away with Ash. Henry will love my grandma. He'll be stocked up on one-liners when we get back. And Daisy will want to show you around. She has a lot of secret spots, you know."

I could have kissed him all night. "I can't wait."

Jake and I were spending the weekend in Duluth. I hadn't been away from Henry for a whole weekend in… Had I *ever* been away from Henry for the whole weekend? It made me kind of weepy as I packed my suitcase. Henry wandered into my bedroom, Game Boy in hand.

He looked like he was embarrassed for both of us. "What's your deal, Mom?"

I tossed some socks in… Did I already pack underwear? "What? There's no deal."

Henry didn't move. He tried not to laugh. "There's *definitely* a deal. You look like Daisy when Purrito walked through her birthday cake."

It looked like I was packing for a month. "Are you sure you're alright with this? Jake and I could do something closer to home."

Henry rolled his eyes. "Jeez, Mom. Don't you *want* to go? Aren't you gonna eat a bunch of dessert?"

"Yes…I *really* want to go." Henry sighed as I pulled him close. "But it's a whole weekend without my Care Bear."

Henry looked like he was going to die right there. "Do *not* call me that."

I hugged him tighter. "You used to like it."

"When I was three."

"That doesn't seem that long ago to me," I said. "I'll miss you. Won't *you* miss *me*?"

"No," said Henry, monotone.

"Come on," I said, jiggling him.

"No." He dug his feet into the floor. "I won't miss you."

"Yes, you will. You'll miss these moments of pure, unadulterated motherly love. You know it." I put on my singing voice. "You're going to miss me, and you know it. You love me, and you know it."

Henry shook his head and squirmed out of my arms. I laughed.

"Alright," he said. "I'll miss you...a *little*. But you're bringing me back a present, right?"

I nodded.

"Then you have to go."

"You should've seen me with Henry," I said. We were in Jake's car, on our way to Duluth. "I acted like I was going to Mars, not three and a half hours away."

Jake gave me a sympathetic glance. "We can stay home, you know. If you want."

"No. Henry already thinks I'm crazy." Jake's face was solemn. "What about you? You must feel this way all the time."

Jake's lips formed a tight line. "The first time Ash came to get Daisy for a few days, it was surreal. I went into her room and looked at all her pictures. Then I sat on her bed and grabbed that stuffed llama of hers. It felt like she had gone off to college." Jake's eyes widened. "When she *does* go to college, I'm going to be a fecking mess."

"I know! It seems like it was just yesterday that I met Daisy for the first time." I rested a hand on his shoulder. "Remember all that hair?"

Jake smiled at the memory. "I didn't realize babies could

have that much hair. It was wild." His eyes drifted to mine. "And it seems like I was just holding your hand when you gave birth to Henry."

I knew my eyes were watery. "That nurse thought you were my husband."

Jake took my hand. We didn't say anything. We didn't need to.

Jake opened the glass door to the restaurant, and we walked in. I felt fancy in my curve-hugging midi dress. It had a red and pink floral design with off-the-shoulder sleeves. Jake didn't look too bad himself with his maroon button-down shirt and brown blazer.

The restaurant had wood floors and chrome furniture. It looked like a coffee house had been eaten by a 1950s diner. We sat at the bar.

"The thing online said that this should be the first stop on the dessert crawl," said Jake.

I couldn't help smiling. "And how many restaurants are on this?"

Jake leaned in. "I think it's eight."

"Are we really going to eat dessert at eight different restaurants?"

A devious grin spread across his face. "We certainly fecking are."

My shoulders relaxed. "Thank God."

We got our drinks and headed over to a jukebox in the corner.

"Aren't you worried that's not going to jive with all the different desserts?" I nodded at his whiskey.

"Slightly. Does whiskey pair with Twinkies?" He gestured to my drink. "Your idea was probably safer."

There was a huge cup of coffee in my hand. I stood in front of the bright red and blue jukebox, looking at the song choices. Jake stood behind me, peering over my shoulder. His breath was hot on my neck. Did he mean to do that? My body tingled in response.

"I'm not drinking because I have to keep my wits about me," I said, flipping through songs.

His lips were only a half-inch from my ear. His voice was rough. "Why would that be?"

I turned so he was hovering over my chest. He gazed to see if anyone was watching, but everyone else was way over at the bar.

There was barely any space between us. I gave him a flirtatious glance. "In case you try to make a pass at me."

Jake took in my comment, his bright eyes sparkling. "Don't you want me to make a pass at you?"

I winked. "I didn't say that."

I turned back to the jukebox. Jake placed his hand lightly on my side. My skin came alive. I pressed the button for "Chuck E's in Love" by Rickie Lee Jones. In a second, guitar music floated through the restaurant.

Jake grinned as I turned back around to him. He leaned in. "What would you say if I told you I was going to make a pass at you in about three hours?"

I bobbed lightly to the music. "I'd probably say...don't threaten me with a good time."

We got small chocolate cakes entombed inside a thick chocolate shell at the first restaurant. The second restaurant was sunny and airy, with a patio overlooking Lake Superior. Jake and I sat chatting in the golden light until the waitress brought us Spanish hot chocolate with churros.

"Look at this." Jake held the end of the churro against the surface of the hot chocolate. It didn't sink. The chocolate was that thick.

"Oh my God," I said, excited. "This is my heaven!" I forcibly dunked my churro into the hot chocolate. I took a bite and nodded. "Holy crap."

Jake was just as giddy as me. "I know! We still have other desserts to try, but I know this is going to be the best one."

"I could eat this every day."

Jake studied his dessert. "I wonder how hard it would be to make."

"If you made this, people would line up around the block. This would be my breakfast. I wouldn't be able to tell Henry he can't have pie for breakfast anymore, because *this* is what I'd be eating."

Jake seemed hesitant. "I'm not sure if I could do it, though."

"Yes, you could." I kicked his foot gently with my heel. "You can make anything."

"You think so, huh? Then I guess we could've spent the whole weekend at my place, curled up in bed with coffee and churros."

I leaned in. "Let's keep that an option for next weekend."

We were quiet for a moment as we ate. The sun was warm on my skin. The light breeze that ruffled my hair didn't even make me chilly.

I stared at Lake Superior. "Think there's a Loch Ness Monster-ish creature in there?"

"You mean a Muckie, don't you?"

I grinned. "Of course. It has to be the Irish cryptid, right? Because he knows *we're* here."

"Absolutely. I'd be a bit disappointed if there wasn't one in there. He could swim through all the Great Lakes and back to the ocean. Give all the sea monsters in the Atlantic the inland news."

"All that hot gossip would make him the most popular and envied cryptid around."

We fell into a comfortable silence. In the distance, seagulls chattered. I rested my head on my hand, watching the ships far off in the hazy distance. When I snapped back to reality, Jake had a serene look on his face. There was a long, thin box on the table in front of him. He pushed it toward me.

I cocked my head. "What's this? A Muckie call?"

"Not quite," he said, playfully raising his eyebrows.

"What for?" I studied the box. "It's not my birthday."

Jake watched me handle the box. Either I was crazy, or his eyes were a little misty.

The transformation of his features made emotion catch in my throat. "But I didn't get you anything."

He gave my foot a playful kick. "I have everything I need right here. Open it... It's not new. It's old."

I lifted the lid. On a foam piece of padding sat a gold locket on a chain. Etched in the center of the locket was a faded red rose. I tried not to tear up as I lifted it out of the box.

His voice was quiet. "It was my mom's. But I had it engraved. Turn it around."

The locket was cold in my fingers. I flipped it over. '*Leah & Jake*' was engraved on the back in cursive writing. I clicked it open. Now I *was* going to cry. It was a picture of us as kids, sitting on our swing. I couldn't talk. Jake came around to my side of the table and sat in the empty chair.

"There aren't too many couples that have a picture together on the first day they met," he whispered.

I wiped away a stray tear. "We're playing our Game Boys and everything." I smiled through my sobs. "I forgot all about this picture."

He placed a hand over mine. "Do you like it?"

"I love it!" I leaned in and hugged him. He held me tight. "But it was your mom's. Are you sure you want to give me this?"

Jake kissed my tear-stained cheek. "I can't think of a better place for it."

It was pitch black when we got back to the hotel. The lake sloshed rhythmically in the distance. We walked hand-in-hand into the hotel and up the stairs.

"Why are you smiling like that?" I asked.

The mischievous grin on his face grew. "Don't you know?" He squeezed my hand as we walked into our room. "I was supposed to make a pass at you an hour ago."

I shut the door behind me and stood against it. "I thought you were sick of me."

Jake leaned in, kissing me deeply. "The fuck you did."

I pulled him tight against me, feeling how hard he was already. He ran both hands down my sides, sending shockwaves through me.

"I love you, Leah." He kissed my neck. "Have I told you that yet today?"

"I love you, too," I whispered back. "And no, I don't think you have."

"I can remedy that by showing you."

He wrapped his arms around me as we made our way to the

bed. But we didn't see Jake's lone shoe in the middle of the floor until we tripped over it and toppled onto the bed, laughing.

Jake let out an annoyed huff and threw the shoe next to his nightstand. "Please, God, tell me that didn't ruin the mood." He threw off his blazer and tugged at his shirt. "I'll murder someone if it did."

I threw his shirt onto the floor. "There aren't any kids around, and I'm still tripping over shoes."

Jake sat on the edge of the bed. He gently held me, and I scooted onto his lap. He played with the locket on my neck and kissed the place where it rested. I ran my hands through his hair.

"Why are you with me?" he whispered.

I smoothed his hair back down. "I just said I love you." I peppered his face with light kisses. "It probably has something to do with that, don't you think?" I draped my arms over his shoulders and looked into his eyes.

"But I'm average. Normal."

"You're wonderful." I kissed a different spot on his face after each compliment. "You're smart. You're funny. You're kind. You're good. You're talented."

His voice was serious. "I'm not talented."

"That's not true. You can make anything, and you know it…" I paused. "What about me? I'm as normal as they come…"

"No…"

"I *am*," I insisted. "I work at a furniture store. I raise my son. I heckle my brother. And I love you. That's it."

"That's not it." He squeezed me. "You can do anything. I've seen you draw. And sing." His eyes met mine. "You're amazing."

"Please… I can sing a little bit, but not that well…"

"That's not true." He kissed my cheek.

"But that's it." I sighed. "I've always wanted to be good at something. To be passionate about something. To take risks. To be one of those elderly hippie ladies sitting with clay all over her hands, happy with some vase or bowl I just made."

Jake kissed my neck. "That sounds like you."

I frowned. "But it's not me yet. I haven't done anything to become that person. And I don't know why. I guess you get caught up in life. Caught up in raising kids. Not that that's bad. But you look up, and a bunch of time has passed. And you're an ordinary person."

Jake ran a hand through my hair. "There's nothing ordinary about you."

"I don't mind being ordinary." I kissed his nose. "Ninety-nine percent of the world is ordinary. Does that mean ninety-nine percent of the world doesn't matter? I love ordinary people." I kissed his chest. "Because when you take the time to pay attention, you realize that everyone is special in some way. It's just whether you care enough about someone to notice it." Jake gave me a hazy smile. "Flowers are ordinary. Flowers are everywhere. But nobody thinks a rose doesn't matter."

Jake pulled me close and gave me a deep kiss. I felt his hard dick through his pants.

"When you're eighty, I'll be seventy-six. And I'll still love you, just like I do now."

There was a contented smile on his face. "We'll still be together when I'm eighty?"

I rubbed him through his jeans. "Unless you get sick of me."

"That's never going to happen," he said in a rough whisper, watching my hand.

I gently pulled away from his embrace. He cocked an eyebrow as I unbuttoned his pants and peeled them off. He tugged down my off-the-shoulder straps and strapless bra. His mouth found my nipples, and I let out a quiet moan as he sucked me.

His eyes lit up. "Your moans are my favorite sound."

I pushed him back onto the bed and threw my dress and bra

away. I grabbed the elastic of his underwear. His dick was pressed against the cotton, begging to get out. I eyed him, and he nodded, ready for me.

I pulled off his underwear and threw them across the room. He lifted his head to watch. I licked his inner thighs, and he shuddered.

"Fuck, Leah."

My tongue made teasing passes around his lower stomach and thighs, never quite reaching the place he wanted.

He grabbed at the blankets. "Jesus."

Finally, my tongue flicked the head of his penis, making him jolt.

"Should I keep doing that?" I asked.

He chuckled. "Yes, please. If you don't mind."

I closed my mouth over the head of his cock, swirling my tongue across it.

Jake's fingers dug into my hair. "Fuck. Yes."

I took him all in, stroking my hand down the last bit of him that didn't fit in my mouth. He groaned as I sucked and stroked him. "Christ. Leah. The way you take me... That's fecking good."

I pulled him out of my mouth, my eyes darting to his. "Why aren't you grinding against me?"

He opened his mouth, at a loss for words. "I don't want to hurt you."

"Don't worry about that. I was grinding against you, remember?" I ran my tongue up his penis. "Fair's fair."

I took him all in again. He gritted his teeth and cursed. He was hesitant for a moment. Then I grabbed his butt and pulled his hips up to me, forcing him to thrust.

"Fuck," he said, finally grinding against me. He held my hair tighter, thrusting into me. His cock brushed against the back of my throat again and again, almost making me gag. He looked like he was losing his mind. I loved that I did that to him. It made me ache between my legs.

"I could watch you fuck me with your mouth all day. Shit."

My moan vibrated against his dick.

That noise must have done something to him. His hands scrambled around, gently pulling me away as he sat up. "Leah. I can't stand it. Let me be inside your pussy."

Our lips crashed together in a fevered kiss as he pulled my panties off. I gasped as his gentle fingers brushed against my ass.

"How do you want to be?" he asked.

I crawled forward on the bed, sliding onto my stomach. I cranked my head around and grinned. "How does this sound?"

Jake's breath was raspy in anticipation. He eased my legs apart and leaned over, his chest against my back. "I'm going to get so deep in you this way."

I nipped at his neck. "I know."

He slid his hands under me, cupping my breasts, which were flat against the mattress. "Is that what you want?"

I moaned as he played with my nipples. "I want you as deep as you can go."

"Fuck." The head of his dick plunged inside me. He stayed like that, teasing me. "I love how wet you are."

"Please…"

His thrust into me was long and luxurious. He took his time so he didn't hurt me. And when I thought he'd hit the limit, he readjusted and went further. He gritted his teeth and groaned when he was all the way in. We stayed that way for a moment, breathing. Then he slowly retreated, almost to his tip, before plunging back inside me again. I clenched my inner muscles against him. He bucked.

"Fuck, Leah. You're so tight around me."

I moaned as he pulled out again, then plunged back in. I

swore, desperate for something to grab onto. "Do you like my cunt?"

He buried his face in the back of my neck. "Hell yes. I go crazy when I'm inside you."

I clamped down on the blankets as I pushed back against him. "Do you know how much I like getting fucked by you?"

"Shit." His lips found mine. He sucked on my tongue as he thrust again. "I see stars when you talk like that."

I wasn't going to be able to take much more. I almost didn't want to come. I wanted to feel this good forever. "Come inside me, Jake."

Our pace increased, and I loved the slapping sound we made.

He lowered a hand to my clit. "Not before you, mo fhíorghrá." I moaned as he swirled his finger around. "You are so good and wet."

"These blankets are going to smell like sex."

His next thrust was long and lazy. I only had a second left. "Good. I want them to. I want all these blankets to smell like your pussy." He rumbled above me. "Come for me, Leah. Come on my cock."

A shockwave went through me, and I pushed myself into him, riding out the orgasm as Jake thrust into me again and again. He yelled my name as he came, clutching himself to my back. Our breathing was rough and shallow as we came to a stop, shaking. We stayed that way for a long time, listening to each other's beating hearts. His heartbeat was like a song I could listen to my whole life, savoring the tune.

"I love you, Leah."

I turned my head, smiling up at him. "I love you, too." I flicked his nose. "Are we still going to do *this* when you're eighty?"

He chuckled. "Even if it's the last thing I do. Yes."

17

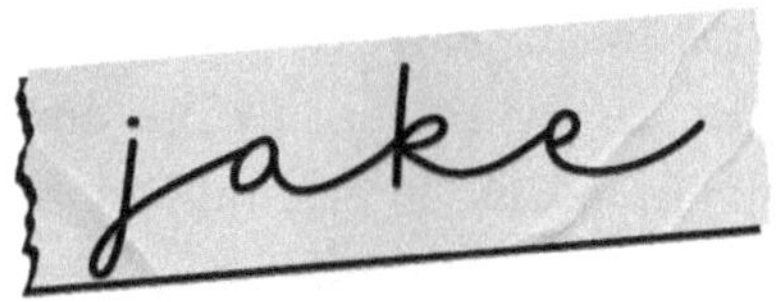

In terms of weather, it was a hot, miserable August. I never cared much for humidity. It felt like you were walking through a heavy mist.

Leah and Henry had been over for most of the afternoon, playing games, listening to music, and eating the caramel corn that Henry and I had made. It was a special request of Daisy's—something fecking normal. Of course, she didn't say *feck* because she was only half me, thank God.

The day started sunny and bright, but by noon, dark clouds rolled in, and the wind picked up.

Daisy pointed at Henry. "UNO!"

Henry ignored Daisy and took another handful of caramel corn. "This is good."

"You have to draw two cards, Henry," I said, shaking my head.

"I don't think so," said Henry.

"You had one card left and didn't say, 'UNO,'" I said. "You know how the game works. You've played it since you were five."

Leah bit her lip to hide a laugh. "He's trying to make the game last forever."

Henry shrugged. "I got all day. There's nowhere I need to be."

Did Leah catch his cadence? He *was* little Steven. It was equal parts surreal and unsettling.

There was thunder in the distance. After a few minutes, it began to rain steadily.

Leah and Daisy sat close together, examining each other's hands.

I waved my finger at them. "Hey, now. There are no teams in UNO. Do I have to get out the rules again?"

But they just laughed at me. After a moment, Henry put down a yellow six.

"You can't put down that card," I said.

Henry was oblivious. "Who, me?"

I stared. "You can either put down a green card or an eight."

"I could get a pen and that six would be an eight in, like, five seconds," he said, deadpan.

I put down my hand, trying not to laugh. "Why is it that I'm the only one who never cheats?" They loved it when I pretended to be perturbed. "Why does the integrity of every game break down after about twenty minutes?" I looked pointedly at Leah, who was doing a terrible job of being serious. "You're at the center of this. I know it. It's mini golf all over again."

Leah and Daisy dissolved into giggles. It was the cutest thing ever. I wanted to keep teasing them so they'd keep laughing.

"I can't help it," said Leah. "I do it because I love that look on your face."

"What look?" I asked, wide-eyed. "Pure desperation? The look of a man at his wits' end?"

"Your face is so cute when you're frazzled," said Leah.

That was the cue for the kids to be disgusted. It was lashing down outside, and we had to speak up to hear each other over the rain.

"Don't do that," said Henry. "I don't think I can handle love right now."

That made Leah and I burst out laughing.

"Plus…Dad's face is *not* cute," said Daisy.

I was offended to my core. "It's not?"

Daisy shook her head. "Your face is weird."

I gathered my cards into a neat pile. "A weird face? Is that so?" I loomed over her. "Well, you know this face is half your face too, right?"

That got Daisy laughing.

I touched my cheeks. "I'd like to know what's weird about it."

Daisy shrugged. "It's pointy."

"Pointy? Are you kidding me?"

Leah wouldn't be able to hold it much longer.

"Your nose and cheeks are kind of sharp," said Henry. "Deal with it."

"My face is in no way sharp." I waved at Leah, now fully laughing. "Do you think my face is sharp?"

"I think it's perfect," and then, under her breath, she added, "and a little pointy."

"Take a good look at Steven sometime," I said. "He's Mr. Cheekbones. He could cut a roast with the side of his face."

The whole table dissolved into laughter.

"Wasn't Uncle Steven supposed to be here?" Daisy looked out the window. The rain came down so hard and fast that everything was a gray haze.

Leah sighed. "He's probably walking in the storm to look introspective."

We listened to the rain and the record player, which was almost drowned out by the former.

"What is this music?" asked Henry, eating popcorn.

"Valerie June," said Leah.

"Your mom introduced me to this years ago." I smiled at Leah. "She's introduced me to a lot of music."

"I'd rather listen to people build Lego stuff on YouTube," said Henry.

"Well, I think your mom has great taste."

"You think that because she's dating you," said Daisy. Henry laughed around his food.

I pointed at Daisy and Henry. "You two are a regular comedy act."

The wind picked up. Light tapping ricocheted against the windows.

Leah's face fell. "Eh, hail!"

A moment later, the music stopped, and the lights went off. We stared at each other in the darkness.

Daisy's small voice cut through the air. "I don't like storms."

"It's alright, sweetie." I gave her shoulder a reassuring squeeze. But a few minutes later, a low siren began thrumming outside.

Henry bolted up. "Sweet! It's not the first Wednesday of the month. This is the real flippin' deal." He danced. "Tornado! Let's go out and look at it."

"Nope," said Leah, guiding her son by the shoulders. "We're all going downstairs."

We led the kids toward the basement steps.

Daisy's posture was stiff. "Dad, I'm scared. What about Purrito?"

I scooped our cat up from her bed in the kitchen. "I've got her, Daisy. It's alright."

Leah grabbed a flashlight from a kitchen drawer and shined it down the steps.

"But what if it wrecks the house?" asked Daisy, all nerves.

I closed the basement door and tried to sound reassuring. "Everything's okay."

The basement was big. The last people who lived in our house had rented it out as an apartment to some cousin of theirs. It had its own living area, a bedroom, a bathroom, and a tiny kitchen. It even had its own separate entrance on the side of the house. Steven had been down here many times to play foosball with me. Before moving into his townhouse, he eyed it as a possible living arrangement, but there was no way in hell I was cohabiting with Steven. After two days, geodes and tambourines would be everywhere.

"Sometimes they start the tornado siren because of strong winds." Leah sat next to Daisy on the basement couch, her arm around her. She shook Daisy's shoulder a little until my daughter relaxed and smiled. Henry plopped down next to them. He still had the caramel corn.

There was something about the three of them sitting there like that. It made my heart feel light and airy, even though the storm crashed around outside.

Henry glanced at the ceiling. "If Uncle Steven's out there now, he's hating life."

I grabbed the weather radio and sat next to Henry. We listened to it as an old clock from my gran ticked loudly on the wall.

Henry crossed his arms. "Did you hear what that guy just said? The rotation was in the sky by Carlos, heading east. Crud. It's not even coming this way."

Leah still had her arm wrapped around Daisy as she rubbed my daughter's back. "See? They just started the siren because we're in the same county."

Daisy looked relieved.

Leah and I exchanged a smile. There was something about her. Even sitting in a dark basement surrounded by a bunch of junk. She made everything different somehow. She made everything better. Daisy loved her. I loved her. There wasn't a way *not* to love her.

Henry was less than thrilled. "I was hoping to see some trees fall."

"You can have a lot of storm damage without a tornado," said Leah.

Henry looked more excited than he should have. "Maybe the hail did something."

The hail did something, alright. It did something to Leah's vinyl siding. Henry pointed out the golf ball-sized holes in it as we all walked around her house. Leah let out a quiet, irritated sigh as she poked around at it. I picked a few stray shingles off the ground.

"Kind of a bummer that none of the windows are broken," said Henry.

Leah gave Henry an annoyed glance. "A dirty shame, isn't it?" She leaned against me. I put my arm around her. "At least I'm insured."

Daisy studied the downed branches in nearby yards. "How come it didn't do anything to our house?"

"We're lucky," said Henry.

I picked up a few larger branches. Henry and Daisy grabbed two sticks and began sword fighting.

Henry whacked Daisy's stick. "I don't get why we even live here." He eyed Leah. "Why don't we move in with Jake and Daisy? We're there all the time anyway."

Kids always knew how to spread an awkward situation all

over the carpet and then leave you to clean up the mess. Leah and I both stood like we had been struck by lightning. I was almost nervous to make eye contact. I wanted to live together so bad I could almost taste it, but I did *not* want to fuck this up. Our relationship had gone from zero to one hundred in about five seconds. That was fine with me. I wanted to spend the rest of our lives together. And I wanted the rest of our lives to start yesterday. But I had no idea if Leah was as crazy as me. I didn't want her to feel pressured. I didn't want her to feel backed into a corner.

Daisy whacked Henry's stick. "Then I can beat you at Scrabble all the time!"

"I don't lose *all* the time," said Henry. He looked at Leah. "Plus, you told me about moving in like forever ago."

My mouth went dry. I got up the nerve to glance at Leah. She bit her lip and glared at Henry. She talked to him about moving in? A hopeful tug pulled at my heart.

Leah ushered her son into the house. Daisy and I followed. I told myself that just because Leah and Henry talked, that didn't mean moving in was something she was keen to do. And her face didn't give anything away. She was trying her best to avoid eye contact with me. That didn't do much for my stomach. Oh, God. Was she dreading this conversation?

Leah pointed down the hall toward Henry's room. "Why don't you go and show Daisy that new card trick Steven taught you?"

Henry grumbled. "I don't feel like—"

Leah cut him off. "Don't make me dust off my mom voice."

"Come on, Daisy." Henry sighed. "It's pretty lame, though."

Daisy followed him. "Can't be worse than the last one."

When the kids were gone, we stood staring at everything except each other. I felt like the floor might sink under my feet. I hoped to God that this wasn't fucked up.

Leah absentmindedly ran a hand through her hair. Good

God, was she nervous? Should *I* be nervous? Who was I kidding? I was already fecking nervous. Was I sweating?

"This is pretty awkward, isn't it?" asked Leah, slowly. "Are you freaked out?"

I was as freaked out as I could get, but not for the reason she thought. Somehow, I managed to sound like a completely calm human being. "I'm not freaked out." I ventured a smile. "Except I'm worried that you're freaked out."

Leah let out a quiet, nervous chuckle. "We really are similar sometimes."

My whole body softened. "You talked to Henry about moving in together?"

Leah fiddled with her locket. "Before we went to the drive-in movie."

Wow. That was a while ago. I found myself stepping closer to her. "What did you say?"

How did I sound so calm?

Leah stood there, fidgeting. "Henry was packing a bag to stay at your place, and he asked me if we were ever moving in with you."

I cleared my throat, unable to talk.

She stepped closer. "I said maybe someday we would."

Relief edged into me. I grabbed her cool fingers. "Is that what you want to do?"

Leah finally looked me in the eyes. A nervous smile crept onto her face. "Yes. I want to move in with you." Her smile brightened. "Does that scare you?"

I wrapped my arms around her. She put her hands on either side of my face. I loved it when she did that. I bent down and kissed her.

"Nothing about this scares me," I whispered. "Except that you might wake up one day and decide this isn't all it's cracked up to be."

"Not gonna happen," whispered Leah. She pulled me down into another kiss.

"Where do you want to live?" I played with her hair.

She let out a laugh. "We're not living in this train wreck. It's not big enough. The kitchen floor is crappy. The bathroom is microscopic. It was never supposed to be permanent. It was just a place to raise Henry for the time being."

I looked around. "I helped you find it."

"Yeah, remember what you said after we toured it?"

Of course, I remembered. "The best of the bad options. And it was. Remember the house with the slanted ceiling in the bathroom? Nothing like standing in the tub and knocking yourself unconscious. I wonder what poor bastard bought that place."

Leah grabbed my hand. "I could get the storm damage fixed and sell this place." I watched as her fingers wove between mine. "So…should we move into your place? You want that?"

I didn't know I could feel so light. It felt like I'd been waiting my whole life for this. "You're damn right, I do."

I sat in bed that night, looking through Leah's book of Emily Dickinson's poetry. She and Henry had brought over a duffle bag each of assorted clothes and things. While I flipped pages, Leah showered in the adjoining bathroom.

I was on my fourth poem when I heard a quiet noise. My eyes drifted to the bathroom door. Leah was singing. When was the last time I heard that? I found myself smiling, straining to hear what it was. The shower turned off, but the singing continued. My grin widened. After a moment, the hairdryer turned on, and all sound was drowned out.

Leah emerged from the bathroom in pajamas with the original Nintendo controller all over them. I loved my sexy weirdo. My arms were crossed as my eyes fixed on her.

She stopped in her tracks. "What?"

"You have a lovely singing voice."

She put her hand out to block me from her vision, but there was a smile on her face. "Don't look at me."

She giggled as I pulled her into bed. She collapsed on top of me. God, she smelled good.

"Why not?" I asked.

"Because I'm embarrassed." She tried to pin me down and tickle me. "I didn't think you could hear me."

I refused to be tickled. I grinned as I held her away with one hand and counter-tickled her with the other. "I *did,* and I liked it."

"I've been singing a lot lately. It's driving Henry crazy." We called a truce, and she lay next to me. "I blame you."

My eyebrows rose. "What did I do?"

She kissed my cheek. "You made me happy."

I stretched out. Leah rested her head on my chest. I wrapped an arm around her.

Home.

"You sing when you're happy?" I asked.

"It looks that way."

"But you haven't sung in a long time," I said.

She looked up at me. "I haven't been this happy in a long time."

My lips found hers. It was a long kiss, our tongues sliding against each other. "Neither have I." We were quiet for a moment. "You could keep singing if you want."

"Now you're pushing it."

She was silent for so long that I thought she had drifted off to sleep. I was surprised when she quietly sang a few verses from a song I didn't recognize.

I kissed the top of her head.

She let out a relaxed sigh. "We're moving in together."
"Yes, we are."
"Thank God," she said.
Home.
The feeling of it, the rightness of it, made my chest swell.
"My thoughts exactly."

18

When I walked into A-to-Z Furniture, Leah looked deep in thought as she frowned at the computer screen next to the cash register, punching keys. Steven was sacked out on a Sleep Number bed.

He lifted his head slightly when I walked up. "I heard you and Leah are shacking up. That's what our grandma used to call it. She'd say that you are sinful little bastards."

I handed him his coffee. "That's right. I'm looking forward to it."

Steven adjusted his sports coat. "In terms of sin, that has to be one of the tamer ones. That and gluttony. Think I'll go to hell for eating all my cousin's birthday cake when I was eight?"

I stared at him. "You seem to be in an even weirder headspace than usual."

Steven drank his coffee. "You two being hot and heavy makes me feel pressured with Danica."

"Is that the banjo player?"

Steven nodded.

"I didn't know she had a name," said Leah, strolling up. She smiled as I passed her the coffee.

"That's because you're too focused on your love bubble," said Steven. "Danica doesn't want to move in together. She thinks it'll dispel our animal magnetism."

Leah cringed. "Please stop talking."

"I *do* love the mystery," said Steven. "And the mystery's pretty much gone when one person sits on the toilet while the other person brushes their teeth." He glanced up and down at us. "I give you two a month of living together. After that, you'll be one of those boring couples that don't care if they ever touch each other again."

I sipped my coffee. "I find that highly unlikely."

Leah and I made eye contact and moved closer to one another.

"Or you'll break up," said Steven.

I jokingly flipped him off. "The power of positive thinking."

We walked to the break room. Leah passed me a sandwich and toasted a bagel for herself. Steven grabbed a large container of leftover fried chicken from the fridge. Leah and I sat next to each other, while Steven slid down across from us, huffing loudly.

"You're surly lately," said Leah. "You act like *your* house is the one with the storm damage."

"It didn't get wrecked in the storm, but I'm still bummed." Steven let out a dramatic sigh. "I finally broke the bank. I'm moving out next week, and I have nowhere to go. If you two move in together, where does that leave me?"

Leah didn't miss a beat. "Screwed."

I bit the inside of my cheek to stop from grinning. "I guess if Danica doesn't want to dispel the animal magnetism, you'll have to move back home for a while."

Steven turned into one miserable bastard as he rested his forehead on the table. "That's horrifying news." He lifted his head again. "How can I live with Mom and Dad? They get up at four o'clock every morning. For no reason."

Leah stared at him. "That's when *you* get up every morning, Steven."

"But when I do it, it's mysterious and sexy," said Steven. "I write poetry, for God's sake. I stare at the sunrise. They're just downstairs banging cupboards and taking the majesty out of the day with subpar coffee. I always thought I'd get that house eventually when they croak—"

"Steven!" Leah cut him off. "That's terrible."

Steven pointed at Leah. "Don't you dare fight me for it, either. I already talked to Mom. I have dibs." He bit into his chicken. "But I don't want to move in *now*. Living with them will make me significantly less sexy." Steven eyed me. "Don't you think so, Jake?"

I put my sandwich down. "I guarantee it."

My agreement egged him on. "See?" He talked around his food. "I could move in with you guys."

I wasn't sure who shook their head faster. We were nothing but a blur of clearing throats and noncommittal noises.

"Not happening," said Leah.

This conversation was ruining my appetite. "Your sex appeal can handle bunking with them for a few months."

Steven crossed his arms. "But you know I've been scoping out your basement apartment for years. I like it, and it likes me. How can you be so selfish?" He narrowed his eyes. "How dare you not let me live with you during your honeymoon period!"

It felt like Leah and I were doing a Vulcan mind meld with each other. We both silently understood that this couldn't happen. The last thing we needed was Steven's Spam collection decorating our living room.

After an awkward silence, Steven decided we weren't giving in. He leaned back in his chair, defeated. "Well, shit... I guess I'll talk to Mom." He looked around. "Where is she, anyway? And where are the kids? They were supposed to help me eat this chicken."

Leah shook her head at him. "Mom and Dad took them camping at Lake Minnewaska for the weekend as their birthday present for Henry. *Remember?*"

"Birthday?" asked Steven, confused.

Leah's expression looked like *hello, Earth to Steven.* "Yes. Henry's twelfth birthday. That was the party we had a few days ago. Remember the water fight? Dad and Jake grilled."

Steven poked at his chicken. "Was I there?"

"That was the thing in the backyard with the balloons." I was deadpan. "And the carrot cake that you ate a lot of."

Realization dawned on him, and he looked at me. "I thought that was *your* birthday."

Leah put a hand to her face, exasperated.

"I did kind of wonder why you gave me that Taco Bell gift card," I said.

"Jake's birthday is December 23rd!"

Steven scratched his chin. "Forgot."

I was monotone. "No worries. You're grand. Everyone with a December birthday understands."

Steven poked at his chicken. "I wouldn't have eaten so much of that cake if I knew it was his. I was just trying to piss the two of you off."

I almost felt bad for Steven. This situation was cutting into his dollar store Matthew McConaughey persona.

"You could start bringing your stuff over to your parents' house tonight while they're gone," I said. "Then, when they come home on Sunday, pretend like you've always been there."

Steven mulled that over. "I guess." He pushed his chicken away. "What a shitty day. First, I need to rebuy a birthday present. Then I buy eighty pieces of greasy, cold chicken and have nobody to eat it with, and now I get to be Dad's live-in dip tester."

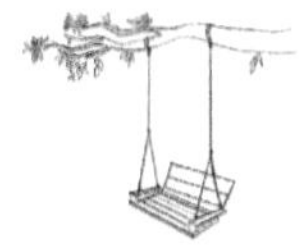

I was finishing cleaning the kitchen at the café that evening when Leah strolled in. I peeked around the corner and grinned.

She stopped dead and narrowed her eyes, teasing me. "Well?" Her voice was filled with anticipation.

"Well, what?" I asked, pretending to be oblivious.

She rushed up and playfully punched my shoulder. "Did you do it?"

I whipped out my phone. "Four tickets to Knock. We leave October 10th."

She stared at my phone, mouth wide. "Amazing!" She gave my cheek a peck. "I'll pay you back tomorrow."

I brushed off her comment. "I'm not worried about it."

"No, no," she said, handing back my phone. "You're not paying for me and Henry's tickets."

"You know how many frequent flyer miles I have?"

"I'm paying you back." She glanced around the dark café. "Are you ready?"

I reached for her hand. "Ready."

We strolled out of the restaurant into the warm, bright evening. There was nothing like walking with her, our intertwined hands softly bobbing in the sun. When the breeze hit us, I smelled Leah's perfume and stepped closer.

She was giddy with excitement. "I can't believe we'll be in Ireland next month!"

Her smile was infectious. It went right to my heart. "It'll be nice to see everyone again. And we'll do a lot of sightseeing too, since you haven't been there in a while."

"I'm already making a list!"

I gave her a playful nudge. "Yeah? What are you looking forward to most?"

She nudged me back. "You."

"Really?" And here I thought you'd say the Wild Atlantic Way."

Leah was about to tease me right back when my iPhone went off in my back pocket. I looked at the screen. "It's your dad."

"Maybe they're having a s'more supplies emergency."

I put the phone to my ear. "Hey."

Dennis said a lot in thirty seconds. His voice was calm the entire time. Everyone knew how easy it was to wind me up, but his even tone didn't help me one bit. It suddenly felt like the sidewalk had turned soft, and I'd sink right in.

"What's going on?" Leah wore a nervous expression. My face must have been a clear giveaway.

I knew I answered him and asked questions, but after the words were out of my mouth, I couldn't remember any of what I'd said. Adrenaline and nerves had taken over. When he hung up, I put the phone in my pocket with a shaking hand.

That's when I realized that Leah was holding my arm. She searched my eyes, looking for clues. "Jake, what's happening?"

I tried to breathe. "We have to go to the hospital. Daisy had an accident."

When we got to the hospital, Gail, Dennis, and Henry were in the waiting room. I burst into Daisy's room like a mad person, with Leah right behind me, but Daisy was all smiles as she sat next to my father. The doctor sat across from them.

I shot toward her, inspecting her from head to toe. There was a black sling around her right arm. "I'm okay, Dad. It was my fault."

"We tried to call Ash, but it went to voicemail," said my dad.

I rubbed the sweat off my brow. "She's in the Florida Keys with Kenneth, remember?"

I hugged Daisy as gently as I could. I still felt shaky. "Are you sure you're alright? Does it hurt? How did it happen?"

"It just hurts a little," said Daisy.

The doctor slid her glasses down onto her face. "It's alright, Mr. Bradley. Daisy's a real trooper."

"Did Dennis say something about a fall?" I asked.

"There was a swinging rope on a tree next to the lake," said Daisy. "Henry went first and swung way out so he could jump in the water. But when it was my turn, I lost my grip. I fell and hit my shoulder on a stump."

Leah rested her hand on Daisy's back to reassure her. "Oh, no!" She cringed. "That sounds like us."

I kissed Daisy's head. "I sprained my wrist kind of like that when I was about your age."

"Daisy is going to be just fine, but she did break her shoulder," said the doctor.

"Broken!" I said. Okay, perhaps I shouted it.

"It's fine, Jake," said my dad. "Kids break things all the time. You should've seen the scrapes I got into at her age. That's why my mother is the way she is."

"She isn't going to need surgery," said the doctor. "But she will have to wear that sling for six weeks. And you'll have to apply ice regularly."

I nodded, trying to keep everything straight in my dazed mind.

"I've prescribed you some pain medicine," said the doctor. "It should be ready at the pharmacy by now. And it's very important to remember to keep all activity gentle. No biking. No sports. No playground equipment. She shouldn't lift anything. And the only time she should have that sling off is while changing clothes or showering."

I nodded. "Thank you."

"I'm sorry, Dad," said Daisy.

I smiled and tried to look calm as I kissed her head again. "Don't be sorry. Everything's grand. You can't be a parent without expecting a few heart attacks."

Leah was already under the covers with her poetry book when I walked into the bedroom that night. She lowered it. "How did Ashley react?"

I still felt the adrenaline pumping through me. "She took it the way I did. She wanted to take the next flight back, but I told her she didn't have to. She's been looking forward to that trip. And everything's fine now, I guess." I breathed out. "I mean, I'm wound about as tight as I can be, but Daisy's fine. I mean, look at the way she joked and laughed earlier. Did you see how much ice cream she ate?"

Leah nodded, patting the bed. I sat down and gathered her in my arms. I closed my eyes and breathed her in. "She said that breaking her shoulder was worth it for that mega malt and the new stuffed animal."

"A girl after my own heart."

I chuckled.

"You remember when Henry was eight and had that rollerblading fiasco?" asked Leah.

I nodded. That was a tense day, too. Leah was nothing but big eyes, worried glances, and whispered cursing on the way to the hospital.

Leah leaned into me. "He was learning to rollerblade. I made sure he wore every pad in existence. Knee pads. Elbow pads. He had a helmet. I don't even know how it happened. Maybe it was a pebble or something. But he face-planted right on the curb by my parents' house. Remember?"

"I held that towel up to his nose. It was drenched. My blood pressure was through the roof." I shook my head. "I thought his nose was broken for sure."

"I thought the doctors would say he had a concussion." Leah sighed. "I was so grateful it was just a nosebleed. It's crazy how days can change just like that. From good to bad."

I couldn't ponder thoughts like that without thinking about Mom. "It is."

Leah's hand slid into mine like she had read my mind.

I could still see the sunny blue day when my mom pulled out of the driveway forever. "I guess that's how it always is. If you knew the day was going to be a horror story, you wouldn't get out of bed." I kissed her cheek. "But you make it better."

"I didn't do much. I saw that look in your eyes when you were on the phone… I thought I was going to throw up, and I didn't even know what was happening."

"You did plenty," I whispered. "You cared about Daisy." I leaned my head against hers.

"I'll always care about Daisy. And I'll always care about you."

"And I'll always care about you and Henry," I said.

We slid down into bed, still holding each other. Leah's face was tucked under my chin. God, that was nice. Her lips and breath were warm against my cold skin. I ran my hands up and down her back. "We didn't even tell the kids about our Ireland trip."

Leah craned her neck, looking me in the eyes. "We'll tell them at breakfast."

"I'll make pancakes."

That made Leah smile. She ran her finger along the side of my face. "When is Ash coming back?"

"She just got there. It'll be almost a week and a half."

We kissed for a long moment. Then I drifted down and kissed that place between her neck and shoulder that I loved so much. I nibbled her there until she let out a breathy giggle.

Her eyes met mine again. "She'll be home sooner."

It was a rainy day in late August. Nathaniel Rateliff played in the background as I stood in the spare room, throwing odds and ends into storage boxes. If this was going to be Henry's room, the spare appliances and tchotchkes had to go. "How did I get all this shit?"

In a couple of days, Leah and Henry were officially moving in. My whole body was alive with anticipation. I could've touched a lightbulb and made it glow through sheer will.

A couple of paint swatches sat on the end table. Henry wanted a blue storm cloud shade for his room. Leah and I planned to paint our bedroom blue too, but something lighter.

I was halfway under the bed, pulling out a storage container of old movies and games, when the doorbell rang.

I heard Daisy's feet march toward the front door, even though she knew I didn't like her answering it. I'd seen enough true crime shows to be paranoid.

I quickly stood up and dusted the cobwebs off. The sound of Daisy and another female voice drifted into the room.

I wandered down the hallway. My eyes widened when I turned the corner and Ash kneeled in the open doorway. She was soaked to the gills from the rain. She held onto Daisy with a firm but tender grip to avoid hurting her broken shoulder.

"I said it's no big deal," said Daisy.

Ashley wiped a tear away. That's when I noticed how raw

her face was. Did she cry the whole way here? "It's a big deal to *me*. I was worried sick. Does it hurt?"

"A little," said Daisy. "Especially when I accidentally roll over in my sleep."

Ash kissed Daisy's forehead. "You have to be careful, okay? Or it'll take even longer to get better."

For the first time since I walked into the entryway, Ash glanced up at me. She seemed almost startled. She stood and ran a distracted hand through Daisy's hair.

I tried to go with it. "Hey, Ash. You didn't have to cut your vacation short."

Ashley shrugged. "I couldn't stand it any longer. I felt so bad sitting there on the beach getting a tan while my little girl was hurt and miserable."

Daisy rolled her eyes. "You two are so weird. Breaking my shoulder was the best. Uncle Steven says he's giving me a free month of guitar lessons…when I'm able to play it." Ash kept fiddling with Daisy's hair. Daisy's face suddenly lit up. "Oh, Mom. Let me show you the picture I did! I found a photo of where you were. I drew it."

Daisy zipped away to her room, leaving Ash and me in the kitchen, awash in awkward silence. I grabbed a kitchen towel out of the drawer and passed it to her. She flashed me a grateful smile as she took it and dried off her face and jacket.

"It was nice that you came back early to see Daisy."

Ash patted the towel against her dark red hair. She frowned. "Yeah, well. I couldn't stand it for another second." She let out a huff. "I was fed up."

What was I supposed to do with my arms? I crossed them. "How's that?"

Ash threw the towel on the counter. An emotion passed over her face. We'd been married for ten years. I knew what that look was. That was the face she made when she was trying not to cry.

"It's okay, Ash. Daisy's fine."

Ashley was quiet for a long moment, staring at the floor. "It's not just that." She let out a bitter laugh. "Kenneth's a prick."

I didn't know what the hell to say. I'd known that since I was ten.

She tried to steady the emotion in her voice. "When you called, I freaked out."

"I know," I said quietly. I wasn't sure how to act. In the past, when she was upset, I'd give her a gentle hug. But how were you supposed to have a heart-to-heart with your ex? Offer her a beer? Did I even have beer?

"When I told Kenneth what happened, it was like he didn't even care. He sat there, drinking his rum and Coke." She gritted her teeth. "I mean, that's his girlfriend's daughter. And you're his cousin. That's his *cousin's* daughter... You'd think he'd care."

No shit, but that was Kenneth. Kenneth was a few years older than Felicity, and when they were kids, one of his favorite pranks was to let her tag along when he was with his friends and then try to ditch her. Once, he ditched her at a friend's house when she fell asleep while everyone watched a movie. Luckily, the friend was nice and told his parents what happened, and the parents called Felicity and Kenneth's parents. Kenneth got into deep shit for that one, and Felicity's face was tear-stained when her mom and dad picked her up. Certified fecking asshole.

"I'm sorry," I said. "Don't let the gobshites of the world get you down."

Ashley tried to smile, but she was tired. "Plus, he's been spending a lot lately."

I felt alarms go off. "Spending?" She wouldn't meet my eyes. "What do you mean?"

For the first time in her life, Ash looked sheepish. "I let him use my credit card."

That's why she acted so weird during all those talks. Kenneth was draining her.

"You don't have a shared bank account, do you?"

"No."

I went wide-eyed. "So, then?"

Ashley picked at her nails. "I don't know. I love him." Her eyes finally met mine. "I don't know why I did it. But we were happy. And he liked going to the casino. It was fun." She frowned. "Don't look at me like that."

My eyes couldn't have gone wider. "The casino? You always said casinos were tacky."

She closed her eyes, embarrassed. "I don't know what got into me. The whole thing was idiotic." She sighed. "He's still the same guy he was back when we first met. I never should have gotten back with—"

It was like a knife cut her words in half. She stopped talking. Her eyes shot to the floor. My lips parted, stunned. I couldn't believe she said that. She looked like she couldn't believe it either. We both knew what her statement implied. Because if Ashley had never gotten together with Kenneth, we'd still be married. And Leah and I would still just be friends.

The thought twisted my stomach. God, the idea of Leah and me not getting together. It was like a crazy alternate universe. This trip back to see Daisy suddenly felt like something entirely different. Something that in no way was ever going to happen. "Ash, you know I'm—"

But I wasn't able to get the sentence out, because she looked at me and said, "You know how much he spent?"

Relief washed over me. Back to the topic of money. A much safer line of discussion. I shook my head.

She let out a tired laugh. "I can't afford my rent anymore. I don't know where I'm going to stay."

Fecking hell.

I suddenly thought of Steven. I considered lightening the mood by joking that they could move in together.

Daisy chose that moment to reappear with a small canvas that Leah bought her at the art store. Ashley was all smiles when Daisy proudly displayed the colored pencil sketch of the beach. Daisy was a great artist. I loved that picture. Leah loved it too. Leah went around the house, trying to find the perfect place to display it. But that made Daisy bashful, and she took it back to her room, saying it wasn't perfect yet.

Ash held the canvas. "It's beautiful, sweetie. It looks like something in a gallery."

Daisy beamed. "I did it with my left hand, too, because it hurts to use the right one!"

Ash was stunned. "You can draw with your left hand?"

Daisy nodded, proud. "It just takes a little longer."

Ash and I gave each other approving glances. I wasn't sure where the art thing came from. The only other people I'd ever known who liked drawing were Leah and Steven.

Daisy gave her mom a puzzled look. "Why don't you have anywhere to live?"

When you ask them to pick up their toys, kids never seem to hear you. And they can be five feet away. But when you try to keep things quiet, they suddenly have superhero senses.

"I have to find a new place," said Ash. "Don't worry. I'll bring all the stuff from your room with me."

Daisy's face turned bright. "Why don't you stay downstairs?"

And just like that, I felt the bottom drop out of something somewhere. I probably looked like a mad person, flailing my hands, shaking my head, and trying to speak. "No, no, no…I don't think—"

"I'm not sure about that, Daisy," said Ash. But she said it with a hopeful glance toward me. I still shook my head. What the actual fuck was happening?

"Come on, Dad," said Daisy. There was a wide smile on her face.

Only childhood innocence could account for how she thought her mother could live downstairs while Leah and Henry lived upstairs, but I wasn't innocent. It reeked of epic disaster.

I gestured for Daisy to come over to me. I bent down and whispered, "Go to your room for a minute, will you?"

"But Dad!"

I lowered my voice. "I'm serious."

Daisy stamped off to her bedroom. My face felt hot. Was it hot in there? It felt like a proper time to pass out.

Ash had that look on her face. I knew that one too. The look of trying to convince someone to do something they didn't want to. She had that look on her face before getting me to go on the Wild Thing at Valleyfair, even though I hated rollercoasters. That hadn't been a great idea, and this idea wasn't great either.

"You won't even know I'm down there," whispered Ash. "It has that separate entrance and everything."

I'm fairly sure that blood vessels were popping in my brain. "I don't think that's going to work." *Line up excuses, damn you.* "I'm pretty sure Steven's moving down there."

Ash let out a short laugh. "Yeah, right. Like that would ever happen."

I put up my hands like I was being arrested. "And you know Leah and I are very serious. We're moving in together. So it's not going to work."

The smile on Ashley's face didn't diminish. "It's only for a couple of months. I'm sure Leah wouldn't mind me being close to my injured daughter for a couple of months." Her smile widened. "Do you?"

She was trying to play me like a fiddle. She made it sound so sensible when, in reality, the idea was batshit crazy. Anyone would call it crazy. Leah would not be okay with Ash living in the basement. And I was most certainly *not* okay with it.

"Why don't you move in with your parents?" I asked. If it was good enough for Steven…

Ashley's smile faded. "We don't exactly see eye to eye after the whole Kenneth thing." She bit her lip. "They always liked you."

That was news to me. Ashley's mom never seemed to mind me, but her dad always acted like talking to me was part of some sentence he had to serve.

There was still hope in Ashley's face. "Please?"

That's when I noticed Daisy out of the corner of my eye. She stood in the doorway of her room. There was a weird look on her face. I gestured to Ashley that I'd be back in a moment and walked over to our daughter. I bent down to her. "What is it, sweetheart?"

Daisy leaned into my chest and put her head on my shoulder. "I want Mom to stay downstairs. I miss her."

Her little eyes looked into mine, and I was instantly gutted. I felt like I was looking back through the years at myself. How many times did I sit awake at night, wishing I had my mother back, if only for a little while? And Daisy was hurt. She wanted her mom while she was hurt. What kid wouldn't? She wanted her mom the same way I had. What the fuck could I say? I understood how she felt. And it was just for a couple of months.

I kissed Daisy on the cheek. "Okay, Daisy. Just for a little while, though."

The house turned to immediate excitement. Daisy and Ash were all hugs and smiles. Like, this was the best thing in the world. But I stood there by Daisy's door, holding onto the frame for dear life. The *okay* was hardly out of my mouth when the horror and foreboding washed over me.

What the fuck is wrong with you? She could have lived with Steven. She could have lived with Margot's cousin, Nadia. She could have lived with her parents. She could have lived in any other damn place but here.

How was this going to look? I didn't even have to ask myself that stupid question because I knew exactly how it would look. It would look ludicrous. It would look like Ashley and I were back together.

Fuck. How would it look to Leah?

The clock on the wall chimed. In two hours, I had to be at the Roths for supper. Then Leah and Henry were supposed to come over to watch a movie and spend the night. They were over almost every night now.

Where did Ash and Daisy go? They were nowhere in sight.

I put my hands to my temples to stop the throbbing. "Fecking idiot." I couldn't get over my sheer stupidity. "Dear God, I think I just fucked everything up."

19

"Aren't we going to Grandma and Grandpa's house?" asked Henry.

We were in my little car, meandering down the block. "I want to drop off these cookies at Jake's house first."

Henry studied the plastic container of cookies on his lap. "You mean *our* house?"

I mussed his hair. "Yep. In a few days, it'll be our house, too."

Henry grinned. "I'm going to decimate it."

I burst out laughing. Where the hell did he come up with this stuff?

I could've brought the cookies over to my parents' house, but I knew how the Roths and Bradleys were with dessert. And Steven was the worst. There wouldn't have been a cookie left for when we watched movies later. And that was the whole point. Henry wanted to surprise Jake. He flipped through four different cookbooks to find a recipe he thought Jake would like. Talk about pulling at my heartstrings. Plus, Jake always made treats for movie night—caramel corn, butter cookies, and those cupcakes that tasted like sugared donuts. So we thought we'd treat him for once.

I pulled into Jake's driveway and took the cookies from Henry. He whipped out his Game Boy and stared down at the screen.

"Back in a second," I said.

As I made my way to the front door, I pulled the house key out of my pocket. We had an extra set made for Henry and me. But when I grabbed the knob, it was loose in my hand. Jake never forgot to lock the door.

I stepped in and was surprised to find the lights on. I put the container of cookies on the counter. "Babe, are you still here?"

I walked to the garage door and opened it. My heart stopped. Jake's vehicle was gone, but a dark Buick sat there. My mind tried to make sense of it. I knew that car.

"Hey," said a familiar voice. I whipped around to see Ash marching up the basement steps with an empty plastic storage container.

She must be bringing stuff over for Daisy, I thought.

I tried not to be awkward, but I failed. I gave her a little wave. "Hey, Ash. How's it going?"

How's it going? What the hell, Leah? Figure out what's going on!

I talked to her like seeing her skulking around Jake's house like Gollum was normal.

Ash wore a sleek blue blouse, dark leggings, and four shiny bracelets. Her hair was a little messy, but she still had that sleek, stick-up-her-butt look going on.

She strategically placed a beaming smile on her face. "How *are* you?"

Amazing, Ash. I'm fucking amazing.

I whipped out my own fake smile and hoped it was convincing. "I'm awesome…" We stared at each other for a beat. "You're back early from your trip. Too hot for you?"

Haha, yes. Pleasant conversation. A great time was had by all.

Ash gave me an innocent shrug. "Things didn't work out with me and Kenneth."

Even my thoughts were sarcastic. *Stop the presses. Shocking news.*

"That's too bad."

"Thanks." She was always great at fake sincerity. "Guys surprise you sometimes. Not in a good way. You know what I mean, right?" A small chuckle. "All those crazy Leah dates."

Very nice. And she kept smiling through the whole statement, like it was completely innocent.

I needed to get out of there.

Instead, I pointed at the storage container. "Bringing stuff for Daisy?"

Ash looked confused. She glanced at the container. "What? Oh, no… I mean, yes, I guess I am. But this was full of *my* stuff."

I stared at her, my face revealing nothing. I felt like she should probably repeat that last sentence. "Uh…what?"

There was that smile again. "I'm a little embarrassed." She looked at me like this was some inside joke. Like we were two pals who were going to paint each other's nails. "I'm having a little money trouble after being with Kenneth." Her eyes widened. "Yikes, right? And I don't have anywhere to go… So Jake said I could stay here."

Do NOT have a heart attack. This woman won't call 911 for you.

My heart pounded against my skull, but I refused to look upset. I kept my breathing steady, even though it felt like I was deprived of oxygen. I didn't want to give Ash any satisfaction. She fed off that shit like an alley cat behind Denny's.

Jake said you could stay? Whatever, Ash. I bet he rolled out the red carpet.

"You're staying here?"

Ashley nodded. "Just for a couple of months, until I get a little money put away so I can get another place."

What the hell had happened in the last few hours? I looked like an idiot for being out of the loop. She slid by me into the garage. She grabbed a large duffle bag from her backseat and came back into the kitchen, setting it on the floor.

"But you never know," she said, her voice chiming. "It could be longer."

There was something about the way she glanced at me. She knew Jake and I were together, but the glint in her eyes slashed through the certainty and permanence of our relationship like a sword through silk. It was an easy disregard that made me feel like Jake and I were just playing house.

I wasn't sure I could speak, but I had to try, so I smiled. "Maybe you should start a lemonade stand to earn extra cash."

She let out a fake, tinkling laugh. She hadn't stopped smiling since I walked in the door, but she hadn't really smiled once. And she had never hated me this much, either. She was never interested enough in my presence to hate me. Usually, Ash walked by me with an innocuous passing comment about the weather or our kids. Usually, she acted like I didn't exist. But now I was in her territory. It was territory she hadn't wanted for the past ten years, but she wanted it now. And she was determined to kick me off the map.

"Is there something you wanted?" asked Ashley.

This is rich. You've got some nerve, bitch.

I pointed to the container. "Just bringing over these cookies for later. Didn't want Steven eating them all."

"Sure," said Ash. "Jake and Daisy headed over to your parents' house ten minutes ago. You just missed them." There was that smile again. "But I'll tell them you dropped by."

I'm sure you will. Because you don't think I'll be back.

Ash pointed at my boots. "Oh, and not to be grouchy or

anything, but you should watch out with your shoes on our kitchen floor. It's not the easiest thing to clean, you know?"

Our kitchen floor.

My body was on fire. If someone threw an egg at me, it would have scrambled in a second. "Sure." We looked at each other for a moment. I took another steady breath. "Well, I guess I better get to supper. You know how they are about punctuality." I smiled. "See you later, Ash."

I'm not sure if she said anything back. I needed to get out of that house. I escaped back into the windy evening. Even though it was sticky outside, the air still felt cool on my face.

Henry stared at me when I got in the car. "What took so long?"

I didn't answer him. I didn't show any emotion.

What the hell is going on? And why didn't Jake tell me?

Jake always told me everything.

I backed out of the driveway and headed toward my parents' house.

I wasn't sure how he knew something was off, but I couldn't fool Henry. "What's going on? Did Purrito have a hairball?"

I shook my head.

"Do you think Karma and Purrito will get along?" Good. He was distracted. That meant he couldn't see my internal freakout. "Is it hard to get two adult cats to be friends when you put them in a house together?"

It was stupid, but the thought of our cats coexisting made my eyes burn. Because I suddenly wondered if they *were* going to live together. I suddenly wondered if *any* of us would live together.

I breathed to stop myself from crying. "They'll be fine."

Henry watched me. "What's up, Mom?"

I mussed his hair again. "Nothing, Care Bear."

I walked into my parents' house completely numb. I didn't feel my feet stepping beneath me. I scanned the house like a robot, looking for Jake. I was scared to find him. I was never scared to find Jake. It felt like something was spinning in my chest, spinning until it broke loose.

Everyone except Jake was in the kitchen, eating Dad's latest dip.

"I like the pickles," said Daisy.

"I don't know if there needs to be a pickle-based dip," said Mom, inspecting it.

"You'll love it," said Dad.

Craig plunged a cracker into it. "It's grand."

Then they noticed me. They froze mid-chew.

I must look like something's wrong.

Steven charged down the stairs, saying something I didn't catch. When he saw me, he stopped and stared.

"Is something wrong?" asked Mom. "You look like you've seen a ghost."

Usually, comments like that made me whip out a fake smile, but I felt too jittery. "Where's Jake?"

"On your swing," said Craig.

I nodded and walked through to the living room. The others stayed behind, whispering something, but Steven was right on my toes.

I looked out the back deck door. Jake sat forward on the swing, his elbows on his knees. The expression on his face matched my mood.

Steven stood behind me. He poked my shoulder until I looked at him. His face startled me. He didn't wear that serious expression very often. "Jake seems weird." He lowered his voice. "He hasn't said much." I made an inaudible noise. "You seem weird, too. Tense."

"I am." My voice was hollow. My eyes were still fixed on Jake, who was rocking slowly.

"What are you going to do?" he asked.

I didn't answer. I kept staring outside. I wondered what I was going to say, what I was going to do, and if I was going to wreck everything.

That's what you do.

The thought scared me. I'd loved Jake forever. In his arms was where I wanted to be, so why did I feel like I'd been ripped from solid ground and tossed out at sea? Why did I feel like I was going to go out to talk to him with an escape plan in my back pocket? I didn't want to escape Jake. Fear pulsed through my veins. What was I doing? I knew I should turn and leave before I ruined what I cherished, before I said words in the heat of the moment that I couldn't take back.

But somehow, I stayed fixed to that spot.

"Maybe you shouldn't go out there right now," said Steven.

He was trying to make sense. He knew how I liked to cut and run at the tiniest sign of trouble.

"Maybe I *should*."

Steven made a throaty noise. "Maybe you *shouldn't*." He lowered his voice even more. "Sometimes things need to air out for a while. You know? Sometimes you have to wait a while so your emotions aren't stupid. I've been there."

I stared into his eyes. Had he been there with Margot? "You're probably right."

Steven's eyebrows shot up. He looked surprised I was taking his advice. He was so relieved that he didn't even have a chance to stop me. I slid open the deck door and charged into the back-yard before he knew I was gone.

Jake was so lost in thought that he didn't realize I was there. Even though it was still summer, the evening was starting to get chilly. I crossed my arms for warmth. When Jake finally looked up, a startled expression washed over him.

He wore an anxious smile. "Hi… You're late. You're never late."

I didn't know what to say. I didn't know where to start.

He looked me right in the eyes. I didn't have to ask if something was on my face this time. From my expression, he knew something was up.

"What's wrong?" There was a nervous tinge to his voice.

"Henry and I made cookies today." My voice cracked. "He's excited for you to try them."

"Cookies?" With how I looked, he probably didn't expect me to start by talking about treats.

I nodded. "You're always so sweet. Making snacks for movie night. So we thought we should bring something this time."

Jake's shoulders relaxed. "That's grand. I can't wait to try them."

The heat slowly rose in my face. "But I didn't want Steven to eat them all… Remember last time? So I brought them over to your house…"

There it was. The horror. Jake went from semi-relaxed to tense in half a second. He rested his hands on his head. "Shit."

"And Ash was there."

Jake opened his mouth to speak, but no words came out.

"And boy, was Ash there alright. In all her glory."

I plopped next to Jake in a huff. Emotions flew across his face. He needed a moment to spill what had happened. That was fine. I loved him. He could have all the moments in the world. But I still couldn't get rid of the nagging fear in my stomach.

"What is Ash doing in your house?" I whispered. "I must've missed the breaking news. She…says she's moving back in."

Jake rubbed his sweaty palms together. "I'm *so* sorry about that. I…was going to tell you everything as soon as you got here. It all happened this afternoon." There was panic in his eyes. "I wasn't trying to keep anything from you."

I put my hand on his shoulder, and he smiled faintly. This was fine. This was good. We were figuring things out. "I believe you."

Jake swallowed. "She cut her vacation short to see Daisy, just like you said she would. But then she started talking about how Kenneth blew all her money at the casino. And she said she doesn't have anywhere to stay because her parents are pissed. And of course, that's when Daisy charged in and told her she could live in the basement for a while…" He took a breath. "It caught me off guard."

My mind took in this information like a computer, trying not to let emotions color the events. *Breathe. Relax.* "What did you say?"

For a long moment Jake's mouth hung open, but he didn't seem able to speak. His big, bright eyes held nothing but fear. "I guess…I told her she could."

I felt like all the air in the backyard had been sucked away, and I was a fish flopping around on the rocks. I kept staring at him.

"You're not saying anything," he said.

My face tightened.

No shit.

"What am I supposed to say?"

Jake swallowed again. "I want to know what you think. I mean…you should have seen Daisy's face. She was so happy with the idea of her mom being downstairs. And with her shoulder… I don't know. It's just for a little while. What do you think?"

Things were starting to happen in my body. I needed to calm down. "I think it's a terrible idea, Jake. That's what I think."

My voice wasn't loud, and my tone wasn't sarcastic, but there must have been a lot of emotion behind my words because

Jake watched me like I was a landmine ready to explode. "It's alright, we just need to figure this out." He said it like he was trying to calm himself down, too. It didn't sound like it was working. It wasn't working for me either.

"You're right about that." I talked faster. This was one of the few things Jake didn't know about me. It was the way I always talked to my Tinder dates whenever things got batshit crazy. "We have to figure things out because this is nuts. What does she think she's doing?"

Jake shrugged. Yep. He was starting to get wound pretty tight, just like me. We needed to breathe. We needed to settle down. "She's just looking for a place to stay." He fiddled with the swing. "And I'm the idiot who answered the door. That's why I hide whenever someone sells things door-to-door. I'd lie on the kitchen floor all afternoon to pretend I'm not at home."

I bit the inside of my cheek. "We're best friends, and I'd love to give you my unbiased opinion…but we've slept together, so I can't do that. So I'll give you my *biased* opinion." Jake stared at me, wide-eyed. I was going a million miles a minute now. "And my biased opinion is that she isn't looking for a place to stay. And she's not here because she has money trouble. And she's not here because her parents are mad and won't let her live with them." I couldn't hide my disgust. "Because what does she care if her parents are mad? For your whole marriage, all she had to do was snap her fingers, and boom, her parents did whatever she wanted—"

Jake put his hand on mine and held it tight. I squeezed it, but I couldn't stop my stupid mouth from talking.

"She *is* here for Daisy," I continued. "I'll give her that. She always puts Daisy first. But she's also here for you."

Jake looked like he'd been kicked by a horse. "For me? No, Leah. She's all wound up about Daisy. Like I was. And she's feeling lost, I guess. You know I'm not—"

"You should've seen the way she acted when I was there," I

said, cutting him off. Jake closed his mouth. "She was telling me to watch out with my shoes on your floor. *Your* floor, meaning both of you. Like she's right back in there again. Like she's your wife again."

Jake looked like he'd been slapped. "I don't know why she said that. I never knew the inner workings of her mind before, and I sure as hell don't know them now." He ran a hand down his face. "I don't know why she said that, Leah. She knows she's just staying in the basement."

My nostrils flared. I looked at him like he was nuts. "She's not just going to be in the basement, and you know it. She wasn't even in the basement when I was there, Jake." My face was hot, but my lips felt ice-cold. "Henry's stuff is in that spare room. What will she think when she sees that? My makeup is in the bathroom. What will she think when she sees *that*? Will she elbow it into the garbage can?"

"Leah—"

Jake was desperately trying to make eye contact with me, to connect at that deep level we both cherished. When I was reluctant to meet his gaze, he could only stare at the ground, light pink creeping up his neck.

My voice lowered as it wobbled. "My copy of Emily Dickinson's *Final Harvest* is on the nightstand. What will she think when she sees that?"

Jake put his forehead against mine. His voice was barely a whisper. "She won't be in that bedroom, Leah. I don't want anyone but you. You have my whole heart, and you know it."

I felt like crying. I brushed his cheek, then leaned in and kissed him. It was so cold out there. How was it summer but still so cold? "Does she know that we're moving in?"

"Of course. It was one of the first bloody things out of my mouth."

I nodded and kissed him again. Our hands were intertwined. "This is so weird. I don't know how we're all going to coexist.

Henry and I living upstairs. Ashley living in the basement." I let out a quiet laugh. "Sounds like a 1980s sitcom."

Things felt calmer, like a merry-go-round finally coming to a slow stop.

Jake gave me a tentative smile and rubbed my palm. "I know. It's complicated… Maybe the timing's not quite right." He cleared his throat. "Perhaps we need to pause the whole moving-in thing for a little while until things are less hectic at the house."

The second those words were out of his mouth, it felt like the hands of a clock came to a stop. The heartbeat in my head was back. It felt like a fist through my skull. I pulled my hands away slowly, angry. I couldn't camouflage the hurt in my eyes. "What did you say?"

Jake was wide-eyed again. He knew he'd fucked up. He instantly realized what those words had done to me. The weight of it made him eerily still. The man was terrified. His mouth was open, but he was afraid to repeat himself. "I think we should wait on that for a little bit."

I didn't feel myself standing up, but suddenly I was in the grass, my arms crossed, looking at everything but him. "I can't believe you said that."

Jake shook his hands as if he was trying to take back his statement. "Wait, wait—"

I put my hands on my head. "Oh, my God. I'm so stupid." I finally looked at him. "You *want* her there."

Jake bolted up and was inches away from me in a second. "No, no. That's not true. *Daisy* wants her there. I don't want anyone but you." He stepped closer. "I don't *love* anyone but you."

"That's what you say, but it's kind of hard to believe you when you want your ex-wife to move back in, but you don't want *me* to." My laugh wasn't happy. "You were Mr. Warp Speed with our relationship until she showed up."

"I don't want her there," whispered Jake. He looked past me toward the house. I didn't turn my head, but I knew what it meant. Our families were peeking out at our train wreck. "Daisy wants her there."

My eyes burned so hard that I felt the sting all over my face. Before long, I'd be crying. I had to escape before I cried. "But you're saying yes to her and no to me."

Jake grabbed my hands again. But he was at a loss for what to say. I let go and turned to walk back to the house. Nobody was at the windows. We must have scared them away.

Jake was at my heels. "Wait." He caught up to me and gently grabbed my hand again. "Where are you going?"

I shrugged, still trying not to cry. I could hardly get the words out. "I don't know. In to eat, I guess."

Jake knew I was about to cry. The realization and pain were all over his face. "We can't go in yet. We have to figure this out." He lowered his voice. "I don't feel like…we're in a good place…with this."

I let out another sad laugh. "You got that right. We're not in a good place." A tear finally slid down my cheek. *Damn it.* "We're not in *any* place…I don't think."

Jake's eyes turned glossy. His fingers nearly shook as they rubbed mine. "Don't say that, Leah. You're scaring me."

"I think you were right, you know?" I was doing a crappy job at fighting back tears. "I've never gone this fast with any guy."

Those amazing eyes were full of nothing but fear. "I didn't mean pausing the move-in forever. I just meant for a little while." His words caught. "Don't do this."

"And I think this was a sign." I tried to steady my breath. "I mean, if we were meant to be, something so stupid wouldn't break us this easily…"

Jake took me in his arms. He rested his forehead against mine again. It felt so wonderful, even when both of us were terrified. I wanted to stay like that, in the happiness that exists right before the tsunami. Before the tornado. In that small pocket of time when there was still a chance that the day could end up bright and beautiful instead.

"Don't say we're broken," he whispered. "I love you so much. Please forgive me." His voice cracked. "I'm an idiot. Don't do this."

I wanted to kiss him. I wanted to forget everything. But I couldn't shake the feeling of rejection. I knew a lot about rejection. When I felt it coming, I always did the rejecting first. Offense versus defense. To protect myself. To feel like I had control.

As we stood there embracing, I smelled the familiar woody scent of his cologne. I felt the texture of his shirt. I held him close, even though I knew I was letting him go. Because that's what I did. That's what I always did. He was letting Ash back in, and he didn't want me there. My heart screamed at me not to be rational about the situation. My heart screamed at me not to make up with him. My heart screamed at me to run. My heart was a jackass.

I pulled away from his touch and stood on unsteady legs. He watched me, hesitating. He looked so raw, like a tall but fragile houseplant wilted from exposure to the first frost of the year. There was still time to fix this, but I knew I wasn't going to. "The timing was always off."

Sadness washed over him. I was breaking his heart. It was happening right now. I could look at him and see it. My heart was a jackass.

"First, we were kids and everything was great," I said. "Then I had a crush on you, but you thought I was a little dweeb. And then I went to college, and you had a crush on *me*, but I decided to date a string of losers instead of letting myself be happy. And then came Lance…"

Jake stared at the ground like he couldn't believe this was happening. I couldn't believe it, either.

"And then after Lance, I was busy with Henry, and we were just friends again. And then, by the time I was ready to be interested in anyone, Ashley was already there." I cleared my throat to stop my voice from wobbling. "So the timing was never right. The only time the timing was right was when I was twenty, and you were twenty-four." My voice shook anyway, damn it. "You loved me then. It would have worked then. I *know* you loved me then."

Jake's eyes shot up. He stared right into me. I'd never seen him so hurt. He furrowed his brow. "I loved you then, did I? *Really*?" His voice rose as his features twisted with pain. He closed the gap between us again. "For your information, I loved you on that very first day." He pointed back at the maple tree. "I loved you when you were six, and we sat up in that tree together. You skinned your knee coming down from it, and we were both terrified of getting in trouble." Tears ran down my face. "So we snuck into the bathroom, and I cleaned it for you. And then you grabbed my hand. You took it like we'd been friends forever, and you brought me into the living room to meet Steven. He had applesauce all over his face." Jake wiped his eyes. I couldn't believe I was breaking his heart. "I was lost after leaving home, you know that? I needed a friend. You came up to me wanting to be that friend." Emotion rippled down his body. "And I loved you for it. I loved you that first day and didn't even know what love was. And I've loved you every day since then, in some way, shape, or form."

I held my arms open. "So love me now. There aren't a bunch of losers from Tinder in your way. Love me now." I wiped my eyes. "Tell her she can't stay. You said we had a good thing. So don't let her ruin our good thing."

Jake stared at me for a long moment. We didn't say anything

as the wind blew between us. It made me feel like we were miles apart.

Jake's voice cracked. "You didn't see the look in Daisy's eyes. She begged me to let Ash stay. A lot of kids wish they could have their mom back." He looked like a knife was twisting inside of him. "A lot of kids beg God in the middle of the night for one last glance. For one last word." His eyes met mine. "So if she wants her mother in the basement for a little while, how can I say no? I know what it's like to miss your mother."

I felt like I'd been punched. He was right. He knew what it was like to miss his mom. Of course, that's why he was doing all this. So what the hell was *I* doing? Was I being an asshole? Could be. There were a lot of former dates who'd probably agree. I looked into Jake's hurt eyes. I wanted to make him the bad guy, but I couldn't. Things had always been different with Jake. Maybe he was doing something nice, and I was punishing him for it. Or maybe he was unreasonable, and I was justified. Standing there on that cloudy summer evening, listening to our porch swing creak as it lazily swayed in the breeze, I realized that I had no idea who was in the right and who was in the wrong. Maybe neither of us was. Maybe *both* of us were. But it made my head pound trying to figure it out. And I was never good at figuring things out. I was only good at running away.

When I finally spoke, my voice was tired. "I understand why you're doing what you're doing. You're a good guy. You're doing a sweet thing for Daisy. You know how I feel about her."

Jake looked surprised by that. He tried to step closer to me, but I backed away.

"Leah. I love you."

"But I think you were right before." I closed my eyes to stop the tears. "I think we need to pause this whole thing…"

He reached his hand out to me, but I wouldn't take it. "That's not what I meant. I meant moving in. And only for a little while."

"It's like I said earlier. It's a sign, you know? That we shouldn't take that trip to Ireland together. A sign that we're just supposed to be friends."

Jake shook his head. "Don't say that."

"It's fine." My face felt taut. "This is the running gag, right? Leah's unlucky in love. Leah is bad at relationships. And here I go again."

I turned to leave, but Jake was right beside me. "Don't go." He finally grabbed my hand. "I love you so goddamn much. I don't want this to happen."

I was about to cry again. "Don't worry. Your heart won't be broken long. And after a while, you'll see. It's better this way."

I couldn't look him in the eyes for another second. So I turned and took unsure steps back to the house. My body shook the whole way. I knew he was still calling after me, but I didn't turn. Because if I looked back, I'd go back, and I couldn't go back. Because how long did happiness ever really last? A few weeks? A few months? And then something happened. Something always happened. Something stupid had already knocked us out. If we got back together, something else would come along. Something always came along. And usually, I *made* it come along.

I slid open the deck door and threw myself into the house. Mom, Dad, Craig, and Steven stood in the kitchen, staring. I walked toward them, scanning my surroundings. Obviously, they knew what was happening because Henry and Daisy were nowhere to be seen. They were probably in the basement watching a movie or joking about my childhood toys and photo albums in my old room.

Thank God.

I zoomed past my family, who watched my every move as they stood by the dip. I looked like I was trying to win first place in speed walking.

"Where are you going?" Mom asked, calling after me.

I sounded like a robot. "For a walk."

"When will you be back?" she asked, confused.

"I don't know!" I raised my voice. "I'm not hungry."

When I got to the front door, I heard the familiar whooshing of the deck door. Jake was in the house. He still wanted to talk to me. I think he even called my name.

But I rushed out into the driveway and down the road. And before long, I was already in town, speeding down the sidewalk. I didn't feel anything. I didn't think anything. I didn't see anything. I just kept walking.

I walked until I made it to the park. My legs tingled. I stood beneath a tree and looked over at a picnic table. It was like all the rest, but it wasn't. Because it was the one we always sat at with the kids. I wandered over and ran my hand along its top. Jake and Henry's names were etched on it somewhere. I could've cried about that.

I sat, my whole body restless and tired. I wondered if Jake was looking for me. He was probably trying to call me. What the hell was I going to do? I was in trouble. Breaking up with Handlebar Mustache was one thing. He lived hours away. All I had to do was delete his number. There wasn't a huge chance of seeing him again, except for the random grocery store sighting. But Jake was different. He was infused into every inch of this town. I couldn't walk down a street without thinking of a time when we walked down it together. And he was infused into every inch of me, too. He had been since I was six. I couldn't get him out, and I didn't *want* to.

What had I done? I broke up with the only man I ever loved…and I wasn't exactly sure why. Was it because he wanted Ash there but not me?

Yes. That hurt.

But did I really think he was going to start something with her again?

Of course not.

So why did I do it? I broke his heart. And I broke mine, too. And it seemed so stupidly pointless.

You don't have to ask yourself why. You know why.

Because nothing good lasted. Because everyone always left. And if they didn't leave, then *I* did before they could. Breaking up with Jake was terrible, but it was better than him breaking up with me five years down the line. Ten years down the line. Because that was probably inevitable. How couldn't it be? After all, I couldn't imagine being in a relationship that long. I never *had* been. Maybe I never could be. Maybe some people weren't built that way.

I wiped my tears away. My face felt sore, the way it did in January when the harsh Minnesota wind whipped against it. I wondered how I got so messed up inside. I wondered why I was so bad at relationships. I wondered why I didn't think I deserved to be happy.

I sighed and shook my head. What the hell had I done? I just made a huge mistake. And I had no intention of fixing it.

20

W hat in the hell had I done? I blew the whole thing up. I watched it collapse underneath me, like I was standing on an ancient bridge. I had hurt the woman I'd loved my whole life. She thought I didn't love her. She thought I didn't care.

Fecking dickhead.

Why the fuck had I told her not to move in? Why had I told her *not* to do the thing that we both wanted so badly? I wanted it to be *our* home. So why had I told her to wait?

Because you're easily wound up, you stupid son of a bitch.

When I saw her disappear into the house, my body went rigid. I thought back to the night I sat in bed, wondering if I should tell Leah how I felt. I prayed to God that it wouldn't get fucked. Well, this was a self-fulfilling prophecy if I'd ever seen one. What a cock-up.

I had to make it right somehow. I needed to tell Ash she couldn't stay.

I frantically walked through the yard, up the deck, and into the house. I heard Gail's voice calling after Leah. I heard Leah shout back, but then the front door slammed, and she was gone.

Dad, Gail, Dennis, and Steven stared at me.

"Son of a bitch!" I lifted my arms in exasperation. I walked in a tight circle as I pulled at my hair. "Fuck! Shit, shit, shit." I stopped mid-freakout. "Where are the kids?"

"You're grand," said Dad. "They're downstairs eating spaghetti and watching *The Mighty Ducks*."

I still paced the room, effin' and blindin' like a mad person. After a moment, I felt a tap on my shoulder.

Gail held out a cow knick-knack. "You look like you need something to throw."

I shook my head. "I wouldn't want to wreck it."

But she insisted. "It's just from the thrift store. I have another one upstairs. Why don't you smash it against the wall?" She lifted an eyebrow. "You might feel better."

Anything was worth a shot. I took the cow, squeezed it tight, and launched it against the living room wall. Chunky shards and bits ricocheted across the floor.

"Any better?" asked Gail.

I let the weight of everything sink into me. "A little. But I feel guilty about the mess. Do you have a broom?"

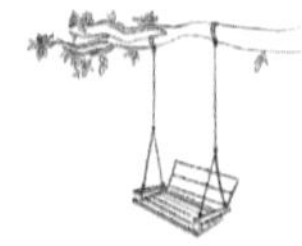

As I swept up the broken cow, our families pressed me for information.

"What happened out there, son?" asked Dad.

"I fucked it all up." I swept up the poor cow's head. "Just the way you all thought I would."

Gail patted my back. "We weren't picking on you specifically, Jake."

"Yeah, we always figured wrecking your relationship would be a joint effort between you both," said Dennis. He took out his wallet and grabbed a hundred-dollar bill. He motioned to Steven. "I guess this is yours."

"That's very nice." I stared at Steven. He had been quiet thus far. And he wasn't sporting his usual devil-may-care countenance. "You bet on whether we'd break up? At least someone's happy."

"I'm not happy," said Steven. He frowned as he shoved the money into his back pocket. "You two have loved each other forever. If you can't make it work, where's the hope for the rest of us?"

We looked at each other, and I gave him a slight nod. He nodded back. I continued sweeping.

"Out of curiosity, how *did* you destroy your happiness?" asked Steven. "Leah looked like she was trying to grind her teeth into powder."

I threw the cow away and stood the broom against the wall. "Ash showed up this afternoon. She broke up with Kenneth. He spent all her money. And she has nowhere to live." The group gobbled up that information with fervor. "So Daisy begged me to let Ash stay in the basement until she's on her feet again. Somewhere between her big eyes and broken shoulder, I agreed."

They exchanged glances.

Steven raised an eyebrow. "That'll do it."

"Are you out of your goddamn mind?" asked Dad.

I put on a humorless smile. "Apparently, I am, yes."

Mumbling and head shaking. There was complete consensus that I was an idiot. Wonderful.

"And then you know how I get," I said. "Tied in knots. Bent out of shape. If I've had too much caffeine, I get overwhelmed choosing an appetizer, for fuck's sake. So then I *really* cocked it up by telling Leah that we should wait on moving in together."

Gail poured herself a glass of wine. "There aren't too many women who want their boyfriends to live with their ex-wives."

"That's fully evident to me now." I rubbed my eyes. "The last half hour has driven that point home. Thanks."

Dad was still aghast. "Why the *hell* did you say yes to Ash?"

"I thought Daisy needed her mother. I was trying to do a nice thing. I don't know. I'm a fool, I guess."

"You've got everything all mixed up with your own childhood." Dad's quiet words made me feel formless, like I might run down the drain. Tension weaved into my forehead. I didn't want to talk about this, but he knew why I thought the way I did. "Ash isn't dead, Jake. This isn't your childhood all over again. A lot of parents get divorced. It's a sad time. It's not easy for kids. But you and Ash were doing everything right until now. Ash and Daisy see each other all the time. If I'd given *you* everything you begged for when you were nine, our house would've had an old McDonald's ball pit, a waterslide, and five Ataris." He lowered his voice. His words drilled into me. "It isn't appropriate for Ashley to be there, son."

His words sank in like a wood stain. He was right, of course. What was I supposed to do now? Why did everything important always crumble?

I sat at the kitchen island and placed my hands on my head. I had to make things right. I'd loved Leah for as long as I could remember. This couldn't be how it ended. Our relationship couldn't be torn up like so many bits of paper over something so stupid.

I took my phone from my pocket and set it on the island.

Gail reached out her hand. Dennis put a hand on top of hers. Dad put a hand on top of Dennis's. Then Steven put a hand on top of Dad's. Then they nodded and pulled their hands away. They acted like it was the most natural thing in the world, like a huddle in a locker room.

I stared them down. "What the hell was that about?"

"We're the Three Musketeers," said Dad. "It's accurate and

everything. In a literary sense, I mean." I continued staring. "There were four of them, you know. Steven's D'Artagnan."

"It means we're going to help you, Jake," said Gail.

"How are you going to help?" I asked, flustered. "This is sort of a personal thing, isn't it? I've got to show her that I love her. That I don't love anyone else. That I'll put her first. How are you going to help with that?"

"We could write some background music for your love speech," said Steven. I blinked. "Don't look at me like that. I'm just bouncing ideas off you."

"We gotta do *something*," said Dennis. "If you two can't figure things out, what the hell will happen with the café? We've been friends forever." He turned frantic. "Will we have to choose sides?"

Gail patted her husband's hand. "It's not junior high, honey. You don't have to worry that Craig isn't going to like you anymore."

Dennis looked relieved. He and Dad exchanged smiles.

"First things first," said Dad. "Should he go find her and apologize or let her cool down?"

The Roths huddled, thinking.

"She needs to cool down," said Steven, finally. "She was acting like that time I broke the Nintendo. Like she's going to fuck you up bigger than Dracula in *Castlevania 3*."

I let out an anxious breath. "What should I do, then? I want to give her space if she needs it. I don't want to come on too strong."

Gail pointed at my phone. "You could call her. That would show you're thinking about her but not getting in her face." She looked at the others. "That seems alright, doesn't it?"

"Call. Don't text," said Dennis. "Whenever I'm mad at someone, and they text me, I never respond."

Steven glanced at Dennis. "You never answer my texts. Does that mean you're always mad at me?"

Dennis lowered his voice. "We'll talk about it later."

I fiddled with my phone. "You think this is a good idea?"

The Roths nodded. I breathed in and called Leah. Each ring of the phone was like an arrow to my brain. Leah always answered right away. I was fucked. The whole thing was totally fucked. After a moment, it went to voicemail. I set the phone down. "Son of a bitch."

"Now you can't call back because you'd look like a psycho," said Steven.

"Or needy," said Dad.

"I got that." I ran a hand down my face, overwhelmed. "I'm aware of the situation."

"We're *not* selling the restaurant," said Dennis. "We're *not* going to stop Daisy and Henry from playing together."

"Calm down, Dennis," said Gail. "And don't worry, Jake. She'll call back. Just give it time."

Steven made a noise that sounded a lot like, *Fat chance*.

For fifteen painful minutes, we experimented with flavors by pairing the pickle dip with the espressos Gail made. It was not good. I contemplated getting plastered but decided a clear head was a wiser choice. Dennis offered me leftover spaghetti, but my stomach wasn't interested.

Finally, after inhaling my second espresso, my phone rang. I stared. "It's Leah." My eyes widened. "I can't believe she's calling me back. Thank fuck."

"See?" asked Gail. "It's going to be fine. You both needed to cool down, that's all."

I nodded and took the phone to the living room. I sat down in their puffy recliner and answered. "Hi, Leah." I tried to keep my voice upbeat, but not too upbeat. I didn't want to sound happy or anything. I didn't want to sound like I was enjoying myself. Because I was *definitely* not enjoying myself. And I was obsessing over how I sounded on the phone.

Her voice was quiet. Tired. Sad. That gutted me. But she

didn't sound mad. "Hi." She paused. "Sorry that it took so long to call back. I had to find my phone."

I swallowed. "That's fine. No worries."

"What are the kids doing?" Concern laced her words. She didn't want the kids to know what was going on. I didn't want that, either.

"They're downstairs watching a movie. They're blissfully ignorant so far."

There was another pause. Why did those pauses scare me so much?

"That's good." It felt so weird trying to analyze her on the phone. I'd known Leah forever, so I'd seen all her moods, and she'd seen all of mine. We were best friends, but that didn't mean we never annoyed each other. But we always quickly laughed it off. Elbowed one another. Teased each other back into good moods. But acting that way now would make me look like I was disregarding her feelings. Not knowing what to do scared me.

"Listen, Leah. I am *so* sorry about earlier. Everything got all mixed up. I want you and Henry to move in. I've never wanted anything more." I talked at warp speed. "When I go home later, I'll tell Ash she can't stay—"

"No." Her voice was soft, like she was trying to console me. "Don't do that."

Now I was confused. "Why?"

"It's good for Daisy. If I were a kid and my shoulder was broken, I'd want my mom."

I wasn't sure how to answer. Where did we stand? "Are you coming back for supper?" I had never been more nervous about a question in my life.

"I…" There was hesitance in her voice. "I'll come back later to pick up Henry and get my car."

Life drained from my face. No harsh words had been exchanged. Nothing strong had been said. But I didn't feel any connection to her on the other end.

I tried to keep the worry out of my voice. "I'm so sorry about everything. Mo ghrá, you have to believe me. I'm an idiot, but I didn't mean any of it."

Her voice caught on the other end. Was she crying? "It's okay." And then I could tell. She *was* crying. I made her cry. Oh, God. I was the world's biggest prick. "I'll see you tomorrow, alright? Are you still coming to the store at noon, like always?"

"Of course, I will." I was so confused. She wanted me to stop by, but that fact didn't seem like a cause for celebration.

"Okay. See you then."

And before I could say anything else, she was gone. I sat there, cold. It felt like someone got out bricks and mortar and went to work building a wall between us. And it was all my fault. I didn't have anyone else to blame.

I wandered back to the kitchen. Everyone watched me, trying to guess how things were based on my body language.

Dennis shook his head. "We're still having our joint Christmas party. I don't care what anyone says!"

Steven stared. "That good, huh?"

I hesitated. "I don't know what to think."

"What did she say?" asked Gail.

"She said she'd see me tomorrow," I said.

"That's not so bad," said Dad. He gave me a firm pat. "A little more time to cool down. So why do you look like you fell in quicksand?"

"I said I was going to tell Ash she couldn't stay, but Leah told me not to." I furrowed my brow. "She told me that Ash should be there for Daisy."

The four of them looked at each other, then at me.

"I don't know what that means," I said.

Steven plunged a cracker into the pickle dip. "It means you're screwed."

When Daisy and I got home, the cookies were on the counter, waiting for us. Like Leah and Henry would be over any minute to watch a movie. I opened the container. They were half chocolate and half peanut butter. I bit into one. They were fecking good. Henry made them with me in mind.

Before the night was over, I was going to throw up.

I passed Daisy a cookie. She took it with her good arm. "Yum."

"Good, aren't they?" I felt like knocking my head against the counter. Or against the floor that Ashley had gone on about.

"How come everyone was so weird at supper?" asked Daisy. "We, like, didn't even have supper like normal."

"Sometimes people aren't feeling so good," I said.

Like me. Right now.

"When are Leah and Henry coming over?"

I didn't want to face this. Leah and Henry were over so often that it was weird when they *weren't*. And just like Leah said, their stuff was everywhere. I stared at a package of dark chocolates that Leah opened the day before. She liked them. So did I. "They're not coming tonight, sweetie."

Daisy stared like I was nuts. "Why not?"

I didn't feel like telling the truth.

Perhaps by this time tomorrow, everything will *be fine.*

Maybe I wouldn't have to sit with Daisy and tell her that Leah and I were broken up.

The words, '*broken up*' seared into me like a cattle brand.

"They're not coming over at all?" asked Daisy.

"Not tonight." I grabbed another cookie. I was going to eat them all.

Daisy looked deflated. "That sucks."

I handed her another cookie. "I know."

She took a few bites, thinking. "Can I go downstairs and see Mom, then?"

I nodded. "Just knock first."

Daisy disappeared downstairs.

I grabbed the cookies and slouched at the table. My whole body felt numb as I absentmindedly ate. "It's going to be a long fecking night."

Most of the night was spent staring at the ceiling, with my hand outstretched, touching the spot where Leah always slept. My forehead was covered in sweat. I tried not to think. I tried not to worry. I was terrible at both.

The next morning at the restaurant, Dad and Dennis seemed as nervous as me. It didn't do much for my confidence.

"What did she say last night?" I asked Dennis.

Dennis shrugged. "Not much. She just grabbed Henry, and they got in the car."

I rubbed my sweaty palms together. "She must've said *something*. She didn't do all that in complete silence."

"When Henry was out of earshot, Gail talked you up. Said you were sorry. All that. And Leah said a lot of *I knows,* and *You're rights.*"

What did that mean? "How was her mood?"

Dennis's throat bobbed. "She seemed sad, Jake."

I was a prick. I paced the restaurant. "Son of a bitch."

"At least the kids are back in school," said Dad. "So they can't see this."

Dennis motioned to us. "Now, remember…we're still having our joint Christmas. You all agreed last night. You can't take it back. Who else would eat my pimento cheese dip?"

It was amazing what the body could do, even when you were nothing but a cesspool of nerves. Somehow, the morning passed. I smiled at customers. I made small talk. I cooked meatloaf. And then, at noon, I got coffee and headed over to the furniture store, my body shaking the whole walk there. Steven and Gail hovered by the end tables near the entrance.

I handed Steven his coffee. "Sorry, Gail. You can have mine."

Gail shook her head. "You know that I don't like to be caffeinated. My family's caffeinated enough for me."

Leah was nowhere to be seen. Was that a bad thing? My leg twitched. I kept my voice low. "How is she this morning?"

"She's been pretty quiet," Gail whispered. It felt like we were in a museum. Usually, A-to-Z Furniture was alive with chatter. Was it too late to pass out?

"She hasn't even fought with me about anything," whispered Steven. "And it's not for lack of trying, either. I told her Hozier wasn't good. And I *love* Hozier. I was just trying to piss her off." He shrugged. "But she wouldn't get pissed off."

"Shit," I said.

Gail pointed. "She's in the break room."

We exchanged glances. Gail gave me a reassuring smile, and Steven flashed me a sad glance that said *good luck, sucker.*

I nodded and walked through the store, past the service desk, and through to the break room. My body felt like it was shorting out. When I saw Leah standing by the toaster, my heart pounded faster. She wore a lacy burgundy shirt and dark pants. Lovely. Her back was to me, but when she heard me, she turned and gave me the faintest smile. Adrenaline surged. And happiness too, despite the doubt. Even in all that uncertainty, there wasn't any place I'd rather be than standing right there with her.

My eyes drifted to her neck. The gold locket still rested

against her shirt, like it did every day. She only took it off when she went to bed. The fact that she still wore it gave me a little hope.

"Hi," she said quietly.

It felt like my heart was going to press right out of my chest. I awkwardly placed her coffee on the table and gave her a small, stupid wave. "Hi."

She seemed at a loss for what to say. So was I.

Why didn't you plan something? What the hell is wrong with you?

After a moment, she pointed at the toaster. "I burnt my bagel again."

I ventured a smile. "Damn thing. You'd think the people in charge would wise up and buy another toaster."

Her smile widened. "I can lodge a complaint against Steven. He's the one that got it."

Optimism trickled into my chest. This felt like us again. Talking about stupid stuff. Making each other smile. Maybe everything would be all right.

"Definitely do that," I said. "Remember when Steven said you stole all the toilet paper from the employee bathroom? This will just be getting him back."

Leah smirked. "I actually did that. I was trying to tick him off. Sometimes he goes to the bathroom for forty-five minutes when he doesn't want to deal with a customer."

I let out a small laugh, but after a moment, everything deflated into an awkward silence. Leah's smile morphed into glistening eyes and a frown. She looked like she was going to cry. I took a step toward her but stopped. Did she want me to do that?

She bit her lip and looked into my eyes. "Can I hug you?"

Her voice was quiet and uncertain. Her question about knocked me down. She acted like there was a chance I wouldn't want to hold her. Holding her was all I wanted for the last twenty-four hours.

"You can definitely hug me," I said, stepping forward. Then things happened fast. We met in the middle of the room, burrowing into one another like we were afraid some outside force might pull us apart. I wrapped my arms around her. She rested her head against my chest. This was where I wanted to be. Just like this. Forever.

I loved everything about her. Her intelligence. Her humor. Her kindness. The smell of her. The feel of her. I never wanted to stop holding her.

After a moment, I could tell she was crying. I kissed the top of her head. "I'm so sorry." My voice was a whisper. "I love you, Leah. I'm so sorry I hurt you, mo fhíorghrá. I'm such a dick."

"You're not a dick," she said, still resting her head against my chest. "You're sweet. You're good to Daisy. That's one of the things I love most about you."

I ran my hand through her hair. She looked up at me.

"I love you so goddamn much it's crazy," I said.

"I love you, too."

I wanted to kiss her so badly, but I didn't want to push it. "And I need you to know I want you and Henry to move in. I need you to know that." I swallowed back tears. "You know that, right?"

She rested her head back on my chest. "I think so."

I rubbed her back. "If you need convincing, I'm totally willing to do that." I gave her a gentle squeeze. "We can get your things and have you moved in tomorrow."

She ran her hand along the side of my face. I took it and kissed it.

"And I'm going to tell Ashley that she can't stay. That whole idea was insane. I'm so sorry about that." I searched her eyes. "I must have lost my mind temporarily. Like back when I thought my Guitar Hero skills would somehow translate to playing the *actual* guitar. They did *not*."

Leah stepped back and leaned against the cupboard. I stood next to her, wondering what she was thinking.

"Don't tell Ash to move out," she finally said. "It's good that Daisy has Ashley when her shoulder's broken. You would have wanted *your* mom there."

I sighed. "I know. But I have to stop projecting onto Daisy. She's not me. Ashley doesn't need to live there."

"You were together for a long time," said Leah, quietly. "It's nice of you to help her."

Leah looked like she wanted to say something more about it but swallowed the comment. This wasn't going the way I thought it would when we hugged. It felt like we were teetering on one leg.

Leah had her elbows behind her, resting on the counter. Her hands hung out. I placed a hand on hers. She didn't pull away. Instead, she gave me a sad smile.

"You know that I love you, don't you?" I asked.

She looked into my eyes and nodded. My heart started beating a little faster again.

"You need to know that you're the only woman I love. Ashley…didn't love me. She told me that. But I wasn't innocent in that marriage, you know. I'm not a perfect person by anyone's standards. It's not as if I pined for Ashley while she was uninterested in me. We had good times, but it wasn't what either of us wanted." I squeezed her hand. "You're the woman I want to be with, Leah. You're the one I love."

Her grip on my hand tightened. She tried to keep her voice steady. "It's always been you, too." Her eyes met mine. "You're the one I love."

Her words should have made me happy. After all, we both sounded like we had back when we were on her sofa with that terrible movie in the background. But even though our words were the same, the feeling wasn't. It didn't feel like we were back on track. It didn't feel like we were together.

I rubbed my thumb against the back of her hand. My voice was hoarse. "I say that I love you. And you say that you love me. But the expression on your face is scaring the shit out of me."

She took a deep breath and let go of my hand. "I'm not sure we should date. Maybe we should just be friends."

Everything in the world stopped. There was no hum from the fridge. No noise from Gail and Steven out on the floor. No hum from the air conditioner. The only thing that moved was my heart. It rattled like a loose bike chain. It felt like we were going to be stuck in that terrible moment forever.

"We both love each other," I said quietly. "And our relationship started at a hundred miles an hour. When you care about someone for so long and are so invested, it's probably not surprising that blips come up." She wouldn't look me in the eyes. "My parents loved each other, but they weren't perfect. They argued sometimes, mostly about stupid stuff. We've both seen your parents argue. I know I messed up, but—"

"You're not the problem," said Leah, cutting me off. "*I'm* the problem. I'm *always* the problem." She stared down at herself. "Look at me. I broke your heart yesterday, Jake." Her eyes flew up to mine. "And *you're* the one apologizing."

I stared at her for a long moment. "I don't think that's how it went. I was an idiot, and you called me out on it."

Her face twisted. "No. I broke your goddamn heart. I saw it in your eyes. After only a few months together. I punished you for doing something nice." Tears were in her eyes again. "What does that say about me? What kind of person am I? Who would want to be in a relationship with someone like that?"

I stepped closer to her. "I do. I love every last little bit of you. There's nothing wrong with you in my eyes."

She wiped her face. "Then maybe you need new eyes." That

was like a knife going into me. "You're sweet. Even when I don't deserve it." She frowned. "I'm sorry that I hurt you yesterday."

I didn't know what to do with my hands. "I forgive you, Leah. I don't think there's anything to forgive. But I forgive you."

She was quiet, staring at the ceiling. "If we stayed together, this is how it would be, you know? It would be just like this. This terrible conversation in this fluorescent room. Every few months, I'd lose it over something, and you'd apologize and say you love me." She looked at me with watery eyes. "And I'd apologize and say I love you. How long could that last? A few years? How long would it take you to think, *This isn't worth it?*"

I leaned in toward her. "I'd never think you're not worth it. And that's not what our future looks like. It's just because our emotions are amped up."

Leah shook her head. "I don't know about that. Look at your longest relationship. *Ten* years. Now look at me. One year with one guy. A year and a half with another. Doesn't that make you a little nervous?" She rubbed her eyes. "Even when I'm with the love of my life, I'm looking for a way to escape so I can't get hurt. I break my heart a little bit now, so it won't *really* get broken later."

I took her in my arms. She rested against me again. "I won't break your heart, Leah. I promise. I messed up yesterday, but I promise I'll never make you cry again. Only happy tears."

She looked up at me. "And what about me? Am I only going to make you cry happy tears from now on?"

Her question startled me. "You've been my best friend since I was ten, and you haven't hurt me so far."

She gave me a sad smile. "Liar."

We stood staring at each other. I didn't know what to say or do. We still loved each other, but I knew she was pulling away. I couldn't keep trying to convince her. I couldn't prod her like that.

"What do you want to do, Leah?" My body stiffened. "I don't want to push you. But…do you truly want to break up?" I was so fecking nervous. "It doesn't feel right to me. We've loved each other forever. Does it feel right to you?"

"It doesn't feel right at all." She crossed her arms. "I make terrible decisions all the time. That's who I am. I dated Lance off and on for a year. I dated Handlebar Mustache for four months. I spent most of elementary school wearing cargo pants paired with plaid shirts. Thanks, early 1990s. I'm nothing but bad decisions. But us breaking up is a good decision for *you*. Because you deserve someone better at love, Jake." She tugged at my shirt. "You're my best friend, and I want you to be happy. *Really* happy. You deserve someone who's not afraid of what will happen two years or ten years down the line. And that's just not me." Her voice wobbled. "I sabotage everything."

Air was caught in my chest. My eyes burned.

Her voice was hushed. "We need to break up… Maybe not forever, but I need time to think."

The world spun madly around me. The blood drained from my face, but I took a breath and rested my shaking hands on her arms. "If you want to break up…then that's what we'll do. If you want time and space to think, then that's what I'll give you. Because I love you. And because you're my best friend." I couldn't hide the pain in my voice. "But if you think I'm going to walk out that door and find someone else to love, then you don't know me as well as you think."

Silent tears trickled down her cheeks. My face was so raw that it was starting to lose feeling. Leah didn't say anything as I took her hand. I studied every freckle on it like I'd never hold it again. My stomach turned when I realized perhaps I wouldn't. Then I gave her fingers a little squeeze and looked her in the eyes. They were big, dark, and wonderful, but full of tears. I couldn't look at them anymore. I couldn't stand there anymore. So I gave those eyes one last glance and let go of her hand.

Before I even realized it, I was out of the room. Before I realized it, I was out of the store. I wasn't even sure if I'd seen Steven and Gail on my way out. All I saw was the warm sun in the sky. It was warm on the day my mother died, too. All my worst days were sunny. Luminous, cheerful, and bright, with puffy white clouds that drifted across the horizon to the tune of my heart breaking.

21

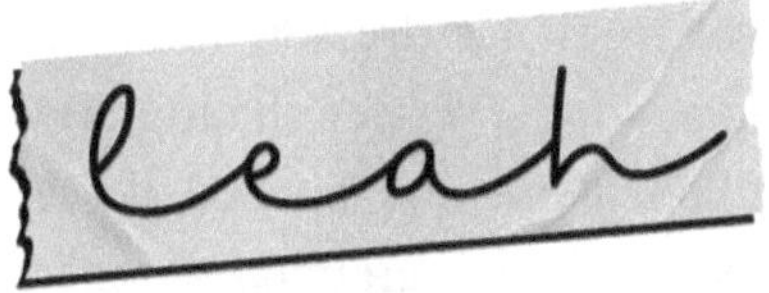

FALL

I didn't go to work the next day. I felt like I had the flu. That's what I told Henry, too. But it was just my life. Just me. I felt like puking up all my stupid decisions.

Breaking up with Jake wasn't stupid. You'd break his heart again eventually. He's better off with someone else.

I wrapped myself in my comforter. "Shut up, stupid mind."

I scooted out of bed with the blanket still bundled around me. I glanced in my dresser mirror. I looked like something that crawled out of a garbage disposal. My eyes drifted to something shimmering on my chest. My necklace.

But it's not your necklace anymore.

I had to give it back. The thought made my insides feel like mush. I unclasped it from my neck and held it with sweaty fingers. I opened the locket, and here we were. I frowned at our childhood picture, running my finger across our faces.

Why was I always afraid to take chances? Why was I afraid to take a chance on love?

I grumbled and closed the locket. I set it on the dresser and walked away. When I reached my bedroom door, I stopped. I looked back at my dresser, then walked up to it again. I reached for the necklace, but then I stopped. "Stop being a jackass."

I walked away from the necklace. But after about ten steps, I turned around, grabbed it off the dresser, and put it back on. "Shut up, Leah."

I didn't move from my dresser, thinking about something else that was engraved. I slid open the top drawer and stared at a small box. I pulled it out and opened it. My dad gave me a watch that belonged to my grandpa a long time ago. Steven wasn't interested in it. He was more interested in Grandpa's pipe. So I took it, not knowing what I'd ever do with it. But after Jake gave me his mom's old locket, I took that watch and had it engraved. I was waiting for the perfect time to give it to him.

Perfect time. That's funny.

I spun the watch around in my fingers. *Jake and Leah.*

I let out a bitter laugh, put the watch back in its box, and shoved the drawer shut.

"Fuck you, Leah."

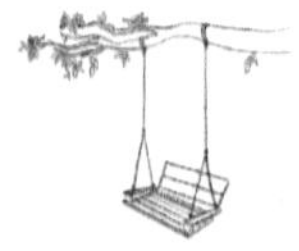

My mom took Henry to school. When the house was quiet and empty, I sat on the sofa in a huff. This was stupid. What was I going to do—eat ice cream and cry to a romantic comedy?

Karma jumped up next to me. I petted her. "Kind of stupid to sit here heartbroken when I did the breaking, isn't it?"

Karma looked at me and meowed.

"You're right. He broke my heart first. He wanted Ash there, but not me. Sure, when he cooled down, he thought it was a stupid idea, but in the heat of the moment, that was his plan." I gestured to Karma. "Don't you think what people do in the heat of the moment is how they really feel about things?"

Karma curled up on the sofa, ignoring me.

I acted like she had a valid point. "That's true. I've gotten bangs twice in my life based on spur-of-the-moment decisions. I blame Monica for the second time. And I guarantee you that, deep down, I *don't* want bangs. So he probably doesn't want Ash to be there, does he?"

Karma stared at me.

"You could be sitting on my lap because you love me, Karma." I scratched her ears. "You would've liked Purrito. She's a sweet girl, too."

I was jolted out of my thoughts by the sound of trucks outside and loud banging on the door. I looked at the clock. Nine in the morning. Was that too early to be robbed? No. That was Kenneth's favorite time.

I thought about hiding on the floor like Jake said. I should've been doing that for years. But instead, I slowly walked to the door, the blanket still wrapped around me.

I peeked through the shade. A stocky guy with a paint-splattered T-shirt stood there.

Oh, shit!

I opened the door and tried to smile, but my face resisted.

"Good morning, Miss Roth… Are you alright?"

I tried to sound light. "Hi, Greg… Feeling a little under the weather. I forgot you were starting today."

"Say no more. My wife gets terrible allergies this time of year." He pointed behind him to four pickups. Tanned, muscled guys got out of them and started milling around. Before Jake, I might have taken a longer look at those guys, but now they were just background noise. *Muscled,* glistening, and perfectly tan background noise. "We're about ready to go. We're siding your house first. It'll take a couple of days. Not too long."

"Sounds good."

"After that, we'll start shingling."

The blanket covering me probably made me look like my old college toga party days. "Thanks."

Greg scratched the side of his head with a pencil. "I feel bad that you're sick. It might get loud later if you're trying to sleep."

"Don't worry." *That's right, Leah. Smile. Pretend everything isn't shit.* "I can sleep through anything."

He nodded and walked to his pickup. I waved at the workers, then retreated into my house. I opened the fridge and looked around, taking out a container of cottage cheese. Cottage cheese in the morning? Nope. I rummaged through the cereal. Nope. I twiddled my fingers while I stared at the bread.

I grabbed it. "Shut up!" I took peanut butter out of the cupboard and snatched jelly out of the fridge. I spread peanut butter on the bread. "Yes, I know. I'm sure people would have a lot to say about this. I'm pathetic." I kept yelling to nobody in the kitchen. "Let me eat my stupid PB&J in peace!"

My sandwich and I headed back to the sofa and my cat. I took two bites when the workers began ripping off the siding. Then there were tearing noises, thumping, and the constant *pow* of an electric nail gun.

I scowled and took another bite. "We're all set, Karma. We can live here for another fifty years."

Karma looked at me and meowed.

"Believe me, I know."

My mom stopped by around two. She walked in like she was tripping over something.

I was still on the sofa with the blanket. Netflix droned on in the background.

"Aren't you hot?" she asked.

"Probably."

My mom pointed at the front door. "There's a man out there who looks just like Dave Bautista. I know your heart is broken and everything. And I love my husband very much. But I thought I'd let that be known." She took a breath. "It's striking."

I wasn't expecting her until she dropped off Henry. I sat up. "Is everything alright?"

Mom sat down next to me. She gave me a casual smile. Mom was never ruffled about anything. "You know it's not alright, honey. It's blown to hell. But nothing's any different than yesterday." She put a paper takeout bag from B&R Café on the coffee table. "I brought you soup. That's what people need when they're sick. It's tomato basil."

I stared at the bag. "Thanks. But you know I'm not sick."

She gave me her patented look. "Duh, honey."

I frowned at the bag. "You went to the restaurant?"

"Where else would I go? It's your favorite place. And there's that little detail of us owning it."

"Was Jake there?"

My mom couldn't raise her eyebrow any higher. "Yes. Like always."

"Did he go to the furniture store today? Did you tell him I was sick?"

My mom leaned back on the sofa and put her ankle boots on the coffee table. "He didn't come to the furniture store. You told him you wanted space, didn't you? You're old enough to know that when you tell a guy crap like that, they take it literally. Like when you rush out of somewhere, wanting them to follow… They *never* do. They think you don't want them to." She shrugged. "They're stupid that way."

"It's a good thing you're not a doctor." I was monotone. "Your bedside manner is terrible."

"And he thinks you're sick because that's when you always get tomato basil soup. Plus, I told him."

Heat engulfed my face. "What did he say?"

Mom rested her head against the cushion. "He said that he hopes you feel better soon."

My eyes felt watery, so I played with my blanket to stop myself from crying.

"Oh, and he said he'd pick up Henry after school when he goes to get Daisy."

Adrenaline rushed through my body. I sat as stiff as a taxidermied animal. "What?"

"Henry and Daisy are still friends, you know. They should be able to play and hang out together."

My posture softened. "I know. I want them to be friends. That's not what I was freaking out about. It's just, if Jake drops Henry off, then—"

Mom gave me a sad smile. "It's okay, honey. He said he wouldn't come in."

I nodded. Tears were right behind my eyes, and I was the one who put them there—the idea. Jake was dropping off Henry but not coming in. I was responsible for that. Jake would never *not* come in. But I didn't want him to come in.

Yes, I did.

Fuck. I *was* a jackass.

"I know it wasn't the best idea for him to ask Ashley to stay," said Mom. "And I know it hurt you that he didn't want you to move in yet. But do you really think he said those things, meaning to hurt you, honey?" She rested her face in her hand. What was she, my therapist? "Do you think that was his intention?"

I balled the blanket up in my hands. Damn. I wanted to break something. I wanted to yell. Maybe at her for being right, but probably at myself for never giving an inch.

"Are you going to give him another chance? He's a good

guy, Leah." She nudged me. "But I don't have to tell you that. There's a reason he's your best friend."

Was she trying to make me cry? Because she was getting there. "I don't think it's a good idea. You know how bad at relationships I am. You guys have been telling me for years."

Mom reached over and rubbed my back. "That's just a running family joke. Like me not getting uppity about anything. Or your dad's bad dips. Or whatever the hell Steven's deal is."

I wanted to laugh but couldn't. "I don't know… I think I'd wreck everything again someday."

Mom didn't respond to that. She stared at the takeout bag. "Better eat your soup before it gets cold."

"Pretty stupid of me to sit here wallowing over a guy, isn't it? Does this mean I'm a terrible representative for womankind?"

She shrugged. "I don't have the handbook in front of me at the moment, honey. But I don't think womankind would want you to beat yourself up about everything all the time. Or constantly look for ways to make yourself unhappy."

That thought settled in my gut like a bowling ball. I placed the takeout bag on my lap. I wondered when I'd go to the café again. I wondered when I'd see Jake again. I wondered if we weren't talking to each other. I wondered if we'd hardly ever text or talk to each other again. I wondered if everything was over.

My eyes hurt. "Thanks for the soup."

How could I ever stay friends with Jake, knowing he wanted more? How could I stay friends with Jake, knowing *I* wanted more? It wouldn't be like it was when we were just friends. It could never be that way again. Now it would be like I was leading him on. I *would* be leading him on. How the hell could I do that? That would be like torturing him. And I'd be torturing myself, too.

I opened the lid of the soup and looked in the bag. Jake always gave me extra crackers. He didn't do that for anyone else.

"I think I just ruined our friendship."

I didn't know what to do when Jake arrived with Henry. The construction workers were still outside, hard at it. I peeked through the blinds like Jimmy Stewart in *Rear Window*. One of the workers walked up to Jake's window. He leaned down, and they talked for a few minutes. Henry stayed in the car, too, saying something. I prayed I couldn't be seen, but what was I worried about? They weren't looking in my direction at all. Plus, who said I couldn't look out my damn window?

I heard faint laughter, and then the worker walked away. Jake was always good at striking up conversations with strangers. The thought of him so close made my legs wobble. I could go to his window and tell him I wanted him back. Everything would be forgiven. We could be like a family again. That's the kind of guy Jake was.

My feet tingled. I knew I wasn't going anywhere. I was too much of a coward.

Henry got out of the vehicle, but he hesitated, talking to Jake. Daisy leaned forward in the backseat. Finally, Henry nodded, waved, and walked toward the front door.

I threw myself back onto the sofa. I held the blanket close and leaned against the armrest. I tried to look like crap. It wasn't hard.

Henry walked in, staring at me. He let his backpack drop to the floor.

"How was school?"

Henry did that *thing* with his eyes. He looked just like Mom and Steven when he did that. He was going to call me out on my bullshit. "Grandma says you're not sick."

Bingo.

I threw the blanket off. "Thanks, Mom. Great."

"What's going on? Why didn't Jake come in? Why did he act so weird?"

I fiddled with the blanket nervously. "What did he say?"

"He came up with, like, a billion reasons why he had to go. Like he'd catch your fake illness. He wasn't worried about getting sick when you actually *had* the flu."

I rubbed my eyes.

Henry plopped next to me. "Why were you guys so weird at Grandma and Grandpa's? What's going on?" He frowned. "Me and Daisy aren't stupid."

I opened my mouth, but the words wouldn't come out. I didn't want to have this conversation. It would make it real.

"Are we going to Jake's tonight?"

I couldn't look Henry in the eyes. "No, sweetie."

His posture was tense. "Are you two fighting?"

I was afraid to answer. I was afraid I'd cry. I reached out and mussed up his hair. But he shoved my hand away, instantly mad.

"No!" He shot up, tugging at my arm. "Get up, Mom. We have to go over there right now and make it better."

He kept pulling at me while tears welled in my eyes. His face was red with anger and fear. He was getting so tall. He could've pulled me off the sofa. But I tugged back slightly, tired. "Henry, no. Wait a sec."

His voice was reassuring. My twelve-year-old son was trying to reassure me. "Mom. It's okay. You two are supposed to be together."

A tear ran down my face. Henry stared at it, wide-eyed.

"Sit here next to me." I patted the sofa. Suddenly, he was a little kid again. He listened to me, like doing so would lead to a positive resolution. I put my arm around him as I tried to sound calm and soothing. "Listen…you and Daisy are always going to be friends. And me and Jake are always going to be friends." I had to pause to let my emotions settle. "But the two of us aren't supposed to be anything more than that."

Henry shook his head wildly. "That's not true! You two are so happy together. We were *all* happy." His eyes were red. "Tell me why we can't be together!"

How could I answer that when I hardly knew myself? "Just because you're an adult doesn't mean you have all the answers." I ran my fingers through his hair. "Your mom isn't always the best at relationship stuff, kid. And I know you've always looked at Jake as…your…" I couldn't say *dad*. The word caught in my throat. "Well…you know. And you don't have to worry. That won't change."

"But it *could* change." He tugged at the blanket. "What if Jake starts seeing someone else, and they end up getting married? He'd have a whole new family." Tears gathered in Henry's raw eyes. "He'd never think about me ever again."

Henry knew how to scare the hell out of me. That's what I told Jake to do, wasn't it? Go find someone new. I gave him that advice, terrified that he'd take it. It served me right. I couldn't tell him it was over and then hope he didn't move on. I couldn't be that selfish.

I held Henry close. "You've known Jake your whole life, kid. He was there the moment you were born. He loves you. And all that time you spend making weird stuff together and laughing… That's not someone who's going to forget you."

Henry stared at the floor. "This sucks."

I leaned into him, and he leaned back.

"I know."

The clock ticked, the workers outside banged on the house, and Henry and I sat together like we had a million times before. But different now, somehow.

"I'm sorry, Mom."

I kissed the side of his head. "I'm sorry too."

I didn't know what to do with myself that night. I stared at the fridge, pondering supper options, when there was another knock on the door.

Why won't people leave me alone today?

Look in the mirror. It's obvious.

My heart caught in my throat. Was it Jake? I hoped not. No, I didn't. Yes, I did.

No, I didn't.

I wandered to the door, biting my lip. I moved the shade, and my heartbeat returned to normal.

Steven stood on my front step with a wheeled suitcase beside him. There were four duffel bags behind him. And a few trash bags. *And* several pillows. *And* his guitar case. *And* a blow-up mattress. And…was that a metal alien statue?

Steven opened his arms like '*ta-da.*' "I guess since you're broken-hearted, I can live with you to keep you company. But if I'm going to be nice and do you a favor, I need a shelf for all my pudding."

I planted a foot on the front step and hugged him with all my might. "Thanks, Steven." I gulped down air to stop myself from crying.

"You see how I did that?" he whispered. "I made it seem like I was doing you a favor. Classic move."

"I got that."

Steven usually exhibited placid emotions. Tranquility. Amusement. Occasionally sincerity. But none of those were on his face. Instead, there was sadness. That didn't happen often.

He was sad at Bonnie's funeral. He'd been too young to

understand death, but he understood that Jake was sad. When he saw Jake crying, little Steven plopped down on the funeral home carpet and sobbed.

He was also sad when Margot left him. That sadness took a long time to go away; maybe it never entirely did.

And he was sad *now*. His voice was raspy. "I teased you like a dick…but I never in a million years thought that you two would break up."

I couldn't do it. It was like a cannonball to my chest. I cried into his shirt.

His voice was low and soothing. "Things have a way of working out." He gave me a comforting squeeze. "You just have to let them work. See what they want to do and let them."

I nodded, pulling away again. "Okay, you hippie."

Steven smiled faintly as I wiped away my tears.

"You think you're crying now. Wait until you help me find a place for all my shit."

I laughed, despite my raw face and mood.

"I've been out here for half an hour taking stuff out of my car and putting it on your sidewalk." He glanced at it. "I thought if it was by the front door for dramatic effect, you'd never deny me."

I picked up his guitar case. "You were right… Plus, Henry will be happy. He's feeling a little down, you know?"

Steven nodded sadly and grabbed a duffel bag. We carried some stuff in and set it on the living room floor.

"Just so you know, I'm going to stay friends with Jake."

"I *want* you to be friends with him. I want *everyone* to be friends with him. We're going to keep doing things the way we always have. Sunday supper and everything."

Steven's eyes bugged out. "*That* won't be awkward."

"It'll only be awkward the first couple of times."

There was Steven's devious smile. "I'll make sure it's awkward *every* time."

I lowered my eyes, pretending to be annoyed. "Don't be a dick, or you can't stay."

"Being a dick is why you're letting me stay." His grin widened. "Leah, the patron saint of weirdos." He winked. "Plus, I *have* to stay Jake's friend. I mean, look at the poor bastard's other friends. There's you… That's not going so well right now. Then there's me. And there are Monica and Tony. Monica will side with you. Tony will side with Jake but fear Monica's wrath. That just leaves the second-string friends, like Margot's cousin, Nadia. And Felicity. Yikes."

I brought in a trash bag. "You like Felicity. You used to have a crush on her when you were a kid, remember?"

The realization dawned on him. "Damn. You're right." He smiled. "Remember how we used to go to Mankato and watch her run track when she was in college? She could do those high jumps like they were nothing. Hot diggity dog."

After a few more minutes, all of Steven's stuff was in the house. I heard Henry open his door. Probably coming to see what was happening.

Steven surveyed his junk. "Now I have to hope you never get into a serious relationship again. That way, I can stay here forever."

I sighed. "I think you're in luck."

"I wouldn't be too sure. Like I said, things have a way of working out."

22

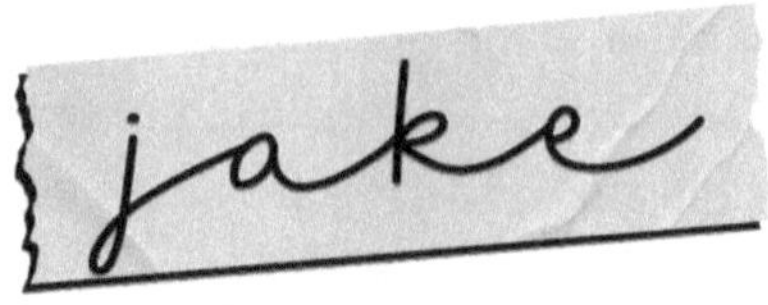

No one ever told me they needed space from me. The thought made me want to find that park trash bin I mentioned to Daisy and throw up.

So I didn't go up to Leah's door when her mom said she was sick. *Was* she sick? Or avoiding me? Or mad? Or all those things?

I assumed space also meant no phone communication, so I didn't send Leah any texts, even though, when we were friends, our phones were constantly going off from the stupid pictures and memes we sent each other.

When we were friends.

We were still friends, right?

"When are Henry and Leah coming over again?" asked Daisy. We were in her room. She was showing me how she could move her bad arm out to the side a little. It was still pretty tender but way more flexible than it had been a week before.

It had been a few days since our encounter in the break room, and Daisy was starting to get curious and annoyed. It was obvious that when we went from spending time with Leah every day to only seeing Henry, something was up.

I scratched my head, unsure how to reply.

Here we go. We're really having this conversation.

I never thought we'd have another one of these talks so soon. We'd also had a conversation like this about me and Ash.

Where was that trash bin?

I rubbed my palms on my jeans. The only sound in the house was Ash speaking softly downstairs to someone on the phone.

I sat on the bed. I motioned for Daisy to sit next to me. She did, readjusting her sling. I grabbed her llama and stared at it.

Daisy looked from me to the llama. "Are you okay, Dad?"

How do you give your child an honest answer to a question like that?

"I'm alright. I'm even better when I have your cool llama here." I tried to smile. "I think I did a rather good job of picking him out. What's his name again?"

"Montgomery," she said.

I chuckled. "That's great. He even looks like a Montgomery, now that you say it."

Daisy stared. She reached out her little hand and held mine. It made my heart want to break all over again.

I tried to keep it light. "Listen, Daisy. Henry's going to keep coming over, watching movies and all that. And he'll spend the night sometimes, too. Just like he always did. But…it might be a little while until Leah comes back."

"Is she sick?"

My throat was dry. "Uh…no."

"Is she going somewhere?"

I tried to swallow. "No."

Daisy petted Montgomery. "Then what's the deal?"

Here we go. "Sometimes, even when two adults love each other very much…well…things don't work out the way you want them to."

Fuck me.

"Like you and Mom."

Hell. I felt like shit. "Kind of. Yes…I guess."

"But I like hanging out with her."

"Me too." I was keeping it together so far. But I didn't know how much longer I could avoid looking like someone about to fall into a black pit.

"Can't you make up?"

I put my arm around her. It felt like a good time for honesty. "Let me level with you. Is that alright?"

Daisy nodded.

"Do you have a dollar for the swear jar?"

Daisy smirked as she pointed to quarters on her dresser.

I nodded. "I fucked up. Big time. Just because you're an adult doesn't mean you don't make mistakes." Wasn't that the fecking truth? "I hurt Leah's feelings, and I feel terrible. I made her sad."

"Why don't you say you're sorry?"

"That's a great idea," I said. "I've done that already, but…"

"Keep saying it."

If only the world were that simple. If only I weren't a fuckup.

"People like it when you say you're sorry. When Lily hit my hip with a basketball in gym class by accident, I was super mad. She said she was sorry like a million times. And the millionth time, I forgave her."

I hoped that worked for me. "That's good to know." I kissed the side of her head. "So I'll keep apologizing, and we'll have to hope that sometime Leah will come back over."

Daisy looked a lot more optimistic than me. In bed at night, I usually stared at the ceiling or over at Leah's book on the nightstand. She never came to get it or any of her other stuff. It felt like she could come in and start reading any minute. That should have raised my morale, but instead, sitting there wrapped in the shadows, that book made hope feel very far away. As moonlight drifted across the walls, I wondered if I'd fucked things up so badly that we'd never find our way back to one another. But as Daisy sat like a ball of enthusiasm, she reinforced my heart. It made me think that hope wasn't such a foolish idea after all.

"We could cross our fingers," said Daisy. She crossed hers.

I crossed mine. "I can do that."

"I can cross my toes, too."

I smiled. "Can you?"

Daisy nodded.

"How did you ever learn that?"

"Steven taught me," she said.

"Now that I believe."

Another puzzle was what to do about Ash. Should I ask her to leave? I probably should. It felt stupid not to.

At first, Leah said it was a bad idea to have Ash live in the basement. And it was. It was probably the worst idea I ever had, right next to the bucket hat I wore all through sophomore year.

But then Leah said Ash should stay because it would be good for Daisy while her shoulder was messed up, and perhaps that was true. Daisy spent a lot of nights downstairs with Ashley, playing Scrabble.

I suspected this was a test I was failing.

A few days after breaking the news to Daisy about Leah, I was making enchiladas for supper. I turned on the oven light and looked in. "It'll be ready in a few minutes, Daisy."

It was Friday. I hadn't talked to Leah since Monday. *Monday.* We hadn't gone that long without speaking since we first became friends.

Should I text her? Should I call her? Should I shut the fuck up?

I'd see her on Sunday night for supper. The thought did weird things to my chest. I wanted to see her so badly, but I was nervous. I wondered what she'd say. What if she didn't look at me all night? Or what if she looked bloody pissed?

It suddenly seemed very hot in the kitchen.

Daisy ran up from downstairs. She rubbed her sling and looked up at me, her eyes shining. Her voice was a whisper. "Can Mom come upstairs for supper tonight?"

Alarms went off in my head. "I don't think that's—"

But suddenly, Ash was there. She gave me a look like, *Yikes, sorry to show up like this.*

I wondered who'd save me when I puked, passed out, and then started to choke on my vomit.

"That's fine," I said.

"I don't have to," said Ashley, awkwardly.

"No. It's okay."

What the fuck are you doing? You've agreed to something you don't want to do. Again. The Minnesota nice thing is starting to chokehold you, moron.

"I brought beer." She had two bottles of something or other. I had never known Ash to drink beer. Wine, yes. Maybe some kind of cocktail. But never beer.

"I'm good, thanks."

Ash put the spare on the counter. "Do you care if I have one?"

"Of course not."

Despite being awkward as hell, supper was filled with standard conversation. We talked about Daisy's shoulder. Daisy loved to retell the tale of how she got injured. Each time, the distance she fell was slightly higher. It made me grin.

Ash glanced at me. "When does she start physical therapy?"

"The beginning of October," I said.

Daisy poked her food. "I don't want to."

"Don't worry," said Ash. "It won't be scary. It's just stretching. And one of us will be with you the whole time."

Then there was silence. This was like a wonky trip into the past. I hated awkward meals. How could you enjoy your food when encased in discomfort?

"I told Mom about Leah," said Daisy.

That got my attention. My eyes darted up from my plate. Ashley's lips were pressed together in a consoling frown.

"I…uh…" I stumbled over my words. "Yeah. It's…a weird time."

"I understand," said Ash. "I've been there."

"Daddy hopes that Leah will come back over sometime."

Ash considered that. "Anything can happen."

Anything can happen? That's even less positive than me.

"Do you think she will?" Daisy asked.

Ashley didn't look at me. "Time will tell."

Daisy disappeared right after supper, leaving at the worst

possible time. Ash and I stood in the kitchen. I opened the dish-washer and started organizing.

"I can do the dishes," said Ash. "Since you made supper."

And I thought the meal was awkward. I felt like running out the door. "That's okay. I can do it."

Ash leaned against the counter, watching me. Why didn't she go downstairs? "Sorry that I came upstairs to eat. I didn't mean to spring that on you."

I rinsed off a plate and put it in. "No problem. It's fine. It's good."

Yep. Fine and good. That was my life at the moment. Fecking fine and dandy.

I tried to think of something inane to talk about—the weather. Minnesotans loved to talk about the weather. We could bitch about how cold it was going to be right after we bitched about how hot it was.

"When did you start drinking beer?" I asked. That seemed safe.

Ashley drummed her fingers against the counter. "I don't know. Kenneth liked it. I guess it's stupid to keep drinking it, seeing that he was a prick and all."

"Sometimes you feel like remembering the good times."

Ashley nodded. We both looked at each other, then looked away. Dear God, this was uncomfortable.

"Think you'll ever get back together?" I asked.

Ash let out a depressed laugh. "I don't know. I hope not."

We both chuckled quietly.

"I'm sorry about you and Leah… Really."

I put a bowl in the dishwasher and stood up. Ashley raised both her eyebrows. She always did that when she felt bad about something.

It felt so strange to have this conversation with my ex-wife, especially when I felt like there was a loaded reason she was here. I didn't think I was ready to discuss my sex life with someone I used to have sex with.

"I thought you guys would go the distance, you know?"

That makes two of us.

I shrugged. "I still have hope, I guess. I don't want to believe it's over yet." She nodded. "I guess it's like that line from *The Goonies*. 'Goonies never say die.'"

Ashley had a goofy expression on her face. "I don't know. I've never seen it."

I almost broke a plate from shock. "You've never seen *The Goonies*?" I pretended to be aghast. "No way. I don't believe it."

She laughed harder. "I haven't. It's like you're speaking another language."

"How were we married for ten years, and you never saw that movie?"

She squirmed, playfully embarrassed. I shook my head and went back to the dishwasher.

Then she put on a particular tone of voice. One I hadn't heard in a while. "We'll have to watch it sometime."

I was fairly certain something was misfiring in my brain. I heard sirens and twisted carnival music in my head. I stood back up slowly.

Leah was right, you fucker.

Ash and I made eye contact. Her face revealed nothing, as was so often the case. I wasn't going to comment on what she said. I was going to pretend like I didn't hear it.

I rubbed my forehead. "I really don't need any help with the dishes."

Ash was as stiff as a post. She wanted to say something but didn't. She hesitated at the basement door. "Thanks for supper."

In a moment, she was gone. It felt like a tidal wave had crashed against my insides. I rested my head against the counter. "What a fucked-up mess. And on top of everything, I'm afraid to ask her to leave. When did I become a full-fledged Minnesotan?"

On Sunday, Daisy and I headed over to the Roth house. I brought over a cherry pie. Cherry was Leah's favorite. I didn't care what Dennis said. Sour cream and raisin pie? Absolutely not. That was Steven's favorite. Probably because it was a fecking weird pie.

I jiggled my left foot the whole way over. I felt ludicrous, like I was headed to pick Leah up for our first date all over again.

I wish.

Gail opened the door and ushered Daisy and me in with an encouraging smile. "She's been talking and laughing a little. And she got pissed at Steven for talking shit about her music taste. So that's encouraging."

Daisy ran ahead into the living room.

"I feel like I did when I picked up Anita Hughes for the prom," I whispered. "I wondered if *she* hated me, too."

I held the pie with a death grip as we walked down the hall.

"Whatever happened to Anita?" asked Gail.

"She's still with Ted Bisby," I said. "They live in Milwaukee. They have *seven* kids."

"No shit?" asked Gail, surprised.

My heart beat faster as Leah came into view. She wore high-waisted jeans with a dark shirt tucked in. The shirt had one of those weird collars. Daisy told me what it was called once. A Peter Pan collar? Anyway, Leah looked good—*really* good.

She didn't see me at first. She was saying something to Henry on the sofa. Daisy ran up and gave her a big hug. Leah wrapped her arms around Daisy, careful not to put pressure on her sore shoulder. As Leah held Daisy, there was a look on her face. Serene. Content. Happy to see Daisy again.

Because she loves Daisy.

It was another moment that reinforced my heart.

"How does your shoulder feel, kid?" Leah asked. She finally noticed me in her peripheral vision. I put the pie on the kitchen island and gave her a tentative smile. Her smile mirrored mine. Was she glad to see me? It made my hands go numb.

"Show Leah what you can do," I said.

With the sling firmly in place, Daisy raised her right hand slowly, then tapped her chest.

Leah gaped, impressed. "Wow, that's amazing!"

"I can get two inches higher than I could last week!" said Daisy, all smiles.

"You'll be throwing a Frisbee in no time." Leah glanced my way again. It did something to me when she looked at me like that. Her expression was a lot more positive than on prom night with Anita. Of course, everyone knew that Anita wanted to go out with Ted. But Ted asked Chelsea Oglesby first.

"I don't think I've ever played Frisbee," said Daisy.

Steven charged down the stairs. "I have fifty of them if you want one. But not the one from 1997 advertising Meyer Plumbing and Heating. That's mine."

While people milled around the kitchen, laughing and talking, I walked into the living room, where Henry sat, still staring at his Game Boy. He was obsessed with it, but it was weird for him to be separated from the group like that.

I sat next to him. He gave me a passing glance. Not his usual self at all. He was bummed, plain and simple.

Leah told him.

Of course, she did. Why wouldn't she? I told Daisy, after all. But Daisy was still hopeful. Henry didn't look like he had an ounce of hope in him. That didn't inspire confidence.

"How's it going?" I asked.

Henry shrugged. It was like a window into how he'd be as a teenager.

"How's school going?"

Henry put his Game Boy down. "It sucks."

"Really?" Sometimes Henry joked about school, but he didn't sound like he was joking now. "I thought you liked school."

Henry didn't seem to know what to say. "I did. But it's stupid now."

Everyone was too interested in Steven's rant about Frisbees to pay attention to the two of us in the living room. Everyone except Leah. She kept looking our way. Was she concerned about Henry's mood? I felt I should say something to him but wasn't sure what. Henry and I had always been close. He was like a son to me. I wondered what he thought about all this. If he was pissed. I wondered what he wanted me to say.

I squeezed his shoulder. He gave me a sad smile.

"We need to think of the next food to try," I said. "Any ideas?"

Henry stared off into space. "Don't know. Haven't thought about it."

I wanted him to know that nothing would change between us. I wanted him to know that I'd always be there for him. "We'll have to think of something. We haven't tried anything for a while." He seemed uninterested, but I ventured on. "I read an article the other day about weird pies. I can't remember where it's from, but apparently, there's such a thing as an avocado pie. That fills my mind with questions. Firstly, *why?* And that's followed by other thoughts. What's the crust? What else is in it? Is it sweet? Is it savory?" I nudged him. "We should find out."

That finally made Henry smile. I dared a glance over at Leah. She looked relieved.

Thank God.

"And I was thinking... You haven't been over in a while. Daisy keeps wanting to watch that weird sequel to *The Wizard of Oz*. You can come over whenever you want. You know where the caramel corn is."

Henry brightened. "Really?"

"*Really*. I can't eat it all by myself. Well, I could. But you should help me."

Henry relaxed on the sofa. "There's this syrup. It's called Coffee Time. In Rhode Island, they add it to their milk to make coffee milk. Like you do with chocolate milk."

"Huh. Never heard of it."

Henry fiddled with his Game Boy. "We could try that too."

I took out my phone. "I'll look on Amazon right now."

Supper consisted of my father and the Roths eyeing Leah and me while trying to keep a steady conversation. There were no awkward silences, but the conversation was batshit crazy.

Dennis pointed his fork at me. "Can you remember the tallest man you've ever seen? I mean, you're tall, but not even close to the tallest guy I've ever seen. The tallest guy I've ever seen was at Crater Lake National Park. The year was 2003. He had red hair. How about you?"

I stared. "Um...I guess I saw a tall guy once at Hy-Vee."

Dennis nodded, fascinated. Now I knew where Steven got it. "What did he look like?"

"Tall," I said. Leah stifled a laugh. "Um…black hair. Glasses."

"Amazing," said Dennis. The kids looked like they were going to dissolve into giggles any moment. Leah smiled at them. "How about you, daughter of mine?"

Leah looked from the kids over to Dennis. "Gee, Dad. I'm not sure."

Dennis frowned. "Don't be like that. You have to remember the tallest guy you've ever seen."

Leah flashed me a glance that screamed, *Help me!* "I think I saw a guy over seven feet at the Denver airport once."

"Nice," said my dad. "That's a good one. Seven-two, seven-three?"

"Probably seven-three," said Leah.

Gail, Dennis, Dad, and Steven nodded approvingly.

"What the hell were you doing at the Denver airport?" asked Dennis.

Leah squinted, trying to remember. "I'm not sure."

"Didn't you and Monica go skiing?" I asked.

Leah's eyes widened as she remembered, and she shot me a surprised glance. "That's right. We were so bad at it. The instructor couldn't convince us to go down the kiddie hill."

We held each other's gaze. She gave me a shy smile. It about knocked me on my ass.

"I can't believe you remember that," she said.

Everyone stared at us. There was that awkward silence.

Steven loved every second of it. "Isn't this fun? Pass the mashed potatoes. I'm going to eat them as slowly as I can. I'm making this bitch last two hours."

"Is there dessert?" asked Henry.

"I brought cherry pie," I said.

Henry didn't look too thrilled. "French silk is better."

"Cherry's my favorite," said Leah, fiddling with her fork.

I knew it.

"I thought it was sour cream and raisin pie," said Dennis. Leah shook her head.

Steven gestured to Dennis. "That's *my* favorite; damn your memory." He turned to me. "I'm in the mood for one. Can I order three?"

"You want *three* sour cream and raisin pies?" I asked. "Aren't you worried the meringue will disintegrate on pies two and three before you've finished the first?"

Steven forked mashed potatoes into his mouth. "Do I seem refined to you?"

"That'll take a lot of room in your fridge," I said.

"I don't care about that either. It's Leah's fridge. Leah's problem."

Leah rolled her eyes. "Thanks."

My heart skipped. Leah and Steven were living together? Why didn't anyone tell me? They told me about the customer who threw a tantrum about orange juice, but they didn't tell me this? "You two live together?"

Was I worried? Did this mean it was *definitely* over, even though Leah said she still loved me? Sometimes Steven lived in several different locations in one year. He said it gave him perspective. On what, I had no idea.

Her eyes widened, like she wasn't the biggest fan of this development.

"Unfortunately."

I decided that joking about it was the best tactic. "My condolences."

"Thanks for thinking of me during this difficult time."

"You know you love me there," said Steven. "I have HBO. You finally get to see how *The Wire* ended. Plus, the other day, I brought home three bags of Fritos. She didn't even ask for them." Everyone stared at him. "You know, for chili."

When it was time to go, I wasn't sure what to say. Luckily, we were able to grab a moment by ourselves when we both went to get our jackets out of the spare bedroom.

I took Leah's jacket off the bed and handed it to her. "Here you go." It smelled like her perfume—spicy and rich. When she took it, our fingers touched. I wanted them to touch longer. I wanted to rest my hands on her waist and kiss her. But instead, I stood there, still feeling the tingle of her hand against mine.

"Thanks." Her voice was unsure as she put it on. "So… I haven't seen you in a while."

I stared at my feet as adrenaline coursed through my body. "Yeah…uh…you said that you wanted space. I…uh…want to give you that."

Her voice was quiet. Like me, she suddenly found her feet fascinating. "Thanks."

"And…I'll do that for as long as you need."

Leah fiddled with her coat. "Okay."

Where did we stand? All I knew was that I didn't want to leave that bedroom. I didn't want our moment alone to be over.

"Your house is coming along. Looks nice. The siding is a slightly different color, isn't it?"

Leah finally made eye contact. "That's what I thought. But Greg said it might be because the other stuff faded in the sun."

"Huh. Weird."

Stellar conversational abilities.

I thought she was going to leave, but she gave my arm a playful pat. She always did that when she remembered something she wanted to tell me. I loved it because I knew she was excited about something. And when she was excited, her eyes crinkled in the sweetest way. "One of the guys working on the house looks like Dave Bautista."

I never would have guessed she'd say that. "Really?"

"Henry thinks so, too. He even told the guy. I guess his name is Connor." She let out a quiet laugh. "Connor doesn't see it."

Leah gave me a wistful smile. Was she just as nervous as me? There was so much I wanted to say, but I didn't want to push her away. I didn't want to open old wounds. "So...has Steven's geode collection made an appearance yet?"

Leah rolled her eyes. "There was one in the bathroom sink the other morning. Not on the back of the sink for decoration. Just literally in the sink. I don't know if he was washing it or trying to be weird."

"What did you do with it?"

"I hid it. He won't see that thing again until he tells me the secret ingredient in his chili. I'm scared to eat it."

We both laughed quietly.

Leah glanced toward the hallway. "I should head out. Steven and Henry want to watch a movie. They put a bunch of weird stuff in popcorn...so..."

I scratched my head. "Sure. Of course." What was I supposed to do? Why were my hands sweaty?

Leah hesitated. She looked me in the eyes. "It was nice to see you."

My heart started beating faster again. "It was nice to see you, too."

"You could text me sometime." She bit her lip.

Was it hot in there? I tried not to sound too eager. "Of course. Definitely."

She tried to hide a smile. How was it the sexiest thing in the world? "Good."

We stood there in that little room. Neither of us made a motion to leave. And somehow, without speaking, both of us understood. We reached out and met in the middle, hugging each other. It only lasted a moment, but it was everything. It felt so right to have my arms around her. To have her head pressed against my chest. It felt like a second and forever all at once. But then it was over, and she stood in the hallway, giving me a little wave. "See you soon."

I hope so.

The next afternoon, I stared at my iPhone. She told me I could text her, but what the hell should I say?

"Tell her you love her," said Daisy. We were at the restaurant. Daisy sat at the counter, eating a grilled cheese.

"I think that might be coming on a little too strong, sweetheart."

"She didn't seem mad last night."

My fingers were sweaty on my phone. "She didn't, did she?"

"So she'll come over soon," said Daisy.

"I hope so."

"Henry says he wants to come over and watch *Speed*. What's that?"

"An action movie."

"Is it old?" she asked.

"It's from '94 or '95."

Daisy frowned. "It's old."

I stuck my tongue out at her. Then I raised my phone and took a picture of the new sticker on Daisy's sling.

"Why did you take a picture of that?" she asked.

"Because Leah used to love *My Little Pony*."

I sent the picture and sighed. I had never fixated on a text so much in my life. What an idiot. Perhaps she didn't even want me to text her. Maybe that was just something to say. I didn't feel certain about anything. Leah wasn't distant at dinner, but we still weren't back to the friendly chatter that used to come so easily.

I decided to stop thinking about it. So I went back to cleaning tables while doing nothing *but* thinking about it. Five minutes later, my phone dinged. Leah texted me a picture of her *My Little Pony* coffee mug. I smiled.

An hour later, she texted me a picture of a geode sitting on the floor next to the toilet with five question marks.

They must like to be near water, I texted her back.

Where should I hide this one? she asked.

Is your shovel handy?

We texted each other off and on for the next couple of days. Every time I got one, it made me feel a little better. It made me feel like perhaps I hadn't fucked everything up completely after all. But what did it all mean? Friends texted all the time, but so did people in relationships. Leah said she didn't want to date, and until she said something different, I had to assume that was still the case. So I didn't go to the furniture store. And I didn't call her. I didn't want to push. And I didn't want to be *that* guy, the asshole who doesn't understand what *no* means. If she was still interested, I wanted her to make the first move.

23

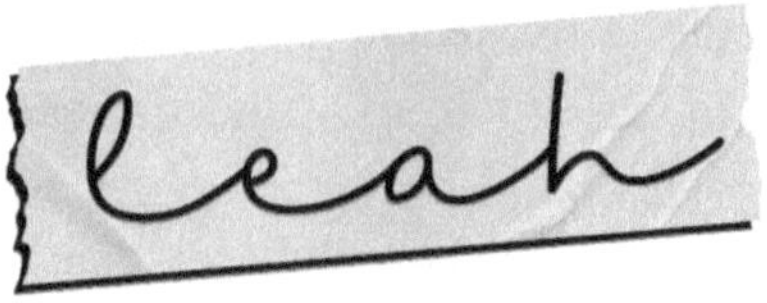

Jake and I were friends again. Were Jake and I friends again? We were texting. Friends text.

Stop kidding yourself, Leah. You don't want to be friends with Jake.

"Shut up, brain."

But my brain was right. Seeing Jake at my parents' house made my chest flutter. My chest didn't flutter for friends. I still wanted to be with him. I still *loved* him. I told him I wanted space, and at first, I did. But as time went on and my emotions settled down, space was like torture. Space was not what I wanted from Jake. I knew exactly what I wanted. And texting was the first step in getting there.

If you don't watch out, you're going to end up in a relationship with him again.

And then what would happen? More tears down the line? Him getting fed up with my bullshit someday?

It was better to stay friends. And if I couldn't be *just* friends with Jake, it was probably better to stay away entirely.

But when my phone dinged and I saw that it was another text from him, I immediately sent one back.

This is going to get me in trouble.

The next weekend, our Sunday supper was canceled because my parents were going out with some friends who were moving to Arizona for the fall and winter. It was their last chance to see them before they hit the road. That meant I didn't have an excuse to see Jake. My mind wasn't sure what to think.

Narrow escape? No. More like, *Shit.*

Saturday evening, I decided I needed a walk to clear my head. I put on my black peacoat with the Peter Pan collar and looked at Steven and Henry on the sofa. "Do you want to come?"

Steven scoffed. "I'm not walking with you. I take a three-hour constitutional every Sunday morning. Plus, I'm introducing Henry to more British programming tonight."

Henry was still quieter than normal, but his talk with Jake had helped.

"Is it something a twelve-year-old should watch?"

"Probably."

I stood there. "I like *Fleabag* too, but that isn't age appropriate."

Steven waved me away. "That's not what we're watching. Leave. You need to work off that nervous energy."

"Nervous energy." I opened the front door. "I don't have nervous energy."

The words were hardly out of my mouth when I nearly tripped down my front steps.

I wandered around until I got to the park. I walked past our picnic table, frowning as I went by.

Get over yourself. You could be walking with Jake, Henry, and Daisy right now. You made things this way.

"Yes, I'm the master of my fate," I whispered, annoyed. "Gee, golly."

I took the path up the walking bridge and snaked through the woods. I liked it in the trees. If you walked far enough, it led to a secluded pond. As kids, Jake and I always liked it there. It reminded me of a place you might find a fairy.

I strolled along the path, getting closer to the pond. September was going at warp speed, and we were losing more light every day. But even though it was fall, I still got warm walking. I unbuttoned my coat, and my necklace jangled against my chest.

I have to give that back.

I glanced at the sky, not wanting to think about the necklace, returning it, or what that meant. The sun was already starting to disappear in the west. And in the thick trees, everything became hushed.

The path in front of me finally opened, revealing the secluded pond. It was so quiet. Even the birds were silent.

I studied the pond we'd walked around so many times, mulberry bushes and lilacs hugging it. But then my foot stopped. I went from relaxed to flustered in a second.

Someone sat on the bench by the pond. He was pointed away from me. I could only see the back of his head, but I knew him anywhere. After all, we'd been friends forever.

Get out of here. But I had another thought at the same time. *Don't you dare go anywhere.*

I wasn't sure what gave me away. I didn't think my feet made a sound, but Jake still turned his head like he was waiting for me. Like he knew it was going to be me. He wore a distressed army-green jacket and dark jeans. And that stubble. Holy shit, he looked good. And I missed him so much.

I'm in big trouble. And I'm getting myself into it.

When he realized it was me, his eyes widened. Like I was something out of a dream. Dear God, that look made my heart flutter again. Before I could react, he stood. Then he walked toward me.

If *his* eyes were large, mine were even bigger. Of all the places I could've walked, I had to take the damn sentimental journey.

That's what happens when you live in a small town. You bump into each other. And you have all the same spots.

My mind was starting to piss me off.

Jake was only five feet from me. He wore a nervous grin.

"Hi." I felt as dumb as humanly possible. And as awkward. "I'm not stalking you. I promise."

His chuckle gave way to a wide smile. That smile and those eyes. "I'll believe you this time. But if you're at the parts store tomorrow buying windshield wipers, I'll start to wonder."

Now it was my turn to laugh. We did nervous stuff with our hands to fill the silence. I knew I should make up some excuse to leave, but I wanted to stay.

"It's been nice…texting you," I said.

He looked me in the eyes. I had to look away. It was just like it was before we kissed the first time. Shit. Did I want him to kiss me? What the hell was I doing? I was going to get my heart broken again. Or I was going to break *his* heart.

"Yeah. It's been nice."

We stepped closer to one another.

"How's Henry doing?" he asked.

I shrugged. "A little quiet. I think he's still bummed."

Jake gave an almost invisible nod. He didn't have to say anything. He was bummed too. So was I.

"But you cheered him up the other day." A breathy laugh escaped me. "He wants to make some weird pie and have coffee milk. Whatever that is."

Jake's smile was soft. "We're going to see what our digestive systems can handle." He paused. "I hope he knows that he can come over anytime. Our door is always open to him…and…"

Jake didn't finish his sentence. He scratched the back of his head and looked at the ground. I knew what he was going to say. He was going to say his door was also open to me. The thought made my chest feel airy, like a honeycomb. He still loved me. He still wanted me. Even now, I could say something, and everything would be forgotten.

But if his door was always open to me and Henry, where did that leave Ashley?

Maybe it's time to let that anger die. For your own good.

"Thanks," I said. "You're sweet."

That comment flew off my lips before I could catch it. I could only gawk.

I told him he was sweet! What the hell?

The effect was immediate. Jake stopped mussing up his hair. Boom. Just like that. His hand drifted lazily to his side. His eyes were on me, and his mouth was open, like he wanted to ask me a question but was too nervous.

But I didn't want to take it back. Jake *was* sweet. He'd always been sweet. And that was something he deserved to know. He made mistakes, but I made them too. That didn't mean he wasn't still something special. Something wonderful.

He just can't be your *something special, Leah. Snap out of it!*

That's when my eyes drifted down to his hand, where there was blood on his thumb. "You're bleeding."

I closed the gap between us.

He examined his left hand and shrugged. "Looks like the old

wooden bench got me again. Remember when Steven and I played chicken on it?"

I half smiled and grabbed a Band-Aid out of my coat pocket.

"You have Band-Aids in your jacket?" he asked.

"I have a twelve-year-old son."

My laughter relaxed Jake. He let out a small chuckle. Lines formed on the outer edges of his eyes. Amazing.

I unwrapped the bandage. Jake lifted his hand, and I pressed it down on his scrape. But then something weird happened. I smoothed it against his skin to make sure it would stick. Then I should have taken my hand away. But I didn't. I kept it on his. I didn't want to stop holding his hand. His hand was home.

Now you've done it. There's no turning back, you idiot.

And for the first time that day, I knew my mind was 100% right. I wasn't going to turn back. I wasn't going to run away. I was going to stay right there, and he was going to know that I still loved him, even though love between us scared the shit out of me. Even though I thought love between us would end in chaos.

I wrapped my hand around his. He stared at our intertwined fingers, then he looked into my eyes. He opened his mouth and only said one thing. Only whispered one thing. "Leah..."

And that was it. I stood so that his chest was right against me. I stared into his eyes. I felt half-drunk again, like the first night we had sex.

He ran his hand through my hair. I missed the way he did that. His voice was a hot whisper. "Can I kiss you?"

I nodded, putting my hand on the back of his neck. He leaned down, resting his hands on my waist and pulling me in gently. I should've worried about the ramifications. I should've thought a little bit, but my heart had scrambled to the forefront and was doing all the deciding.

When Jake's lips finally touched mine, I didn't think about anything else. It was just us, holding each other again, loving each other again. Our kiss was slow and thorough, his tongue grazing against mine. I didn't want this moment to end because I didn't know what was going to happen afterward. I knew what my head thought, and it made me afraid. So when it seemed like Jake might stop, I pulled him closer and kissed him more deeply. He made a throaty noise and grabbed me with a firmer grasp. A quiver of heat ran up my body. Our kiss became needy. I broke away, licking his neck as he groaned again.

I don't know how long we stood there, wrapped around each other. It was almost dark by the time I gently pulled away. Now I *really* felt drunk. And out of breath. His mouth was still close to mine.

"We're doing a bad job at staying broken up," I whispered.

His chest rose and fell. I almost couldn't stand it. He looked like he wanted to take me right on that bench. "You think this is bad. I know how we can be even worse at it."

Heat vibrated through me again, and I pulled him in for another kiss. He whispered my name as he nipped my neck and ear. We had to stop, or I'd let him strip me naked right there. It was like Jake sensed my thoughts, because he reluctantly pulled away, keeping his hands on my waist. He rested his forehead against mine. "I didn't think this would happen when I went for a walk. If I could rate this park, I'd give it five stars."

"I miss you." I could hardly get the words out. My voice wobbled.

That emotion caused an instant reaction. Concerned lines formed between Jake's eyes. He cradled me closer. My skin tingled at his touch, even though two layers of fabric separated me from his hands. "I miss you so goddamn much." His eyes scanned down. "You're still wearing the necklace."

I took it in my fingers and nodded. I couldn't hide it. And I couldn't hide how I still felt, even if I wanted to. Even if my rational mind told me I'd end up ruining the relationship that meant the most to me.

I looked at the locket in my fingers, then my eyes drifted back toward Jake. He stared at me like there was no place he'd rather be. And I wanted him so much. But I was terrified. How could I be sure that it wouldn't come crashing down again? How could I be sure of myself? How could I be sure of anything? I knew I should get out of there before I got us in too deep again, but his kind, patient eyes were still on me. So I stood there, letting all my thoughts drift away. "That space thing wasn't very fun. I kind of hated it." I raised an eyebrow. "How about you?"

His pupils were wide as he huffed a breath. "I'd rate that more like one star."

We stood staring at each other. We both had faint smiles on our faces but seemed unsure about what to do.

"I don't want to assume anything." He gently rubbed my lower back. Wow. That felt good. "What does this mean? What do you want to do?"

I broke eye contact. "I don't know. My head and my heart are telling me two completely different things."

A shadow passed over his face, but it only lasted a second. "Isn't that the fecking worst?" His voice was upbeat, but my stomach still twisted. "I guess we better sort that out."

"I just can't shake the feeling that we shouldn't be a couple. That I can't hack it in a long-term relationship, you know?"

Jake looked at me like he understood. No judgment.

I felt like a jackass—a jackass to me and a jackass to him. "I feel like I need more time to think. Is that okay?"

He still rubbed my back. "That's okay, Leah. If time is what you need, I'll give you time. There's nothing wrong with that."

He didn't look upset. Good grief, I felt like a jerk.

"That doesn't seem fair to you," I said. But he shook his head, dismissing my comment. "Isn't that selfish? It's like I'm letting you hang there. Aren't you mad?"

Jake pretended to think for a moment. He still had that amused expression on his face. "Oh yeah, I'm totally pissed. I'm as mad as when they got rid of that freezer-burnt cheesecake ice cream at the stand downtown."

I felt like crying. "Thank you."

"And if you need some reading material to try to sway you one way or another, Daisy now knows how to make brochures on her computer, like the kind you pick up outside a monument to tell you how great it is."

I sniffed back tears and smiled a little brighter. "Sounds interesting."

His fingers moved in circles on my back. "It is. A pamphlet about our possible relationship would have different sections, of course. One about eternal love and understanding. Another about the joys of growing old together." He winked. Something in me fluttered again. "That bit's my favorite. And maybe another one about sex. Because everyone knows sex sells."

I shook my head, smiling. "You're the best. You know that?"

"I don't know," said Jake, hesitating. "I don't think so. I think I'm looking at the best right now."

I pulled him in and rested my head on his chest. He wrapped his hands around me and held me tight.

"What do we do now?" I asked. "I hope you have some idea because I'm jittery."

"Good thing you came to Mr. Cool, Calm, and Collected. Because we both know that feeling overwhelmed is not what I'm about at all."

We dissolved into laughter, and he playfully traced his fingers along my back again. "How about this... You said you didn't like the whole space thing, right?"

"Okay..."

"But you're still not convinced about the dating thing?"

Where is this going?

"Then I think there's only one sensible answer," he said.

"Does it involve your homemade pizza?"

"God, I hope so," he said, almost laughing. "No, I was thinking…we should do some friend shit."

My heart lifted.

He looked right at me, his eyes glowing. "What do you think? We could watch a movie. Get you away from Steven and his geodes."

"Now he's hiding his Spam collection all over the house."

"Lovely."

I tugged on Jake's jacket. "But what about Ashley? Won't it be weird if I come over?"

Jake thought for a moment, then shrugged. "I think it sounds hilarious." I raised an eyebrow. "No, really. There are definite comic elements to us all being in the house together."

I couldn't help giggling. "I can see that. It'll be weird…" For the first time, I looked at him and refused to break eye contact. "But I think it sounds fun, too."

His smile was eager. "Yeah?"

"Yeah."

He ran his hand through my hair again. "Daisy will be so excited to see you. She misses you too. She has a bunch of new drawings to show you. She did one of Karma."

"Aww," I said, touched. "I can't wait to see it."

Jake looked hesitant. "So…you want to, then?"

My body felt warm. I nodded. "Sounds good."

I rested my head on his chest again. I didn't know what I was doing. I didn't know if this was right or not. But I also knew I couldn't stay in the same static place, wondering whether to go forward or run away. I had to do something to make me decide.

"Do you want me to walk you home?" he asked.

"Yes."

24

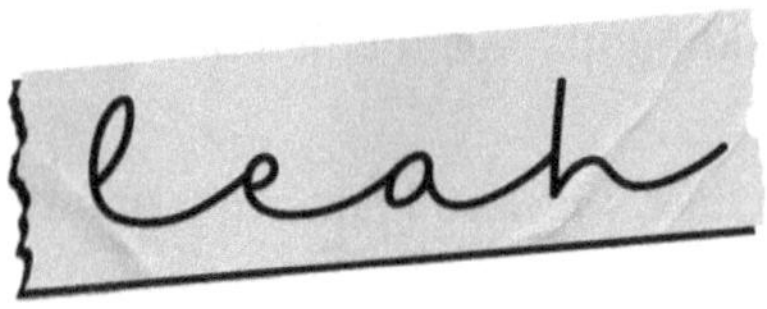

Henry was downright animated. It scared the crap out of me because he was animated about us going to Jake's. He hummed in the passenger's seat.

My hands got sweatier on the wheel.

He had a plastic container on his lap. "I knew these cookies were a good idea." He opened it and took one out. They were the same half-peanut butter, half-chocolate kind that we brought over before, when I discovered Ash. "Jake says they're lit."

I stifled a laugh. "He said *lit*?"

Henry took a bite. "No. He said whatever you old people say. But he likes them."

"When did he say that?"

Henry shrugged. "When we texted the other day." I raised an eyebrow. "What? We text all the time."

"I know…but I didn't think you had been lately."

"I haven't," said Henry. "Not until you two got back together."

There was the pounding headache, right on time. And the hot flashes. And it wasn't my period, damn it. It was nerves. The weight of expectations. Gee, how could anything go wrong?

"Grandma and Grandpa said I didn't have to worry. They said you were bound to get back together. And if you didn't, they were planning stuff. With Steven."

I needed eight cups of coffee.

Nothing like your whole family meddling in your personal life. Sounds like a delightful recipe for relationship bliss!

I stopped at a light and mussed Henry's hair. He looked at me like I was the most annoying person in the world. I loved it. It was a lot better than the solemn teenage angst he'd given me lately.

"Listen, Henry." I hesitated. *Nothing like breaking hearts, Leah!* "You know that me and Jake...aren't...exactly dating, right?"

Henry gave me one of his patented sassy glances.

"What?"

"Sure, Mom."

I took a right. "We're not, Care Bear..."

"Don't call me that."

"We're just friends for now, but we're seeing how things go. We're seeing if we might want to get back together eventually."

Henry's expression didn't change. "That's the lamest thing I've ever heard."

"I'm sure you've heard lamer things. Wait...why is that lame?"

We were almost at Jake's house. Henry fiddled with the cookie container. "That's dating but saying you're not dating."

Uh-huh. "No. It's two totally different things." I glared. "And stop talking like Steven. It creeps me out more and more each day. It's like a weird funhouse mirror."

And just to seal the deal, Henry flashed me a smile that reminded me so much of my brother that I wanted to take a picture.

I pulled into Jake's driveway and sighed.

"You're meant to be together, Mom. Deal with it."

Henry got out of the car. I followed behind. Everyone seemed so sure that Jake and I were written in the stars. If we were such a sure thing, why couldn't I convince myself? Why, deep down, did I still think I didn't deserve happiness, even though I had touched it, all aglow with warmth and comfort?

Henry shoved the cookies into Jake's hands.

"Fantastic." He smiled down at the container. "There's a chance I ate six of these in a row last time."

Jake and Henry exchanged a smile. Then Jake focused on me. Was I blushing? Good grief. Was I seventeen?

"Your old container is still here. Sorry that we didn't get it back to you sooner."

I pretended to be sinister. "That's okay. We know where you live."

Jake got a kick out of that. The way he looked at me was… yummy. I didn't know what to do, so I glanced away. This was getting silly. Henry rolled his eyes.

Jake stirred the soup on the stove. "Daisy, they're here."

Daisy bounded up from the basement and hopped over to me. "I have a picture of Karma to show you!"

"That's what your dad said. I can't wait to see it!"

Daisy beamed. She seemed to have more movement in her arm, even though it was still in a sling. I gave her a gentle hug before she ran over to Henry.

And of course, Ash was right behind her. Just like I knew she'd be. Because the new, Leah-hating Ash couldn't resist showing a little fake niceness. I kind of missed the old Ashley, the one who didn't seem to realize that I was a resident of the planet.

Ashley opened the fridge. "Don't mind me. Just looking to see where Daisy hid my orange juice."

Jake and I exchanged a quick, entertained glance. The kids didn't notice. They were already at the table, looking at the dessert Jake had made.

Ashley grabbed her juice from the fridge and finally made eye contact with me. "Hi, Leah. You're back."

Time for a fake smile. "What can I say? Jake knows his way around soup. And I'd eat his bread any day. How could I stay away?"

My mouth hung open. Dang. Did that sound dirty? Jake looked like he was biting his lip to stop from grinning as he focused on the soup.

Ashley looked at me like I was a classless bitch. She hadn't seen anything yet. I felt like showing her my old college party photos.

"Sure. Uh-huh." She glanced at Jake. "Would you mind coming down and looking at my dryer later? It's doing that thing again where it makes noise but doesn't spin. And it gets hot. I think it needs a new belt."

Jake looked slightly uncomfortable but nodded. "Sure. I'll take a peek."

Ashley slapped a look on her face that was like a robot trying to mimic happiness. "Thanks. See you later, then." She was about to walk away but stopped. She pivoted to me again, pointing at the counter. "Oh, and that cookie container has been here for a while. We don't have the biggest kitchen. It gets cluttered easily, you know."

Jake was a bundle of contradictory emotions. He looked embarrassed as hell, but he was also wide-eyed, like he wanted to laugh. He swallowed his amusement as Ashley traipsed back to the basement.

The kids still weren't paying attention. Henry looked over

Daisy's shoulder as she showed him something on her Game Boy.

I stepped closer to Jake. "That's how she was *that* day."

"I believe it." Jake took the loaf of bread out of the oven. "She's been weird since day one."

I nudged him. "Maybe she thinks you'll have a sexy dryer rendezvous later."

Jake reddened for a moment, scratching his eyebrow. "It'll be quite raunchy. First, I'll stare into the back of the machine and say it *does,* in fact, need a new belt. Then I'll scurry back up the stairs, terrified."

Good answer.

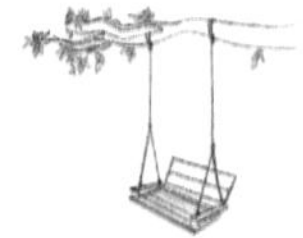

What can I say about lunch? It was nice. The four of us laughed and joked around while eating Jake's homemade chicken and wild rice soup. It was like before.

"I still think the poutine was awesome," said Henry.

Daisy shook her head. "I don't even like gravy on potatoes."

Jake winked at Daisy. "Wait until you try the avocado pie."

Daisy looked at me, and we both laughed.

"I don't think I *am* trying it," said Daisy.

But somehow, in the back of my mind, I couldn't shake the feeling that I was having lunch in a memory. It felt like this was something I'd never get back, even though I was experiencing it in real time.

When the kids hunkered down to watch *Speed*, Jake and I wandered back to the kitchen to make popcorn. I kept feeling Jake's warm glance settle on me. The idea of sitting next to him on the sofa for a two-and-a-half-hour movie was nice but getting him off alone to talk seemed better.

Or not. Depending on how you mess things up.

The air popper drowned out our quiet talking.

"How are you?" asked Jake.

Fidgety.

"I'm good." His grin melted my tension. "How about you?"

"I'm fecking fantastic." He playfully bumped my arm. That got my heart fluttering.

When he took the popcorn out to the kids, I told him I was going to grab one of my burgundy sweaters out of his bedroom closet. I left it there when we thought we were moving in. I kind of wanted it back for work since it was starting to get cooler outside.

But the real reason I went to the bedroom was because I had something in my back pocket that felt like it was burning a hole down to my butt. It was something we'd barely discussed since that day in my parents' backyard when I broke Jake's heart.

When I got to the bedroom, I took the envelope out of my pocket. I peeked inside, just to make sure the money was all there. It was the cash for the plane tickets to Ireland. I had tried hard not to think about it, but the day when we were supposed to leave was coming fast. I needed to give that money back.

You need to give the necklace back, too!

"Shut up, brain."

I tried to decide where to stash the money. I knew Jake would never accept it. I planned to hide it and then casually mention it to him on the phone later.

But I was already too late. His footsteps came down the hall. I abandoned my mission and reached into the closet, grabbing my sweater. When I turned around, Jake was right in front of me.

"Shit," I said. "You scared me!"

An awkward laugh escaped him. "I'm sorry. I didn't think you were actually coming in here for your sweater. I thought—"

He looked so sexy when he was nervous and embarrassed. I could've eaten him with a spoon.

I raised an eyebrow. "You thought what?"

That sheepish look wouldn't go away. "I thought you wanted me to follow you in here and, you know…kiss you."

I had been trying *not* to think about Jake kissing me. Because we were supposed to be doing friend stuff, right? I was afraid we'd start going at warp speed again. And I was afraid that I'd like it.

"That's not what I was thinking," I said. Jake doubled down on that embarrassed look. I poked him gently in the chest. "But…um…since we're here. And alone. I guess we could see if we still like it."

Jake laughed quietly. "Still like it?" He stepped closer. "With your lips and tongue, it isn't even a question."

Man, he always had the right answer. I grabbed his waist and pulled him slowly to me. His eyes flashed with need, and my skin heated. He leaned in, his lips slowly settling on mine. Everything relaxed when we kissed. My thoughts drifted away like morning fog. My worries didn't seem so big when his lips were on mine. It was *after* the kissing that the problems began.

Jake's fingers made lazy circles on my neck, then drifted down my back. His touch sent a shiver up and down my spine. He noticed and made a breathy noise, pulling me closer. What was I thinking? I *wasn't* thinking, not when I could feel how hard he was.

All of a sudden, his hands stopped.

Oh, shit.

Jake pulled away, a curious smile on his lips. "What's in your back pocket?"

"Uhh…"

He tried to peer around me, but I backed up.

He was loving this. "What is that?"

"It's…uh…the other reason I came in here."

He inclined his head as if to say, *Well?* I sighed and pulled the envelope out of my pocket.

"Is that a thick letter for me?" He blanched. "Because if it is, I'm slightly nervous."

"No… It's just…I knew you wouldn't take it if I tried to give it to you."

I held it in the still air between us. We didn't move.

"Listen," I said. "I know things have been weird with us lately. It's getting better, but…"

Jake put his hands on my sides, gently rubbing. "It's okay, Leah."

I tried to smile. But there was a big mass of guilt lodged in my stomach. "We haven't talked much about our trip to Ireland. And I…" I looked at the floor. "It doesn't look like we're going to make it, since we're supposed to leave in a couple of weeks."

Jake's hands came to a stop, but he still held them on my sides. I was afraid to look him in the eyes. When I did, his face was open, waiting for me to continue.

I rested the envelope on his chest. "So I thought I better give you this. And say that I'm sorry."

Jake took the envelope with a reluctant hand.

"It's the money for the plane tickets," I said.

"You didn't have to do that." He did a double take when he opened it. "Holy shit. You look like a bootlegger giving me all this cash."

I let out an awkward chuckle.

Jake scanned the money, perplexed. "Leah, this is the money for *all* the tickets, not just yours and Henry's." His forehead creased. "Why are you giving me this?"

My eyes turned hot, but I wasn't going to cry, damn it. "Because I ruined the trip. I feel terrible." I could hardly get the last words out. "And we were looking forward to it."

Jake placed the envelope on the bed and took me in his arms

again. "It's okay." He kissed my cheek. "Ireland's not going anywhere."

That kiss was so soft. I felt like complete garbage. "Are you and Daisy still going?"

Jake tried to look nonchalant, but I could see the sadness in his eyes. "I don't think so."

Shit.

"But you haven't been back home in a while. You hate going this long between trips."

It was clear he didn't want to talk about this. "I don't think right now is a good time."

"Why not?"

Color crept up Jake's neck. "It doesn't matter."

My mind went back to the day when I was sick. I squeezed his arm. "You can tell me the things that bother you."

Jake's eyes focused on mine. He remembered saying that. He smiled faintly. His voice was quiet, but he tried to sound light. "It wouldn't be a very practical time. Daisy's supposed to start physical therapy…and…" He was nervous. "It's just that I told some friends I was bringing you… Matt…was excited to see you again after all this time."

I blinked back tears. "I'm sorry, Jake. I fucked things up big time."

Jake quickly tried to combat my fears. "Don't say that. Don't think anything like that. I shouldn't have told you about telling people. That's like me trying to pressure you. Tell me to fuck off, Leah."

I chuckled as I held him close. He rested his forehead against mine. It felt so good. Fuck the movie.

"Just because we're not going now doesn't mean we'll never go," whispered Jake.

I made a noise of agreement, half hypnotized by his touch.

"And you know… There's no rule that we can't go as friends. We have before, right?"

I pulled away, trying to smile. "Yeah."

Because friendship was what I wanted, right? That's why I kept looking for opportunities to kiss my friend. Who the hell was I kidding?

"So don't start thinking I've forgotten my promise to bring you to the ocean," he said.

I couldn't believe how sweet he was. That wasn't true. I knew exactly how sweet he was. He'd been my friend since I was six. But something else was bothering me. I touched my locket. "I guess I should give this back, too."

But Jake shook his head. "Don't even think about it. That was a present. That's yours."

My chest tightened. "Are you sure?" I felt nervous keeping the locket but even more nervous about what it meant to give it back. As if in response, Jake pulled me back in. I rested my head against his chest as he held me.

"Thank you," I said.

We stood wrapped up together for a long time.

When I finally pulled away, Jake had a playful look on his face. "I'm pretty sure the kids paused that movie a long time ago. They're waiting for us."

"Then I guess we better get in there before the popcorn is gone."

Jake made for the door like it was a race. I followed, laughing.

"Fuck the popcorn," he said. "I'm getting those cookies."

I told Henry he could spend the night. He got a new Lego Star Wars set for his birthday that he wanted to put together with Daisy.

When it was time for me to head home, Jake and I stood on his front steps. My logical mind told me I had to go, but my heart wanted to stay. And it would have been easy to stay. After all, I still had a toothbrush in the bathroom. I still had pajamas and clothes in the bedroom. My poetry book was still on the nightstand. Jake didn't say anything about me taking my stuff back. And I didn't bring it up.

Why don't I get that stuff out of his house?

You know why.

"Thanks for coming over," said Jake. I saw it in his eyes. He wanted me to spend the night. But he'd never pressure me to do anything, and…that made me want to stay even more.

"It was fun." I fiddled with the locket. Jake watched me, a smile tugging the corner of his mouth. "But I guess I better get back. Steven was threatening to make homemade peanut butter when we left. I better see if I have to buy a new food processor."

Jake chuckled. But we both stood in a strange holding pattern. I wasn't sure what to do.

Should I kiss him again? I wanted to, but we'd been kissing a lot lately. Yikes, I was going to get myself in too deep again.

Like that's not what you want, you idiot.

My palms were sweaty. I stepped toward him, stood on my tiptoes, and kissed his stubbly cheek. On my way back onto my heels, my face passed in front of his. His hazy eyes gazed into mine. I felt half-drunk all over again. He took my hand and gave it a little squeeze. There was something about it—instant comfort, understanding, and love. I gave him a soft smile and squeezed back.

"See you soon?" I asked.

"Absolutely."

When I got in the car, I leaned back and sighed. How did I feel? I think I felt okay. Maybe everything was going to be fine. We'd hang out like this for a while and then slip right back into dating. Maybe my worries would drift away, and I'd feel steady on my legs again. It would be one of those funny stories we'd tell the grandkids someday.

Something caught my eye. The envelope of money sat on the passenger's seat. I picked it up and shook my head, laughing. When did Jake sneak it in here?

I was about to back out of the driveway when I noticed someone walking toward me. Ashley. She'd used her basement exit. Talk about posture. She was like one of those 1940s movies where women did ballet with books balancing on their heads. I lowered my window.

She gave me a non-smile. "Heading home?"

"Yep. My public service to the block is not leaving Steven unattended for too long."

"Sure." She was weirdly normal. I was waiting to be the punchline. "I thought I should catch you before you go. There are some things of yours in the house. We don't like messiness, you know? We like minimalism."

That was a new one. I didn't think Jake's two hundred baking books and kitchen gadgets counted as minimalism.

I was baffled. "Okay."

"So here you go. Just trying to get organized."

She passed me something through the window. I knew the dark blue and brown cover instantly. *Final Harvest* by Emily Dickinson. My fingers were ice-cold as I held the book. Ashley's elbows rested on my open window. She was uncomfortably close, and she knew it. She *meant* it. This was some kind of weird intimidation.

There were a lot of things I wanted to say. Ashley knew what she was doing. She took my book out of Jake's bedroom. She wanted me to think about that. To wonder why she was in there.

She wanted me to assume she was in there all the time, but I knew that wasn't true. It made me want to laugh in her face. The idea of her and Jake getting back together was comical. No, it made me upset for a whole different reason. Just when I was starting to feel a little better about me and Jake, uncertainty walked onto the stage and belted out a show tune in my ear, like "Some Enchanted Evening."

Was it always going to be this way? Was there always going to be some little pesky *something* that made me nervous to commit?

Take a wild guess.

I was right back where I started. Why did I spend the afternoon with Jake? This was all going to end in a tidal wave. He was my best friend, but nobody's patience is limitless. Pretty soon, all my fucking around was going to make him crazy. How long can someone wait around before they want to move on?

A cool breeze drifted into the car. It rustled Ash's hair. I smelled her perfume. Swank. She smiled. I smiled back.

"Thanks, Ash."

The days passed in a blur. Ashley's stunt made me as apprehensive as a kid playing Operation, waiting for the loud buzz. Jake started coming back to the furniture store at noon. And I was friendly. I *was*. But I didn't give him the sense that it would go any further than that. I acted the way I had back when we were friends. Perhaps a little chillier than that, but friendly just the same.

When he said something that made me want to flirt, I didn't. Instead, I sipped my coffee or changed the subject. And when we were alone, I filled the silence with random blabber, so there was no chance of kissing.

Did Jake notice? Maybe. Probably. But he didn't say anything.

We kept texting. We kept hanging out. But everything was PG.

One night, Monica came over to watch a true crime show, but she brought along a bunch of pampering crap. She held up a whole container of nail polish.

"Do I look like someone who thinks about my nails?"

"Tonight you do."

I wasn't convinced. Monica lifted a case of hard lemonade.

I grabbed one. "You win."

We were just starting to paint our nails when Steven jumped onto the sofa with us.

"Watch it," I said, shielding my nails. "I thought you were hanging out with Danica."

"She's visiting her cousin in Brainerd." He frowned. "How come nobody offered to paint my nails?"

Steven pulled off his socks. I cringed, and Monica laughed as he put his feet on my lap.

"Do you think I want your smelly feet on me?" I asked.

"They are *not* smelly," said Steven. "I guarantee it. You could eat off those bastards."

"What color do you want?" asked Monica.

Steven considered. "What can you offer me in a shade of green?"

Monica sorted through her nail polish while I continued painting my fingers a dark plum.

"There's this light green," said Monica. "It's very in this year. It's called matte meadows."

"Hell yes," said Steven, turning so Monica could paint his nails. "Danica loves to do charcoal sketches. And one of her latest subjects is yours truly. Gettin' classed up like this will have her motor running."

"I don't want to hear about my brother's sex life," I said.

But Monica was all ears. "I have three kids under six. You can talk to me about your sex life all you want."

Steven and Monica laughed. I shook my head.

"Speaking of sex life," said Steven. "What do you think about the current Leah and Jake drama?"

Monica rolled her eyes. "I think they need to get their heads out of their butts, roll in the hay, and get back together."

"Amen. Then people can stop talking about them and start talking about me and Danica."

"There's no drama." I tried to keep my hand steady as I applied the polish. "We're friends."

Steven and Monica exchanged a very pointed look.

"That's not what I heard," said Steven. "A little birdy told me that you two were doing friend things for a while, trying to decide if you should be a couple again."

I put down the nail polish. "You've been talking to Henry."

Steven admired his toes. "No shit…but it doesn't seem like you're headed in any particular direction."

I felt Monica and Steven's eyes on me. "What do you want me to say?"

"Actually, I think you've been a little cooler than average toward him," said Steven. "Frosty. Like a Klondike Bar forgotten at the bottom of the freezer for five years."

"That's damn frosty," said Monica.

I huffed. "I'm not that frosty. I'm perfectly friendly."

"And it's eating you up inside," said Steven. "You want to ride that weirdo so bad you can almost taste it." Steven thought.

"You've been strange ever since you came back from his house that afternoon."

Monica sat straighter. "What happened? I love hot gossip."

I blew on my fingers, trying to ignore the oncoming headache. "Nothing."

"Shut up and spill it," said Steven.

I glared at him. "Fine. Ashley took my book off Jake's bedroom nightstand and gave it back to me. And Jake doesn't know about it…I don't think."

Monica and Steven exchanged another look.

"Wow," said Monica, monotone. "I can see why you're furious."

Steven blinked rapidly. "I think it must be the whole context of the thing. Because otherwise, it's stupid. Stupid, but interesting. I'll have to look into that."

Look into that? What the hell did that mean? I started doing a lot of weird hand gestures to get my point across. Stupid hard lemonade. "She wants me to think that she's sleeping with Jake. Or that she's *going* to sleep with Jake."

Steven's smile was hazy, amused. "She's not sleeping with Jake. She'll never sleep with Jake again. She hardly slept with Jake before, poor bastard."

My face felt hot. I didn't like to think about Jake sleeping with anyone else, past, present, or future. "You don't know that."

"The hell I don't," said Steven.

"Now it's getting good," said Monica. "I can't wait to tell Tony."

"I don't get you." Steven wiggled his finished toes. "Jake was gonna ask Ash to leave. Why didn't you let him? A sucker for drama?"

I avoided his glance. "It's nice for Daisy."

"If we had a bullshit meter, it would be humming like a tornado siren."

"Shut up, Steven. You jerk."

Monica sipped her lemonade. "Don't stop talking."

"I think you want the path toward love to be difficult," said Steven. "I don't think you want Ashley to leave. You want her to be an excuse for why you two can't be together. Because if she leaves, you'll have to come up with another excuse. Because you could never let yourself be happy. That would be too nice. Too relaxing."

Stupid Steven!

I hated it when he was right. I sipped my hard lemonade.

Steven watched me. "She's not the villain of the piece, you know. Her one goal in life is not to sleep with her ex-husband."

"Shut up, Steven," I said. "I hate when you make sense, you know that?"

"I don't know what she's after, but it's not Jake," said Steven. "Some people get all twisted up until they don't know what they're after anymore. And after being with Kenneth, she's probably as twisted up as she can get. She's a lost soul trying to find her way. Cut her some slack."

I hated when Steven was nicer than me. "She's not cutting *me* any slack."

Steven shrugged. "If she's in a bad place, you probably shouldn't use her as a model of how to exist. Instead of worrying about her, you should focus on not getting all twisted up yourself."

Monica and I looked at each other. This was supposed to be a fun, pampering night. And now here I was, taking advice. Yuck.

"I hate you." I dabbed nail polish on Steven's nose.

We tried not to smile at each other. I lasted about five seconds. Steven didn't even try to wipe the polish away.

Monica focused on her nails again. "You're kind of deep, Steven." She paused. "In a Snapple lid kind of way."

Steven leaned back. "It's funny you say that because I have a collection."

25

Daisy finally got her sling off and started physical therapy. And Leah and I were friends again. From the outside, everything seemed perfectly fine.

But from the inside, I was fecking paranoid.

I thought our afternoon of movie-watching and stolen kisses went pretty well. It wasn't like I was expecting us to go back to picking out wall colors or anything, but it felt like we were moving in a good direction.

Then I showed up at the furniture store on Monday. Leah was friendly. Friendly, but weird. Weird, like she didn't want to be alone with me. She came up with every excuse under the sun for Steven or Gail to be in the room with us. That got the two of them eyeing each other.

We still texted. We still talked. We still spent time together. We still laughed. We didn't kiss, but that was fine. If she wanted to slow that down, I understood. We were supposed to be doing friend shit, after all.

But I couldn't shake the feeling that something was off. Something didn't quite click.

I was closing up the restaurant. I studied the paint on the walls while Dennis and Dad tidied up the tables.

This wall needs help, I thought.

I turned to find both of them in my face. "Jesus." It took me a second to recover. "You two look like you're thinking about something. I don't want to know what."

They had their arms crossed.

"How's she cuttin', son?" asked Dad. "With Leah and all?"

"Couldn't say."

"That doesn't sound good," said Dennis. "Do we have Tums around here?"

Dad still eyed me. "What's up?"

"She said we could spend some time together and see if it goes anywhere. But I don't know." My stomach sank just saying it. "I think she's cooling on the idea."

Dennis rubbed his chest. "How come?"

I fiddled with a napkin holder. It looked like I was trying to break it. "Let me panic in peace, will you?" I huffed. "I don't know, guys. I probably did something to fuck it up again." I slammed the napkin holder back down. "Damn it. Now *I* need Tums."

Dad wrapped one arm around my shoulder and the other around Dennis, like a huddle. "It's okay. We'll figure this out."

"No, no." I shook my head. "There is no *we*. This is something that me and Leah have to figure out. The two of us are the only *we*. None of the rest of you are in any way involved in the *we*."

"But we did the Three Musketeers thing," said Dennis. "You saw it."

"That's not a binding contract," I said, feeling slightly unhinged. "You don't have to feel obligated to do anything."

"Sure, sure," said Dad. But he winked at Dennis.

"I need to focus on something else. There are a lot of things that need to be fixed, you know. Like this wall. Look at the state of it. I hope customers don't stare at it too hard. We were going to paint this place four years ago. What happened?"

"Got lazy," said Dennis. "That's why Gail and I don't put out flowerpots in the summer anymore."

I felt the urge to do a thousand DIY projects. "Things need to change around here."

"By painting?" asked Dennis.

I ran my hand across the faded wall. There were certain things in life you couldn't control, like the weather, traffic, and the way people felt. But as I stood there, my fingers grazing the bumpy paint, it became very clear that there were a lot of things I *did* have control over. So why wasn't I doing anything about them?

It's happening again. Just like Ash said. You're letting life happen to you instead of making it happen. You're wandering in a daze as time floats by.

I lowered my hand and realized something. I couldn't make things happen with Leah. It wouldn't be right. I had to let her decide. I couldn't push. But that didn't mean I couldn't make *anything* happen.

I walked to the back and grabbed my jacket. Dennis and Dad were right on my heels.

"What's going on?" asked Dad.

"Hold onto your butts," I said. "We're revamping the baked goods in the display case."

"Shit," said Dennis. "What are we getting rid of?"

"The muffins," I said.

Dennis shrugged. "C'est la vie."

Dad grabbed my arm. "Where are you going so fast?"

"I have to make some changes."

I was about to knock on the basement door when I heard faint laughter downstairs.

It almost sounds like…

Bizarre.

I gave a tentative knock.

"Yeah?" asked Ash.

I opened the door a crack. "Can I come down and talk to you?"

There was that laugh again.

"Get the hell down here," said Steven. "Now it's a party, Ashley."

What the actual fuck?

I walked down the stairs, totally bewildered. Ash and Steven were sitting on the sofa, drinking beer. I stared, still dumbfounded. There was a deck of cards between them.

"We're playing poker," said Steven. "Want to join?"

I arched an eyebrow. "I think I'll pass."

"Not strip poker," said Steven, smiling at Ash. "Even though I know she wants a peek."

Ashley laughed but pretended to grimace. She took a sip of beer. "In your dreams, Steven. I don't want to see your gangly little body."

Steven and Ash had a weird relationship. They didn't talk very often, but when they did, their conversations were full of jokes about how much they hated each other, with the subtext of them actually enjoying each other's company. It made you dizzy.

"I thought I'd steal some of her money to bring back those warm, fuzzy memories of Kenneth."

"Fuck off," said Ash, snickering. "I don't know what your girlfriend sees in you. Are you sure she's not a blow-up doll?"

"Not this time," said Steven. They both leaned forward and laughed. Steven wiped away a tear. "I don't know what this beer is, Ashley. It gets the job done, but it's bad news. I didn't know the dollar store sold booze."

"It was Kenneth's favorite," said Ash.

"So you *did* get it from the dollar store," said Steven.

Ashley leaned forward again, hardly keeping it together. "No. I stole it from the grocery store!"

They were almost doubled over with laughter. It was infectious. I hadn't seen Ashley laugh that much in years. It was nice. I hoped that wherever life led her, it was in a place that kept her laughing like that.

"Maybe I should come back later." I smiled as I backed toward the stairs.

"No, no," said Steven. He got up quickly and put the cards on the end table. "I've gotta go anyway. Have to keep my sister in check."

He bent over and gave Ash a pat on the shoulder. She pinched his cheek.

Steven pointed at her. "Now…you think about what I said."

What's that about?

Ash pointed back at him. "And you think about what *I* said. But don't think too hard. You might sprain that little brain of yours."

Steven swayed a little. "That's true. I have to be careful. I only have about five functioning brain cells. One is used up on the guitar. One is used up on nineties dance moves. One is being fucking weird. And one is distracted by sex. So that doesn't leave me much left to do damage to." Steven thought for a moment. "Did I do that math right?"

I shook my head and chuckled. Steven and Ash gave each other a high five as a parting salute. How drunk were they?

As Steven passed me, he gave me a secret wink. What the hell did that mean? What the hell was going on? And why did I think it had something to do with musketeers?

I still heard Steven's voice outside as the basement door slammed behind him. "Don't worry. I walked here."

Ash stayed sitting on the sofa. We stared at each other for a long moment. An easy smile was on her face. I didn't know where to start, but I was glad she was happier again.

Finally, she sighed. "It's time for me to go, isn't it?"

I nodded. "I think so. I hope that's okay."

She looked at her lap and lightly chuckled. I sat next to her.

"So…my half-hearted attempt at getting you back didn't pique your interest, huh?" she asked, amused.

What do you say to that?

"Sorry…I did find it a bit strange, seeing that you told me in the car to go after Leah."

Ash played with the fabric of the sofa. "The dumbest part of the whole thing is that I don't even want you back." She frowned at me. "Sorry."

I chuckled. "Don't worry about it. We might as well be honest, right?"

"I guess." She paused. "You're a way better guy than Kenneth." Her eyes lit with amusement. "I doubt you'd ever steal a brisket."

"I guess it depends on how well it was prepared. Is this hypothetical brisket dry?"

Ash let out a quiet laugh. She hadn't laughed at anything I'd said in a long time.

"So…what's this all been about, Ash?"

Her smile faded. "Has Leah been weird lately?" She didn't look at me. "Quiet? Upset?"

Perhaps I'd need those Tums after all. "We haven't been clicking lately."

Ash picked at her nails, nervous. "That might be my fault." I stared. "Sorry…I kind of…stole her poetry book out of your bedroom and gave it to her the day she was here." My eyes were getting wider by the second. "I was kind of insinuating that we were sleeping together, or that I *wanted* to sleep with you."

My mouth hung open. At least if I passed out on the sofa, I wouldn't bang my head against anything hard. "I thought Leah took her book back that day. Jesus… What the hell, Ash?"

"Sorry." She rubbed her forehead. "I know. It was stupid. But…she can't in a million years think that we're actually sleeping together, can she?"

"I fecking hope not."

We stared at each other for a long moment. Finally, Ash dissolved into laughter.

This is different.

"I'm glad this is funny to you," I said, still agitated.

Ash was amused but tired. "Yikes. How stupid, huh?"

I leaned back on the sofa. "If you're not interested in me, why did you do that?"

Ash shrugged. "Because I was mad at you two, I guess. Because…right now I think that love is a big bunch of bullshit, you know?"

"Okay…" I said slowly.

"Love isn't how it is in movies or books… Why can't it stay how it is in the beginning? That's what I like. Those first couple of months. When every joke is hilarious. When they find you fascinating, and every touch feels like lightning because you've never been touched by them before." Ash stared off into space. "But it never stays that way. The jokes get old, or they start to annoy you. And you get used to their hands on your body. Everything ends up feeling like a worn path in the grass, you know?" Her eyes darted toward me. "Sorry. I'm not trying to be a jerk. But maybe I am. Because *you* were the path."

I gave her a faint smile. "Don't worry about it. It's fine."

"You don't feel that way about love? Like, after the thrill is gone, it turns into routines and boring habits?"

I thought about Leah. "I think it's nice…being with someone for years. Being with someone until they're able to read you like a book. Your ins and outs. Being totally known. Totally understood." I grinned. "I think that's the best bit."

A little smile spread across her face.

"Perhaps you just haven't found the right person yet," I said.

"I don't think I want to find anybody else. Not right now." She studied her hands. "I think I want to find myself instead."

I nudged her elbow. "Then I hope you find her."

We sat there for a moment, not saying anything.

"Can I ask you one question?" she asked.

I shrugged, trying to keep the mood light. "Sure. But no geometry. I'm already agitated because of that book thing."

She rolled her eyes, a faint smile on her face. "You've loved Leah since she was twenty. You loved her before I even showed up. So why in the world did you marry *me*?"

That was complicated. I scratched the back of my head. "I dated on and off in college. Then, right before graduation, I met Hannah. Remember me telling you about her?" Ash nodded. "We were together for quite a while. But then she wanted to move back to the Cities to be closer to her family. And for some reason, it was never a question of whether I'd go with her. We knew we'd break up. And I was bummed. But not heartbroken."

Ashley's eyes were gently fixed on me, listening. The only real, honest conversations we'd ever had were after it was over between us. Life was funny that way.

"Then I met Kali. She had a great sense of humor. Big nerd." I took a breath, remembering. "But then one day Leah asked if I wanted to get coffee and meet one of her new college friends.

When I got to the place, I opened the glass door and there she was…with a big, bright smile. Eyes crinkled. Laughing with Margot's cousin, Nadia. And it…hit me. We'd been best friends forever. I always loved her. But I never noticed her *that* way. So when Kali and I broke up, my heart wasn't broken then either." I sighed. "When I dated, I told myself I didn't know what I was looking for. But that was a lie. I knew *exactly* what I was looking for. I just didn't think she was looking back."

"And then you met me."

"And you looked back. And you kept looking back." I smiled. "Do you remember what you said to me on our second date?"

"Yikes. I said a lot of things. Most of them probably weren't true. How drunk was I?"

I let out a silent chuckle. "You said you wanted to go on an adventure with me. That was new. I'm not the adventure type. I'm the type that waits while other people zip-line."

Now it was Ashley's turn to laugh.

"I guess I thought that's what I needed," I said. "Someone the opposite of me. Someone to knock the cobwebs off. They always say that opposites attract."

Ashley fiddled with her bracelet. "That worked out well, didn't it?"

We both got a kick out of that.

"We didn't go on too many adventures, though, did we?" asked Ashley.

I shrugged. "We didn't go zip-lining. Thank God—"

"I did get you to go on that roller coaster."

I pretended to be annoyed. "Yes. I hated you that day."

That got us going again.

"And we didn't hike any mountains," I said. "But we had Daisy. And I couldn't ask for a better adventure than that."

Ashley's eyes turned misty. Her voice cracked. "Agreed."

We were quiet for a moment, staring off into space.

"I don't think you need someone who's the opposite of you," said Ashley. "And I don't think you have cobwebs. I think you need someone *similar* to you. Someone you can laugh with while watching bad movies. Someone who knows you in and out and deep down." Her eyes met mine. "You need to be with a friend."

My eyes felt hot. "I hope you're right."

"And I hope I didn't wreck everything," said Ashley. "Tell her I'm sorry, will you?"

"Will do."

Ash gave me an unsure look. "Oh…and sorry about tomorrow. I know how hard it is."

I always tried not to think about *that* day. But I never succeeded. I wanted to get away from that subject. After a moment, a thought occurred to me.

"What was Steven talking about? When he told you to think about what he said?"

Ashley rolled her eyes. "He told me that we could be roommates. It would be like an *Odd Couple* thing."

"People might pay to see that," I said, feeling lighter. "What did you say?"

Ashley let out an amused sigh. "I told him something my grandpa always used to say. I told him I'd rather drink turpentine and piss on a brush fire."

We both laughed. Ash kicked my foot. "I think things are going to be okay with you and Leah. Give it time."

I hoped to God or any other momentarily available higher power that she was right.

After talking to Ash, I wanted to run over to Leah's to explain everything. But it was late. And a text or call wasn't going to cut it. It would have to wait until the next day. So I had a fitful night of sleep, thinking about her and the day I always dreaded.

After dropping Daisy off at school the next morning, I zoomed over to Leah's, hoping to catch her before she headed to work. We'd already had an emotional conversation in the A-to-Z Furniture break room, and I wasn't up for another.

I was about to knock on her door when it opened.

Leah stood there, giving me a startled smile. "Hey. I was just heading to the restaurant to see you."

That made my eyes temporarily grow larger. "You were?"

She nodded. "Do you want to come in for a minute? Steven brought Henry to school. It's their new thing. I think they both eat three fast food breakfast sandwiches before he drops Henry off."

I tried to give her a lighthearted smile, but I was surprised. This was the most Leah had talked to me in...*how long?* And she hadn't wanted to be alone with me in a while, either. Did she already know that the book thing was a bunch of bullshit?

We sat on her puffy sofa. I sank into it, remembering. This was where I told Leah I loved her.

No, it wasn't. I didn't tell her I loved her that day. I was afraid that was too fast. I told her I had feelings for her, but I *did* love her that day. I loved her that day and *every* day.

We sat there, awkwardly looking around. Leah's purse was still slung over her shoulder.

Say something, you idiot.

I scratched my head. Why did I always do that when I was nervous? "I'm kind of surprised you were coming to see me."

She sounded hesitant. "You were?"

"I...uh...thought you weren't talking to me." I swallowed. "I mean, we've talked and everything. But it doesn't seem like we've clicked lately."

"I guess that's true." She put her purse on the floor and grabbed something from it. "But today is different."

She handed me a paper lunch bag. I gave her an amused look and took it.

When I peeked inside, my eyes turned hot. "It's a peanut butter and jelly sandwich." My voice cracked. "You know what day it is, don't you?"

Leah's lips formed a tight line. She rested a hand on my knee. The gesture made my eyes burn even more. "I do… Did you sleep last night?"

I shrugged, placing the paper bag beside me. "Not very well. I had stuff on my mind. Not just that." I took a deep breath. "You know, a while back, my dad said I was older now than she ever was." I glanced at Leah. "Both of us are. By years." Tears were right on the verge. "Isn't that weird to think about? Isn't that fecking stupid?"

Leah scooted closer to me. "Can I tell you a story about your mom?"

That made me want to cry and smile at the same time. "I wish you would."

Leah took a deep breath. She looked like she was going to cry, too. God, I loved her. "When I was little, your mom was babysitting me and Steven. It was the summer. You and me were going to have a water fight in the backyard."

I loved hearing stories about my mom, even if they hurt. I loved that Leah remembered her. I loved that we could both look back together.

"I was wearing a white *My Little Pony* shirt," she said. "I loved that shirt so much. I think I got it for my birthday or Christmas or something." Leah smiled at the memory. It made me smile, too, although sadness was right on its heels. "I had my swimsuit on under my clothes. I was so fixated on that shirt that I folded it up all nice and neat and put it on their deck table. And then we had our water fight. Do you remember?"

I strained to think, but it wasn't registering. "I don't think so."

"So you and I played for however long. When we were done, I went to get my shirt. But Steven was playing with finger paint. He got hold of my shirt with his little blue and red fingers. Paint was everywhere. I screamed like crazy." Leah laughed. "You don't remember?"

I looked into her eyes. "I don't know how I *don't* remember."

"Well, Steven is an idiot so often. All the memories probably blend together."

We shared a laugh. Her eyes got squinty in the way that always knocked me out. She grabbed my hand. And suddenly, we clicked again. Like the weirdness between us never happened.

"Your mom felt so bad about that shirt. She washed it five times with all these different products. But the paint didn't come out. I went home with all those spots on my shirt. I was so bummed…"

Tears welled up in Leah's eyes and ran down her face. That was it. It was all over. I felt tears in my eyes, too. I batted them away, but they kept coming.

Leah's voice was strained. "A week later…your mom came up to me with a little bag. She had this big smile on her face." I squeezed her hand. She squeezed back. "I opened it, and there was another *My Little Pony* shirt. It was the *exact* same one. I don't know where she got it. It's not like we had big stores around here back then. And you couldn't buy stuff online. It must've been a pain in the butt to track it down. But she found it." Leah held my gaze. "*That* was your mom."

She used the sleeve of her sweater to wipe away her tears. I used the back of my hand.

"Jesus," I said, hardly getting the word out.

My face felt raw. We looked at each other for a moment,

understanding. We leaned in, hugging each other tight. I never wanted to let go.

"Thank you, Leah."

We were hesitant to pull away from each other. When we did, Leah leaned her head against my shoulder. "I'm sorry about today."

My voice was strained, but her weight on my shoulder comforted me. "I wish I could forget today. I wish I could just remember her on her birthday, not the day she died. I used to be sad on her birthday *and* today. But then, as time went on, at least I found a way to be happy on her birthday." Leah sat up but stayed close. So close, I could smell her perfume. "But I still can't forget today. I guess if I haven't forgotten it yet, I never will."

Leah took my hand again, twining her fingers through mine. "You might never forget today. But I'll always be here for you. To listen. And to remember."

I wanted to kiss her so badly, but I didn't know if she wanted that. And I had to explain things. I didn't know if she thought me and Ash... "Listen." Leah's eyes drifted to mine. "Ash moved out. I thought I should tell you that."

Surprise washed over her. "Really?"

I nodded. "She started packing up last night. She's moving in with her parents for a while."

I couldn't read her expression. But she squeezed my hand again.

"I want you to know..." I felt awkward and unsure. "Me and Ash...we never slept together. She told me about the book last night. How she gave it to you."

Leah's eyes were huge. "Seriously?"

"Yeah. She wanted me to tell you she's sorry about that."

I don't think she could've looked more surprised. "She did?" Leah searched for the words. "That was nice of her."

I rubbed her hand with my thumb. "I know I've said it

before, but perhaps it bears repeating." I scooted a little closer. "You're the only one I want to be with."

Leah looked like she was going to cry again.

"Did you think we slept together?" A surge of adrenaline shot through me.

Leah shook her head. "No."

She looked like she wanted to say more, but something stopped her. She stared over at Karma.

I was nervous to ask the next question. "Then why weren't you talking to me?" I could hear my heartbeat in my head.

Leah opened her mouth but hesitated. My heart beat faster.

"That whole thing with Ash and the book made me nervous about us all over again." She pulled her hand from mine. My heart sank. "It feels like every time I'm ready to dive in again, something scares the shit out of me."

I looked at her, trying to decide on my words. She fiddled with her shirt.

"And it's not fair to you. I know you want an answer. You deserve an answer. You should be able to get on with your life. I just… I don't know…"

I swiveled toward her. She stopped fidgeting.

"If time is what you need, I told you before that I can give you that," I said, my voice quiet. "I'm happy to give you that." I couldn't hide my nerves. "But I…I have to know something. I'm terrified to ask this…but…is time what you need, or is this your way of letting me down gently?" My face was on fire. "Or you're scared to tell me that you don't love me anymore." Leah opened her mouth, surprised. "Because if you don't love me, I won't bother you about this anymore. But you have to tell me."

I held my breath, but I didn't have to for long. Leah touched my arm. When her fingers grazed my skin, each little hair stood up.

Her eyes were red. "I can't tell you that I don't love you, because I've never loved anyone more." My heart started beating faster again. "That's why I'm all freaked out about this, Jake. This right here is the most important relationship to me. We've been friends since we were kids. What'll happen if we date again…and something goes wrong?" A tear slid down her cheek. "Maybe next time you'll get fed up. Then where will that leave me? I won't just be down a soulmate; I'll be down a best friend too."

I wrapped my arms around her. She rested her head on my shoulder again. My heart clanged against my chest. I was elated and gutted at the same time. She still wasn't sure about us, but she called me her soulmate. A tear dotted my cheek.

"I'm hurting you, aren't I?" she whispered.

Our faces still hovered near one another.

Soulmate.

I thought I better be honest, even though I was terrified. "It does kind of hurt that you don't have more faith in us."

Her eyes widened. "I'm so sorry."

I felt like a dick. Why the fuck did I say that?

"I have faith in you," she said. "I just don't know if I have faith in *me*."

I kissed her hand. "It's okay. That was a jackass thing for me to say."

She looked at her lap, thinking. She hesitated, then reached around to the back of her neck. I knew what she was doing. The necklace I gave her was there, under her burgundy shirt, where it rested every day. She unclasped it and held it in her hand. She tried to give it to me. "If I'm going to be wishy-washy, I need to give this back. Until things are certain."

I swallowed hard. I felt like a spinning top, wobbling on the kitchen floor. I didn't take it. "If you keep trying to give that necklace back, you *will* break my heart."

Her hands stilled, and her eyes became glossy again. After a moment, she nodded. I gently took the necklace. Then I leaned in so close I felt her breath on my cheek. I reached around and put it back on her.

There was a wistful smile on her face. "I'm such an idiot. I don't know what I want." She hesitated. "That's not true. It's like I want something written in stone guaranteeing that everything will work out. That I'm not going to want to run again at the first sign of trouble. That you're not going to get sick of me…" Her voice faltered.

I ran my hand through her hair. "I can't show you the future. I can't tell you what's going to happen or how things will go. All I can do is promise. Promise to love you." Her eyes met mine. "Promise to always be there. That's what love is, Leah. A promise."

She nodded, but her face was downcast. "Unfortunately, people go back on their promises all the time."

My finger grazed across those freckles on her cheek that I loved so much. "And some people keep them." She smiled a little more at that. "So I'll give you the time you need, for as long as you need it…and I'll try to stay out of your hair a little more, so it doesn't seem like I'm pressuring you." Something flickered in her eyes, but she said nothing. "And maybe someday you'll look up and believe you can trust me with your heart. And that you can trust *yourself* with mine. That you can believe in us. That you can place a bet on us."

Leah rubbed her eyes. Her voice was unsteady. "What if I never get there?"

My heart beat so fast, I could feel it everywhere. But I laughed it off, not showing my anxiety. "Then I guess I better adopt another cat." She bit back a laugh. "Also, I'm planning enough random projects to keep me occupied until I'm eighty."

Seeing her eyes crinkle cheered me up. She reached out, pulling me in again for a hug. Her hands were warm on my back.

"For whatever it's worth," I whispered, "I think of you as my soulmate too."

Leah's breath caught. I felt her nod as she kept her head on my shoulder. When she finally drifted away from me, she planted a kiss on my cheek. When her face passed in front of mine, we looked into each other's eyes. I rested my hands on either side of her face and kissed her forehead.

The clock on the wall dinged. We looked at it. Then we looked at each other. We had to go. We were already late.

Leah grabbed her purse off the floor. "Projects? You never told me you were starting a bunch of projects." Her slight grin brightened my heart. "Like what?"

I winked. "Making churros."

26

Jake was giving me time. And he thought he needed to stay out of my hair.

So I was pretty much miserable.

That's your own fault.

We only texted each other about three times a week. And his visits to the furniture store slowed to a trickle. He was friendly, and we shared jokes, but it wasn't like it used to be.

Is he as miserable as me?

Jake was trying to let me figure things out. And I knew that's what I needed. Somewhere in the cream filling of my loneliness and uncertainty Oreo, I realized that to figure out what I wanted with Jake, I had to figure *myself* out. Who was Leah? What made her tick?

Great question. Tell me when you find out.

Suddenly, October 10th was staring me in the face. The day we were supposed to leave for Ireland. I woke up ready for a shitty day, and it was. It started with me staring at the calendar, thinking about what the day could've been like if I wasn't such a scared jackass. I drank my coffee and frowned.

Where would we be right now?

I glanced at the clock.

At the airport. Getting a snack before the flight. Henry would be complaining about the long layover in New York.

Henry caught me off guard as he came into the kitchen. I quickly looked away from the calendar attached to the fridge and focused on a magnet.

Smooth.

I wasn't fooling anyone. Henry knew what day it was. He'd been looking forward to our trip, just like all of us. He looked both downcast and sassy. But he was silent as he poured Cocoa Pebbles and stared at me.

Steven walked in, still half-asleep and scratching himself. He must have read the atmosphere in the room because he poured a cup of coffee, leaned against the cupboard, and observed us. He blew on his mug. "Who died?"

"Joy," said Henry. "Family. Love. Happiness."

"Is that all?" Steven drank his coffee, relaxed as ever.

I rubbed my face. "Come on, Henry. Don't be like that."

"How come we stopped hanging out with Jake again?" He pushed away his cereal. "How come you guys hardly text?"

"It's complicated, Care Bear." I was already tired, and I had just gotten out of bed. That was a good sign for the rest of the day. "I need to figure things out. But you're always welcome there. You know that." Then it hit me. "How do you know how often we text?"

Henry shot me another annoyed look. "Because I steal your phone and check...duh."

Steven smiled at his coffee. "From the mouths of babes." His eyes bounced to Henry's cereal. "What are you doing, bud? What about our breakfast sandwiches?"

I pointed at my brother. "Ha! I knew it!"

Now it was Steven's turn to look annoyed. He set his cup

down. "Son of a bitch… Wait, I don't care if you know we get fast food every morning. Speaking of which… Come on, Henry. Let's roll. Knowledge is power, and all that."

Henry stood up, hardly looking at me. I didn't like this bad crap between us. Henry and I never fought. And I rarely had to play the mom card with him. We were pals. He was upset with me over the whole Jake thing, and I couldn't blame him. Usually, Henry didn't get much of a glimpse into my dating life. That was on purpose. To protect him. I told him a few stories, basically enough to make him laugh. Enough for him to get an idea of the weirdos I'd encountered. But I didn't tell him much else. I didn't want him to think someone was going to be permanent and then take it back. But Jake was different. Henry and Jake had been close forever. It was impossible to keep that relationship from him.

And now I'm breaking his heart too.

"Shut up, brain!" I said.

Steven and Henry were halfway out the door. Steven cranked his neck and looked back at me. "What did you say?"

I let out an exasperated, squeaky sigh. "I said eating three breakfast sandwiches every day is going to wreak havoc on your cholesterol!"

Steven shrugged. "I'll worry about that in another thirty years."

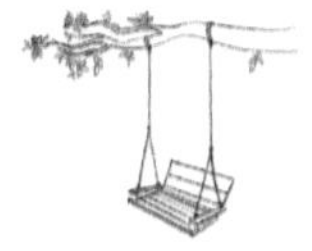

There was a weird vibe at the furniture store. Whenever I spoke with a customer, my eyes would drift around the floor to find Mom and Steven whispering about something. Whispering and looking at me.

Great.

What the hell were they talking about?

The better question is: what are they plotting?

"They better not be," I said, under my breath.

My paranoia was interrupted by my ringing phone. The panic was immediate. It was Henry's school.

Did he get in a fight? Did he fall from the jungle gym? Is he sick?

I answered it and listened to the voice on the other end. As my heart tried to calm down, a bitter grin spread across my face.

"You've got to be kidding me."

That night, I held three tests in front of Henry. We sat at the dining room table as he rested his chin on his hand.

"When the school called, I thought you were puking your guts out," I said, "or that you had a freak accident in shop class and cut the tip of your finger off. But this? Tell me what this is, Henry."

Henry shrugged. "Tests I failed."

I tried to stay calm. "In English. *English.* Your best subject. Mrs. Murray says your grades are slipping worse than ratings on a TV show where they decide to kill off the main character but still come back for another season."

Henry lifted his head, finally interested. "Wow. Mrs. Murray said that?"

I thought about throwing the tests in the air. "No! I embellished for comedy. But it's still true."

Henry's interest soured.

"Cut the kid some slack," said Steven. He was in the kitchen, assembling a sandwich that would've made Scooby-Doo proud. "Don't pressure him into being an A student or anything."

"He doesn't have to be an A student," I said, annoyed. "He knows that. And if he was doing bad at gym, I wouldn't bat an eye. Because he hates gym. But he *loves* English. And he always does well in English." I glanced back at Henry. He looked bored. Totally, completely bored. "What's going on, Henry? We studied together and everything."

Henry stared at the table. "I didn't try."

What the hell was happening? He didn't even make a lame excuse.

I was dazed. "What was that?"

Henry traced the grain of the table. "For the last three weeks, we've had a test each week. They're all multiple-choice. I don't even read the questions. I don't look at the answers. I randomly circle a letter and see how many I get right."

I sat like one of the taxidermied animals from *Psycho*. I hadn't been a perfect student. And I didn't always get along with the popular girls. But I was a test nerd. I took the SAT three times. Blowing a test on purpose made my inner child shudder.

Steven didn't try to stifle his loud cackle. "That's too funny. That's the kind of talk that'll give your mom the cold sweats, kid."

Henry watched me, waiting to see what I'd do. What *was* I going to do? I fiddled with the tests, biding my time. "Why did you blow those tests?"

Henry was quiet. I eyed him. Steven ate his sandwich, also watching. It was like a high-stakes poker game. Except I couldn't play poker because when I got a good hand, it was all over my face. The only person who was worse was Jake.

Henry stared. "I wanted to make you mad."

I bit the inside of my lip to stop any emotion from coming forward. Steven and I exchanged a glance.

"Why did you want to make me mad?" I asked, keeping my voice steady.

Henry stared at the table, mumbling. "Because we were supposed to go to Ireland together."

There it was. I really hated today. I wanted today to be over, and not that long ago, I wanted it to be today so much.

Steven suddenly found something fascinating about the inside of the fridge.

I sighed and picked up the tests. I nodded at Henry and ripped them in half. Then I put them together and ripped them in half again. Henry stared, his mouth wide open. I shoved the test fragments toward the edge of the table. Steven poked his head out of the fridge, an equally surprised look on his face.

"I'm not in trouble?" asked Henry.

I couldn't remember the last time I felt so drained. "No."

Henry was totally confused. "You're not even mad?"

"No, I'm not mad."

Henry looked at Steven. Steven shrugged.

"How come?" asked Henry.

I sighed. "I don't think you deserve it…Do you?"

Henry bounced out of his chair and slammed into me. I held him tight. Steven walked by and mussed up Henry's hair before making his way to the living room.

"I'm sorry, Mom."

"I'm sorry too, Care Bear." I scratched his back as I hugged him. I always used to do that when he was little to make him laugh. He didn't laugh this time, but that was fine. Things didn't seem all that funny. "Sorry that your mom isn't as good at relationships as she used to be on tests."

"Maybe you need to study more." Henry gave me a sarcastic smile. From the living room, my brother laughed.

"I'll borrow one of your uncle's dating books," I said.

"No, you won't," said Steven.

On Saturday night, I was stretched out on the sofa, staring at the ceiling. Steven sat in the puffy recliner, tuning his guitar. Henry was in his bedroom, playing video games.

"You've been quiet for a long time," said Steven, finally. "Penny for your thoughts."

I kept staring. "Just wondering who I am."

Steven stopped tuning for a moment. "That wasn't what I thought you'd say." He played a few notes. "If you don't know, who does?"

I let out a bitter laugh. "To be completely honest, I don't know what there is about me to fall in love with."

Steven's head was down, but he gazed up at me from under his eyebrows. "That's some damn fine confidence right there."

"I told Jake that I love ordinary people. That there's something special about everyone if you take the time to stop and notice. But…I don't know… I'm not feeling all that special right now. I feel stagnant."

Steven played a few more notes. "Want to know my philosophy on life? I don't think you have to convince anyone of a fucking thing. If you think you have to convince people that you're interesting enough for them to pay attention to, you've already failed." He played a little louder. "I've met a lot of people, and I haven't found an uninteresting human yet. You know how mathematically ridiculous it is that we all exist on this planet in exactly this form at exactly this time? We're anomalies spinning around on a big orb. I think that makes all of us, by default, interesting."

I lifted my head and cracked a smile. He got a little too much satisfaction from it.

"I get what you're saying, but I think it's a little woo-woo for me. But…do you get what I mean? I'm stagnant. I used to have hobbies. I don't have hobbies anymore."

"Why?" asked Steven.

"I don't know. I go to work, come home, make supper, take care of Henry, watch an hour of TV, and go to bed."

Steven's eyes stayed fixed on his guitar. "You draw."

"Don't make me laugh. I haven't drawn in years."

"You sing."

A garbled, amused noise came out of my mouth. "I haven't done that in years, either."

"If you want to draw, get out some paper," said Steven. "If you want to sing…" Something lit up inside Steven. *Uh Oh.* "Hey, I've got the guitar right here."

Before I could react, Steven was out of his chair and over with me on the couch. He pushed my feet aside. "If you want to sing, sing."

I shook my head so violently that it hurt. "I don't think so. You know I'm not confident about my singing voice."

"You got a folky voice, and I have a fucking guitar. Let's do this thing."

Steven strummed, smiling.

Now I was shaking my head *and* throwing my hands around. "No way."

"Why not? You used to be in choir."

"With a hundred other people. Not on my own."

Steven glanced around the living room. "Yeah, I can see why you might have stage fright. The spider over there in the curtains might be watching."

I stuck out my tongue. "I don't want you to make fun of my voice."

"Yeah, it's right up there on my list of things to do. We tease each other all the time, but I'm not going to make fun of your voice. I'm not a total dick. Plus, I've heard you sing before. We grew up together, remember? I was in the room down the hall. Just like now."

I refused to respond.

Steven wore a devious smile. "I bet you sing all the time when you think nobody's listening. I bet you do more than that. We have the same DNA. I bet you've *written* a song. Something you only sing in the shower. Maybe a heartbreak song from your twenties, when you were pissed at Lance."

He looked at me. I looked at him. After a moment, I blushed.

"Holy shit!" His enthusiasm pissed me off. "You *did* write a stick-it-to-Lance song."

I tried not to smile. "No, I didn't. I wrote one-fourth of a stick-it-to-Lance song."

"Sing it. I'll play."

"I'm not going to sing it," I said.

"Why not?"

"It's not even good," I said.

The notes he played were relaxing. "I don't *even* care. It's like a Kurt Vonnegut thing. Not everything has to be a masterpiece. Do it because it's fun. Do it because you love it."

I sighed. "Stop saying things that are the truth, Steven. It makes me hate you."

He raised his eyebrows. "Well?"

"You don't even know the tune! How can you play along with me?"

He gave me the look that Henry had inherited. "Gee, Leah. I don't know. I've only played the guitar since I was thirteen. Give me a little credit. Start singing, and I'll catch on."

Why did I feel so embarrassed? It was only my brother. And if I were telling the truth, I did want to sing. If I were telling the truth, I loved those old days in choir. I'd always wanted to sing again, but at the same time, it scared the shit out of me.

Finally, I nodded. "Brace yourself. I'm going to sing now."

Steven was tickled. "You go right ahead. I'll pretend you're a disembodied voice."

I rolled my eyes. Then I took a few seconds to get up the courage. Finally, words came out of my mouth that only usually came out in the shower. My voice started wobbly but got stronger as I went along.

"I'd like to say I told you so…so I will."

Steven got a knack for the melody. There was a crooked smile on his face.

"I'd like to say I told you so, so I think I will. I guess I'll be a really bad winner. I guess that girl ate you for dinner." Steven laughed quietly. "I'd like to say I told you so, so I will."

"So vindictive. I love it," whispered Steven, still playing.

I stared off into space, pretending I was alone. "It doesn't make me sad to think of your heart as broken. I wish I could have been there when the wreckage was still smokin'." Steven smiled again. "I'd like to shake any girl's hand who could turn you into a heartbroken man. I'd like to say I told you so, so I will…"

Steven played for another few seconds, but by then I'd stopped singing.

I shrugged. "That's it. I never finished it. I was too busy doing everything short of taping bubble wrap to Henry because he was learning to crawl."

Steven wore a smile as wide as a cartoon character.

"What?" The smile made me a little nervous.

"We're gonna be like *The Partridge Family*."

I put up my hands again. "Absolutely not. Don't look at me like that. We're not forming that band you always dreamed of—"

"The Big Damn Deal! Don't tell anyone that name, either. I don't want someone to steal it." He was downright giddy. "Now we just need three or four more members. Because otherwise, it's not big, and that would be false advertising. And we've got to get someone who can play the trumpet."

This was amusing and terrifying at the same time.

"I am *not* joining a band with you, Steven. I know you probably have visions of the two of us finishing that song and getting a double bass involved, but it's not going to happen."

Steven waved his hand. "Forget the song. Hear me out. Do you like to sing?"

It didn't seem safe to answer one way or the other. "Obviously, but—"

"And you want a hobby, right?" asked Steven. "Internal growth and all that jazz?"

"Steven—"

"Well, you're in luck. Because the Silver Dollar has karaoke and an open mic on Saturday nights during happy hour. Nothing gets people singing like cheap booze." He motioned to the clock. "And damned if it isn't Saturday night."

And just like that, my body seized up. "Hell no!" Welcome to Panic City. "Tonight's not a good night for a heart attack."

"Come on. It's not like the place is packed. I should know. Danica and I play there all the time. It's a handful of people you've known your whole life."

"I am *not* going to sing in front of people while you strum away." My hands were doing crazy things. "I need to practice first. I'm not going to wing it. I want to sound good."

Holy crap. What was I doing? My protest hardly even sounded like protesting. It sounded like an excuse to do it later. Did I want to do it later? What the hell was wrong with me?

Jake always liked my voice. But he loved me. When you love someone, you almost have to lie about things like that.

Steven's face scrunched up like he was planning something. Why did it make me feel like bracing for impact?

Finally, he nodded. "What you're saying makes sense. We

should practice a few songs for a couple of weeks and then go in and play when you're more comfortable."

Steven said it in such a calm way that I almost thought about it.

Oh, my God. How are you actually considering this?

A smile spread over his face. "What do you think?'

I didn't say anything.

"Let me ask you this." He strummed again. "If you knew that nobody was going to make fun of you…and if you knew you wouldn't get nervous on stage, would you do it?"

I opened my mouth. Holy shit, what was I about to say? "I… uh…I guess so."

Steven's smile widened. "So what you're saying is that you want to do it. You're just afraid?"

I held my breath, then blew air out of my cheeks. "Shit."

Steven patted my shoulder. "You're in luck. We can practice the stage fright right out of you. And there's something else we can do to take the edge off. Do you trust me?"

I leaned forward, giving him the most sarcastic look I could. "Of course, I don't! No. Absolutely not. I don't trust you at all."

But Steven laughed. "The first step to getting over stage fright is being up there with a couple of people. Safety in numbers, you know? Then you work your way down."

"What the hell does that mean?"

Steven glanced at the clock again. "Like I said, the Silver Dollar has open mic and karaoke on Saturday nights. You're not ready for open mic. But we could sing karaoke together."

Time to shake your head frantically again.

"I don't think—"

"Come on," said Steven, coaxing. "Just one song. I'll be right beside you, singing along. Like I said, safety in numbers. And hey…you think Monica's there tonight?"

"Since her husband owns it, probably," I said, sarcastically. "She's there every Saturday, helping out."

"There you go. We can snag her for a minute. You know that Monica never turns down karaoke."

That was true. She had a thing for Cheap Trick's "I Want You to Want Me."

I sat there, feeling unsure. That stupid, coaxing smile wouldn't leave his face.

"Fine!"

Steven jumped up and held his guitar high in triumph. His laugh was like some cross between a hyena and a witch's cackle. I had a pretty good feeling that I'd regret this.

The laugh was enough to get Henry out of his room. He peeked around the corner, like we were losing our minds.

"Get your phone, Henry," said Steven. "You're going to want to film this."

"It sounded like someone was throwing up," said Henry.

I crossed my arms. "Not yet."

"We're going to sing karaoke at the Silver Dollar," said Steven.

Henry was shocked. "Mom too?"

"Yes." I felt like I was having an out-of-body experience. "Don't ask me how. It happened so fast."

"Were you drinking hard lemonade?" asked Henry.

Steven laughed. That's when I realized he was on his phone.

"Who are you texting?" I asked.

"Uh…Monica," said Steven, concentrating. "Telling her to get ready for us."

"What song are you going to sing?" asked Henry.

"That's a great question," said Steven. I hadn't seen him this excited since Margot gave him his first geode. "We could sing something I serenade Danica with before…" Steven looked at Henry. "…the…uh…mood strikes. Like 'Body Like a Back Road' by Sam Hunt or 'Want to Want Me' by Jason Derulo."

"Before the *mood* strikes?" asked Henry, frowning. "That's nasty."

I cringed. "Agreed. We're not singing one of your baby-making songs, Steven."

"Fine," said Steven. "You choose one. Something fun. Something silly." His eyes darted my way. "Don't look at me like that, Leah. I know you have something in mind."

I glanced between Steven and Henry. I didn't want to smile, but I couldn't help it.

That made Steven giddy again. "What are we singing?" He stood behind Henry, jiggling my son's shoulders until he smiled.

I laughed. "Chevy Van."

27

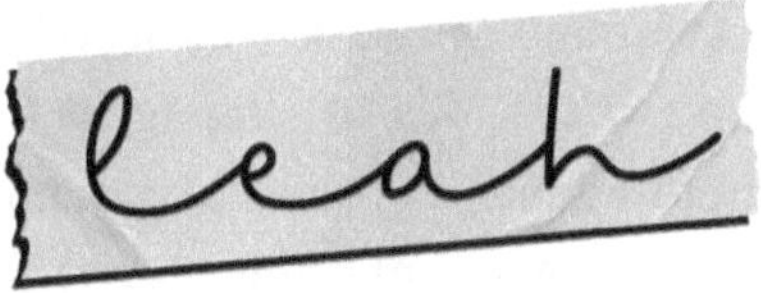

"This is my favorite bar in town," said Steven.

The Silver Dollar wasn't much to look at. It was a dive, I guess. But it was *our* dive. The place was dark, with multicolored lights hanging just down from the ceiling. It had a wooden bar in the middle and a small stage in the back.

"You just say that because it doesn't smell like puke," I said.

Steven, Henry, and I sat at a table near the stage. There were probably only thirty people in the place. It was a cold night in October. Between football games and the lure of warm sofas and streaming TV, it made for a slow night. And Steven was right—I probably knew everyone in there. But it was dark, so it was hard to make people out. And I was scared to try. I didn't know if singing in front of strangers or friends was worse.

A couple was on stage singing "I Believe in a Thing Called Love" by The Darkness. It made me feel a little better. What they lacked in talent, they made up for in drunken enthusiasm.

"I should sing this one to Danica," said Steven. That grossed Henry out all over again.

Hands reached out of the darkness and shook Henry's chair.

He laughed and turned to find my parents standing there. Craig was next to them, doing a little dad dance to the music. If looks could kill, my eyes on Steven would have melted his face.

"Steven! You said you were texting Monica!"

"I did," he said, crossing his arms. "And everyone else."

Everyone else?

My eyes flew around the dark bar, searching for Jake. Oh, God. I didn't know if the idea of singing in front of him made me calmer or more agitated. As my eyes squinted through the shadows, I realized I wanted him there. After all, I sang to him in the shower. And in bed.

Now is not a good time to think of the two of you in bed.

Steven leaned toward me. "I don't think he's coming, sis."

I looked at my brother, confused.

"He's the only one who didn't text back."

Blood rushed from my face. Jake didn't text Steven back? What world were we living in? Jake texted everyone back in a heartbeat. He said he was going to give me space, but we still talked and texted…sometimes. And we were friendly toward each other. So what was going on?

Oh, shit. This is it. He's sick of how I'm on the fence about us. I mean, how long can you wait around for someone? How long would you wait around for someone, Leah? It would be easier for him to find someone who is not afraid of commitment.

I put on my best fake smile. Steven wasn't buying it.

"I wasn't looking for…anyone…" I said.

Before Steven could say anything, Dad and Craig sat down and started talking.

"Right up there," said Dad, pointing to the stage. "That's where it happened. Paint them the picture, Craig."

"The year was 2003," said Craig, reminiscing. "It was the B&R Christmas party. Me and your dad were *not* drunk—"

"Yes, you were," said Mom.

"And we sang the best damn karaoke version of 'Wonder-wall' that you've ever heard. People cried."

"People cried because it was that bad," said Mom.

"Jake thought it was great," said Dad.

"Jake's nicer than me," said Mom.

I couldn't stop myself from letting out an airy laugh.

Craig and I made eye contact. He shrugged. "He must be busy with something. I'm sure he'd be here if he knew."

I waved away his comment like it was the furthest thing from my mind. But my whole family stared at me, including Henry, who didn't look too happy about Jake *not* being there. I didn't think I could handle much more of this.

I eyed the bar. "I think I need a drink."

Dad, Craig, and Mom shifted away from us slightly, busy with their own hushed conversation. I prayed that it had nothing to do with me.

"From the way you're flipping out, a sedative might do you good," said Steven. I sat on my hands. "You're making way too big a deal of this. It's not like you're going up there to get married."

I stood up, nearly tripping on my chair. "It's your fault. Inviting everyone." I cleared my throat. "Do you want anything?"

Steven smiled. "I'm calm all on my own."

"Good for you," I said, monotone. "You want a Coke, Henry?"

Henry took a picture of me. "Sure."

"Stay away from that hard lemonade, though," said Steven.

"Shut up, Steven."

I made my way toward the bar. Tony Moore, Monica's husband, was a stocky guy with thick, dark hair and a bushy beard. He always bartended.

He nodded when he saw me, grinning. "Monica told me what you were up to. Did you lose a bet?"

"That sounds better than admitting that I'm doing this willingly." I held my hands on the bar to stop them from shaking. "I need a Coke. And your wimpiest beer."

That got Tony laughing. He grabbed the drinks.

"Trying to see if you can burn a hole in your gut, Roth?" asked a voice from behind me. Now, if this were a movie, I would've turned to find Jake standing there. And all my fears that he was fed up with me would have vanished. It would've been a night of stolen glances and him whistling from the crowd to cheer me on. But this wasn't a movie. And there was only one person in the whole damn world who called me Roth.

I cringed and turned around. Lance stood there with that stony gaze of his. Everything about Lance was unyielding—his posture, his stillness, his eyes. Yep, back in the day, I was all for Mr. Intensity.

Lance was...*different* from other guys I'd dated. It was hard to see what Henry had inherited. Lance's head was shaved and shined up like a bowling ball. He always wore silky polo shirts that accentuated his chiseled physique. His arms and chest were ridiculous—tanned, toned muscles and woven, abstract tattoos. The guy was one step down from looking like he was going to roll in oil and fight another gladiator to the death. For the year we dated on and off, quite a few women and men probably ended up in the ER from twisting their necks to look at him when we walked by.

"Don't tell me Steven texted you," I said.

Lance let out one quick, abrupt laugh. "Nope. Jackson Barnard's bachelor party."

Yikes. I scanned the bar. "Where's everyone else?"

Lance didn't take his eyes off me. "I went rogue. Plus, those dudes are losers."

I eyed his weird green drink. "What's that?"

"Spinach. Bee pollen. Cucumbers. Flax. Bunch of other shit. Tony is the master."

"Don't order one," said Tony, stone-faced. "For the love of God. My blender is never going to forgive me."

I laughed at Tony, then my eyes went back to Lance. We stared at each other. It had been a while. I didn't know what to say. And his dark eyes wouldn't move from my face.

"How are things?" I asked.

"Marvelous. Imagine greatness, and greatness is what you will manifest." He took a breath. "That's what it says right above my gym door."

"Huh." I paused. He stared. "I see you stopped standing an inch away from people when you talk to them."

Lance gave a quick nod. "Personal growth. Plus, my last hookup told me it was off-putting." He stepped closer to me. "How come you never told me it was off-putting?"

"You're in the red zone, bud."

Lance looked at the distance between us, nodded, and stepped back. "Good to note. Thank you."

Those unrelenting, wide eyes kept watching me. I was about to tell him that was also off-putting when he cleared his throat. "How's Henry?"

I gestured through the darkness and haze over to our table. Mom, Dad, Craig, Steven, and Henry all had their eyes on us like they were throwing darts. Could the night get any weirder? Between getting dragged here to sing, the whole Jake thing, then the whole Lance thing...

I suddenly felt nauseous.

Shit. I still have to sing!

I put my hands on my face. "I'm about to sing in front of Henry and everyone else. It's going to be terrible. And our kid's going to record me. Ever have one of those moments where you know you're going to regret something for years, but do it anyway?"

Lance blinked. "No."

I threw up my arms. "Okay. Well...that's about to be me."

"No, it won't. You are going to destroy them like they're your blood-sworn enemies. And you'll sing great."

I lowered my hands. "You think so?"

Lance sipped his drink. "Yes. And if you don't, everyone here is drunk. So who cares?"

That was actually pretty sound logic. But I couldn't help wondering what Jake would have said, standing in front of me. He would've told me that my voice was pretty, and I didn't have anything to worry about. And I would have said that was a nice lie. But Jake wasn't here. And I had to stop expecting him to show up, especially when I didn't know what I wanted.

The stage was quiet and empty. When did the last people finish singing? I knew it was time to face the music, as literally and stupidly as possible.

"We should go over to your family," said Lance. "It's time to dominate. And I should see if Henry liked the Lego *Star Wars* thing I gave him for his birthday." He readjusted. "I was thinking I should bring him somewhere to make up for being in Tallahassee on his birthday."

I felt a jolt. Lance wanted to do things with Henry? Usually, getting him to parent was like getting Henry to cool it on the pop. What the hell was going on?

But I pushed that thought aside and realized something else.

"You're strong," I said. We both looked at Lance's bulging arms.

"Yes. That's accurate."

"If I pass out on stage, will you use your massive hands to break Henry's phone into five pieces?"

Lance stared at me, then took a sip of his drink. "Consider it done."

How the hell did I get here?

The night started with me staring at the ceiling. And now I was on stage with Steven and Monica. Steven stood in front of us, eating up the crowd. Monica stood near him, looking perfectly calm. After all, she'd done this a hundred times before. I tried to hide behind them.

Am I really going to come back here and sing alone?

The idea of Steven strumming his guitar and me stumbling over a song was enough to make me feel like throwing up.

That wimpy beer was a bad choice.

Steven grabbed a microphone and then passed two to me and Monica.

"Hey, everyone," said Steven. There were murmurs from the audience. Steven laughed and pointed at people he knew.

Dear God.

"Well, what can I say?" asked Steven. "It's my lucky fuckin' day, bitches, because somehow, I got my sister up here to sing with us. Why don't you clap for her? She's terrified."

"Jesus Christ," I muttered under my breath. Monica quietly laughed and patted my back.

The small audience broke out in a cheer. My eyes drifted toward my family's table. Jake wasn't there. Jake wasn't coming.

Get over it, Leah.

It was crazy how much I wanted him there. I took a deep breath to try to calm myself down.

Lance sat next to Henry. Everyone at the table stared at him, but he didn't care what anyone thought. He never had. They looked at him while he looked at me. Then he raised his glass and nodded. And suddenly the music was playing.

Shit.

The whole thing started in a blur. Steven sang up in front. Monica and I acted like background vocalists. I was fine with that. I didn't want to be seen, damn it. I couldn't feel my lips. Or my toes. Or my chest.

Lance sat back, relaxed, taking me in.

Henry's recording this! I thought, glaring at my son. He was enjoying this *way* too much.

I'd belted this goofy song out a thousand times, but now it felt like it was never going to end.

Everyone's smiling. The world isn't going to end.

And just when I started calming down, just when the song was almost over, Steven was suddenly next to me. He threw one arm around my shoulder. Then he pointed to me with his microphone. My stomach sank. I knew what he was doing. The fucker wanted me to sing the last verse alone. I looked at him like his death would be imminent and painful. But there was nothing I could do. The music kept playing. So I hesitantly opened my mouth and sang lyrics about dropping a woman off after having sex, not knowing if their paths would ever cross again. I didn't look at the audience. I stared at Steven the whole time. I hated his guts. He watched me, grinning like the Joker.

Then it was over. Steven hugged me. Monica whooped. And out there, in the audience, Lance was on his feet, whistling. Seeing him like that made me wonder what year it was.

The audience clapped. My legs felt like jelly.

I did it! Holy shit!

I didn't want to admit it, but it felt good. "That was mean, Steven!" I pretended to glare at him. But he could tell I enjoyed it, the jerk.

We walked off the stage toward our family, Lance, and Craig.

Lance handed me my beer. "You did great." His eyes went up and down me. "No broken phones or anything."

Despite myself, I smiled back at him. Everyone stared at us. When Lance looked at them, they suddenly became fascinated by the nearby tables.

It felt bizarre to hang out with Lance. But nice…sort of. "Thanks."

"And I have it forever," said Henry, flashing his phone. Lance let out a small chuckle and put his arm over Henry's shoulder.

Note to self: steal Henry's phone.

Talk drifted away from me. Steven struck up a conversation with Lance and Henry, while my parents and Craig talked to Tony and Monica. I stood off to the side, staring at the stage, smiling.

My feet were walking out the door before I even realized what I was doing. When I stepped into the night, the frigid air was a shock to the system. I only wore my gray, distressed sweater and black jeans, but the cold was a relief compared to the thick, stale air of the bar.

I leaned against the stone building and stared at my phone. I knew I shouldn't do it, but I did it anyway. Because we were best friends. And when something happened to you, you told your best friend first.

Jake's phone rang and rang. After a moment, I got his voicemail. I never got Jake's voicemail.

When the sound beeped, I hesitated and licked my lips. "Hey, Jake. Sorry to bother you. I just…Well… You'll never guess what happened to me tonight…"

Music thumped inside the bar again. Somebody else was doing karaoke. Probably Steven. Hopefully not Dad and Craig.

I sighed into the phone. "I…uh…think I might be the newest member of the Big Damn Deal."

28

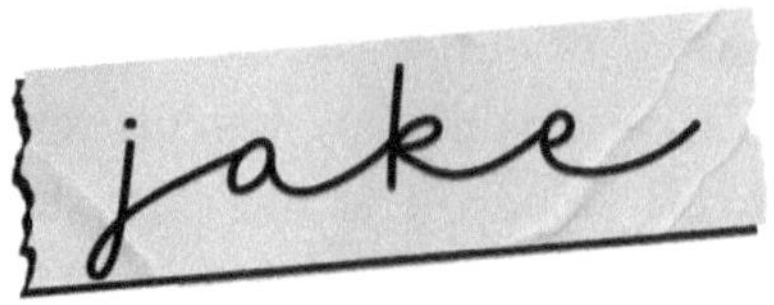

I don't know what the hell's wrong with me. I must have the worst timing of any man in history. Daisy and I decided to go see a movie on Saturday night. Simple. Straightforward. But, like a grandpa, I put my phone on airplane mode when we went into the theater.

I should've left it on, volume up, like the dick in the front row.

Afterward, we went for ice cream. And, of course, I forgot to take my phone off airplane mode. Actually, I forgot to take my phone off airplane mode until I was brushing my teeth before bed. At about eleven-thirty.

Suddenly, Daisy rushed into my bathroom, iPad in hand.

"What are you still doing up?" I asked, mid-brushing.

She was as hyped as that time Ash and I accidentally gave her coffee ice cream at 9:30 at night. "Did you see the video Steven sent?"

I spat out my toothpaste. "What video?"

Daisy hopped up and down. "Of Leah singing!"

"What?" I asked, totally confused.

Then it dawned on me.

Your phone.

I grabbed it, turned off airplane mode, and was suddenly inundated with messages. It was like the Ents releasing the river. I got four texts from Steven, two calls from my dad, one call from Dennis, and…

My chest froze. I had one missed call from Leah.

I stared at my phone. "What the fuck?" Daisy giggled. "Sorry, sweetie. I shouldn't have said that."

The first three texts from Steven told me to get my ass down to the Silver Dollar to hear him and Leah sing karaoke.

Karaoke? What the feck?

The third message included a video of the song. I stood there, watching it, my bare feet glued to the hardwood floor. Leah was singing—in front of people—and I missed it.

Daisy danced around, laughing and watching it again and again. "Steven was a jerk to make her sing that part alone."

My mind could hardly process it. I went to my voicemail and listened to Leah's message.

"Hey Jake, sorry to bother you…"

Bother me? Jesus.

"…I just…Well… You'll never guess what happened to me tonight…"

Daisy turned up the video and nodded her head to the music. "This is a weird song."

"I…uh…think I might be the newest member of the Big Damn Deal."

Steven's nonexistent band?

I realized I was smiling. Leah was going to sing more. She was having fun.

Good.

But what the hell had happened in the last six hours?

"Hey Dad, did you watch the end of the video?"

Did I? I didn't seem to be thinking straight.

"Look at the guy next to Leah and Dennis," she said. "Isn't that Henry's dad?"

My mouth hung open as I watched Lance and his shiny head make pleasant conversation with both of our families. Leah laughed at something he said.

Was it really hot in my bedroom?

"What in the fuck?"

"She asked Tony for the wimpiest beer he had," said Steven. He laughed into the French onion dip. Dennis pulled it away to avoid Steven's spray.

It was Sunday night at the Roth house, and everyone was regaling me with the story of Leah's first karaoke experience. I wanted to call her right away on Sunday morning to hear about it. That's what I would've done before. No, that's not true. I would've gone right over to her house to hear the story. But now that I was giving her space again, I questioned every move I made. I was afraid of crowding her or annoying the hell out of her.

"Shut up, Steven," said Leah. "I was nervous. I didn't expect everyone to be there."

Leah flashed me a look. Was it a nervous smile? What did a nervous smile mean? Was she upset that I wasn't there? Was she *glad* that I wasn't there?

Jesus Christ. Calm down.

"Too bad we went to that movie," said Daisy. "It wasn't even good."

"Too bad you had your phone on airplane mode all night," said Steven, cackling. "It's time to buy Daisy a phone so she can teach you how to use it."

He was probably right.

Leah and I sat on our swing. It was almost completely dark out, and the air was chilly. Leah pulled her hands up into her fuzzy green sweater. It reminded me of the night when I could have told her everything but didn't, afraid that I'd ruin our friendship. But maybe I ruined our friendship anyway, and our love along with it.

Optimistic bastard.

"I'm sorry I missed you singing." My breath drifted out into the night. "Stupid phone."

"That's okay." She played with her hands. "You can watch it anytime you want, thanks to Henry."

"And I will. You were great."

Leah finally made eye contact. It was easy to see that there was something on her mind. "I shouldn't have called you last night." She hesitated. "And bothered you. That was dumb."

I nudged her playfully. "You didn't bother me. Don't be silly."

"It's just…You said you were going to stay out of my hair… We haven't talked as much lately… I mean…we talk. And you come to the furniture store sometimes. But…I don't want you to feel like you're forced to do something just because I ask you. You know?"

She was talking a mile a minute. I grabbed the swing to steady myself. I wasn't sure what she meant. Was she unhappy that I was giving her space? Or did she like it? Should I ask her?

I tried to keep it light. "You've never forced me to do a thing."

"You sure?"

I smiled a little more. "I wish I could have been there. What are friends for, right?"

She nodded and ran a hand along the swing. The white paint was starting to come off. Between that and the warped arms, it needed an overhaul.

"Unless me being there would have bothered you."

"You only would've bothered me if you were drinking something as gross as Lance's smoothie."

We grinned at each other but then awkwardly glanced away into the cool darkness. This was how our talks always went now. We could be chugging along, all smiles, and then suddenly we were both at a loss for what to say. But we weren't really at a loss. The problem was that we had *too* much to say but didn't know how to say it or whether it was a good idea. It was too bad this wasn't a movie. I'd know what to say in a movie. I'd be able to tell her that she could trust us to stand the test of time without looking like a broken record or an insistent creep. And if this were a movie, I'd be wearing a coat I could drape over her to keep her warm. But this wasn't a movie, so I sat there stiff and self-conscious, unsure whether Leah even wanted me to say or do anything.

"So...Lance," I said, breaking the silence. My blood pressure rose just mentioning his name.

Leah's eyes widened. "Yeah. I wasn't expecting that. He was in town for a bachelor party."

I nodded, trying to look nonchalant.

"He sat with everyone while I sang. It was like going back in time to a bad stage in my dating life."

"Does he still do the beady-eye stare?"

"Oh yeah. He's Mr. Intensity. And his arms are even bigger than last year. I don't know how, but they are."

"Jesus," I said. Muscled bastard.

"But he learned about personal space. He doesn't almost stand on your toes when he talks to you anymore."

My head swung around. "No shit?"

My surprise made Leah break out laughing.

"How are we going to make it for the rest of our lives without smelling his garlic breath?" I asked, trying to hold it together.

She laughed so hard that she swatted my leg. The unexpectedness of it made me laugh along with her.

"You think that was bad. For half the time we dated, he was on a horseradish kick. That was fun to kiss."

See? Everything is fine. Calm the fuck down.

When her laughter finally subsided, she let out a long sigh. "But you know what was the weirdest part of him being there?"

"That he didn't take pictures of his dick?"

Leah tried not to laugh all over again. "He seemed decent." Something stirred in my chest. "I know, I know. But he actually wants to take Henry out for his birthday since he wasn't in town."

That *was* surprising. Lance always insisted he wasn't dad material.

"Really?"

"I know. Isn't that strange? And he reassured me when I was nervous about singing."

What the hell?

"He was like a football coach," she said. "Trying to pump me up to go on stage."

I had no idea what to say. Nervousness crept back in, despite my best efforts to squash it. "It would be nice for Henry if he came around more."

"It's almost enough to make me forget that he went behind my back and sent all those dick pics while we were going out. And then hooked up with that blonde while I was at my parents' house."

I stared at her. She stared at me. After a moment, we both started laughing again.

"Okay," she said, shaking her head. "I still kind of hate him."

We drifted back and forth in the swing. It was getting colder, but neither of us mentioned going in. I didn't want to move from that spot next to her. I wondered if she felt the same way.

"How's Daisy doing?" she asked.

"Sometimes she has to ice her shoulder after physical therapy. It can get a little sore. But her movement is better each day."

Leah smiled at the faded swing. "That's good."

A light breeze blew through us. She scooted a little closer. I wasn't sure if the move was conscious or unconscious.

"How about Henry?" I asked.

All signs of Leah's smile were gone. Her lips were a long, tight line. "He isn't doing too well in school."

"Daisy hasn't said anything."

"He's kind of bummed, you know?" She didn't look at me. But I knew what she meant. "That's not just me saying that. He pretty much said it himself…"

My stomach felt like it was being tied in a bunch of fisherman's knots. I knew Henry was unhappy that day when we talked about the pie. But I thought things were better. But his texts to me lately had been short…

I wondered what I could do to help him.

"I don't know what to do," she said. "The only time he's been happy lately is when he took that video of me. And when you guys were talking about that pie and coffee milk."

Now *I* was the one scooting closer to her. I didn't even mean to do it. Leah didn't move away. She gave me a light smile that made me woozy.

"Has he been texting you lately?" she asked.

"Not as much."

"But he sent you the video."

"Steven sent me that." Leah frowned at me. "What?"

"That's kind of weird, don't you think? Why didn't Henry send it? You guys are buds."

We were buds. But everything was weird now. Complicated.

"He should come over," I said. Leah's face brightened. "Tell him the coffee syrup came. It's sitting on the counter, waiting for us."

"Really?"

"Of course. And coffee milk might be about the only thing we've ever made or tried that Daisy won't be grossed out by."

Leah laughed quietly. "Yeah, but I don't think she'll try the pie."

I grinned. "Hell no, she won't."

Her fingers were only an inch from mine. We sat in anticipation of something that both of us were frightened to do. But neither of us moved. We were close together, but I guess not quite close enough.

"Henry's going to be fine," I whispered. "Everything's going to be fine."

My words drifted to her. She closed her eyes and took them in, nodding. For a moment, I thought she was going to reach out and grab my hand, but she was only tucking her hair behind her ear.

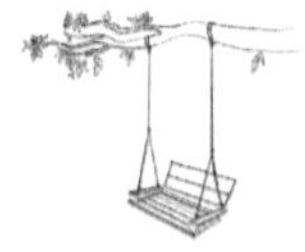

B&R Café was closed for painting. Dad, Dennis, and I spent one whole day taking crap off the walls and putting up painter's tape that ended up being, as my grandma might have put it, a big load of bollocks.

"This is a nice, cheerful color," said Dad.

"Way better than the tan," said Dennis.

"Hey, I picked that color back in the day," said my dad.

The three of us had settled on a nice light blue. I dipped my roller in the color and tried to paint as close to a window as possible. The sun peeked out from behind a cloud and lit up the new paint. I cocked my head. It was similar to the color that Leah and I picked for our bedroom when she was supposed to move in.

I stopped and stared. Okay…maybe the exact same.

Good God.

"How are things going with Leah, son?"

"You don't have to ask him how things are going," said Dennis. He was wound up in a second. "This is, what, round two of giving her space? I think that means it's going like shit."

Pressing the roller as hard as I could against the wall suddenly seemed like a grand plan. I didn't breathe. It took me a moment to realize that Dad and Dennis were right behind me, watching.

I turned. "Is there something I can help you with?"

"See?" asked Dennis, nudging Dad. "It's going like shit."

I put down the roller. "It's not going like shit." The fuck it wasn't. "I told her I'd give her time. And that's what I'm doing."

"But time is money, kid," said Dad.

I threw up my arms. "Those words don't even mean anything put together in that context."

"He means that the longer you two spend apart, the more likely you are to *drift* apart," said Dennis.

"Exactly," said Dad. "What if you wake up and, boom, it's two years from now? You could end up dating other people but pining for each other the way you two always used to."

"That would be shitty," said Dennis.

These guys always thought they were offering me great advice, when all they did was amp me the hell up.

"And you weren't with us the other night," said Dennis. "Lance and his beady little eyes were looking Leah up and down like a possum about to romance a dish of cat food."

Just what I want to hear. Fecking Lance. Mr. Four Minute Mile. Mr. Dick Pic. All these years later, he's still haunting me with his shiny bald head!

I wiped my hands on a rag. "What do you expect me to do?"

"Proclaim your love," said Dad. "Like in a romance movie."

I stared at him for a long moment. Then my hands flew up again. "Do you need to look at the script to jog your memory, Dad? I've proclaimed my undying love several times. If I do it again, I'm going to look *fecking* nuts. I can't tell her I love her again unless I somehow receive 100% confirmation from Leah that she wants to be in a relationship."

Dennis and Dad shook their heads.

"How are you ever going to get that?" asked Dad.

My ears were ringing. "Great question!"

"That's not what taking a chance on love is about," said Dennis. "It even pretty much says so in that song."

I collapsed into a nearby chair, Dad and Dennis following suit. We had a selection of day-old treats and coffee on the table.

"It's not like it is in the movies, you know," I said, peeling the cupcake liner off my muffin with the finesse of a tiger. "In movies, when a guy keeps proclaiming his love, it comes off as romantic. In real life, if you keep telling a woman you'll love her forever…and she's not sure the relationship is a good idea… You look like a needy psycho. You look like a bloody stalker."

Dennis and Dad contemplated this.

"He might be right," said Dad.

"Shit," said Dennis.

"I told her I'd give her space and time, and that's what I'm doing," I said. How many espressos had I had? "Because if I do anything else, I look like I'm trying to push her into a relationship. And that is not kind, healthy, or sexy."

We sat there quietly eating day-old baked goods.

"We should try this from another angle," said Dad. "Work on Leah a bit."

Dennis frowned. "Steven's doing that, remember? Pretty sure Gail already gave up scheming so she could play pickleball with Lois."

"Excuse me?" I asked. My mind blinked back to Steven winking at me after he was done talking to Ash. "Perhaps you should stop meddling!"

They weren't listening. To be honest, I'm not sure if they realized I was still sitting there.

"They need more excuses to casually bump into each other," said Dad. "That always happens in movies."

Dennis was pumped. "Yeah, like they're both at a party. Then they turn. They gasp. They see each other from across the room—"

"Both looking hot to trot, don't forget that," said Dad, cutting in. "By that time in a movie, everyone's pure sex."

"Exactly!" said Dennis. "Then it's nothing but stolen glances. Words unspoken. Sparks flying! Baby-making music is playing in the background."

What the hell was happening to these two?

"And parties have low, sexy lighting," said Dennis, insisting. "Strobe lighting. It's blue. It's red. It's sexy." He gave my shoulder a light slap. "You're young; you get it."

"We could have strobe lights at the Christmas party," said Dad. "That's months away, though."

I rolled my eyes. A Christmas party with strobe lights and Steven sounded like five hours in hell.

"We could have a Halloween party," said Dennis. "We haven't done that in a while. And nothing says sexy like Halloween. Halloween costumes are sexy even when you don't want them to be. Even when they *shouldn't* be. They force it on you."

I wiped crumbs off my hands. "I don't think any of us should be attending a party where we have to look sexy."

Dennis was outraged. "Speak for yourself!"

"Don't sell yourself short, son. You're not Mr. Body Builder like Lance, but I'm fairly certain you're sexy. You have my genes, after all." He eyed me. "You have muscles. Look at those arms. And you're tall as fuck." He looked at Dennis. "What do you think?"

Dennis scanned me, considering. "For Halloween he could dress up like a sexy tall puppy. I could see Leah liking that."

"No Halloween party," I said in a stern voice. What the hell was I saying? I didn't mind a Halloween party. I wanted to bump into Leah as much as possible. I just didn't want to dress up like a sexy tall puppy. What would that even entail?

Dad and Dennis had already moved on.

"What are some other romance tropes?" asked Dad. "We need to think of more ways they could get back together."

I sighed. "Jesus."

"That depends," said Dennis. "Are we talking romance movies or romance *novels*? Because romance novels are probably a whole different thing."

"That's true." Dad thought for a moment. "Romance novels can get damn spicy. If this was like the fantasy romance I'm reading, someone would've fucked a dragon by now. And the guy you thought was evil would be fantastic at oral sex."

I stared him down. "Dad! What book is that?"

Dad looked pleased with himself. "Your gran sent it to me. It's good. I'll lend it to you when I'm done."

We all took a moment to breathe. I didn't know about them, but I was more confused than ever.

Dennis took a bite of a day-old cookie. "Have we figured anything out?"

Dad scratched his chin. "I don't know that we have."

29

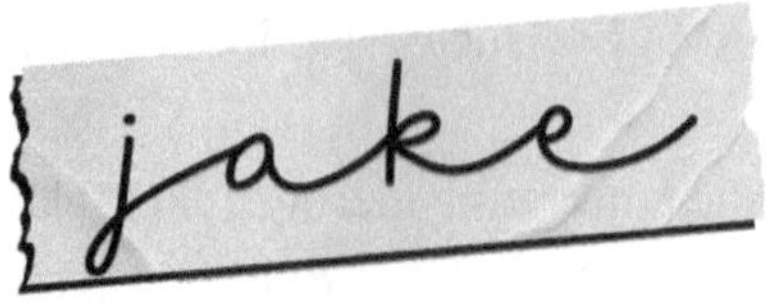

I lifted a kitchen towel to reveal the ingredients. "We have avocados, cream cheese, and…I can't believe I'm saying this… Here's the sweetened condensed milk."

Henry and Daisy inspected everything for the avocado pie. Daisy wasn't too impressed. Henry had looked underwhelmed since his arrival, but he brightened when he saw the coffee syrup and everything for the pie.

"This is gonna be kind of gross, isn't it?" asked Daisy.

I cracked a smile.

"It sounds like something Steven would eat," said Henry.

"It does kind of, doesn't it?" I asked.

While the graham cracker crust was in the oven, we mashed the avocados and beat them in the mixer with the cream cheese, sweetened condensed milk, and lime juice. After the crust cooled, we dolloped the filling into it and put it in the fridge.

Daisy got out the milk, and I grabbed the coffee syrup. We poured milk into our glasses and then squirted in the syrup.

For reasons I didn't understand, the clinking of my spoon against the glass reminded me of a heart palpitation. I was nervous to have Henry over. How stupid. He'd been over a thousand times and spent the night more times than I could remember. But now everything felt weird. I felt like I had to entertain him. Or maybe impress him? At the very least, I felt like I had to put on some kind of show in an attempt to prove that everything between us was fine. But as Henry's bored, downcast eyes scanned the house, his expression said what words didn't have to. We were *not* fine. And if making stuff together didn't mend our relationship, I didn't know what would. That was the way we had always bonded.

Daisy took a tentative sip of her coffee milk. "This might be the first thing that doesn't totally suck."

Henry and I gaped at her. Usually, Daisy found a reason to hate every weird thing we tried. Henry and I exchanged a glance. After a long, quiet moment, we both laughed.

Okay, he's laughing. Everything's fine.

Henry took a big gulp of the milk. "I think it's fire."

I took a drink, then stirred it a little more to incorporate the syrup at the bottom of the glass. "I like it. I think I might have gone a little heavy on the syrup, though."

Henry's face brightened a bit more. "You'll have a stomachache later."

I took another sip. "If I'm lucky."

That made all three of us laugh.

"I wonder if it has caffeine?" asked Henry.

"We'll know if we feel like running Grandma's Marathon later," I said.

This isn't the apocalypse. Everything's good. Shut your mind off, you idiot.

Now that the coffee milk experiment was over, we had a big swath of time to fill until the pie was set up enough to eat. But I had no idea how to fill that time.

The kids figured that out for me. They sat on the sofa, coffee milk in hand. In a few minutes, they were engrossed by a YouTube video to help them figure out how to beat some level in

The Legend of Zelda: Link's Awakening. My shoulders relaxed. Maybe everything *could* be the way it was. Or close enough to happy, anyway.

It seemed like a good time to look through my cookbooks for tips on making churros. When I returned to the living room a half hour later, the kids weren't there. Music wafted from Daisy's bedroom, so I wandered over. She sat cross-legged on her bed, talking to her Game Boy as she played.

"We figured it out," she said, smiling up at me.

"That's good," I said. "Where's Henry?"

Daisy shrugged. "He said he was going to find you. To see if you remember this level."

I nodded and left the room. Why was my stomach churning? *Too much coffee milk.*

It didn't take me long to find Henry. The door to the room that was supposed to be his was cracked slightly.

Now my stomach is really fucked.

Henry stood by the window in the nearly empty room. There was a bed, a dresser, and not much else. I never put my stuff back in after the move-in fell through. His card of paint samples still sat on the nightstand. He had his back to me and didn't hear me come in. He put down his coffee milk and picked up the paint sample.

After a moment, he put it down again and tried to open the top drawer of the dresser. It fought him every step of the way.

"That drawer always sticks," I said. Henry glanced at me as I walked up. "I used that dresser when I was a kid. The drawer did the same thing back then."

Henry didn't say anything. He only nodded.

"I heard once that you can rub a candle along the inner part of the drawer," I said. "Something about the wax is supposed to make it easier to run on the track. But I've done that a couple of times. It doesn't help."

The drawer finally opened. There were a couple of Game

Boy games in it. When did Henry put them there? He shoved them in his pants pocket. "Maybe a YouTube video could help you fix it."

I smirked. "That's a good idea. We'll have to look it up."

It suddenly felt too quiet. It was enough to drive you nuts.

"Not right now, though," said Henry.

I didn't know what to do. Henry stood there, so unlike himself. No jokes. No laughter. No sarcasm. It made something catch in my throat.

"No worries," I said, just for something to say.

Henry pushed the dresser drawer back in. It squeaked the whole way—like nails on a chalkboard—but neither of us laughed or commented on it.

When the drawer was finally closed, Henry let his hand drop. He stared at me, sullen. "This was stupid. I want to go home."

My eyes widened. Before I had time to say anything, Henry was out of the room.

God, that kid's fast when he wants to be.

He sped by Daisy's room, with me trailing behind. Daisy was so focused on her game that she didn't notice us.

Henry snagged his coat out of the closet like he was the Enterprise at warp speed.

I grabbed mine and followed him out the door. "Come back inside. We haven't even tried the pie."

"I don't give a shit," said Henry. He turned on the sidewalk and scowled.

I stopped dead. I'd heard Henry swear a few times, but this was different. There was so much anger in it. I was speechless for a second. "I don't think your mom would want you talking like that."

"I'm *twelve*," said Henry—nothing but sarcasm.

My feathers ruffled. "Congratulations! You're good at math. Come back in the house."

But Henry kept walking until he reached the road. He sat on the curb and took his iPhone out of his coat.

I tried to sound calm and open. "Daisy will wonder what's going on."

Henry cranked his neck. That kid's biting voice could've drained the life right out of me. "Daisy knows *exactly* what's going on."

For a comment that didn't contain a single swear word, he sure made me feel like I'd been kicked in the stomach.

"Everything is stupid now," said Henry. "Everything is stupid, and you and Mom don't care."

Jesus. What was I supposed to say to that? It was easy to see why Leah had kept her dating life and Henry separate. I'd never seen him like this. I felt like I was losing him, and it scared the shit out of me.

I edged closer. "I know things are hard now, but they'll get better."

Henry texted someone. He didn't look up. "They haven't yet."

I looked at him for a long moment. He barely looked back. "You have to give it time."

We stayed that way for a while. I wondered if I should try to coax him back in. But he was like a lawn ornament fixed to that spot.

"Do you want me to call your mom?" I asked.

Henry's face became nothing but dark eyes and bushy, angry eyebrows.

Shit. That was the wrong thing to say.

"No!" He stared me down with the intensity of a volcano. "Why do that? You guys don't even *like* talking to each other."

I stood my ground. "That's not true at all."

"That's what it seems like to me!"

I tried to sit down, but Henry slid further down the curb.

"I texted Steven to pick me up," said Henry. "So you don't have to stay out here with me."

The sky was cloudy and the air was cold. There were always snowflakes in Minnesota in October. The snow didn't often stay; it was usually only a flake or two, but there *had* been a big Halloween blizzard our first year here. Leah, dressed as a witch, climbed up snowbanks far taller than she was. As I stood there with Henry, the dim autumn light wrapping around us like a heavy sheet, it felt like it could snow anytime.

I stepped closer to Henry again, but he stood up and walked further down the sidewalk.

"Go away!"

His angry voice was like a shockwave in the air. I was at a loss. A child had never made me feel this way. He hated me, and I knew kids hated their parents sometimes. I remembered times when my dad annoyed the shit out of me. But I had never felt it from this end.

And Henry's not your child.

But my heart had different thoughts on that.

After a moment, I walked straight at him. His eyes widened with surprise. He must have thought he'd scared me off.

I held his shoulder. "I won't stay out here if you don't want me to." I saw my whisper in the air. "But I'm going to watch you from the kitchen. So don't you leave this yard until Steven gets here."

Henry stared at the ground. Just like that, he was a kid again. He gave a small nod.

I stepped away like I was heading back to the house. But then I stopped. "Things are going to be alright, Henry. You'll see."

Now I had to make myself believe that.

I stood in the B&R kitchen with my dad, Dennis, and, inexplicably, Steven.

"What are *you* doing here?" Dennis asked Steven.

"I can't stand being at home with Leah. Between her worrying about Henry and worrying about Jake, it's been nothing but stress and sad love songs."

"Is she also listening to 'Animal' by Neon Trees?" asked Dad. He motioned to me. "Because *he* has it on repeat."

"That's not true," I said.

It was.

Steven nodded. "Except she mixes it up sometimes and plays Niall Horan's 'Heaven.'"

"I don't get what we're doing here," said Dennis. "We're missing football."

"This is more important than football," I said, grabbing the flour.

"Bite your tongue," warned Dennis.

"I need you guys here to help me," I said. "And Steven too…because what the hell else are you going to do?"

Steven ate a cookie. "That's true. What's shakin', bacon?"

"What's shakin' is that my life is imploding," I said. "Henry hates me. And I'm not sure if Leah will ever want to take the plunge with me again."

Dad stepped closer. "So, what are we doing?"

My eyes met his. "We're going to do the same thing we did when Mom died."

Dad stared at me for a long moment, then finally nodded. He was ready. "We're going to bake some shit."

Steven leaned against a counter. "Isn't it neat the different ways people process grief?"

"This must be what you meant about changing up the bakery case," said Dennis, worried. "Oh, God. You didn't just find different muffins to try, did you? It's going to be complicated stuff that makes me tired just thinking about it."

I ignored him and lifted a piece of paper. "This is what we're going to make. Churros—"

"Are you kidding?" asked Dennis. I stared him down. After a moment, he relented. "Keep going."

"A chocolate cake reminiscent of the one from the movie *Matilda*," I said.

Steven made the surfing hand gesture. "Fuck yeah."

"Some kind of chocolate chip cookie that's a copycat of the one at Levain Bakery," I said.

"Jesus." Dad stared at the ceiling, looking almost wistful. "I heard that whole block smells like cookies all day long. That's the dream, isn't it?"

"And éclairs," I said, voice rising. My face was dead serious as I glared at them all. "And we're going to call them éclairs, damn it. We're not calling them long johns."

My dad had his hand up like he was waiting to be called on. "We can't do that. We can't call them éclairs. People around here won't know what the fuck we're talking about."

"What's wrong with long johns?" asked Steven. "Yummy, yummy custard filling."

"It's an éclair!" I threw up my hands. "I don't know where the term 'long john' came from, but the rest of the world thinks you're a load of goons."

"I will fight any man who says an éclair and a long john are the same thing," said Dennis. "Totally different. Not even close."

We all stared at each other for a moment.

Steven was the only calm one in the room. "That's it? That's how we're going to stave off melancholy and the fear of heartache?"

Steven gave me a dubious glance as he wiped crumbs off his shirt.

I shoved a cookbook in his hands. "You're fecking right. Get the measuring cups."

30

Steven sat next to me on the sofa, strumming his guitar. Henry was in the puffy chair, his arms crossed.

"I can't believe you acted that way with Jake," I said, frowning. "You know he loves you. He was worried about you on the phone. You better apologize."

The phone call with Jake had been friendly but brief. Something about his voice made me antsy. Was he annoyed? Was I finally annoying him?

Good grief, Leah.

What was I freaking out about? He had a right to move on if I couldn't figure things out.

You're a mess, girl.

Henry's shoulders dropped. "Can't I send him a letter?"

Steven laughed, still strumming. "That sounds like something I'd say."

"I know," I said. "It gives me nightmares." My eyes bounced back to Henry. "And no, an apology in person, thanks."

It was seven at night, and we were waiting for Danica to show up. Somehow, I fully agreed to Steven's plan. I was going to practice a few songs and sing them at the Silver Dollar.

Steven wouldn't be singing with me this time. He'd be playing the guitar. But even though we'd still be on stage together, the idea of singing alone freaked me out. Steven asked Danica over because he thought the Big Damn Deal needed a banjo.

"Three people isn't that big," said Henry.

I tried not to laugh.

"No shit." Steven furrowed his brow. "I'm working on it."

The idea of watching his mom, uncle, and uncle's girlfriend play instruments and sing must have sounded lame, because Henry wandered to his bedroom.

"I'm worried about him," I said.

"Give it time," said Steven. "That's what Jake said, too, right? You can't rush anybody about their feelings."

"I guess that's true." *Really* true, since I was the one being wishy-washy about what I wanted. And it didn't help that we weren't talking much. Space didn't do shit last time. Why did I think it would help now? It made everything feel worse. Was Jake even interested anymore? If I went to him with an answer, would he even want to hear it? And what answer did I want to give him? Was I sure I wouldn't run away again?

"Shut up, mind!" I said out loud.

Steven didn't take his eyes off his guitar. Mr. Relaxation. "You do that a lot lately."

I ignored that. "When is Danica going to get here?"

"She has to feed her Irish Wolfhound first."

I listened to Steven play. The song wasn't familiar.

"You always want to talk about my love life," I said, tossing a throw pillow at him. "Let's talk about yours."

He batted it away. "You trying to make me blush?" His eyes glistened. "Fire away."

I settled into the sofa. "Do you ever see Margot?"

Small lines formed between Steven's eyes, and his playing stopped. "She was at Felicity's wedding."

I sat up straighter, shocked. No wonder Steven was so

moody at the reception. "She *was*? I didn't see her." I scanned my memory. "She wasn't in the bridal party with me."

Steven's voice was unnaturally quiet. "You know she doesn't like that stuff. Bridesmaids and all that. But she was there." His jaw shifted. "Her hair isn't red anymore. It's black."

I watched minuscule emotions on Steven's face. "It must be hard living in the same town, knowing you might bump into each other."

The subject of Margot was the only thing that made Steven lose his characteristic cool. "I'm pretty sure Margot has devised a schedule whereby she never has to bump into yours truly." His eyes drifted to the floor. "Except when we run into each other at Caribou. She can't calculate whether we might both be in the mood for a depth charge at the same time."

I didn't expect him to look this way. To look so sad. "I'm sorry, Steven. Everyone thought you were going to get married."

Steven fiddled with the guitar strings. "You don't have to tell me... I know what they thought. The two of us thought that, too." There was hurt in his eyes. "But sometimes the road to love is like that county road seven that they turned back into gravel because of all the potholes."

Now both of us felt bummed about love. I scooted closer, staring until he made eye contact.

He met my gaze. "What?"

"Was she the love of your life?"

Steven gave me a wary look. "I'd be a pretty big dick if I said another woman was the love of my life while simultaneously dating Danica." He didn't look away. "I don't play games that way."

I nodded. "Does that mean Danica is the love of your life?"

An emotion I couldn't decipher flashed across Steven's face. It disappeared, and he started strumming again. "Danica and I are great. We know exactly what to expect from each other. Nothing complicated, but lots of understanding."

That didn't sound too bad, but as I thought back on my love life, it was clear that I preferred things as complicated as they could get.

"What about you, Leah? What do you want?"

Good question.

Like you don't know.

"A love that will last."

Steven nodded. "Great song. We could practice that one too."

We smirked at each other.

"You can have that, you know," he said.

I stared at my lap. "I don't know if I'm made that way."

Steven played a little louder. "That's the beautiful thing about people. They get remade every day."

Danica had straight blonde hair that went halfway down her back. She wore a white sundress and a brown vest. When she put down her banjo and smiled, she reminded me of Shelly Duvall.

She was way taller than I was. She bent down to my level when we talked, like when you talk to a toddler. "Hello there." At least, I think that's what she said. "Nice to meet you."

I had to step closer. I'd never heard someone with such a quiet voice. Everything about her was as chill as Steven. It wasn't hard to see what had attracted him. She was Margot's polar opposite. Margot was a lot of fun and a lot of things, but chill wasn't one of them.

"Nice to meet you, too," I said.

We shook hands and everything.

"This might be out of the blue." What was that? "But are you happy with your current living arrangements?"

I glanced around at the small house I hated. I was supposed to be living a couple of blocks away with Jake.

Then what are you doing here?

"To be honest, no."

She gave me a hazy nod and pulled a business card out of her dress pocket. "We should talk. But I can't give you a discount because I'm sleeping with your brother." Her eyes disappeared in her smile. "I wish I could."

I looked at Steven. He looked at me. He was pretty damn satisfied with himself.

"Good to know." I raised an eyebrow. "So…you're a banjo-playing real estate agent?"

"And I sing." She put a hand on her throat. "I've been told my voice is very quiet when I talk."

I acted surprised. "Really?"

"It's louder when I sing." She put her hand down. "Steven says that you're having love troubles?"

Talk about an abrupt change in topics.

I shot Steven my death eyes. "Yes. Thanks for that, Steven."

"No problem, sis."

Danica put her hand on my shoulder. "That's wonderful. Heartbreak is great. It makes your singing more emotional. And it builds character."

I had so many comebacks, it was like I was at a buffet. "If heartbreak builds character, I must be Orson fucking Welles."

Danica let out a tiny laugh. "I don't know who that is, but I can sense your joke must be funny."

Then, just like that, she wandered over to the rocking chair to fiddle with her banjo.

Steven kicked my foot. "What do you think?"

"She's better than the one who made the butter sculptures."

My singing adventure wasn't going great. Everything was fine when it was just Steven and me, but now I felt pressured. My voice was so quiet, it felt like I was mimicking Danica. I had the strong urge to grab the nearby throw blanket and hide under it like Henry when he was three.

I stopped singing and cleared my throat.

Steven and Danica's playing came to an abrupt stop. Steven sighed.

"She doesn't know me very well," said Danica. "I think I'm making her nervous."

Everything made me nervous. Singing in front of Steven's girlfriend, the idea of singing in front of everyone without the silly karaoke music and other singers to hide behind…and of course, Jake. If I were honest, Jake was the main thing on my mind. I couldn't get him out. Was I letting him slip away because I was afraid?

"I feel stupid," I said, ignoring my thoughts. "A lot of people sing better than me."

Steven rested his arms on his guitar. "You act embarrassed that you're a beginner. But that's the way everyone is at everything." He gave me an understanding nod. "You can't skip a step and be an expert. To be good at anything someday, you have to be a beginner today."

Danica nodded. I couldn't believe he said that. Why was Steven making so much sense lately?

Was he making sense, or was I spending too much time with him?

"That was actually profound," I said.

"Get to know me, sis." He studied me. "And another problem. Why are you sitting hunched over like that?"

He took the end of his guitar and gently pushed it against my chest, forcing me to sit up straight. "You act like you're trying to hide, and you're the singer." He was loving this. "I know this might scare you, but people are there to listen to singers, so hiding won't work."

I was instantly defensive. "You're hunched over, too."

He chuckled. "That's because I'm playing the goddamn guitar. I'm supposed to sit here like a moody son of a bitch. But if you sit hunched like that, you're not going to get good airflow."

"Try some breath work before going on stage," said Danica.

"And you know how else you get *not* nervous?" asked Steven. "We do this over and over. You sing in front of people over and over. Until it's as scary as making a piece of toast."

"Remember that most people aren't there to judge you." Danica smiled. "They're distracted by sad questions in their own lives. Like, why doesn't my wife love me anymore? Or why can't I get the asking price for my house?"

I stared at her.

"Not caring what people think is a good option, too," said Steven.

I fiddled with my shirt. "I'm nervous because my voice isn't stellar."

"Not everyone's going to be Adele," said Steven. "You have a folky voice. A weird voice. And lucky for you, we're going to sing some folky, indie, slow shit. It'll be like that coffee shop channel on Sirius XM." Steven strummed. "So calm down and enjoy yourself."

They were right. I needed to relax. "What songs should we do?"

"I think we should do a slowed-down version of 'Amadeus' by Family and Friends," said Danica. "That would suit her real good."

Steven nodded. "I like that." Then he looked at me. "What else?"

"You're asking me?"

"You're the singer," he said.

I nearly laughed. "But I don't know what I'm doing."

"You like a lot of music," said Steven, coaxing. "What do you want to sing?"

I thought. Then I thought some more. And when something obvious raised its head, I knew I was thinking *too* much. I knew I should ignore my idea, but I said it anyway. "Maybe some Bob Dylan."

"You're speaking my language. Which song?"

I couldn't help it. I thought of Jake and me in bed. It felt so long ago, even though it wasn't. The place where we told each other our secrets. Gave each other our hearts. Touched each other. Made each other feel loved. And now I wasn't sure we'd ever be in that place again, even though I wanted to be. Because I wasn't sure it was right, even if it felt good.

I thought about Jake pulling me close and telling me there were a lot of songs about me. I wondered if he still thought that. I wondered if he still thought about me when he listened to *that* song.

My eyes met Steven's. "'Girl from the North Country.'"

31

It was a chilly Saturday, and people were lined up around the block.

Steven packaged treats for people. "Am I getting paid for this? I could be working my *actual* job."

I handed treats to Mrs. Jacobs. "You never work on Saturdays."

"You could still pay me, if you want."

I nudged him out of the way to grab cookies. "Tell yourself you're doing a good deed."

Steven wasn't amused. "I sure have been doing a lot of good deeds for you and Leah lately."

"How is her singing going?" I was eager to hear her at the bar. I loved that she was doing this, even though I knew she was probably nervous.

"Henry would say that she's fire." Steven paused. "Fire with a little stage fright."

When there was a pause in the action, Steven poured us each a cup of coffee. "By the way, Leah's coming over later. I told her about all the new stuff you've been making. She's excited to see it."

That got my attention. "She is?" I became as fidgety as a teenager on a first date. Were my hands numb?

"Thought I'd mentally prepare you." He looked me up and down. "Good thing I did. Look at you. Don't you want to see her?"

I took a coffee cup from him, annoyed. "Of course, I want to see her. We haven't talked since my call to her about Henry. And I know I sounded like a fecking idiot on the phone." I mentally kicked myself. "I didn't know if I should offer to come over and talk to him to figure things out."

"You seized up like improperly tempered chocolate."

He had been spending too much time at the restaurant. I guzzled the coffee and poured myself more.

Caffeine should help, right?

"Yes, I seized up. I didn't know what to say or do. Pressure has never been my thing, you know that." I held the coffee cup with a death grip. "I can't even stand the pressure at the ALDI checkout. They hardly have your stuff in the cart before they're onto the next person, and there you are, scrambling to grab your lettuce. It's too fast."

"I've always considered the ALDI checkout a metaphor for life," said Steven.

"That's how it was with the whole Henry thing. Too fast. And then I didn't know what to say to Leah."

"She'll probably be here in ten minutes, so while you're pondering what to say and do, you might want to switch to chamomile tea."

The bell at the top of the door chimed for the millionth time that morning. But this time was different from all the rest. Because this time, when I looked up, it wasn't just anyone walking toward me. It was Leah. There was surprise on her face as she took in all the people and the energy in the café. We made eye contact, and she gestured to everyone. Her grin widened as she approached. Her eyes sparkled as she studied the bakery case. She was happy for me. She was thrilled for me. I couldn't help but smile back as she gave me a thumbs-up. Things might have been weird with us, but she was proud of me. I wondered if she knew what that meant. How that feeling nestled in my heart. She really was golden.

A wistful, happy look was stamped on her face. "You did it."

I reached into the bakery case and took out a churro.

Her eyes got bigger when she saw it. "I didn't even see those!" Were her eyes watery? "Do you remember what I said?"

Of course, I remembered. I needed to watch out, or my eyes would get watery too. "You said that if I made churros, people would be lined up around the block."

Leah turned her head and looked at all the people in the restaurant. Then she looked back at me and cracked a smile. "I was right…because you can make anything."

Then she did something I didn't expect—something she always did when we were friends. She came around the counter and reached out her left arm. My heart beat faster as I reached out my right hand. We met in the middle and gave each other a half hug. Her head rested against my chest, and I was right back in those months when we were together. When everything felt like a wildflower haze of us laughing, of us opening our hearts and sharing secrets, of us stretched out, our bodies intertwined, of us knowing we'd last forever. I breathed in her perfume for the brief moment that we hugged. I told myself to take it all in. Hold it all in, in case this was the last time we ever held each other.

When the moment was over, Leah glanced up at me again.

Her eyes were still watery. I wondered what that meant. All I knew was what my heart wanted it to mean.

She lifted the churro and took a bite. I knew that look. She closed her eyes and nearly laughed. "This is even better than in Duluth."

My cheeks felt warm. "You think so?"

Her eyes narrowed in a sweet, pensive way. "Definitely."

Steven, Dad, and Dennis stared at us from the kitchen. I fought the urge to ask if they wanted us to record our conversation. Unconsciously, Leah and I both walked to a quiet corner of the restaurant. Dad took over the register. The Musketeers continued watching. Leah rolled her eyes at them.

"Do you have hot chocolate to go with the churros?" asked Leah when we sat down.

"I haven't quite cracked the recipe yet."

She playfully kicked my foot. "You will."

I appreciated her confidence, but I'd already tried three recipes. "If you like the churros, I guess this means Henry gets pie for breakfast."

Leah tried to smile, but I could tell she was still stressed about Henry. "Did he ever apologize?"

Oh, shit. Can't lie about this.

I felt a little nervous for Henry. "No." Leah sighed. "But he doesn't have to. I was…wondering…if there's something I could do. Should I talk to him? Would that make things worse?"

Leah stared down at her churro. "That's sweet of you… I don't know what to do either. That's the other reason I'm here…"

"Oh," I said, slightly confused. "Well…I'd love to help."

"That's great…" She tapped her fingers on the table, nervous. "But…um…I'm actually here to meet Lance. He wants to be more involved with Henry, and I thought this was a good time." I made my face emotionless. "Maybe he can say something to him, you know?"

In my heart, I knew that made sense. Fathers should want to be involved with their children, but it was hard for me to think of Lance as anything but a first-class prick after the way he cheated on Leah and mostly ignored Henry's childhood.

"I'm sorry we're meeting here," Leah added. "It was Lance's idea."

I bet it was.

"He hasn't been here in a while," said Leah.

You bet he hasn't.

"And he said it's his favorite restaurant in town," she said.

That was rich. Lance never liked me. The feeling was mutual. He always stared me down when Leah and I shared a joke or when we spent time together.

Because he knew how you felt.

I swallowed that thought. "Don't worry about it. I hope he can help Henry. And I'm glad you came in to get that churro."

"Are you kidding?" she asked. "I'm coming in every day to get these bad boys." She sounded like she meant it. That felt good. "Could you watch the table for a minute? I want to use the bathroom quick before Lance gets here."

"Sure."

She smiled, got up, and slipped away to the restroom. I glanced at the register. The Musketeers seemed pleased. I gave them the finger, which made them smile more.

Idiots.

I didn't have to look up. His cloud of cologne announced his presence. Fecking Lance. And Leah was still in the bathroom, so I had to talk to the prick.

Holy shit. I did a double take. He looked like the joke Leah and I made about exercising seventeen hours a day.

He wore a gray polo shirt and khakis. No coat.

Probably not. Gladiators are impervious to the cold.

He made beady eye contact with me, and there was that smile. The condescending one. Yep. A changed man, alright. Against every urge in my body, I motioned him over. I turned my head for a second to look at Steven, Dad, and Dennis. Steven was downright tickled. He winked. But Dad and Dennis looked like they needed to find the Tums.

Lance sat across from me and stared me down, just like old times. And just like old times, his look made me guess that I was two minutes away from him attempting to make me feel inadequate.

"Leah's in the bathroom," I said. "She asked me to save this table for you."

Lance nodded. "Perfect."

Talk about the personality of a cardboard box.

He reached his hand across the table. Were we going to shake? I reached out my hand. It felt like he was trying to break my fingers.

Dick. But I smiled.

"It's been a while," he whispered.

"Henry's eleventh birthday."

I've been to all his birthdays. Where have you been?

He got a kick out of that. He leaned back in his seat, watching me.

Here we go—the changed man.

"It's funny," he said slowly. "After all these years, you still have your eyes firmly plastered to Leah's ass."

I let out a humorless laugh and patted the table. "Leah told me you'd turned into a gentleman. Nice to see."

"And I hear you couldn't keep her." He leaned forward, his voice quiet. "I told you back then, and I'll tell you again, Jake.

She's too much woman for you. Women like that don't go for guys like you." He leaned further. "Were you even able to make her moan?"

It wasn't the first time I had daydreamed about smashing Lance's face in with a café chair. He always brought out the best in me. "Go. Get. Fucked."

Lance chuckled lightly. "I *have* changed, you know. But… there's something about you, Jake." He traced his hand tattoo. "Your goody-goody act…"

I didn't see Henry anywhere in him. "Then why are you intimidated?" I crossed my arms. "And you're the last man on Earth who should comment on keeping Leah."

Lance shot a casual glance at the register. The Musketeers made a point of looking busy. "They all think you're a great guy, but great guys don't dream of fucking another man's woman. Especially when she just had a baby."

Jesus. There was a lot to unpack in that sentence. I hadn't been in many fights, but this fecking idiot was pissing me off worse than a particularly eventful night at the bar when I was twenty-four. "I'm well aware I'm not perfect. But if you want to talk about great guys and fucking around, remember who you were with and what you were doing while Leah was changing Henry's diapers."

There was no reaction on Lance's face. Not surprising. The man was a robot. He leaned back. "You want her back, don't you?" I felt the heat rise within me. "You think she'll want to go round two with a man-child?" Lance chuckled. "Time to give it a rest."

Then something clicked. It all made sense. "Good Christ. You're only agreeing to spend more time with Henry to get to Leah, aren't you?" I shook my head. "How typical. Go to the bollocks, you moron."

"Maybe I want both. I want us to be a family."

Bitter amusement slapped me. "That's rich. I've heard the

way she talks about you. Keep dreaming. She'd never get back with you."

"You sure?" I nodded, but I couldn't stop the uncertain twist in my stomach. "You're not the only one who's loved Leah all these years." It felt like a weight had been dropped on me. *Holy fuck.* "I messed up. But I changed. And I changed for *her*. And I plan to make it right."

My body was nothing but twisted anger and heat. Lance. Why was it always Lance? "People like you never change."

"Keep telling yourself that." He enjoyed every second of this. "And I'm just as patient as you. I can wait for her for five years or ten. If she ever wants me, I'll be there." His smile drilled me. "And even if you get back together, I'll always love her." My palms turned sweaty and cold. *Shit. Shit. Shit.* "You'll never get rid of me, Jake. I'll always be around."

That was enough. I stood up. Nobody looked at us. Despite our mutual hatred, we'd been quiet.

"It kills you, doesn't it? That Henry is my son and not yours."

I stared down at him. "DNA doesn't make him your son. *Time* does. You never understood that."

A cocky grin. "I'm getting that time thing figured out right now."

"For Henry's sake, I'm glad."

I tried to walk away, but Lance turned toward me. "Yeah, you're the saint, aren't you? I bet you *fucking* love how we'll spend time together."

A knowing calm came over me. "I *do* want you to spend time with Henry." I leaned over. "But I know you'll fuck it up, just like you fuck up everything else. That's what fuckups do."

32

Lance handed me a piece of paper. "These are activities I could do with Henry."

Being at B&R Café meant I had to pretend I didn't have peripheral vision. Dad, Craig, and Steven watched me like I was a good substitute for whatever game they were missing. Jake tried to shoo them into the kitchen, but I could see the heat on his face. Had Jake and Lance argued? It was no secret that they hated each other. I guess it was hard to be a big fan of someone when they broke your best friend's heart. But if Lance finally wanted to be a part of Henry's life, I didn't want to tell him to stick it.

I grabbed the paper. "We could've met somewhere else."

Lance sipped his decaf coffee. "That wouldn't have been as fun."

I raised an eyebrow. "What do you mean?"

Lance turned and looked Jake square in the eyes. Jake stared back, his face a stony mixture of annoyance and amusement. He shoved cookies in the bakery case.

Lance turned back to me, smiling. "I can tie him in knots like he's a set of Christmas lights."

I didn't hide my disappointment. "You picked a fight with him."

That smile. He didn't even try to deny it. And there was that shine in his eyes. That mixture of danger and anger was what attracted me when we first started dating. I got tired of it quickly. Where was that guy from the bar when I sang? The guy who seemed so different. I was an idiot.

He knew I was pissed. His face softened. "I'm sorry." That was new. "That guy pisses me off… Probably because you crushed so hard on him the whole time we dated."

I felt like laughing. "Crushed?"

Lance fiddled with his coffee cup. "Don't deny it, Roth."

I looked toward Jake. His eyes met mine and held my gaze, making my body woozy. He shot me a goofy smile.

You will never not love him.

"Okay, maybe I did," I said. "But you weren't exactly lonely or heartbroken. Not with that blonde sitting in your lap."

Lance's expression tightened.

I ignored it and pointed to an item on his list. "You want to take Henry fishing? Have you *ever* been fishing?"

"When I was fifteen."

"Did you like it?"

Lance didn't move or blink. "No. But Henry might."

I read through Lance's other activity suggestions. "Chanhassen Dinner Theater?"

I wanted to be a fly on the wall while Lance stared, stonefaced, at people singing and dancing.

"They're doing *Jersey Boys*," said Lance.

I smiled, remembering our old joke. "I didn't realize they let the Tin Man into musicals."

There was a spark in Lance's eyes. "C-3PO. We agreed years ago that I could be C-3PO."

I laughed. "You can't be a robot from *Star Wars* when you've never seen *Star Wars*." We stared at each other, our laughter slowly dying away. "Thanks for spending more time with Henry. He's been bummed since Jake and I split up."

Lance nodded, leaning forward. Everything went still. "Of course." Did he hesitate? "I *want* to spend more time with Henry…and you."

He gently placed his hand on top of mine. I didn't have to look to know that Jake had stopped putting churros in the display case, his attention totally on us.

I slowly pulled my hand away, dread creeping in. "What's happening?"

Lance looked nervous as hell. "I want to ask you out."

I felt dizzy. I could have ripped up that list. "Oh, my God. That's why you're here." I tried to regain my bearings. "We aren't hooking up." Disgust settled in my stomach. "Good grief. Are you even here for Henry? Or is this just to get to *me*?"

There was a pleading look in his eyes. "I don't want to hook up. I want to spend time with you." He took a breath. "I want us to be a family."

I felt like I was through the looking glass. What the hell was happening?

"I'm not that same guy anymore."

I stared him down. "Henry says you're with a new woman all the time."

"Sure. I date a lot. Just like you date a lot, Roth." I felt clammy. Was my whole family watching? "I know you don't believe me, but I'm not that same guy anymore. Cheating on you was the worst thing I ever did. I wish I could take it back. Because then we'd still be together."

There was buzzing in my ears. I wanted an escape button. "You think we'd be together if you hadn't cheated?"

"Yes." He took a breath. His voice was constricted. "I love you, Leah."

Shit. Lance meant it. I could see it all over his face. My chair squeaked on the hardwood as I backed out to run.

"Please don't go," he whispered.

And shit, I couldn't. I needed his help with Henry. I hesitated, then scooted back up to the table. My whisper to him was exasperated. My eyes were crazy. "We're *not* getting back together."

Lance's jaw tightened. "Is it because of *him*?"

My eyes drifted to Jake moving around the kitchen. The muscles in his long arms flexed as he grabbed heavy trays out of the oven. Holy shit, he had good arms. And a good heart. He had *good* everything. It made it hard to breathe.

Lance's voice was gruff. "What's so great about him? He's predictable. Boring."

That was a good way to piss me off instantly. "Is that how you're going to win me back? Insult my best friend?" I gave him an irritated smile. "Interesting tactic." I saw the regret in his eyes, but I didn't care. "You know how many times he's had my back over the years? The trips to the hospital when Henry had a fever as a baby? Driving fifty miles out of his way when my car broke down? And there are a thousand other examples I could give you. He's been a father to Henry for years, Lance. When you were MIA." The color drained from him. "Boring and predictable? Get a fucking clue."

Lance leaned back. He looked like I'd slapped him. "I'm… sorry."

And I thought he meant it, but I was overheated and needed to get out of there. "I want you to spend time with Henry. But that's it. You have to forget all this about you and me."

Lance stared. I couldn't figure out what his expression meant. His voice was quiet. "Alright."

I didn't believe him for a minute.

I nodded at his list and put it in my purse. "I like these ideas. You can pick Henry up Friday after school."

Lance wouldn't stop looking at me. "If Jake is so great, why did you break up with him?"

Jake's face lit up, smiling at something Steven said.

My eyes met Lance's again. "Because people like us don't deserve people like him."

Where did the time go?

It was the night before I was supposed to sing. Between the performance, anxiety over Jake, and annoyance over Lance, my legs felt like they were going to buckle. And the dumbest part was that deep down, I wanted to sing.

You're an idiot, Leah.

Danica placed her banjo back in its case, ready to head back home after our night of practicing. Steven held her gently by the elbow and pulled her in for a kiss. Then she winked at him and headed toward the door.

"Thanks again for suggesting 'Amadeus,'" I said. "I love singing two songs that are strangely topical and slightly uncomfortable."

Danica waved on her way out. "No problem."

I threw myself onto the sofa. Steven slid down next to me, untroubled. "I can't sing two songs about love and loss. I'll look crazy."

"All songs are about love and loss. Calm down."

Did I look as freaked out as I felt? "I think I'm getting sick. Do I feel hot?"

Steven felt my forehead. "Just as I suspected. Scared shitless." He took his hand away. "Don't worry. I felt like that before my first EI competition. Ironing while downhill skiing."

I eyed him. "How did it go?"

"Remember that time I sprained my wrist?"

I crossed my arms. "Great."

"You'll be fine. We've practiced so much that the words have lost their meaning. Plus, Jake's excited to hear you."

That didn't help. I could still see Jake's wide-eyed horror as Lance held my hand. Did he think Lance and I were back together?

Oh, God. Another thing to worry about.

Henry hurried into the kitchen and grabbed a granola bar.

"Bud, tell your mom she's going to do great tomorrow."

Henry flashed me a knowing look. "You're not getting out of it. I've had to listen to you sing the same two songs for how long?" He tore open his bar. "You're doing it."

As Henry walked away, I shouted after him. "I'll do it if you apologize to Jake! You still haven't done that!"

"Yeah, yeah," he mumbled as he disappeared into his room.

"I like his style," said Steven, grinning.

I grabbed my brother's arm in a quiet panic. "Listen. I need a favor."

Steven was intrigued. "How much are you willing to pay?"

"I'm serious."

"So am I."

"You need to tell Jake not to come hear me sing tomorrow night." My eyes were still on the hallway. I didn't want Henry to overhear me.

"Bullshit," said Steven. He glared at me. "You know how much I've been at the café lately. He talks about you singing all the time. What the hell, Leah?"

"'Girl from the North Country' is the song he used to listen to when he thought about me. I was such an idiot to pick it. I don't know why I did."

Steven lifted his eyebrows. "I know why. You want him to be your sexy tall puppy."

I couldn't have been more confused. "What the hell are you talking about?"

Steven ignored me. "Aren't you trying to tell him something by singing this song?"

"I was missing him when I picked that song. It was stupid. I must have been dehydrated." I was getting more flustered by the second. "And I *always* miss him. But the song's not supposed to be a come-on."

If I wanted that, I'd sing "I Could Write a Book."

"So why choose that song? What does it mean to you?"

I could've pulled my hair out. "I don't know. That's the problem! That's why I'll probably puke three times before tomorrow night." I sighed. "It means I wonder if he's still thinking about me. And I don't even have the right to wonder that because I don't know what answer to give him. You have to tell him not to come."

Steven studied me for a long time. "What excuse should I give?"

"You're fucking weird, Steven. I'm sure you can think of something."

Steven rubbed his chin. "That's probably true." He paused. "This is only going to freak him out more. He's wound pretty tight after seeing Lance. It might send the wrong message."

Stupid Lance. I rubbed my temples. "I know. But if he's there, I'll have a total freakout."

We were quiet for a long moment. Steven leaned back. "You know you can't avoid him forever."

I frowned. "You and Margot have avoided each other for five years."

Steven put an arm around my shoulder. For some reason, it almost made me want to cry.

"I don't think you should use me as a blueprint for what to do and what not to do," he said.

33

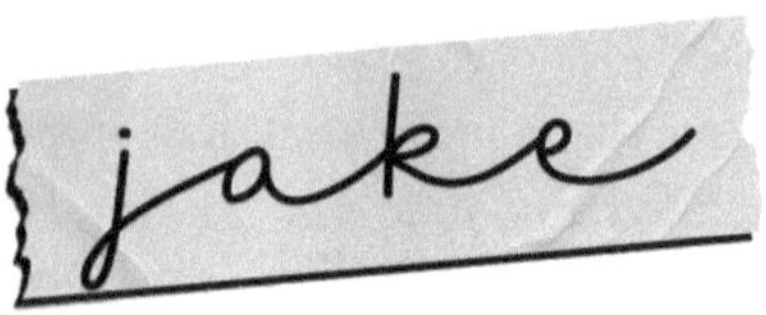

Daisy was at Leah's house, hanging out with Henry and getting ready to hear Leah sing that night. So when the doorbell rang, I was instantly suspicious.

Time to pretend I'm not home?

Then the door cracked open.

"We're not selling bad pastries for a school fundraiser," Gail called out. "It's just me and Steven."

I met them at the door, wondering what was up. Gail and Steven stepped inside, taking off their scarves. A rush of cold air came with them.

"Is everything okay?" I asked. "Is Daisy—"

Gail sighed. "Daisy's fine. It's you and Leah that are the problem."

"Mom's pissed." Steven walked around the kitchen, opening cabinet doors. "Got any snacks?"

"I'm not pissed," said Gail. "I don't get pissed. But you and Leah *are* directly responsible for throwing off my pickleball game. And that's something I take seriously."

I looked back and forth from Steven to Gail. "Am I missing a page from the script? Because I have no idea what's going on."

"Leah doesn't want you to come tonight," said Steven, matter-of-factly.

My mind went to a thousand different places in under a second. "Are you serious? Why not?" I was stunned. And then it hit me. Lance said he'd always love Leah. That he'd always be around. *That guy's a fecking bollox.* "Don't say it's because of Lance! Please don't tell me that spending more time with Mr. Personality has turned into something. Because if it has, I'll be throwing up very shortly."

"Of course not," said Gail. "You know Lance. He'll probably get distracted by a shiny object and wander off like always." I took a deep breath. "Leah doesn't want you there because she chose a song that she's embarrassed to sing in front of you." Gail was deadpan. "Because she misses you, you idiot."

Now my mind was off in another direction. Thank fecking hell it wasn't because of Lance. But how did I feel about her choosing a song she was embarrassed for me to hear?

I grabbed the countertop unconsciously for support. "What song?"

Steven opened his mouth, but Gail shushed him. She narrowed her eyes. "We're not telling you. Because I think you should be there to hear it. You two need to figure things out. You're more confused than Steven when he started out as a math major in college."

"That was a strange time," whispered Steven. He opened the cupboard above the sink and snatched the store-bought chocolate frosting hidden behind the cereal. "What's this trash? You must be slipping. You won't even eat pancake syrup."

I stared off into space. "I always have a secret stash of shit frosting for times of total chaos." Steven grabbed a couple of spoons and started chowing down.

"You can lurk in the shadows by the exit," said Gail. "She won't see you. It's like Bella Lugosi's crypt in there."

"Okay…" I said. The word was stretched out. I rubbed my

eyes, confused. "I think I need to sit down." I plopped onto a kitchen island chair. Gail and Steven stood, observing me and eating frosting. "So…she's singing a song that means something to us, but she doesn't want me there. Does that mean she doesn't want me back, or that she *does*, but she's nervous?"

"She doesn't know what she wants yet," said Steven, licking his spoon.

I didn't know where my head was. "You two know how to make me feel great."

"Anytime," said Gail.

"What should I do?" I asked. "Am I supposed to ask her about the song? Do something because of it?"

"That's for you to decide," said Gail.

Steven slid the frosting over to me. I grabbed the clean spoon.

"Huh," I said.

"What?" asked Steven.

"Oh, nothing," I said, eating a large mound of frosting. "I'm really curious about what I'll do."

Dad, Dennis, Gail, Steven, and the kids were already at the Silver Dollar when I quietly slipped in through the side door. It had been a while since I'd been there.

God. Is it always this dark?

Dad and Gail must've been waiting for me. They passed me on their way to the bar, nodding. Dad gave me a pat on the shoulder when he walked by. It was supposed to be comforting, but it made me nervous.

It was busy in there. If I had to sing in front of that many people, I would have pissed myself. And there was Lance, cozying up to the bar. He gave me a passing, snide smile. I took a page out of my dad's playbook.

Téigh ithe cac, I thought.

I was trying to shove Lance out of my head when Henry walked up. We'd barely spoken since he stormed out of my house. He didn't look in a better mood. His arms were crossed, and he had a defeated look on his face. It made my heart lurch.

"Henry." I wanted to say a lot to him but didn't know where to start. "How are things?"

"Steven says Mom doesn't want you here. Is that true?"

He was getting taller every day, but standing there, he looked just like he did when he was seven.

"Yes," I said, but I quickly added, "I think she's nervous."

Henry stared holes into me. "If she's nervous, she should want you here the most."

That made my heart ache.

"It's going to be okay," I said, but Henry shook his head. My eyes popped to Lance. How long had he been staring? He was enjoying himself.

"Forget you," said Henry. Then he turned and charged back into the crowd.

"Henry," I whispered, reaching out for him. "Henry, wait—"

But he slipped between some people and was up by our families in a second, taking a seat next to Daisy.

I stepped back into the shadows, resting my head against a pillar that went from the floor to the ceiling. A headache cemented itself at the base of my neck. Everything was so fucked up. Lance sat in full enjoyment of my misery. Henry hated me. What the hell was I going to do?

After a few quiet moments, Danica walked up the steps and took her place on stage. She had eaten at the restaurant a couple of times with Steven. Either she was incredibly quiet, or I was going deaf.

My body was tense, and my heart ached, but then everything stopped—my fears, Lance's pointed glares. It stopped.

Leah walked into the shimmering light, Steven trailing behind. She took in the crowd, then glared at her brother. She didn't look like she knew what to do with her hands. All clear signs that she was nervous. My heart went out to her, but I knew she'd be fine. Better than fine. She'd be fecking amazing.

"Alright, everybody," said Steven, talking into the mic. His voice was casual, relaxed. "You know me. This is my sister, Leah. And this is Danica Walters. And we are the Big Damn Deal. We're going to play a couple of songs for you tonight. Just two, because I know Monica is excited to get out here and do her karaoke rendition of 'Kiss From a Rose.'"

There was quiet laughter from the audience. Monica gave him a thumbs-up from behind the bar.

Steven strummed his guitar. "Oh, and we're always recruiting for the Big Damn Deal. To make it, you know, *big*."

During Steven's speech, Leah stood next to him, staring at her brother like she didn't want to acknowledge the crowd. The dim light set off golden and auburn tones in her hair. She had bright red lipstick and wore a dark plaid dress that hugged her waist. She looked fecking wonderful. Sexy. Haunting. Artsy.

What'll she sing? I wondered. I realized I wasn't breathing.

"I'm guessing a lot of you will know this song." Steven strummed away. "If you don't, your Minnesota driver's license will be revoked."

There was more quiet laughter from the audience. I didn't have time to register what Steven meant when the tune on his guitar changed. It was slower than the original version, but I knew that wonderful goddamn song anywhere. It was "Girl From the North Country" by Bob Dylan.

Leah stepped up to the mic and gazed down at her family. My heart felt like it would bust in half. Then she opened her mouth and started singing the words I knew from front to back

—lyrics about a woman who lived in the cold north, who used to be the singer's true love.

I leaned my head back against the pillar. I could hardly see her from the tears welling in my eyes. She was singing the song I had listened to a thousand times while thinking of her. While falling in love with her. It was the song that ran through my head as I held onto her hand while she gave birth to Henry. The song that ran through my mind as I sat on her sofa, nervous to tell her how I felt. The song that ran through my mind when she reached for me in the night. There were a lot of songs about Leah, but this was *the one*. The one that told me everything was okay. The one that told me everything was falling apart. The song that bolstered me. The song that gutted me. And she sang it fecking perfect. Her voice was crackly and jazzy. I could have made love to her tone.

I took a deep breath as she got closer to one particular verse. The one that meant the most to me. The question that had crossed my mind so many times over the years. The question that still crossed my mind now. Tears were already sliding down my cheeks when she got to the part where the singer spends days and nights wondering if the girl ever still thinks about him.

The rest of the song was a blur as I wiped my face. Nobody noticed me back there in the corner. Not even Lance. Everyone's attention was on Leah, just like it should be. Because she was golden. Absolutely golden.

Everyone clapped. There was a surprised expression on Leah's face. Steven and Danica gave her exuberant pats on the back. She looked amazed that she had done it. Happy that she had done it.

Good, I thought, *because you were brilliant.*

But the surrounding air was starting to feel tight. Lance eyed me again, then disappeared closer to the stage and our families. I felt boxed in. Leah was starting her second song when I knew I had to get out of there. I threw open the heavy side door and was smacked by the chilly night. I stood on that darkened sidewalk, hands on my hips, trying to get some air back in my lungs. My chest was frozen.

The door squeaked open behind me, and Gail and Daisy shot out.

Daisy grabbed my arm. "Wasn't Leah great?" The bright smile on her face faded when she saw me wiping the last of my tears away. "Are you okay?"

"I'm fine," I said, trying to get myself together. "Everything's fine."

I knew I should smile to be more convincing, but I couldn't.

Gail didn't have her normally placid countenance. "I think your dad needs a hug."

Daisy grabbed me around the middle. I held her, trying not to lose it all over again.

Gail stepped forward. "Can a mom give you a hug, too?"

That did it. A stray tear ran down my face. "I'd like that."

They both had hold of me. We stayed that way for a while, our breath disappearing into the blackness. When Gail pulled away, she kept her hand on my back. "I know I don't say this a lot because I'm from Minnesota, and we don't do emotions…" She raised an eyebrow. "But you know I love you, right?"

I nodded, smiling slightly.

"You can have a mom hug from me whenever you want."

"I might take you up on that."

Daisy stared at us, puzzled.

"So, what do you think?" asked Gail.

I was quiet for a beat, then pointed at the bar door. "I don't know what happens after this life, but I know one thing. I'm not going to love Leah until the day I die. I'm going to love her a lot longer than that."

Gail cracked a smile. "What are you going to do?"

I stared down at Daisy. She gazed into my eyes, all excited.

I grinned. "Me and Daisy are going to sneak into your backyard and steal the porch swing."

Daisy frowned. Gail was dumbfounded. They exchanged a look, and then Gail let out a little laugh. "Steven and I wondered how you'd react, but neither of us guessed you'd say that."

"Why steal the swing?" asked Daisy.

"We're going to fix it up," I said. "Then give it to Leah on Christmas. What do you say?"

Daisy jumped up and down.

Gail gave me a crooked smile. "I say hell yes."

An hour later, Daisy and I stood in our garage. The faded, warped swing sat on the floor in front of us.

"What do we have to do?" asked Daisy.

I circled the swing, inspecting it. "Well…I think it needs new arms. Unless they can be fixed. Some of the planks on the back of the swing are loose, too. We might need to buy some power tools. And the whole thing needs a coat of paint."

"But Dad…do you even know how to fix stuff like this?"

I shrugged. "No, but that's what the YouTube gods are for."

We examined the swing again.

"We're going to buy a bunch of tools to fix *one* thing?" asked Daisy.

That was a good point.

"We should fix something else, too," I said.

Daisy smiled. "There's that dresser in Henry's room."

My body felt lighter. "You've got something there."

34

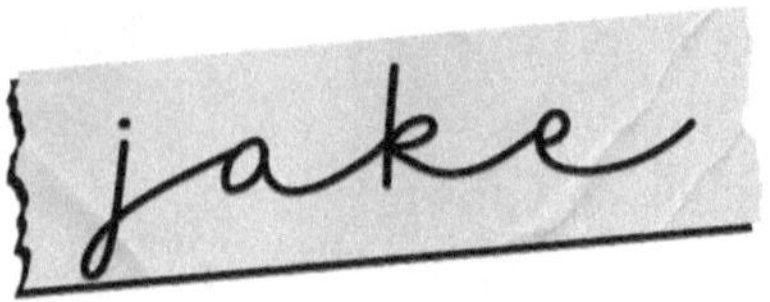

The next day, I sat in the living room, watching clips on my iPad about how to fix the swing. Daisy saved a few videos before Ash picked her up to go get hot cocoa.

As I watched a very helpful woman from the south tell me why I should invest in wood filler and an electric hand sander, I heard a strange sound. I looked up from the video, trying to figure out what it was. After a moment, I shrugged and stared back at the screen. But then the noise returned. It was muffled. A kind of strange plopping sound. I paused the video and stood up, trying to figure out where it came from.

Suddenly, something banged against the kitchen window, rattling the glass. I zoomed over to the closet, threw on my coat, and opened the front door. I ducked as something flew two feet to my right, hitting the siding and house numbers. I stared, wide-eyed.

It was mud! A thick clod of mud.

My vision shot over to where the mud came from. Henry stood on the sidewalk with a five-gallon pail. His hands were caked. His face was red and stained with tears. He reached into the pail, grabbed another mound of mud, and threw it against the house. Then he looked at me and screamed.

I flew out into the yard and examined the house.

Fecking shit!

Apparently, he'd been at this for a considerable amount of time before I heard him. The siding looked like something dragged through a swamp. My mind spun in disparate directions. I was worried about Henry, nervous about how the old vinyl siding was holding up, and also somewhat proud of Henry's dedication to his art form. This was the kind of thing my dad got up to when he was a child, which said a lot about why my Gran was the way she was.

I slowly approached Henry, my hands raised like I was trying to calm down a tiger. But the situation was probably closer to looking like an old Western showdown at high noon. Henry reached into his bucket again and grabbed a huge clod. When he narrowed his eyes at me, I could have sworn I heard that whistling theme song from *The Good, the Bad, and the Ugly* somewhere in the background. The only thing we needed were toothpicks hanging from our mouths.

"Now wait a minute," I said, hands still raised, but Henry drew first. I only had time to widen my eyes as he threw a wet clod squarely at my chest. It ricocheted, splattering not just my chest, but my face and arms as well. Then he threw one at the sidewalk by my feet. The mud slammed into the cement, splattering both my legs.

"I hate you!" said Henry, throwing more mud at me. It was caked under his fingernails and on the wrists of his coat. "I hate you and Mom. We used to be a family. Now we're nothing."

I stood still, letting him splatter me. He didn't need me to soothe him, not yet. He needed to yell at me. He needed to get it all out. He needed to hate me before he *needed* me.

"And you know what's stupid?" asked Henry. "Lance is taking me ziplining. *Ziplining.* I don't want to go ziplining! I want to make poutine with you. I want to make homemade spaghetti with you!"

I waited to see if he was going to say anything else, but he stood there, tears dotting his eyes, waiting for me to react.

"It's good that Lance wants to do things with you," I whispered. I might have hated the guy, but Henry deserved time with his father. "He needed to step up. He needed to make an effort. You know that. It's good that he wants to be there for you."

Henry started to say something but stopped. Tears slid into his gaping mouth. He ran a dirty hand through his hair. "He didn't care when I was five. He didn't care when I was ten! But *now* he cares. And because he cares, *I'm* supposed to care?"

I stepped closer to him. The cold air stuck to us like glue. "I know you and Lance haven't had the best relationship. But maybe now it'll be better, Henry. This is a good thing."

But Henry wouldn't stop crying. "I'll go ziplining with him. I'll go fishing with him. But he's always just going to be Lance, my friend. I don't want him to try to be my dad." He shook his head. "He doesn't get to suddenly be that. I don't want him to be my dad. I want *you* to be my dad!"

The tears in my eyes made him look like he was underwater.

Henry kicked the pail over into the brown autumn grass. "You were there for me when I was five. You were there for me when I was ten. You've *always* been there. You were gonna be my dad. You were supposed to be my dad! And now I'm nothing to you. You'll marry someone else, and have a new family, and forget all about me."

I stepped right up to him and got down on my knees. My face was red from the tears trickling down my cheeks.

I put my hands on his shoulders and looked him right in the eyes. "You listen to me, Henry." I could hardly get the words out; my voice was so strained. "I love you. I have always loved you, and I *will* always love you. Nothing in the world is going to change that." Our sad, bleary eyes looked into each other's. "I don't really care what the birth certificate says, do you? You're my son, do you hear me? You are my son." I put a hand on my chest. "That's what my heart tells me, and it's never going to change. I'm never going to leave you; I'm never going to abandon you, and I'm always going to love you. You are my son."

I pulled him into me, resting a hand on the back of his head as he cried into my shoulder. He reached his arms around me and held me tight.

"It's okay, Henry," I whispered. "I'm never going to leave you."

His sobs were muffled in my coat. "I love you."

"I love you, too," I said, holding him tighter.

We stayed that way for a long time, holding each other. Finally, Henry pulled away, wiping the tears from his face.

He pointed to my coat. "I got you all dirty."

I was covered in mud from head to toe. But it was all over him, too, from our hug. I smiled and shrugged. "Who cares? But I am a little pissed about one thing."

I winked, so he knew I wasn't actually angry.

"What?" he asked, his voice raw.

"Halloween was the perfect chance to throw mud at the house." I raised my hands in exasperation. "What were you thinking?"

Henry laughed through his tears. "Next year."

I chuckled quietly. "And ask Daisy to help. She loves group activities." I surveyed his pail of mud. "Where'd you get that anyway?"

"The dirt's from my grandparents' yard. I added water. It was hard dragging it here."

"I bet."

"Grandma loves spying on neighbors when they argue in their yard." Henry glanced around. "People are probably watching us."

I stayed on my knees. "Feck 'em." Henry smiled at that. I rested my hand on his back. "Listen, did you notice that the swing is missing from your grandparents' backyard?"

Henry nodded.

"Daisy and I took it. We're going to fix it up and surprise your mom on Christmas. Do you want to help?"

Henry's face lit up, though it was still puffy from crying. "Yeah."

"Great." Then I sighed. "Do your grandparents know where you are?"

Henry looked like he'd been caught.

"Does your *mom* know where you are?"

Now, Henry really looked nervous.

"Henry, Henry," I whispered, pulling him in and hugging him again. "You probably have everyone terrified." As I stood, I mussed up his hair. "We better get you back home. Your *other* home. Because this is your home too, okay?"

"Okay," said Henry, smiling. But it didn't look like it would take much to get the tears flowing again. He leaned into me, and I put my arm around him.

"Hey, do you want to eat some chocolate frosting quick before I bring you back?"

Henry didn't miss a beat. "Sure."

35

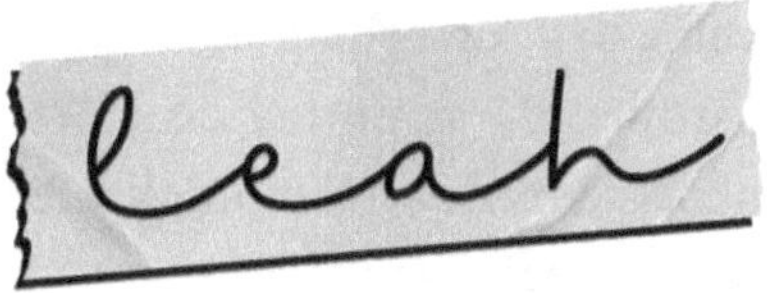

There was a light knock on the door before it opened. Jake and Henry walked in with dry mud plastered all over them. I stood like an idiot, mouth open. The fantasy novel Craig lent me fell to the floor with a dull clack. "What the hell?"

Before I could say anything else, Henry slammed into me and gave me a big hug. My mouth was still open as I hugged him back. I stared at Jake, completely confused. Did he look a little nervous?

"You guys can tell me what's going on now," I said. "Should I be scared?"

"I kind of hated you and Jake." Henry held me tight. "But I don't hate you anymore."

I wanted to laugh and cry at the same time. "I'm so glad. It makes me sick when my Care Bear hates me."

Jake looked like he might cry, too. It almost made my insides turn into that green slime from *Double Dare*. Quiet tears ran down my face. I was still half wondering what was going on.

Henry pulled away from me slowly. "I'm sorry, Mom."

I wiped a tear from both my cheek and his. Then I kissed his forehead. "I'm sorry, too, kid. I love you so much."

"I love you, too."

I sniffed in my tears and picked at the gunk on Henry's coat. "What were you guys doing?"

Jake smiled. "Henry threw mud at my house."

Everything came to a screeching halt. "What?"

Jake shrugged like it was no big deal. "It looks better with the mud. Like modern art. Don't you think, Henry?"

Henry laughed. "I decimated it."

Steven sauntered in. "Holy shit." He ate a bowl of Cocoa Pebbles, watching Jake and Henry with mild interest. "You two look like you tried your hand at professional mud sculpting. I did that for a while. It was a smellier hobby."

"You were supposed to be at Mom and Dad's," I said to Henry. "Do they know where you are?"

He cringed. "Well...they know I'm still in town... probably."

"Henry!" I said, freaking out. "Are you serious?"

Steven gestured Henry over. "Come on. We'll call the GPs so they don't have a shit fit. And I'll show you some pictures of my mud sculptures. I did a whole series on Hayao Miyazaki characters."

Before he left the room, Henry's gaze shot to Jake.

Jake grinned. "I'll see you tonight at your grandparents'. And then tomorrow after school. Don't forget."

"I won't!" said Henry.

Henry smiled. A *real* smile. I hadn't seen him like that in a long time. I gave Jake an over-the-top look of surprise when Henry was gone. I put my hands on my hips. "Are you going to tell me what's going on?"

Jake felt the mud on his cheek. "Henry was mad at me. Well...he's been mad at me for a while. You know that."

My smile faded as I stepped closer to him.

"It's okay," he said quickly. "Don't worry. He came over to throw mud at my house, but we made up. We're good now."

I gave him a puzzled look. "You're good now?"

"Yeah."

My skin felt hot. It had been a while since Jake and I were alone like this. "What did you say to him?"

Jake opened his mouth, then closed it. Was he nervous? "Do you really want to know?"

My pulse went up. I took another step closer. "Of course, I want to know."

Jake tried to find the right words. "Well…he was mad at Lance. Lance wants to do stuff with Henry, and Henry's fine with that. But Henry said he doesn't want Lance to be his dad."

My heart wobbled. I still wasn't sure if Lance's offer to spend time with Henry was genuine or if it was just a way to get to me. Stupid Lance.

Jake looked tense. Wistful. He came closer. "Jesus. I hope this doesn't upset you or anything because I'm pretty sure I overstepped like crazy, but…Henry said he thinks of me as his dad because of all the time we spend together. And he was scared that I was going to forget about him."

Keep it together, Leah!

But I couldn't keep it together. Jake reached out and rubbed my arm. It sent a shockwave through me. I never wanted it to stop.

"I told him that I'll always think of him as my son. I told him that I'll never leave him and that I'll always love him."

And just like that, the weirdness between us didn't exist anymore. I buried my head in Jake's chest. He wrapped his arms around me and gently rubbed my back, the way he always used to. He'd always love Henry. Did he know what that meant to me? Did he know what that did to my heart? Did he know that made me love him even more? It made me want to act on things, despite the fear lingering in my heart.

Jake's breath was warm on my face. I almost couldn't stand it. I wanted to kiss him so much. "Can you please stop giving me space?" I was moving one step closer to the thing I was scared to do, but I was doing it anyway. "It's even worse than last time. I thought it would help me think, but all it does is scare me. I can't figure anything out when we're apart like this."

Jake held me tighter. I felt his breath catch. His surprise. "You want me to come around more?"

He looked down at me. His bright eyes sparkled.

"Yes." Was I flirting? Damn right. "If you don't mind."

Jake gave me a nervous smile. With my chest right up against his, it was easy to feel his heart beat faster. "I think I can manage that."

I rested my head back on his chest, breathing him in. He smelled a little earthier than usual. I'd forgotten all about the mud on him. So did he.

"Oh shit." Jake pulled away. "I've probably made a disaster out of you."

There was only a little dry dust on me. "I'm fine. But look at you. We should clean your coat."

We stood in the bathroom with a couple of soapy rags. Jake had his leg up on the tub, wiping the dirt from his jeans. I had his coat over the sink, trying to scrub streaks of mud away.

My eyes darted up to Jake's reflection behind me in the mirror. Whenever he looked at me, I looked down at his coat. Whenever I looked up at him, he looked down at his jeans. But his face was getting redder by the second. He had on that brown button-up shirt that showed off his long, lanky torso.

What the hell is it with the two of us and bathrooms?

"You don't have to clean off my coat," said Jake, breaking the silence. "I can get it after I'm done with this."

I lifted it. "I think this is more than a rag can handle anyway. We have to stick it in the washing machine."

Jake and I made eye contact. I wondered if we were thinking the same thing. Was he going to stay while his coat tumbled around in the washer and dryer? My fingers were suddenly tingly.

I was still uncertain about whether Jake and I should be together or whether I could hack a long-term relationship. But for some reason, as I felt his warm presence behind me, I realized I wasn't going to run away this time. I wasn't going to hang out with him, pretending that we were friends but wanting something more. I was going to keep flirting with him and see where it went, even if I was nervous it would all fall apart again. I was going to see what evolved.

If your heart gets broken again, it won't be the first time, I thought. *And if you break his heart, it won't be the first time for that, either.*

I almost laughed at myself as I looked at the care instructions for Jake's coat.

A little optimism wouldn't hurt, you know.

"What's so funny?" asked Jake.

"Huh?" I looked up. "Oh, just my stupid mind."

Jake nodded. "I've been there."

There was something I needed to say, so I threw it out there. "I'm not interested in Lance."

Jake's jaw shifted. His eyes lifted to mine.

"I'll never be interested in him." Our eyes stayed locked. "Just so you know."

Jake gave me a crooked smile. Heat flashed in my chest. Finally, he nodded.

I absentmindedly mushed Jake's coat into a ball in my arms. "I'll go downstairs and throw this in the washer." My Lance comment did something to him. He had an intense expression on his face. Enamored. Smitten. It made it hard to speak. "Do you want to stick around while it's in there or...I could loan you one of Steven's coats until tonight. Except the arms probably won't fit right."

Jake took a step closer.

Good. Night. Those. Eyes.

"I can stay. If you're sure you want me around more."

I'm pretty damn sure about that. Thank you.

"That sounds great. We can think of something to do."

You didn't even mean for that to be a come-on!

"I mean...uh...with the ten thousand streaming services and everything..."

Jake chuckled. I shook my head like I was an idiot as we both went down to the basement. Steven and Henry walked around upstairs, talking loudly about *Spirited Away*. They sounded like elephants marching. Jake took his coat from me and threw it in the wash. I put a hand on the dryer, twiddling my fingers, and being all around awkward.

"I meant to tell you..." said Jake, slowly. He looked nervous again. "You were wonderful last night."

I felt my blood pressure drop. There was a ringing in my ears. Jake was there?

Shit!

I couldn't do anything but stare, open-mouthed.

"I was at the bar. Hope that's alright. Steven said you didn't want me there, but...your voice was beautiful, Leah."

Holy crap.

I could tell by his face that he was worried I might be mad that he came. I rested a hand on his to reassure him. His eyes widened.

"It's not that I didn't want you there. I always want you... there." There was that look again. Engrossed. Transfixed. "I was embarrassed…because you used to listen to that song and think about me."

He didn't get any closer, but somehow his warmth surrounded me. His voice lowered. "I still listen to that song and think of you."

Those whispered words sent a tingle up my spine. My eyes burned. If he said anything else, I'd be crying.

"I don't know why I sang it. I hope I didn't hurt you. I think…maybe…it was a shitty thing for me to do."

"Don't say that." We were barely a foot apart. "I loved it. But…uh…you don't have to worry that I'm going to flirt with you or anything because of it."

The implication hung between us. His eyes were on me, wondering what I'd say.

I shifted, playing coy. "You're not going to flirt with me at all?"

He didn't take his eyes off me. When he talked, I could hardly hear him. "Do you want me to flirt with you?"

Was my heart still beating? "A little, I hope."

He took a deep breath. I became aware of his chest, rising and falling. "I can do that."

I smiled, staring at my feet. "I guess…I sang it because I miss you. I…uh…I still don't know what to do. But I miss you."

He stood there like he was contemplating something. Finally, he reached out and ran a hand through my hair. Now *I* was mesmerized.

"That's okay," he whispered. "I said you could have all the time you needed." He leaned near my ear. "But it's nice to be missed."

There was that tingle again. We weren't going to kiss. Not today. Even though I wanted to. Even though it looked like he wanted to. We needed to bake a while longer.

"You thought I did okay?"

"Your voice was amazing. Fecking beautiful."

I tried to play it off. "You always say that. But it's probably the weakest voice in the room. The most average."

"No." He touched my hand. I wound my fingers through his and held them. "Your voice did something to me."

I tried not to look bashful. "Really? Like what?"

Jake's throat bobbed. "First, it broke my heart. Then it did something else."

I raised an eyebrow.

"I don't think I can say," whispered Jake. "There's a kid around."

My whole body flushed as I playfully kicked his foot. "I don't think anyone can hear you down here."

But that was cosmic timing for you because the words were hardly out of my mouth when Steven charged down the stairs with a toothpick in his mouth. Jake and I separated like we were radioactive.

Steven leaned against the wooden railing and took us in. He chewed on that stupid toothpick, looking happy with himself. "We're going to watch *Kiki's Delivery Service* and feel great about the world…if you want to join us."

Jake scratched the back of his head. "Yeah…sounds great."

Steven narrowed his eyes, like he really knew something. I hated that.

"Why are you staring at us?" I asked.

Steven almost laughed but kept messing with that toothpick. "Just thinking."

"Thinking about what?" asked Jake, raising an eyebrow.

We followed Steven back up the steps. When he was nearly at the top, he looked back at us. "Just thinking…hot damn."

"Shut up, Steven."

36

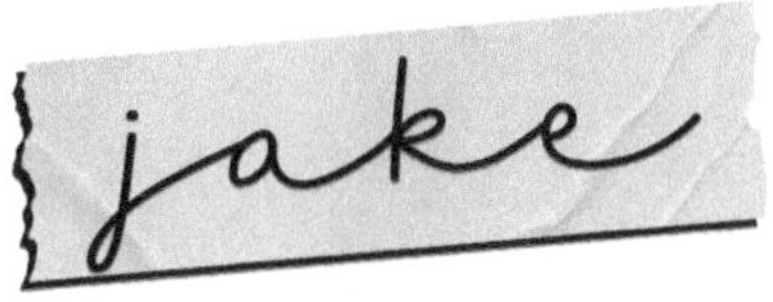

Henry and I smoothed wood filler onto the arms of the swing while Daisy took pictures of our progress.

"Why do we need so many before and after photos?" asked Henry.

Daisy rolled her eyes. "You don't understand girls. It's romantic. Leah will love them."

"She did watch a lot of home renovation shows when you two were little," I said, considering.

When the holes in the arms were filled in and smoothed out, we stood up and inspected our work.

"Now we only have a thousand other things to fix on it," said Henry. "How do we fix those weird loose boards on the back?"

"The internet," I said.

"But we can't do anything else right now," said Daisy. "The instructions say we have to let it dry."

Henry put down his trowel. "Great. Let's eat cookies."

I grabbed his shoulder. "Put on the brakes. There's something else we can do."

"I hope it doesn't have anything to do with this garbage,"

said Henry, giving a disgusted glance at the wood filler. "This stuff sucks."

I laughed at Henry's scrunched-up face. "No. We're going to fix your dresser."

Henry looked at me the same way he did when I told him I wasn't going anywhere. "Cool."

November was a busy time for the Roths and Bradleys. Leah's birthday was November 16th, Daisy's was the 19th, and Steven's was the 24th, the day after Thanksgiving. We decided to have a little shindig for Leah and Daisy the Sunday before Thanksgiving, since I had Daisy that day. Then on Steven's birthday, he wanted everyone to go down to the Silver Dollar to listen to the Big Damn Deal…and that little bastard wanted me to sing karaoke with him.

Good luck.

When I brought Leah and Daisy's cakes to the dining room, Leah couldn't hide her surprise. I made the café's new chocolate *Matilda*-esque cake for her and a marble cake for Daisy.

"You didn't have to make me my own cake!" That grateful shimmer in her eyes made me want to kiss her right there.

Steven gestured to our parents and did a kind of Groucho Marx thing with his eyebrows. My dad winked at him. Musketeers, indeed.

"My birthday is December 23rd, Leah," I said, sliding the cake up to her. "I know how it is. You get your own cake."

Daisy blew her candles out in a second, but Leah took her time. I watched her through the sparkling light. She bit her lip and blushed. What was she blushing about?

Sweet Jesus.

Things had been fairly flirty with us lately, leaving me both thrilled and stunned. I wasn't going to question it, worried I'd jinx it somehow. I was at A-to-Z Furniture every day at noon again. Whenever Leah saw me pass through the doors, she sauntered up in her snug burgundy dress. The way she looked at me made me want to pull her into the employee bathroom. I had to think about toxic sludge and multiplying fractions to stop my body from embarrassing the fuck out of me.

After everything that went down with Henry, I felt braver somehow. And when Leah said she didn't want space from me, and then made that comment about flirting…Well…fuck… I didn't deserve her. But I wanted her. Bad.

Gail drummed her nails on the table. "You better blow out those candles before the frosting is half wax."

"Fine," said Leah. Maybe it was my imagination, but I swore that her eyes darted to me a second before she breathed in, made a wish, and blew them out.

After Daisy opened presents from my dad and the Roths, the kids ran into the chilly backyard to play. Leah and I followed. We sat on the replacement swing.

Leah wasn't impressed by it. "This isn't the same." She frowned at the chipped, gray wooden seat. "Dad said a friend of his is fixing our swing. It better not be that Ted guy. He fixed Mom and Dad's fridge, and they had to buy a new one the next day."

Daisy, Henry, and I shared a covert knowing glance. Henry had a hard time not laughing.

"What's so funny?" asked Leah.

Henry went wide-eyed. But he recovered quickly, pointing at me. "Give Mom that present, Jake."

"Present?" asked Leah, surprised. "I already got presents."

"But Dad has one that's just from us!" said Daisy.

I unzipped my coat and pulled out a small package.

Leah smiled and shook her head. "You guys are spoiling me."

"I don't think that's possible," I said, meeting her eyes. Her face turned soft and bashful. I handed her the present, and she ripped it open with curiosity. When she saw what it was, her eyes were like fireworks.

"Pretty sure the kids are never giving us back our old Game Boys," I said. "So we decided as a group that you and I needed two of our own to relive our glory days. Thank God for eBay."

"Heck yes!" Leah grinned, her eyes squinting. She put her arms around the kids and pulled them in. Then she flashed me a look that sent a shockwave through my chest. "I'm going to kick your…butt…at *Contra*."

"Well, we all know how you love to cheat, so you probably will," I said.

She burst out laughing. "That's just at mini golf."

I caught her again! "You have to stop admitting that you cheat at mini golf! We need a rematch."

We laughed so hard that Leah was wiping away tears. She touched my arm, and I felt her fingers even through my coat. Good God. I didn't know why she was flirting so much, but I hoped it would never stop. "Thanks, everyone. I mean it." A sly smile spread over her face. "But I'm not the only one who gets a surprise extra gift."

Daisy's posture turned straight as a pin. Her mouth became an "o," excited to see what Leah got her. Leah pulled a flat present out of her coat and handed it to Daisy.

The air in my throat caught from the way Leah's look morphed from happy to bittersweet. Her eyes turned misty.

Henry stood in front of us. I slid closer to Leah, putting my hand on hers. She wrapped her fingers around mine.

With her other hand, she tapped the present on Daisy's lap. "Now…this is a silly present." Her voice turned wobbly. I held her hand tighter. "Just a sentimental thing, okay?"

Daisy picked up on Leah's mood. She nodded and ripped open the gift as carefully as possible. When I saw what it was, my heart wanted to shatter and sing at the same time. Leah was wonderful. Completely amazing.

Daisy lifted the *My Little Pony* shirt in the air. Her smile was wide. "I love it!"

Leah's nose was pink, and I didn't think it was from the cold. "This is a special shirt. A long time ago, your grandma went out of her way and found it for me when Steven ruined the original. I took very special care of it because I was so grateful.…and because…who doesn't love *My Little Pony*, right?"

Daisy giggled as she and Henry examined the shirt.

"That was your grandma, Daisy," said Leah, wiping away a tear. "She was wonderful. If you ever want to hear stories about her, just ask me, okay?"

Daisy nodded. The emotion in my chest felt like it was trying to slam its way out.

"I'll take good care of it, too," said Daisy.

"I know you will." Leah leaned in and hugged her. "I love you, sweetie."

Daisy wrapped her arms around Leah. "I love you, too." I took a mental picture of that moment. All of us by the swing. Laughing, crying, and loving one another. I'd remember it forever.

When the kids ran off to get more cake, I took a deep breath and wrapped my arm around Leah's side. I didn't know if it was going too far, but with the way she'd been acting lately, I felt like taking a chance. She leaned against me, and my whole body hummed. Her warmth was pure comfort.

"Thank you," I whispered in her ear.

She ran her hand down into her coat, fiddling with the locket she still wore. The locket I gave her. "Anything for Daisy." She smiled. "You know how I feel about her, right?"

I nodded. She relaxed against me more, her proximity making my whole body tingle. "The same way I feel about Henry."

The cool air wafted against us. It felt good against my hot, sticky skin.

"Are you sure you liked my present?" I asked.

She leaned forward and giggled. I had given her a new black jumpsuit to replace the one ruined by Steven and the blue frosting.

"I love it," she said. "I think I'll wear it to Steven's birthday party."

"I have it on good authority that the frosting dye never came out of the other one." I raised my eyebrows. "Have you noticed that Steven's wrecked a lot of your clothes?"

"I know! Just think about the stuff I don't know about!"

We laughed, our gaze settling on each other. Then Leah's glance darted away, shy. I loved that.

"When you saw the black fabric, you weren't hoping it was something else?" I asked.

Was she blushing?

God, I hope so.

"Like sexy lingerie?" she asked, whispering. "Or a corset nightie that's a little bit too short?"

I remembered a nightie like that. It did things to me just thinking about it. The way it hugged her curves. Damn. Was it wise to keep talking and thinking about this?

Hell yes.

"But if I get you anything like that, it can't be black," I whispered. "Plum, right? That's your color, isn't it?"

Leah's giggle was nothing but air. "I guess that gives you Christmas ideas."

I stretched out my legs to relieve the tension. "That won't work. I already have your Christmas gifts all covered."

"No, you don't." But when I didn't stop staring, her expression changed to one of surprise. "Really? You got me something already… Wait…did you say *gifts*…Plural? You're not supposed to get me more than one thing for Christmas. That's our deal."

I crossed my arms. "I'm afraid I'm breaking our deal."

"You sneaky tall nerd." I laughed. "I better step up and get you something awesome."

I looked her right in the eyes. "I have everything I need."

37

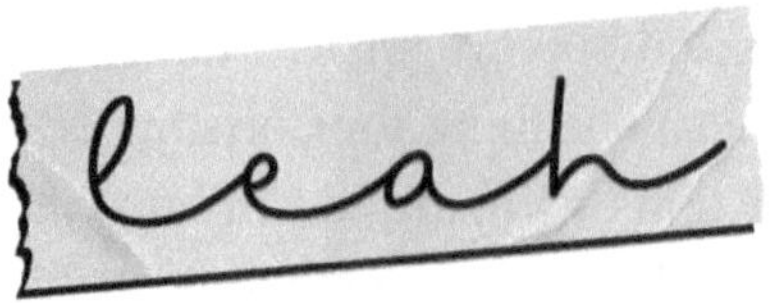

I should have been nervous about flirting with Jake. I mean, that was why I'd (kind of) avoided him the last couple of months, right? I was still nervous. He wasn't some random guy who could leave without it bothering me much. The two of us together meant something. It was like the difference between looking out at a beautiful day and standing directly in it. Being with him was something I wanted. Something I'd wanted for years. And the more I wanted something, the more it could hurt me. The more *I* could hurt *him.*

But whenever I got nervous, it seemed like he knew it, and he'd give me a reassuring smile. It made me want to keep moving forward, no matter the consequences.

On Thanksgiving, I helped my parents with the turkey, stuffing, and potatoes while Jake brought the macaroni and cheese and pecan pie. He came alone. Daisy was at Ashley's for Thanksgiving. I tried to ignore how weird it was without her there.

I was sarcastic as I looked at the spread. "I'm worried we might not have enough carbs."

"I got it covered," said Steven. "I brought dinner rolls. Danica's sister made them."

I touched Jake's arm. My fingers on his skin made him perk up. "And Henry has a surprise for you." I gestured to Henry. "Show Jake."

Henry ran to the fridge and was back in a second with a pie in his hands. He had such a big smile on his face that I could've shoved a whole donut in there.

I nudged Jake. "Henry made it all by himself."

"Hell yes," said Jake, excited, and I knew he meant it, too.

"I know you made pecan pie," said Henry, handing Jake the dessert. "But I found this online and wanted to surprise you."

Jake inspected the lattice top and the filling poking out. His eyes were full of surprise. "Is this a mince pie?"

Craig leaned over, shocked. "Holy Christ. I didn't think anyone in the Midwest knew what the shit a mince pie was... I mean... Sorry about the swearing, Henry."

"It's not a mince pie," said Henry. "It's a funeral pie."

Steven rubbed his hands together. "Now we're talking. I don't know what that is, but let's eat it first."

"Didn't we all decide a couple of hours ago to call it a raisin pie?" asked Mom.

"It's just raisins, brown sugar, cinnamon, and butter," said Henry.

Jake nodded approvingly. "Fair play. It looks delicious."

Henry's smile got even bigger. "Daisy would probably say raisins aren't even good in trail mix."

"We made too much food again," said my mom.

I was super full, and I hadn't even gotten to the pie yet. But I was still going to have a slice, damn it. A big one. Henry did what the kids usually did—ate fast and then took his pie downstairs to play games with sticky fingers.

Jake sat next to me. "How do you like the macaroni and cheese?" We weren't even that close to each other, but it felt like there was some force field around him that I rubbed against.

"I love it. Especially the topping. It's my favorite part of Thanksgiving."

Jake didn't look so sure. "I think I remember you saying that something else was your favorite part of Thanksgiving."

Yep, he remembered. I told him that *he* was my favorite part of Thanksgiving. I willed myself not to blush like a teenager.

"It's the cranberry sauce, isn't it?" asked my dad. "That's your favorite part. I could put that stuff on everything. And I have."

Needless to say, we were entertaining our families. Steven and Craig exchanged a knowing glance. Mom rolled her eyes. Jake scratched the back of his head, amused.

I cleared my throat. "Next year we should cut down on the sides."

"You can't have too much food," said Steven. "Give it to me. I'll put it in our fridge and eat it for the next two weeks."

Jake looked up from his potatoes, horrified. "That's not how that works. You could get very sick doing that."

"You're just saying that because you want to take it to Felicity's next weekend." Steven piled more mashed potatoes on his plate, like he thought Jake might take the rest.

"I guarantee I'm making all new food for next weekend," said Jake.

"Don't mention next weekend," said Craig as he pushed his plate away, looking sick. "We have another Thanksgiving to go to. Bollox."

"What's the big deal?" asked Dad. "More cranberry sauce. Score."

"I don't want to talk about it," said Craig.

Jake gave me a look that screamed *save me!* "We're going to Felicity's in Mankato. Felicity and Mark will be there, of course. Joe and Helen, too." His eyes widened. "But guess who else?"

Steven let out a cackling laugh before Jake could finish.

Mom was stunned. "No."

Jake gave an exaggerated nod. "Yep. Kenneth will be there too." A ticked-off noise escaped his throat. "Fun times, huh?"

I tried to be deadpan. "I don't see the problem." Jake and I held eye contact for two seconds, then started laughing. "Nothing like a super awkward Thanksgiving."

Craig didn't think it was so funny. "It'll be hours of complete silence." A heavy sigh. "Staring at our plates. Wanting to joke about whether Kenneth stole any of the components of the meal. A total farce. Tabhair foighne dom."

"I'm surprised Felicity wants him there," said Mom.

"She doesn't," said Jake. "Joe and Helen want to move past the stealing and the…"

"Breaking up your marriage?" asked Steven, finishing Jake's sentence.

Jake stared my brother down. "Thanks, Steven. I was trying not to be tacky, but yes."

Steven grinned. "No problem."

"We've been trying to think of ways to get out of it," said Craig.

Jake shifted to me. "If you want to help us with excuses, we'd be eternally grateful." Why did that make my skin flush? "Want to suddenly take a road trip to a huge ball of yarn? Or I could go with you to the dentist. You don't even need to have an appointment. We can sit in the parking lot for two hours drinking coffee."

I let out a small laugh. "I can probably think of something."

Jake's voice turned quiet. "Yeah?"

It was an innocent question, so why did I feel like blushing again? "It's supposed to snow a lot tomorrow." I tried to ignore the fluttering in my chest. "First snow of the year. Don't shovel your driveway. Let it get hard and packed down."

Craig looked like he saw the light. "That's it! The snow is too deep to leave the driveway. Can't shovel. Bad back. Too cheap to pay anyone else to move snow."

"But what about me and Daisy?" asked Jake.

I shrugged. "I can shake the pipes below the kitchen sink until they're loose."

"That won't take much," said Steven.

I ignored Steven. "Then you can say you have to help me fix it."

Jake's eyes were freaking amazing. "I like the way you think."

Our families stared at us again. Jake ignored them, focusing on me.

"You know what I'm thinking about?" asked Steven.

Jake cringed. "Nobody knows. That's the thing that frightens everyone."

Steven rested his chin in his hand. "Remember that time you two decided to be a couple, then fell madly in love with each other…and then broke up for no reason? Remember that?"

Jake flipped off Steven, and my brother chuckled.

I leaned forward and kicked Steven under the table. "Shut up, Steven. That's not funny, joking about my fear of commitment. Asshole."

But Steven howled with laughter. "It's a hereditary thing, sis. We're the same."

"I don't think so," I said, still pretending to be mad.

Jake's eyes were on me again. Did he smile?

38

WINTER

On Steven's birthday, the snow started at ten in the morning. By 1:00 p.m., there were four inches on the ground. It came down like thick feathers, lazy but constant. When it was almost time for Steven's party, four inches had turned into eight. The streets in Alexandria were so quiet and deserted that you could've made snow angels on the road without worrying about cars.

I loved winter. I loved the way the moon glowed down on untouched snow and lit up the night. You could have wandered through town without a flashlight, perfectly able to see the trees and houses around you.

"Sorry about the party," I said to Steven when it was almost time to leave the house. Steven got texts from friends throughout the day saying they couldn't make it because of the storm. By nightfall, the party had shifted from the Silver Dollar, which was closed due to the weather, to our parents' basement. And the only people coming were us, the Bradleys, Danica, and Monica and Tony, who were bringing their home karaoke machine.

Steven was the opposite of bummed. "No sweat, sis. I can hang out with you guys tonight and everyone else next weekend. Plus, Daisy's coming over here for a sleepover with Henry after the party, and they're asking for another edition of Steven's Fine Films."

"Age-appropriate fine films," I said, monotone.

Steven sighed. "I realize now that *Peeping Tom* was a mistake."

"Why don't you move the whole party to next weekend?" I asked.

Henry walked in. "Get with the program, Mom." So much sass. "If he has a party with us this weekend and one with his friends next weekend, he gets double everything. Double cake, double presents."

"You understand, bud. Plus, double booze. That's where my head's at."

"Old people don't get double birthdays very often," added Henry.

"Hey, now," said Steven. "I thought we were on the same side."

Henry laughed and ran back to his bedroom to grab his iPhone.

Because he has to record me again.

"Plus, if hardly anyone's there, maybe I can get Jake to do karaoke."

"Fat chance," I said.

I examined myself in a mirror above the hutch, adjusting my jumpsuit and fiddling with Jake's locket. After a moment, I felt eyes on me. I looked behind my reflection. Steven sat on the sofa with his guitar case leaning against him.

I turned around. "What?"

"You nervous about singing tonight? We haven't practiced as much."

I almost laughed. "No."

Steven furrowed his brow like an old professor. "How come? Did we practice the nerves right out of you?"

I slid down next to him on the sofa. "I don't know. Maybe. Plus, we both know the song. We only heard it a million times when we were kids. And, you know…we're singing at our parents' house. So what's there to be nervous about?"

Steven cracked a smile. "This from the woman who was nervous about singing in front of just me and Danica."

That struck me. He was right. I *had* been nervous about singing in front of two people. But for some reason, it didn't bother me as much now. The nerves weren't totally gone, of course. But I didn't feel like I was in *Alien*, with a creature about to burst out of my chest.

I didn't know what to say, so I shrugged again. "I guess that's kind of weird, isn't it? That I'm not as nervous anymore."

What was that goofy expression on Steven's face? "That's not weird. That's good. You pushed past the fear and did something you wanted to. Now you know you can do it."

We sat in silence. What was taking Henry so long? That kid was never on time.

Steven stared out the window. "I don't know why, but winter always seems like the time for telling secrets. Everything is silent and muffled. No bugs, no birds, no sounds at all. And the way it gets dark early… When the snow gets thick, it feels like insulation around you. Like you can yell your secrets to the night, and they'll just disappear into the shadows. You don't have to worry about anyone taking them, twisting them, and using them against you."

I didn't take my eyes off my brother. What was going on? "Do you want to tell me a secret, Steven?"

A complex expression flashed across his face. He looked amused and heartbroken at the same time. "Margot sent me a text a couple of hours ago. Wishing me a happy birthday."

Holy shit.

I wasn't expecting that. "But she hasn't said anything to you in, like, forever, has she? Doesn't she still actively avoid you?"

Steven nodded. "Pretty much. And yeah, it's been a long time."

I sat, stunned. Margot and I had been pretty good friends for a while there. We *all* had been. After a moment, I swatted his arm. "See? You two can be friends after all, huh? Maybe the whole gang can get back together. Or the whole band, like in *The Blues Brothers*."

I thought Steven would laugh, but that frown was glued to his face. "But that's all we'll ever be now. *Friends*." He stared at his guitar case. "Do you know why me and Margot broke up?"

I nudged his elbow to cheer him up. "Because you're freaking weird?"

He let out a sad laugh. "Yeah, Leah. That's why."

I was stunned into silence again. The way he said that…

Steven played with the handle on his guitar case. "I love weird people. Everyone should be exactly what they want to be. And Margot got me. She liked that I was who I was. I mean, damn, we went to the Spam museum together."

"But?" I asked.

It felt like Steven was afraid to look me in the eyes. That didn't happen very often. "But…you know how I am. I move from one hobby to the next pretty fast. Not much of an attention span. One of those old novels in Margot's store would probably describe me as flitting from one thing to the next, with nary a thought of tomorrow."

I shot him a crooked smile.

"Of course, the thing about moving from one thing to the next at the speed of light is that you give off this aura of not being too serious about anything. Not too committed to anything. And Margot wondered if that meant her too."

Oh, shit, I thought. I knew where this was going. Commitment issues. *We* are *alike*.

I rested my hand on his. "Oh, Steven…"

I didn't know if it was my words or me trying to comfort him, but he let out a bitter laugh. "Yeah, you get it now, don't you? It's like I said at dinner yesterday. We're so alike, it's scary. Deep down in my heart, I knew I wanted to marry Margot. I knew I wanted to be with her forever. But she thought I wasn't serious about her. And then, suddenly, I was afraid to tell her I was. Suddenly, I was afraid that I couldn't hack it in the long run. I thought I'd fuck it up someday. So instead, I fucked it up *that* day."

I squeezed his arm to reassure him. I knew how he felt, and it wasn't pretty. "I'm sorry. I didn't know."

He shook his head, angry with himself. "What sense did that make, Leah? I'll tell you, no fucking sense at all." Finally, he looked straight at me. His eyes were so direct that I almost wanted to look away. "I don't want you to be like me. And I know *you* don't want to be like me. Love scares us because it can hurt. But it's worth it, too. Take it from someone who threw it all away."

I realized I was sitting like a rigid action figure. Tears dotted my eyes.

Stupid Steven, being philosophical. And on his birthday, too.

Wasn't he supposed to be drunk on his birthday? My mind didn't know what to think, but suddenly everything felt urgent. Everything felt like it was going to happen tonight. What was I going to do? Let it all slip away, or grab what I wanted and never let it go?

Steven patted his case. "'He who fears he will suffer, already suffers because he fears.' I can't remember who said that, but I saw it once in the inspirational quotes section of Pinterest." That made me laugh through my tears. "It's true, though, isn't it? And that's what we're both doing. We're afraid that tomorrow might be bad, so instead we make today bad."

I wiped away my tears. "And it's so dumb because Jake and

I have been friends forever. And it's not like we never got annoyed with each other. But I never worried that our friendship wouldn't last. So why am I so worried that our love won't?"

"Because it's high stakes. And the higher the stakes, the harder it can hurt."

"And those other guys never really meant anything," I said, sighing. "We had fun, but I never let them get close enough to break my heart. I left long before then. Or they did. But Jake's different. I've wanted to be with him for a long time. And I don't want to fail at something that means so much to me."

Steven shrugged. "So don't."

My tears were dry. I let out a small laugh. "Just like that. You think it's that easy?"

"It might not be easy every day, but if it's important to you, it'll be *worth* it every day. When something fills your heart, you put in the time. You put in the effort. You make it happen. I think the only thing more depressing than the hard days of reaching for a dream is turning your back on it and knowing that it'll never come true. Look at your singing. That dream scared you, but you made it come true."

My ears popped like there'd been an elevation change. Holy shit. Steven was right. And I hated it when Steven was right!

Singing again had always been my dream, but I pushed it down and hardly thought about it because it terrified me. Six months ago, if someone had told me I'd sing at a bar in front of a hundred people, I would've told them they were nuts. And if someone told me the next time I sang, I'd barely be nervous about it, I wouldn't have believed that either. But now I knew I could make my dreams come true, even the ones that scared me. So why was my dream of being with Jake any different? That scared me, too, but being with him was worth the fear. Spending our lives together was worth the fear. Loving each other was worth the fear.

So make it happen already!

I bolted off the sofa. "Shit!" I turned and kissed my brother on the forehead. "Don't ever shut up, Steven."

I sprinted toward my bedroom.

Steven followed, dumbfounded, but entertained. "What the hell is happening?"

"You and your fucking truth bombs," I said, riffling through my dresser. I called out into the house. "Henry! Where are you? Turn off that PlayStation. We have to go. Now!"

"What are you looking for?"

"Grandpa's old watch," I said. The watch box warmed my hand when I grabbed it from the dresser. Then I sped down the hall, with Steven hot on my tail. Henry stood by the door, a wide-eyed look of confusion on his face.

"Grandpa's watch?" asked Steven. "What for?"

I smiled wider than I had in a long time. "To make another dream come true."

Steven rolled that comment around in his mind. A Cheshire Cat smile spread across his face.

"What's going on?" asked Henry.

Steven patted a still-confused Henry on the shoulder. "Damn, Leah. What can I say? Ha cha, cha."

39

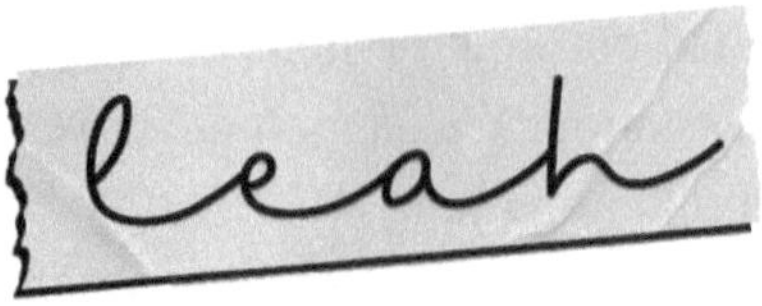

We all got to my parents' house at the same time, filling the normally quiet basement with food, laughter, and energy. Monica and Tony were in the corner, setting up the karaoke machine and makeshift stage. When they saw Steven, they walked up with presents in hand. Steven's usual cool exterior melted. Was that a tear in his eye? He was full of surprises tonight.

I knew the second Jake walked in with Daisy. I felt the pleasant prickling on my skin before I even raised my head and made eye contact. He strolled over, sheet cake in hand.

"You're not going to drop that on me, are you?" I asked, acting afraid.

Jake winked, looking me up and down. "No, that's Steven's job."

"You're damn right it is," said Steven. "Holy crap. Danica, look at this."

We all stood around Jake's creation. The cake was decorated to look just like a Spam label. I grinned as my eyes focused on Jake.

"I hope it doesn't taste like Spam," said Daisy.

"No worries there," said Jake. "It's red velvet. Steven's favorite."

"That must be the most normal thing you like, Hun," Mom said to Steven.

"Yeah, he's the only one who'll touch my ketchup dip," said Dad.

Steven gave Jake a face like, *Aww, shucks.* "How did you know that red velvet is my favorite?"

"I *am* your friend, you know. Plus, whenever you're at the restaurant, you ask for it." Jake and Danica made eye contact, almost laughing. "Also, Danica told me."

"Damn," said Steven. His eyes didn't know whether to focus on Danica, Jake, or the icing. "I guess I'm not the only sneaky bitch."

Craig nodded at Daisy and Henry. "He didn't mean to swear, kids."

Steven took the cake from Jake, set it down, and then gestured to him.

"Wait, are we hugging?" asked Jake. He hardly got the words out when Steven grabbed him tight around the middle. Jake was speechless. But after a moment, he wrapped an arm around my brother. "Happy birthday, Steven."

"Thanks… And you don't have to say anything. I know we're best friends." Steven lowered his voice. "I won't tell Leah."

When he was done hugging Jake, Steven embraced Danica in a way that made our mom do a double-take, impressed. They hugged for so long that the rest of us were a little weirded out. Then Danica gave him a light kiss and whispered something in his ear. I'm not sure what she said, and I don't want to know, but whatever it was, it made any remaining speck of Steven's blue Margot mood from earlier completely disappear.

"I wanted to do 'Rainy Day Women #12 & 35,'" said Steven into the microphone. "But Danica and Leah vetoed that. So instead, here's 'One More Cup of Coffee.'"

I stood on our basement stage. Steven and Danica were beside me, and our families sat in the middle of the room at a few card tables, eating cake. Henry recorded me, so I made sure to stick my tongue out before we started.

Danica strummed her banjo, and then Steven followed with his guitar. Pretty soon, I was singing. And I didn't mind. Actually, I was having fun. *Again.* And this time, Jake was there. That was the best part. He leaned back, taking me in. He looked proud of me, even if I was just singing in the basement. Because I'd sing at the bar again, and he knew it.

His eyes didn't drift from mine. And it hit me, about halfway through, that I was looking at the man I was going to spend the rest of my life with. My soulmate. If he was still interested.

Because now I knew I could do the scary things that were important to me.

When the song was over, Monica and Tony started the karaoke machine. That made Craig and Dad happy. They belted out "No More 'I Love You's'" and "White Wedding" at the top of their lungs. Poor Mom stared at her cake, shook her head, and laughed with Monica. The kids sang with Steven and Danica. And holy shit, Danica's voice *was* louder when she sang. Jake and I sat with shocked expressions. But as the song went along, Jake became more uncomfortable. Probably because Steven pointed at him like *you're next.*

"I don't want to sing." Jake frowned. "I *don't* sing. I only sing in the car with you…badly…to Megan Trainor songs. It's just a you and me thing."

I leaned toward him, smiling. I loved the hard line of his jaw when he was annoyed. So sexy. "I'm singing with you. It'll be awesome."

Jake made a frazzled noise and took a sip of beer. "I'm not sure about that."

I rested my hand on his. He stopped, mid-sip. His eyes drifted toward me. I leaned in more, my voice quiet. "What if I hold your hand the whole time?"

It felt like he was stripping me naked with his eyes. His breath was warm on the side of my neck. The world went hazy. "You're going to hold my hand through a whole song while we stand in front of everyone?"

I gave him a sultry whisper. "Yes, I am. So…what do you say?"

Jake's voice turned gravelly. "I'm suddenly in the mood to sing."

I wondered if my face was as red as it felt.

Jake stared at our interlaced fingers. "You were amazing, by the way. Not sure if I told you that."

My smile took up my whole face. "Really?"

"Fecking fantastic."

I was true to my word. When it was our turn to sing, we made our way to the makeshift stage next to Steven. I didn't hesitate as I took Jake's hand in mine. He gazed at me, a warm smile on his face. It made my body temperature rise even though we were in a winter weather advisory.

About half a second after our hands touched, both of our families took notice. They perked up like they were sharing a vat of strong coffee.

Steven winked. "Okay, everybody. I got my Bob Dylan choice blocked, but it's my damn birthday, so I get to choose the song that the three of us sing." Steven gave me and Jake a very specific look that I couldn't interpret. "These two know this song because they listen to it while eating Rocky Road."

After a second, familiar music wafted through the speakers. Steven chose "Animal" by Neon Trees. Jake and I hardly got through the first verse with all our laughter.

Way to be obvious, Steven.

We stood there singing about love and longing in the most over-the-top way we could. Our families cheered. Even my mom lifted her hands like she was into it. And if Jake was nervous, he didn't let on. Maybe it was because we teased each other on stage the whole time. Or because we never once let go of each other's hands. All I knew is that when I stood there, I was home. In every sense of the word.

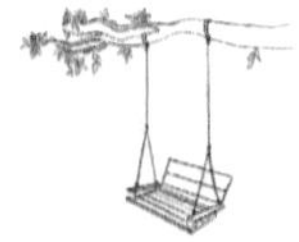

As the night went on, the karaoke performances dwindled. Instead, people chatted, ate, and avoided Dad's dips. The kids were more interested in the snow outside than anything else. Actually, everyone was. Another four inches had fallen since we got to my parents' house. Since everyone was obsessed with standing in the driveway to measure the accumulation, I got an idea.

I strolled up to Steven. "When Jake gets out of the bathroom, can you put a song on the karaoke machine for me?"

"Sure," he said, poking at his huge slice of cake.

I took a breath. "And then, can you make sure everyone stays outside?"

Steven put his fork down and studied me. "It's happening now, isn't it?"

I nodded.

Steven ran a hand through his crazy hair and whistled. "Damn, Leah. You must be singing one hell of a come-on. Is it En Vogue's 'Don't Let Go (Love)'?"

"No." That got me thinking. Steven's idea was on point. "But damn, Steven. Now I wish I was."

"Songs don't get sexier than that."

I weighed the options. "I think I'll stick with my jazzy pick, though. 'I Could Write a Book.' Frank Sinatra. I used to sing it in choir."

Steven's eyes widened. "You don't have to tell me. Rodgers and Hart. That should about do it, sis."

"Shut up, Steven." I grinned. So did he, but then he threatened to slam his cake into my outfit. I dodged his hands and shoved him toward the karaoke machine.

When Jake finally came down the hall, he scanned the nearly empty basement, confused. He spun around. "Where is everyone?"

"They're outside, fascinated by the snow," I said, walking up.

Jake rolled his eyes. "You'd think you'd all be used to it. You see feet of snow almost every year. You know how much snow I used to see? I should be the fascinated—"

Jake stopped talking when he realized how close I was to him. His eyes turned hazy. I knew he wanted to reach out and hold me but wasn't sure if he should. So I took his hand and pulled him to the makeshift stage.

"What are we doing?" he whispered.

"I'm singing to you," I whispered back. "You can listen… then tell me what you think."

Jake looked like he was in a trance, and I *felt* like it. "What song?"

Music started playing gently in the background. In my peripheral vision, I saw Steven walk up the stairs and quietly shut the basement door. My pulse raced.

This is it, Leah. Now or never.

"Steven thought that when I sang 'Girl From the North Country,' it was me proclaiming my undying love for you. And I like that song. But if I wanted to proclaim my undying love for you, I think I'd sing this one instead."

Jake's posture changed instantly. He became rigid, and his eyes widened. Was that a good sign? My legs wobbled.

Jake rubbed my elbow. I missed that. My heart raced so much that I thought it would drown out my singing. I held the microphone to my mouth and stared into his eyes. I didn't have to look at the monitor as I sang that old, familiar tune, lyrics about all the tiny nuances that made someone special—so special that a book could be written about them.

Whose eyes got misty first? We stared at each other, trying to hold back tears. They were happy tears for me. I hoped they were happy tears for him. His light touch on my elbow became a firmer grasp. Did he want to pull me close? Kiss me?

And then I got to *that* verse—the one about how people shift from friends to something more. Jake turned pale as the words came out of my mouth. His body was nearly shaking.

The music played on, but somehow everything else stopped. I felt every particle of air between us. I felt the heat coming off him.

"So…what do you think?" I asked.

His whisper was strained. "Darling." The word bounced around in my chest. He ran his hands up my bare arms. I shivered. "I think I feel like I did on your sofa when we first kissed. I think I'm in a dream." Jake rested his forehead against mine. He almost vibrated with need as he held me. "If this is a dream, Leah, please don't let me fecking wake up." He pulled me close, and I was reminded how well we fit together. His breath turned ragged. "I want to sleep here forever with you."

I got rid of the microphone and took his face in my hands. He closed his eyes at my touch. He rested his hands on my back as I guided his mouth to mine.

How long had it been since we kissed? Somehow, it seemed like forever and only a moment ago. But when his lips touched mine, it felt like the first time all over again. His kiss was tender and tentative, but when I let out a small sigh, it morphed. He pulled me closer and deepened the kiss, nipping my bottom lip and taking his time, like I was something worth worshiping. He kissed me like he never planned to let me go. His arms desperately ran across my jumpsuit, reacquainting himself with every inch of my torso and every noise I made. And I didn't want him to stop. I didn't want any room between us. I wanted his heart against mine. His soul against mine. His skin against mine.

When we finally pulled away, his eyes sparkled, and his voice was still a whisper. "I have something to tell you. But I can't do it here." I hovered close to him. "Will you meet me somewhere?"

"I'll meet you anywhere." I kissed him again. His lips were sweet and soft. By the time I pulled away, I was almost out of breath. "Where?"

Jake smiled. "At our swing."

I let out a breathy giggle. "I don't have to go far."

"Just give me a twelve-minute head start. There's something I need to do."

I wanted to say more, to kiss him again, but there was a light knock at the top of the stairs.

Steven charged down the steps with his hand in front of his face. "Are you decent? I know how you are with basements."

"Shut up, Steven," I said, smiling.

Steven pointed back upstairs. "Our parents are out in the

street talking to the Abbertons. So that should last for two hours or so." Steven studied us. We stood close together. *Very* close. "I'm going to drop Danica off and then bring the kids back home so we can start that movie. Does that sound reasonable?"

Jake scratched the back of his head. "That's great, Steven, thanks."

We all stood there, looking at each other, about as awkward as we could get. Finally, Steven leaned against the wall and nodded.

"Something on your mind?" I asked him. That was a dangerous question.

Steven shrugged, pleased. "Just admiring my work."

Jake and I burst out laughing.

"You think you did something?" asked Jake.

"Hell yes, I did," said Steven, adamant. "You know I did, damn it. Both of you. From where I'm standing, I look like the goddamn master of ceremonies. But you don't have to thank me. It's all part of my job."

Jake and I exchanged a skeptical glance.

"Oh, God. What job is that?" I asked.

Steven moseyed back up the steps. "Haven't you figured it out yet? I'm Steven Roth: Lover and Friend."

He chuckled as the basement door closed behind him.

"There's a thought," said Jake, contemplating Steven's catchphrase. "Jesus. I better try not to think about that one." Then he rested his hand on my arm. "Twelve minutes?"

I winked. "Not a second more."

There was a thin, shoveled path winding to the swing. The snowflakes had transformed over the last few hours from thick and heavy to sporadic dots of glitter. The moon and stars were hidden from view in the heavy nighttime clouds, but with the shimmer of the snow, I could easily see Jake sitting on the swing. My feet didn't make a sound as I approached him. I don't think I was breathing. I felt like I was stepping into a wish we both shared.

Jake watched me approach. He looked at me like I was a wave of love, and he was ready for me to crash against him. My eyes were glued to his for so long that, at first, I didn't notice he was holding something.

He handed me a thermos and a paper bag as I sat down. I studied them with curiosity.

"We always end up out here," said Jake, nodding to what he handed me. "I thought we needed snacks. I had to hide them so Steven couldn't find them. I'm excited for you to try what's in the thermos."

I opened the paper bag. I shimmied in delight. "Churros!" My eyes darted to the thermos. "Does that mean—?" I took a sip. "Oh. My. God. You did it!"

I loved that crinkle between Jake's eyes. "It took me ten recipes, but I think I got the hot chocolate right."

I dipped a churro into the chocolate and took a bite. Holy crap. Then I dunked it again and offered a bite to Jake, who gave me a hot, intense glance.

My toes went numb, and it had nothing to do with the cold. "This is freaking good."

"It's not quite as good as in Duluth, but—"

"Yes, it is," I said, swatting him. "It's perfect. It's better."

Jake slid closer. "You think so?"

I felt nervous, but I stared into his. "Everything you make is better."

Suddenly, the churros and thermos were out of my hands. Jake set them aside and pulled me into him. A rush of longing stirred inside me. This was happening. Good.

I couldn't tell where I ended and he started. He kissed me long and deep, his tongue brushing against mine. I let out a shudder and dived deeper into his mouth. I could've stayed out there for hours and not felt anything but warmth and love.

But when we finally pulled away, I frowned.

Jake stroked my face. Those fingers. Rough and smooth at the same time. "What's wrong?"

My eyes burned. "I'm so sorry. I'm sorry that I didn't believe in us. I'm sorry that I left you hanging for all those months." I could hardly get the last words out. "…And I'm sorry that I broke your heart."

Jake kissed my forehead with such tenderness that I almost swayed.

"There's so much I want to say I'm sorry for," I said. "But *sorry* doesn't seem good enough."

"Don't be sorry. You never have to be sorry for making up your mind. And if you want to be sorry, you have to get in line behind me. I'm the one who started all this, remember? With Ash. I'm the one who's sorry, Leah."

I shook my head. "If it wasn't Ash, it would have been something else. Something else would've scared me away…"

His fingers slid down to my neck, warming me. "I think it all happened the way it was supposed to, mo fhíorghrá. Because we were apart, I remembered how much I liked making things. I've always loved it, but you pushed me to bake things I wouldn't have tried. Who knows how long the bakery case would have been filled with boring muffins? We were stuck in a rut, and now we're out of it. And business has never been better. I was pushed to make my dream come true. And you're the one who pushed me. So thank you."

I rested my head against that spot between his shoulder and neck. I loved it there. He rubbed my back.

"And you pushed me to sing," I said, sitting up again. "You helped me believe in myself. And I guess…if we weren't apart for a while…maybe I never would've gotten up in front of those people. So thank you."

Jake wrapped his hand around mine. "See? Everything happened the way it was supposed to."

I gave him a light kiss. His hair was dotted with snowflakes and his lips were cold, but after a second, he warmed up. "There's still so much I want to say…"

His fingers twitched. "Me too. It's the whole reason we're out here, actually… I've wanted to tell you this for a long time."

He took a deep breath like he was trying to find courage. I rubbed my thumb against his.

He patted the wood beneath us. "Too bad we're not on our old swing, but this will have to do." He glanced at the snow. "I want to tell you a story. We've been friends for so long… We know most of each other's stories, but I've never told you this one."

I followed his gaze out into the darkness. "Tell me."

He squeezed my hand. "Do you remember that one Halloween party? Where Tony and Monica met?"

"That was right before I met Lance and got pregnant."

Jake pulled my hand onto his leg and rested it there. "That was a very important night for me. Do you know why?"

I shook my head, curious.

Jake swallowed, his jaw tightening. "I'd been planning it for weeks. That was the night I was going to tell you how I felt. *Finally*. I even planned what I was going to say." His eyes drifted to mine. The sadness in them made my stomach flop. "But then we got out here…and I lost my nerve. I didn't want to ruin our friendship. And I didn't know if you felt the same way. So we just sat here. Do you remember that? We sat out here for so long in the cold. In the dark."

Now *my* eyes were watery. I kissed his cheek.

"That night haunted me," he said. "Like an idiot, I'd think about it before I fell asleep… How I'd do it right if I ever got another chance." He sighed. "But I had millions of chances, didn't I? And I let them all slip away."

I held his hand tighter.

"But after a while, I rationalized it. I told myself that there was no chance you felt the same way. That you were just my friend. That you probably didn't want to hear what I had to say anyway. So life went on…"

A ball of sorrow filled my chest. I let go of his hand and brushed it across his face. He leaned into it. "Do you remember what you were going to tell me?"

His bitter laugh rang out into the cold. "Every word."

I took his arm and wrapped it around my back. "Will you tell me now? Now that you know I want to hear it?"

His eyes had never sparkled quite like that. He took a deep breath. "This is what I would have said. What I felt. What I *still* feel now, and what I'll always feel for you." I leaned into the calming pressure of his hand on my side. "The thing about people is that they're not one thing. They're like a mosaic. A lot of different pieces…and sometimes those pieces contradict each other. But all those bits still fit somehow, and when you stand back, they make up a person." Jake rubbed my side through my coat. I didn't take my eyes off him. "And when you love a person, you have to love all those pieces." His eyes shot to mine. I was already almost a blubbery mess. "There isn't a piece of you I don't love."

He kissed my forehead again. I wasn't sure if the tear on my face came from him or me. "I love your heart, your kindness, your sense of humor… I love that you have zero patience when queuing for anything." I let out a loud laugh. "It's true, mo ghrá. You see a line at the coffee shop or the DMV and go into a blind rage. And I love that you're a million times better with electronics than me. You can fix my cellphone." We grinned, trying to keep it together. "I love that we started as friends. I love that we grew up together. And I love that my family is your family…"

I knew he was thinking about his mom when he said that. He pushed my hair behind my ear, his face red. "I don't know if you feel the same way…but I thought I'd let you know that you are inside me all the time. When we're not in the same house, or the same city, or the same country. You're the first thing I see when I open my eyes in the morning. I open my eyes, and they're full of you. You're reflected everywhere. You're sparkling everywhere."

I couldn't hold it back any longer. I put my hand up to my eyes. My face was completely wet.

Jake kissed my tears, his voice a whisper. "We make a pretty good pair, Leah. And I want to be a pair with you for the rest of my life."

He embraced me with arms I knew would never let me go. We sat like that for a long time, holding each other and feeling our hearts race. Finally, my eyes drifted up to him. I could still hardly speak. "That was amazing. You were going to say that to me on Halloween?"

Jake nodded, his eyes still red. "I've recited that speech in my mind so many times it feels like I'm rehearsing for Broadway."

We both laughed. I shot him a devious smile as I reached into my coat pocket. Curiosity spread over Jake's face as I took out the small box. "Just for the record, I feel the same way about you. You're reflected everywhere, too. You're such a big part of my heart that there's no getting you out of me."

Jake's lips met mine again, the kiss deep and breathy. I gave him a mischievous nibble on his upper lip. There was a quiet rumble in his chest that made me want to keep going.

But I pulled away, handing him the box. "I was going to give this to you right after you gave me my locket. But then everything happened." I rested my hand on his wrist. "I hope you like it."

There was a content look on his face as he took the top off the box. The gold watch shimmered in the dark.

"It's not expensive or anything," I said. Jake's eyes widened as he stared down at it. "My grandpa gave it to my dad. Look at the back."

Jake turned the watch around to see the engraving. *Jake and Leah.*

He took a deep breath and pulled me close again. I closed my eyes, breathing him in as his lips ran up the side of my neck. Short, sweet kisses. His voice was low as he talked between them. "I love you, mo fhíorghrá."

A lone tear rolled down my cheek, but Jake rubbed it away. "I love you, too." I tried to laugh. "And you're not getting rid of me again."

His chuckle was deep and quiet. "Thank Christ."

I don't know how long we kissed, making up for lost time, but I needed more. I needed all of him, and I was going to get it. Time didn't matter on that swing, at our spot. It was just us.

When we finally separated, Jake nodded toward the deck. "I'm fairly certain your parents and my dad have been spying on us from the sliding deck doors for some time."

I grinned as my gaze followed his. It was dark in the house, but I still made out shadows scurrying away from view. "I know. I was going to say something during your speech, but it was so sweet. You were on a roll."

Jake's jaw flexed again. Damn. Why was that so sexy? He leaned in toward my ear, his lips brushing against it. A tingle shot through me. "The kids are at your house with Steven." I nodded. Everything turned soft and hazy again. "Do you want to spend some time alone together…for a little while?"

I raised an eyebrow. "Only a little while?"

His smile was eager. "Or a *long* while."

I reached my hand through his coat and under his shirt, tracing my fingers along his firm stomach. His breath caught. "What do you think?"

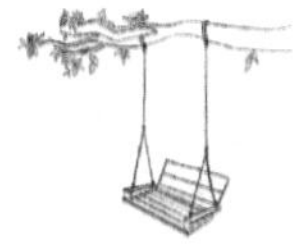

We were a tangled mess of kisses as we entered the house. When the door shut behind us, we threw our coats off, and I pulled him to me, my back against the wall. I thrust my hips into him, feeling how hard he was under his pants. "I see that you still like me."

Jake let out a low chuckle. "Do you want me to show you how much?"

He pulled my left leg around his waist and pressed into me, leaning over and nipping my ear. I easily felt him through my flimsy jumpsuit. I let out a quiet moan.

Jake's breath turned raspy. "Leah, I fecking missed you."

Something about the way he said it brought tears to my eyes. He stilled as our gazes locked, resting his forehead against mine. "Baby, I love you."

He took my hand, and we walked to the bedroom, not taking our eyes off one another. We stopped by the side of the bed, kissing slowly and sweetly. He wiped away one of my stray tears. There was so much longing on his face. He looked grateful to be with me. Grateful to love me. To *know* me. I hoped he saw the same thing in my eyes.

Our kisses turned deep and feverish. We were eager to hold, to take, to give, and to remember. I needed every part of him against me.

Jake trembled as I unbuttoned his shirt. It fell to the floor, and I ran my hands across his chest. His lips trailed down my neck, kissing me until I couldn't feel my legs.

I unzipped my jumpsuit. It pooled at my feet. Jake's gaze went up and down my body as I stood before him in my lacy strapless bra and panties. I took his hands and settled them on my hips. He stroked his fingers across them until I let out a shallow breath.

"We're not going to waste any more time. I promise."

He ran his hands up my sides. "I like the sound of that."

I unzipped his pants, pulling them down. His hard dick pressed against his underwear. I ran a finger along him over the cotton, and he swallowed. "God. Leah. I want you."

I sat on the bed, my eyes on his. "If you come here and take me in your arms, I'll never let you go again."

I never saw Jake move so fast. He was on the bed in less than a second, holding me. He laughed. "How's that for telling you how I feel?"

I ran a hand through his hair. "You're my soulmate. It's always been you. I don't want to spend my life with anyone else." I kissed his mouth, then leaned over and nibbled his ear. A little spasm rippled through him. "I don't want anyone else to touch me or taste me or take me."

Jake kissed me long and deep, then reached around and undid my bra. He threw it away and cupped my breasts. "I'm not the richest man in the world. I don't go to glittery parties…and I don't know important people. But everything that I am—my body, my soul, my heart, and my life—is all yours. Forever. You're the only one I want, Leah. I'm all yours, for however long you want me."

I slid my panties off, then helped him pull off his underwear. "What if I want you for the rest of my life?"

His fingers trailed down me, and I let out a small gasp. "Then I'm one happy bastard."

He gently slid his finger inside me. We eyed each other as he added another. His breathing picked up as he watched me squirm with pleasure.

I rode his hand hard, watching as his fingers plunged into me. "Look how good I fuck your hand, Jake. Look how much I want it."

His voice was strained. "The way you move. I could come just watching you."

I nuzzled into his neck.

"I want to lick you out so bad. I want to taste you for a week."

He peppered the side of my head with kisses as I writhed.

"That's it," he whispered. "Just like that. Come for me, Leah. You're so perfect."

The orgasm came fast. I moaned louder than I meant to. I probably made Jake's ears ring, but he didn't seem to mind.

Blood pulsed in my ears, and my heart thumped as the tremors subsided. We gave each other lazy kisses. His rock-hard dick was jammed against my leg. His eyes looked hazy with need.

I couldn't handle it for another second. I climbed onto him. He looked at our bodies, at where I hovered over him instead of settling down.

I leaned over, my chest against his. My lips were an inch from his mouth. "I want to make you feel so good."

"This is definitely the way to do it."

He looked so damn happy. So damn in love.

With me.

I wanted to cry. He took my face between his hands, gazing at me like a sacred object.

"I love you, Jake."

He breathed out, trying to keep himself together. "I love you, too." He lowered his voice. "Being with you is like discovering that magic is real. You're magic, Leah."

I fought back tears as I kissed him deeply.

Finally, I slowly settled myself down onto him.

He watched his cock slide into me, rubbing my hips again. "Fecking hell. These hips."

I lifted myself again. Slowly. Jake's eyes narrowed. I lifted until only his tip was inside me, and then I slowly slid back onto him.

Jake met me with a slow thrust of his hips. "I love watching every inch of me go into your pussy."

We picked up the pace. Sweat dotted his brow. The muscles in his arms and chest flexed. It drove me wild.

"Do you want me?" I asked. "Do you want me to make you come?"

"Not before you."

I squeezed my breasts together. He groaned. His hands moved to my ass, rubbing me as we met each other.

"Am I good at fucking you, Jake? Am I as good as you dreamed I'd be?"

He reached up, tugging my nipples gently. I moaned. "Better. Nobody's ever done me like you. Fuck my brains out, Leah. Do it."

With one final fluid thrust, I was done. My body felt like it was cracking in half as my back arched.

Jake was still rubbing my breasts. "That's it. Keep fucking me. Don't stop yet."

Jake came a moment later. He fisted the blankets as his whole body shuddered.

We panted in the dark room. Our bodies glistened with sweat, even though there was a blizzard outside. After a moment, I drifted down toward him, resting my chest on his. He met me with open arms, wrapping them around my back. We held each other, content, listening to each other's beating hearts.

It was so quiet in that house. There was no sound except breathing. My eyes drifted up to his. "Forever?"

My whole body felt alive with electricity as Jake's sparkling eyes met mine. "Longer than that."

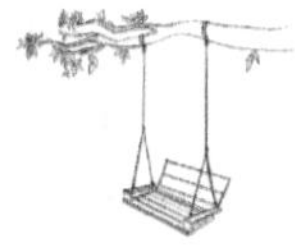

We sat tangled in bed, my head against his chest. I didn't want to, but I glanced at the clock.

Jake saw me check the time. "I know Steven's watching the kids, but I suppose I better get you back home."

I shot him a sneaky smile. "Yeah. We better be fast."

Jake pretended to be insulted. "And here I thought we had some afterglow going on. Sick of me already?"

I playfully pinched his chest. "No. I'm excited. We have a lot to do."

"A lot to do?" asked Jake, curious. "You have plans?"

"You bet. First, we have to go to my place. We should probably tell the kids that this is a forever kind of deal." Jake gave me a long kiss for that. "And then I'm guessing everyone will want hot fudge sundaes. Our families celebrate everything with food. And your hot fudge is the best."

"I'm liking all this so far," said Jake, running a lazy finger around my locket.

"Then we have one busy weekend."

Jake's finger traveled down to my stomach, making me shiver. He smiled, amused. "Is that so?"

"Damn right." I exhaled, pretending the whole thing was a lot of work when it was actually my dream come true. "Tomorrow, we better take the kids to get a Christmas tree." My eyes flashed to his. "Our first Christmas tree as a family."

That was the right thing to say. Jake was on top of me again, kissing me all over until I thought I'd melt out of his arms. When he pulled away, his grin was devilish. "What else?"

I gave him a gentle bite. "While we're getting a tree, we might as well pick up a couple of cans of paint." I pointed at the walls. "So we can paint this room and Henry's room."

Jake had a very specific smile. Bonnie described it to me once. He looked like a cat who stole the cream.

"If you still want me and Henry to move in, that is," I said.

Jake looked downright diabolical. He played with my locket before pulling me against him. "I think this is shaping up to be the best weekend of my life."

40

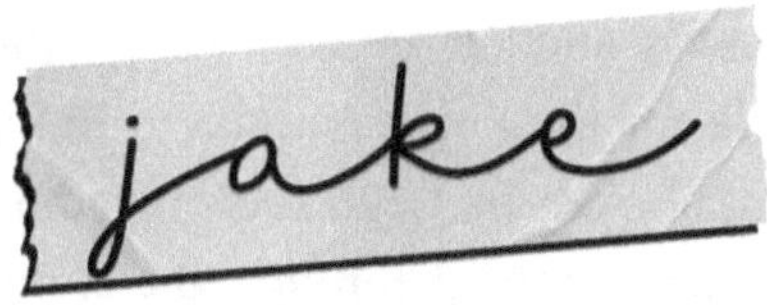

It didn't take long to get them moved in. It was five days of packing boxes, somehow losing shirts and toys packed in those boxes, finding them in *other* boxes, plus cleaning, painting, and braving the wind and snow to do it all.

I loved ever fecking minute of it.

While we painted Henry's room, we listened to Prince as loudly as my scratchy old iPhone could handle. When Leah's phone rang and she saw it was Felicity, Henry cranked the music louder. Leah stifled a laugh and took her phone to the living room. I followed.

"Uh-huh," said Leah into the phone.

I came up behind her and slid my arms around her waist. She leaned into me, and I breathed her in. I was never going to get tired of having her in my arms.

"Remember what I said," I whispered. "Hold firm. We're going to be too busy having sex to go to their Thanksgiving tomorrow." Leah playfully pinched my side. "We have a few months to make up for, damn it."

"What was that?" Leah asked on the phone. She turned and ran her finger down the buttons of my shirt. "Uh-huh…Yeah,

I'm sorry, Felicity. The house is a disaster area." Leah and I glanced around the tidy living room. It wasn't hard to get things in order when we all helped. "Henry's games and toys are everywhere. I can't see the floor."

I crouched down on the hardwood and pointed at it. "It's right here, mo fhíorghrá."

Leah suppressed another laugh. "And I think it's going to take a little while for the kids to adjust to living together. They fought this morning over the Lego soccer stadium."

Just then, Henry zoomed through the living room, hauling Daisy on his back. They giggled as they disappeared into the frigid backyard. Leah grinned as she watched them throw snowballs.

"Plus, something is wrong with the pipes in my old kitchen." She tried her hand at a fake sigh. "We better fix that."

I leaned against the sofa. "That's what happens when Steven goes after them with rebar."

"What's that?" Leah asked Felicity. "Yep. A hassle, alright."

Leah winked. That was enough to get me back in her arms.

I kissed her neck. "I wouldn't wish this hellscape on anyone."

She grinned, running her free hand through my hair. "Thanks for understanding… I hope we can hang out soon. Give our love to Mark, your parents, and Kenneth."

She didn't miss a beat when she said my cousin's name.

"All the love in the world to that gem," I whispered. Leah tried her best not to laugh.

She threw her phone on the sofa. "There. We got out of that."

"You're a miracle worker," I said, going in for a kiss. Leah's light touch on the back of my neck made my whole body numb.

"What about your poor dad? He has to go by himself." She narrowed her eyes, teasing me. "Don't you feel terrible?"

My lips hovered near hers. "Haven't you heard? He's all snowed in. Bad back. Can't shovel."

It was still dark when we awoke on Christmas morning. Leah's head rested on my chest. She reached up to my lips and planted a delicate kiss.

I stroked her face, smiling. "Merry Christmas."

"Merry Christmas. Our first as a family." Her eyes turned misty. So did mine. "Any bets on when they'll wake up?"

I rubbed the sleep out of my eyes. "What time is it?"

Leah glanced at her phone. "Six-thirty."

I gave her a long kiss. "I can't believe the chaos hasn't started already."

Five minutes later, there was a loud bang on our bedroom door. Daisy and Henry entered, in a panic about when they could open presents. Leah and I smiled at each other. Did she remember our first Christmas together when we were kids? The two of us didn't care about anything except what was underneath the wrapping paper. Leah wore a green velvet dress and had permed hair. I wore a short-sleeved shirt with a long-sleeved shirt underneath it.

In one of my photo albums, there was a picture from that morning. We were taste-testing Dennis's blue cheese dip and not enjoying it at all. Steven was on the floor, pulling at Leah's dress. My mom was off to the side in a blue blouse with puffy sleeves, laughing at our grossed-out reactions.

That was life. Little moments. Silly moments. Things that didn't seem like much to outsiders looking in, but when you stepped back, you realized you were staring at some kind of magic.

We were all in the living room wearing our matching red plaid pajamas when Steven burst through the basement door. He wore the same pajamas but with a red Santa hat.

"Merry Christmas, family," he said.

The kids greeted him but were quickly distracted by the presents under the tree.

Leah pretended to be annoyed as Steven put an arm around both of us. "Isn't this nice? A big ol' family Christmas. It's like a picture. Like a cupful of merriment. Don't you think?"

Leah rolled her eyes. "Sure is."

"Thanks for getting us the pajamas, by the way," I said.

"No problem," he said. "It's the least I could do. This is a great area of town. Not by a lake, but still good. Danica says it's prime real estate. Plus, my commute has never been easier."

I raised an eyebrow. "Yes, a flight of stairs and two blocks is fairly simple."

"And I can walk to work," he said.

Leah's voice was monotone. "You walked to work before."

"But now I'm coming at it from the other side, so it's a fresh perspective on life."

The kids charged up to Steven with a present in hand.

Steven didn't hold back his surprise. "Dang, guys. You didn't have to get me anything. Good thing I stopped at the bank and the candy store, or I'd look like a grade-A jackass."

Steven sat on the recliner and ripped the present open like he was ten again. He lifted the flaps on the box and peered inside. A wicked smile spread across his face as he pulled out the gift: two fedoras. One hat was blue with a yellow ribbon around the brim, and the other was black with a brown ribbon. Steven plucked the Santa hat off his head and put it on Daisy, who giggled and stuck it on Henry. Steven looked like he was crowning himself as he placed the blue hat on his dark, unkempt hair.

"Damn. I feel like Frodo the first time he held the One Ring. It's meant to be."

"But wasn't the One Ring bad?" asked Henry.

Steven adjusted his fedora and shrugged. "Semantics."

Leah pulled at my pajama sleeve to get my attention. She nodded to a rather large and obvious present sitting by the wall, wrapped in reindeer paper. She shrugged, wondering where it came from. I winked, and her eyes widened.

"What did you do?" Leah shot me an accusing look. I could tell she was pleased, but she never liked big gifts.

I kissed her cheek. "What can I say? I told you in November that we had your presents all taken care of." I nodded to the others, and they smiled.

"Wait...*we*?" Her eyes darted to each of us. "You're all in on this?"

"Yep!" said Daisy. "We've been planning it for, like...ever."

"And you didn't suspect a thing," said Henry, smug.

That made Leah laugh. She gave the kids each a hug and sat down beside the present.

"I'm not in on it," said Steven. "I have no idea what the hell's going on."

"What is it?" asked Leah, touching the gift. "It's huge!"

Emotion pinched at my chest, but I only shrugged. "Guess you'll have to open it and find out."

Leah looked like she still wanted to scold us, but she grinned and tore into the present. In ten seconds, the repaired and painted swing was revealed. Leah couldn't decide if she wanted to laugh or cry, but crying won out. Tears slid down her cheeks as she ran her fingers along the swing. She looked at the kids, then at me.

Her voice cracked. "Is this *our* swing?"

I kissed her forehead, brushing away the tears. She wrapped an arm around me.

"We fixed it all up," said Daisy.

"And we found out that wood filler smells real bad," said Henry.

A small chuckle interrupted her tears. "When did you do this?"

"The night you sang for the first time at the Silver Dollar," I said, running my finger along her cheek. "We stole it from your parents' backyard."

Steven gave a low whistle. "Holy shit. And here I was creeping around people's yards, thinking someone took it."

A grin spread over Leah's raw face as she pulled all of us in. "Thank you. This is the sweetest thing ever. I don't think anything could top this."

Daisy and Henry shot me knowing, amused glances.

I grinned and yanked an envelope out from under the tree. Leah wiped away the last of her tears, watching me with suspicion in her eyes.

I kissed her as I placed the envelope on her lap. "Since you're already crying…"

Her exasperated glare looked a lot like, '*I'm going to spank you later for this.*'

That sounded grand to me.

"Have you lost your mind? Why are you getting me all this?"

"Buttering you up." I acted nonchalant. "Plus, I believe that day I said you were getting *presents*…Plural."

She shook her head as she smiled. The kids egged her on to look in the envelope. She tore it open, like something might jump out.

Steven played with his hat, studying her. "What is it?"

Leah pulled a folded sheet of paper out of the envelope. As her eyes scanned the page, they turned glossy. Her face was a mixture of shock and joy. "It's ticket information."

"Tickets! To where?" asked Steven.

Leah leaned into me, holding her breath. She closed her eyes and smiled. "We're going to Ireland."

The kids cheered. You would have sworn they'd already eaten all the candy from their stockings.

"I can't believe you did all this." Leah's face was wet with tears again as she kissed me.

"Believe it." I flicked the end of her nose with my finger.

"This kind of makes all those KitchenAid attachments you got Jake for his birthday look pretty weak, Mom," said Henry.

Leah burst out laughing. "You're right."

I protested. "No, I love kitchen gadgets." I held Leah close. "Nothing excites me like a garlic press."

Steven leaned back in the recliner and whistled. "This is the best Christmas since the year I got that Super Soaker." He played with his fedora. "When do we leave for Ireland?"

Leah let out a mock laugh. "Sorry, Steven, but…" I cleared my throat and pointed to the sheet. Leah raised the paper, studied it, and went wide-eyed. "Oh…I mean… I guess you *are* coming with us, Steven."

Steven was pretty damn satisfied with that. He pointed at me. "What did I say? Best friends."

Leah gave me a long kiss. "You're the nicest guy in the world."

"I'm not that nice," I whispered back. "He's not sitting near us on the plane."

Leah giggled. "Joke's on you. He'll like that better. He can talk to strangers about EI kayaking."

As the kids opened their presents and showed them to Steven, it struck me that most of the people I cared about were in that room. And I'd see others later that day at the Roth house. And the rest…Well…I'd see them in January when we boarded the plane. It made me smile, knowing we were all united by the invisible thread that connected everyone to those they love around the world—those still here and those already gone. It gave me comfort, somehow. Like, none of us were ever alone, not really.

I could say that was how it ended—the five of us opening presents on Christmas morning, with light snow whipping around in the frosty Minnesota air—but that wasn't true. There were a lot of things to happen yet. Surprises to experience. Laughter to experience. Life to experience. And maybe I got wound up at times, but as I stared into the shimmering lights of the Christmas tree decorated with Daisy and Henry's homemade ornaments, I felt like opening my arms to it all. I couldn't wait, not for any of it. Because I knew we'd all be there for it together.

I rested my head against Leah's. "Are you excited?"

She turned to me, eyes bright. "For the trip?"

The kids and Steven laughed as they poked around the kitchen, hunting for the donuts we were going to have for breakfast.

I smiled at her freckled face. "For all of it. For everything we're going to do together. See together. For all the stuff we don't even know about yet."

My enthusiasm made Leah laugh, her eyes squinting. The light that came off her could have warmed me for a hundred bleak winter days. Steven, Henry, and Daisy's happy chatter in the background mingled with that look in her eyes, and I knew this was a day to remember. This was a picture, even if there was no camera in sight.

Leah rested a hand on the back of my neck and drew me in for a kiss, but before her lips met mine, she gave me a wink. "You better believe it."

acknowledgments

You GUYS. This is my second novel! And you're reading it! Or at least you flipped to the acknowledgements page. Either way, thank you!

This is the novel that I came up with during a blizzard. My head was full of fantasy stories that wanted to be written, but this book pushed them aside, scowled at me, and tapped its foot. So I plotted it out while I shoveled snow in a coat good for negative forty conditions, with five scarves wrapped around my face and hand warmers shoved in my boots. I either looked like a yeti or the kid from *A Christmas Story.* You decide.

This book was so fun to write. I hope you had just as much fun reading it. A huge thanks to all the people who read this book in its various stages. I'm so grateful!

Thanks to Cassidy at Cassidy Hudspeth Editing and Proofreading for helping me wrangle this story. Your comments were so helpful.

Thanks to Emma Craven for proofreading…and art advice… and blurb help. Basically, thanks for ALL THE THINGS.

Thanks to Halle at AJ Wolf Graphics for the lovely cover and interior formatting. You knocked it out of the park!

Thanks to my parents and family for being wonderful and for understanding how important baked goods are to me.

Thanks to Billy for love and books. They are the two best things in the world.

And thanks to YOU. If I could send you a pan of cinnamon rolls with the power of my mind, I would.

XOXO
Amanda

As a child, Amanda Braun-Boe could often be found playing too much Nintendo, watching old movies, reading in a hammock swing, and daydreaming about fictional worlds. She obtained her M.A. in English and decided to start putting those worlds down on paper. When not writing, she enjoys baking, reading, searching for the best donuts in whatever town she's in, filling her phone with cat pictures, and testing the limits of how much coffee a person can consume in one day. She lives in rural Minnesota with her husband and their sofa-stealing furry friends. For more, visit her website at amandabraunboe.squarespace.com or find her on Instagram and TikTok.